The Office of Innocence

Also by Thomas Keneally

Fiction
The Place at Whitton
The Fear
Bring Larks and Heroes
Three Cheers for the Paraclete
The Survivor
A Dutiful Daughter
The Chant of Jimmie Blacksmith
Blood Red, Sister Rose
Gossip from the Forest
Season in Purgatory
Victim of the Aurora
Passenger
Confederates
The Cut-rate Kingdom
Schindler's Ark
A Family Madness
The Playmaker
Towards Asmara
By the Line
Flying Hero Class
Woman of the Inner Sea
Jacko
A River Town
Bettany's Book

Non-fiction
Outback
The Place Where Souls Are Born
Now and in Time to Be: Ireland and the Irish
Memoirs from a Young Republic
Homebush Boy: A Memoir
The Great Shame
American Scoundrel

For Children
Ned Kelly and the City of Bees

THOMAS KENEALLY

The Office of Innocence

SCEPTRE

First published in Great Britain in 2002 by
Hodder and Stoughton
A Division of Hodder Headline

A Sceptre Book

1 2 3 4 5 6 7 8 9 10

A CIP catalogue record for this title is available from the British Library

ISBN 0 340 62473 6

Printed and bound in Great Britain by
Mackays of Chatham plc, Chatham, Kent

Hodder and Stoughton
A division of Hodder Headline
338 Euston Road
London NW1 3BH

To the memory of Sergeant Thomas Keneally,
Third Australian Squadron, North Africa,
World War Two

Acknowledgements

The author's thanks go to the customary midwives: Judith Keneally, wife and reader, Deborah Rogers, agent; Carole Welch, editor and Amber Burlinson, editorial assistant.

CHAPTER ONE

ENITENTS, KNEELING IN the confessional, can be divided into predictable categories. The tennis-playing young priests at White City on Mondays, drinking beer supplied, despite war rationing, by a Knight of the Southern Cross who owned a hotel at Edgecliff, often did so. They spoke only of generalised types of sin and sinner, being careful not to violate the strict seal of the sacrament of penance. So, there were, for instance, the self-congratulators, muttering minor sins; the shame-hot boy masturbators; the guilt-obsessed, so hungry for pardon that they would confess, if given a chance, many times a day.

Among priests, as among the laity, the confessional was a focus of humour, just as, privately, it was a focus of dread and hope. The curates sitting by the tennis courts all agreed that hearing the utterly predictable confessions was an ordeal, and boring. Young priests groaned through their Saturday after-noons, leaving their radios, the staccato of horse races, the reports of Sheffield Shield or rugby league at the Sydney Cricket Ground, to do their personal penance in confessional boxes too hot in summer, too cold in winter. Then a quick meal and their Saturday evening stint in the box began, with all the banal confessions of disobedience, small theft, secret desire, shifty touches and self-soiling.

Frank Darragh, a pale, lean-faced young man of quieter disposition than the other curates, had had an early experience which caused him not to think so cynically, either of the boxes or of those who entered them in piety or desperate guilt. It had occurred on St Patrick's Day, 1939, a few days after Hitler invaded Czechoslovakia. It was, in so far as any day ever was in the seminary, a day of special meals in the refectory, and a day of remission from the Lenten fast which had recently made the seminary bill of fare more frugal than ever. But with an abscessed tooth, he had not been able to do much feasting and was walking down the long driveway towards Darley Road, with a pass from the rector, to go to the dentist. Because he was a young man close to being ordained a priest, he would be treated free and for God's love by either of the chatty Cusack brothers, who had a dentistry practice down the hill in Manly.

His naïve soul was in some turmoil that day, and it was not to do with missing what passed in the seminary's dour cuisine as a special meal. It was this: should there be a war, he would feel he was being tested to become a volunteer, as his father, Sergeant Darragh, had been in 1915. That which in him made him relish the communal life of the seminary would dispose him, he believed, to enjoy the ordered fraternity of the army. He could tell this from the demeanour of his deceased father, who had a lung condition as a result of both a shrapnel wound and gas intake, but whose eyes gleamed beneath his freckled dome whenever visitors mentioned the life they had shared in Great War rest camps, after having come alive out of the line. At other times, Darragh's father was politely secretive, yet then uttered unexpected war tales, stories in which Darragh thought absurdity and savagery swamped the humour his father thought to be the real point. From all this, the child Darragh supposed the Great War to have been the most exalting, horrifying, humbling and valid stage of his father's life. In both darkness and light, it was the measure of who he was. And thus, Darragh's mother said once, there were dead men in France and Flanders who knew his father best, better than she and Frank did. The truth of his father was dug down with the bones of valiant fallen into the soil of unreachable places with names like Bullecourt, Hamel, Albert, Mont St Quentin.

And now that war asserted itself again, thought Darragh the student, how can I be measured? Within a year he would be a priest. He feared that those who did not understand would consider him an evader of warrior duties, of the duty of being measured. As silly as such a feeling might have seemed to world-lier men, on the way to the dentists' it rankled within his innocent chest and ate away at his virgin heart.

Before he had traversed the long driveway with its deep-green sentries of Norfolk pine, and as he approached the iron gates with their wrought designs of harps, mitres and Celtic crosses, from the archbishop's house on the far side of the road emerged an arduously creeping old priest. He was a familiar sight on the bitumen surface between the archbishop's house and the semi-nary driveway, and local trucks had been known to steer around him considerately as he stood, contemplatively catatonic, in the midst of the road. It always seemed as if, in walking, the old man was held back by a gravity greater than that of earth. The story was that he had flung incarnate evil, the Devil, out of souls in China when he was a young missionary. Now, in vengeance, the Devil and his minions fiercely delayed the old fellow as he crossed

Darley Road on his way to the St Patrick's Day feast. It had been known for him to take three hours to pass four hundred yards up the driveway, and students who encountered him knew better than to extend a hand to him and thus enrol themselves in the close combat between him and the Evil One. All Darragh, with a dental appointment in the temporal world at two o'clock, said was, 'Hello Monsignor, Happy St Patrick's,' to the old man, who was at this moment, as at most, inhabiting another scale of time and place, and passed on.

Darragh accepted that, though many inches taller, indeed nearly six feet, he was an insignificant figure in the exorcist's land-scape. But before he had gone five paces past the barely moving old fellow, a thunderous voice emerged. 'Wait!' Darragh turned and the old man had him fixed with two blazing eyes set in his block-like Irish head, a skull which seemed to come from another age, from the duecento—reputedly the greatest of centuries, Darragh knew, apart from the diseases people had, of course. The old man's eyes were exactly the sort which, seconds before or eons ago, had transfixed the Evil One himself.

'You, son!' the old priest further roared. Darragh stopped, and his callow student soul blazed in his face. He was not ready yet for such an august summons.

'Monsignor?' he pleaded. He could not tell what would be demanded of him, but his pre-dentist nervousness was gone, replaced by a terror more absolute and transcendent.

'You must be a merciful confessor!' It sounded as if the old man had been struck by a message from another sphere, a suggestion that Darragh, unless warned, would not be at all merciful.

Darragh took his black hat off and straightened the black tie he hoped soon to exchange for a clerical collar. 'I pray I will be, Monsignor,' he assured the old man.

But the exorcist waved his hands in a cut-out-the-claptrap way. '*You must be a merciful confessor!*' he insisted.

'Yes,' said a terrified Darragh. He knew this answer had no chance of satisfying the terrifying old exorcist. 'Help me,' he heard himself bleat like a despicable creature, a coward, a sinner, a silly boy as well.

Though the monsignor did not answer, the fury went out of his eyes, and he seemed content that an essential message had been passed. Turning back to apply himself again to the driveway, and advancing by half-inches, he might make the main building by pudding.

This was the most exalted message Darragh had received in all his preparation for the priesthood. As a revelation, it suited him. He'd carried from childhood a sense of the augustness and aura of the sacrament of penance. He was aware of how the penitent, having been absolved, emerged into a new and better light. A trivial Saturday afternoon in a remote place called New South Wales—remote from God's apparent eye, anyhow—was connected to eternity by the exercise of this sacrament so mocked by an unknowing world, so essential to the inner peace of a pilgrim soul.

And, in the summer of '41–42, now that Darragh had been ordained and was Father Frank Darragh, he was still an enthusiastic confessor, and recognised an extra radiance to the light of day, or on rainy winter afternoons an unexpected warmth about the shadowy penitential pews, as he made his way to his confessional box on the western side of the church. He was thus secretly at a loss at Monday tennis, he did not try to contribute to the ironic classifications of Saturday penitents his confrères came up with. He sat, he smiled, he listened without adding anything. He was well respected by his fellow priests for smiling and holding his tongue. And he *was* a merciful confessor.

'My aunt says old Frank's got armies of sinners lining up outside his box,' said a smiling tennis-champion curate from Hurstville, as if to have armies of sinners was just typical of Frank Darragh.

'Of course he does,' said one of the other muscular young priests. 'If I'd robbed a bank, I'd want to go to Frank.'

'Or if you ran away with a housekeeper?'

'You haven't seen our housekeeper.'

Their waspishness had fondness to it. They respected that mixture of secretiveness and warmth of nature he had inherited from his late father. And the parishioners seemed to respect it too. It was not a wonder that the lines outside his confessional occupied perhaps a sixth of the seating in the church. Entering the church with Monsignor Carolan, who manned the confessional on the east side of St Margaret's, his name above the door—*Monsignor V.J. Carolan, Parish Priest*—and Darragh himself, the curate, occupying the hotter box on the western side, Darragh was half-embarrassed to see the extent to which the four or five pews of his penitents outnumbered those outside his parish priest's box. He took no glory in it, because that would be the most stupid vanity. And he knew most experienced priests mocked men who attracted too many penitents. It was a sign of some weakness in a priest-confessor, and a characteristic of a particular type of young one. Nor did Monsignor Carolan, his threads of hair sleek across his fine skull, in any way envy Frank. 'You'll have to put in for overtime, Frank,' Carolan would tell him, all without an edge to his voice.

As a confessor the monsignor appealed to men like himself, grizzled old jokers from Homebush or Strathfield who wanted to be absolved for bread-and-butter sins—taking the Divine Name in vain, making an unseemly joke about an office girl to a companion—all without fuss. Men blessedly unburdened by vaster guilt. Pragmatic, faithful, self-certain fathers of families. Women, too, of similar sunny and practical cast of mind. Monsignor Carolan's finance committee generally went to him to be shriven.

To Darragh, merciful confessor, came many souls troubled by war. Terrible questions had been generated by the time. Men who wanted to know whether, should the Japanese come, they had divine leave to kill their wives and daughters to save them from violation. When Frank conventionally told them that they 'must trust in the will of God, which cannot be foreseen by us,' he could feel the warmth of doubt begin to rise from them, like condensed water from some scorched surface. He would say, because it was true, 'I know I'm a young man, and I do not have your experience. But it seems to me that in these times, when we can predict nothing, that the safest road is blind faith. It will give us all more light than any prediction will.' He would say also, 'You must depend on God to save you from such terrible acts. He understands why you are tempted. But He wants you to be hopeful! It's not as if the Japanese have captured Singapore.'

It was not *yet* the case, he should have said. These Japanese, who had made so many Jesuit martyrs in the sixteenth century! Could it be believed that in plain old Strathfield, among the Federation houses or against the red brick wall of St Margaret's, they would convert himself and Monsignor Carolan into similar martyrs? His own honest fear as a mere human animal moved frankly in him, and the men who were considering the murder of those nearest to them felt he had taken their impulse off them and onto himself, and were consoled.

To Frank Darragh's confessional too came, these fraught days, a fair number of girls from the bush who had come down to

Sydney to work in war factories far from the control imposed by
their severe country fathers. They were bewildered, intrigued,
delighted and morally confused by their first kisses and caresses
at the hands of more-travelled and opportunistic soldiers and
civilians.

As for wives and husbands, the keen chance of Japanese invasion had made people not more wary but more reckless. Darragh
knew what was said of priests in these matters—they knew
nothing of marriage yet arrogantly traced out the law for lovers
and the married. His closest physical contact with a woman had
been a blunt and clumsy kiss he had landed on the cheek of a
Rose Bay convent girl when he was sixteen. It had heated his
blood, but it had not caused him to suffer one of those stupefying erections. And that, apart from the love of his mother and
Aunt Madge, was all! Though he would admit without quibble
that to advise on matters of marriage and physical desire he
needed guidance from the Holy Spirit, he believed it to be super-
abundantly forthcoming to him in his role as confessor. Sometimes he was surprised by the tenor of the advice which rose
unbidden to his lips. To the new race of female riveters, sheetmetal
workers, welders, for example, these green and pleasant girls who
would have remained under their parents' care but for the war, he
might say this: 'God has given you in trust the incalculable treas-
ure of your womanhood. Since He has given you free will, you
must honour and guard yourself in His place. Remember that one
day you will be a grandmother, and your grandchildren will look
to what you did when you were young for a model of their own
youth.' More conventionally he would tell them to turn to the
Virgin Mother of Jesus for succour, counsel and example.

The troubles of the war-working girls were nothing to those
of soldiers' wives. Sydney suburbs were populated by American

soldiers who had arrived well-fed and confident straight from the United States without passing through the filters of war. They had not been humbled by the defeats and hardships of the Philippines. They wore sharp-creased uniforms unstained by battle, yet, as far as fabric could, promising gallantry. They had access to hosiery and chocolate, both of which seemed to mean so much to women, and would kindly bring into the lounge rooms and kitchens of every parish the glossy magazines of American Mammon. What might be most dangerous was that compared to Australian men, the Americans were said to be courtly. Occasionally, after Sunday Mass, one or two of them would present themselves at the sacristy door with a pleasing frankness, courtesy and respect. One GI had given Darragh a stipend of a pound note and asked him to say Mass for 'me and the boys of my section'. Darragh told the soldier the normal Mass offering in Australia was five to ten shillings. But the boy—he could have been little more than twenty—said, 'No, no, Father. I want you to say a real good Mass.' This mixture of innocence and worldliness was of a different order than that of Australians, and that gave the Americans fascination.

Some women's husbands had been absent for the better part of two years—the chief divisions of the Australian army were in North Africa or in Singapore. It was utterly according to nature, as Darragh could see, that with the sudden triumph of the Japanese in the last two months a woman on her own, with small children, should be tempted to interpose some American soldier between herself and the chance of invasion, violation and disembowelment during the coming winter.

Even after the Japanese drove the British and Australians down the Malayan peninsula, the confessional remained Darragh's obscure duty in war. He had learned to embrace it. It assuaged more easily than he expected his occasional self-consciousness about not being a soldier.

As with the life of a soldier, much of Darragh's duty was drudgery—dealing, for instance, with the surprisingly numerous platoons of self-abusers. In the spirit of the aged exorcist's advice to him, Darragh despised this crime while understanding the sinner. He'd been a rare sinner himself, twice, although in one case, during a fever, his full intent had been lacking. He exercised a self-discipline based on not thinking about the thing, and upon resigning control over his animal nature to God. Before he was ordained a priest, he had thought the sin far less common among young males than the confessional now indicated to him it was. For a moment sometimes, he wondered where he stood in relation to these young men who could sin fourteen or more times a week. Was their malice greater than his had been at that age? If so, why did they come to confession? Or were they, or he, deficient in some medical way, they for being so regularly tempted, himself for being tempted so little? He had divine grace to fortify him, and he had his sense of outrage. In Noldin's famous six-volume work, *Summa Theologiae Moralis*, the Latin name of the sin had been based on its capacity to unhinge and to damn. *Manustrupatio.* Hand-rape. An assault upon one's own temple. Hence it had—by title—a profound irrationality and danger, and yet occurred as commonly as the pride, the appeasing lies and the small meannesses and envies to which respectable older women most commonly confessed.

Some wisdom greater than himself had him telling these boys that they were better than their sin—that they were not hateful in God's eye, that they should not fear but should resign themselves to divine help and the intercession of the Virgin Mary, forces which made all things possible. Made it possible, among other miracles, he told the sinners, for priests to keep their vows!

Because he saw no sense in thundering at them, the adolescents of the parish, boys from the Christian Brothers' school a mile away who might in a short time be fighting the Japanese, milled to his confessional.

Back in the presbytery on Saturday evenings, between confessional sessions, over Mrs Flannery's chops, peas, potatoes and carrots, Monsignor Carolan always sooner or later advised him, 'Don't wear yourself out, Frank. I've seen fellows like you—great confessors, but it wears them out. Men who take the world's sins on them.' Unless the rite was performed in a brisk, functional way, the monsignor saw the confessional as a possible danger to all concerned, particularly to the vain or the excessively pious. His talents were directed to building the physical kingdom of God— brick by brick. In the month before the war began, he had completed the little school next door to St Margaret's. Classrooms, playgrounds, toilet blocks were Monsignor Carolan's chief visible sacrament. Frank Darragh suspected he lacked the fundraising gifts of a Carolan, and thus had little chance of becoming one of those wise, competent managers of parishes so admired in the archdiocese.

At seven o'clock each Saturday night, he was back behind the door of his confessional box, seated in his chair, facing the dim beaded glass of the door which had closed with a smooth ball-bearing click as discreet as God's mercy. Either side of him lay the sliding shutters which gave onto the space occupied by the penitent on the left, and the one on the right.

On the other side of the church, in *his* confessional, Monsignor Carolan tried to serve the needs of his penitents in good time to hear the 'Sid Stone Variety Show', on the Macquarie Broadcasting System at eight o'clock. The monsignor's favourite variety turns

were yodelling and bird calls—he enjoyed a full-throated kooka-
burra, the most difficult bird call in the world to achieve with
utter authenticity. He had an aged uncle who had done kooka-
burras and currawongs on the 'Amateur Hour' years before, and
been praised by the compere. The joy of Christ shone appealingly
in Monsignor Carolan's eye when Stan Jones teased husand-and-
wife yodelling teams.

CHAPTER TWO

O N SUNDAYS THE merciful confessor Frank Darragh normally said the early Masses, the six-thirty and the eight o'clock. The monsignor, with the debt on the school to repay, said the more populous and strategic nine and ten o'clock Masses. For these he attracted the bulk of the parish with the briskness of his recitation and of his sermon, which never failed to refer to the reality that the parish was burdened with the primary school debt and the maintenance of St Margaret's.

St Margaret's was indeed a splendid, almost basilica-like church built in the most modern style during the prosperous 1920s by an Irish parish priest named McHugh, and improved and paid for in his memory by the younger Australian cleric, Monsignor Carolan. It put the modest Methodist chapel and even the Anglican church of St Anne's in the shade, which had been the intention of the late Father McHugh and the inheritance of Monsignor Carolan. Behind its main altar, which stood high above marble steps, a fresco of the Assumption of the Blessed Virgin into Heaven had been painted by a team of Italian artisans who had travelled the length and breadth of the Australian continent filling churches with iconography in the style of Raphael. These artisans, and the families they had acquired in Australia, had recently been interned, but the Papal Nuncio in Sydney had been working to have them released so that they could continue their benign craft even in wartime.

There were in St Margaret's as well two handsome side altars, one to Our Lady of Perpetual Succour, the other to St Anthony of Padua, everyone's favourite miracle worker and finder of lost objects. None of this had come cheaply, nor had the slate roof and the rafterless cement-and-steel-reinforced upper reaches of St Margaret's. St Margaret's had a grandeur then which outshone many Sydney parish churches, including the one at Frank Darragh's first posting, in Stanmore. The next-door parish to Strathfield, Flemington, within reach of the dust from the livestock saleyards, possessed an extremely humble and dowdy church by comparison, barely more than a cement-rendered hall, undistinguished architecturally, with murky varnished cedar buttresses and rafters, and bare gestures towards ornamentation and statuary. It was not that Darragh would be unwilling to serve in such a place, but that he was pleased exceedingly to find himself the unwitting beneficiary of the energy of Father McHugh, native of Tipperary, and Monsignor Carolan, native of Tamarama.

Darragh took a little longer than the monsignor over his Mass, since he considered it a work of serious articulation. In the seminary he had acted Mark Antony in Shakespeare's *Julius Caesar*, and had been an admirer of the iambic pentameter. Since he needed to give the Latin of the Mass at least the same weight and rhythmic enunciation as he had Shakespeare's metres, he found it hard to finish the eight o'clock Mass and fit in a sermon in fifty-one or two minutes. But the monsignor had made it clear that

that was what he required—Frank was to be back in the sacristy and out of his heavy Mass vestments by about seven minutes to ten. The monsignor wanted peace in which to recite privately the pre-Mass prayers while parched summertime altar boys took turns drinking water from the washbasin which sat in the sacristy's corner.

Within the limits the monsignor placed on him, Frank Darragh was a happy young man, dazed and delighted with his sacramental duties. Dried out from the weight of his vestments that summer, he ate little more than toast at the end of his Masses, despite the insistence of Mrs Flannery that he needed more. He drank plenty of tea, and left the substantial breaking of his Saturday-night, Sunday-morning fast until he reached his boyhood home in Rose Bay, to which he returned on most Sundays.

This Sunday was in humid February. He had no car, but travelling by public transport gave him a sense of fraternity which he knew he would lose when and if he acquired the skills appropriate to a car, and a vehicle to go with it. Hard-bitten fathers of families raised their hats to him on Strathfield Station, implying, 'We are one with you in the Faith.' He made in return a half-embarrassed gesture of raising his black felt hat to them. They were the ones who had fought the fight, had raised their children in a harsh decade. But a fraternity of respect was established, even as people shuffled together towards the doors of the red electric trains.

In the crowded Sunday-morning carriage, young leading aircraftmen tilted their forage caps, and he nodded. The Communion of Saints on the Western Line thundered towards Central Station amidst showers of sparks from the electric lines above. Of course, from much of the population of the trains, those not party to the mysteries of faith, there were surreptitious stares and blankness. Mystification. A mute hostility to which he was utterly accustomed.

A beautiful young woman in a floral dress drew her six- or seven-year-old son off the seat opposite her to allow Frank Darragh to sit. She held the child between her knees and told the boy in a lowered voice, 'Say hello to Father.' The boy had a small scatter of freckles on the same fine-grained skin his mother had.

Darragh said, 'Thank you for the seat.' The mother had that air of grace, and a particular light in the eye. She was not frightened of him. It was good not to be feared.

'My daddy's in the Middle North,' said the boy.

'The Middle East,' his mother corrected him, and kissed the rim of his ear. Darragh tried to remember if such easy exchanges had operated between himself and his mother. He decided briefly and with some unease that his mother might not have been so casual in the presence of a priest. 'Your father is a brave man,' Darragh told the boy.

Darragh saw that the woman nearly shrugged, as if Darragh's compliment did not serve her and her son much.

'We're going to Clovelly,' said the boy, resting easily against his mother's thigh. As the train rolled, this young woman evoked in Darragh the usual sharp and not too frequent pain of celibacy. His spiritual adviser, an elderly, gentle soul named Dr Cahill—for every seminarian had to choose a spiritual adviser from the staff of the seminary—had once said, 'The institution of celibacy is not a mere sacrifice of pleasure. It asks of a man that he will consent to be the end of the line. That he will not pass on his embodied nature.'

Darragh considered this apparently perfect, archetypal young woman who faced him. Besides what he read as an air of confident innocence, she had the character of having suffered without being given a choice. History, without asking her, had claimed her husband and put him at a fabulous distance from her.

On a rowdy stretch of the line near Macdonaldtown, she leaned forward by just a margin and told Darragh, under her breath, that she and her son lived closer to Flemington parish, but belonged to St Margaret's and preferred to go to Mass there. So she had recognised him as the curate of St Margaret's. Was she one of the young soldiers' wives who had confessed loneliness or temptation to him? Had he, unconscious of her loveliness, absolved her and imposed a penance: 'Say one decade of the Joyous Mysteries.' Darragh nodded, and the woman settled back and resumed a secret whispered conversation with her son.

Central Station that dangerous February was a melee of Sunday people, children in light summer hats, beach-bound with their parents. Skylarking soldiers bearing kitbags made their way towards the steam trains which would take them—who knew?— to some banal camp in the bush, or to immolation in the Pacific. These warriors among whom he could not be counted! On the broad concourse at Eddy Avenue, a larger amy of sailors, airmen and soldiers posed for the pavement photographer on the arms of their mothers, wives or girlfriends. The papers talked about Australia being stripped of troops, but there seemed enough to raise substantial regiments waiting with their womenfolk for the Bronte and Bondi trams.

And, some distance away, among the crowd by the tramline stood the mother and son. She had the air of a woman who was used to waiting, of not resenting queues and crowds. Probably a country girl, he thought, building a history in his mind, whose husband had brought her out of the bush to the city, looking for some work in the Depression. Darragh saw her lift her son onto the running board of the Clovelly tram. A militiaman who looked

perhaps sixteen stood, doffing his slouch hat, and offered her a
seat. She took it with a frank smile, and with a steely howl the
tram bore her and her tribe of fellow travellers away to Elizabeth
Street. When his Rose Bay tram came along five minutes later, he
boarded it, and a boy in a school blazer stood up to offer him his
seat. Some instinct that he should now separate himself from the
memory of the lovely mother, and that this was better achieved
in the discomfort of standing, caused Darragh to smile and say,
'No, I'm perfectly fine, thank you. You sit.'

To the edification of any Catholics who might be on the tram,
and the mystification of others, he pulled from the pocket of his
black jacket his *Breviarium Romanum*. The volume he had was
marked *Hiemalis*—Winter—since it was winter in Europe, winter
in the Vatican surrounded by Italian Fascists, winter in Russia
where Hitler's men correctly suffered at the hands of Soviet
troops, winter over the bomb sites of England, and of course over
the neutrally undisturbed and poverty-stricken farms of Ireland,
from which his own ancestors came. This word '*Hiemalis*' in dull-
gold lettering on the spine of the beautifully printed little book,
when taken in conjunction with the humid summer day, told you
that Australia was in a remote and inverted relation to the well-
springs of the European faith, to the locales of monasticism and
mysteries of faith, and of strategic importance. That was the basic
question which *Smith's Weekly* and the *Telegraph* kept asking:
Could Mr Churchill be made to take an interest in the destiny of
a place so distant? So far off that a priest, reading the *Hiemalis*
volume of his daily breviary, felt no shiver of northern wind but
sweated instead into his black serge, in the close air of a tram
beneath a ruthless February sun?

Each day, diocesan priests like Frank Darragh were required to
recite their breviary—the office, as it was called. In the tradition

of those monks who sang in plainchant the sundry so-called hours of the office—named Matins, Lauds, Prime, Terce, Sext, None, Vespers and Compline—busier souls like Frank and the monsignor were allowed merely to recite the psalms, hymns, lessons, versicles and collects making up the text which, according to one of Darragh's seminary professors, sprang from ancient Jewish tradition and had been formally recited from the second or third century in Christian monasteries. The office thus possessed a worldwide breadth and a historic depth, but that did not prevent comparative speeds for its completion being discussed by young priests on tennis Mondays, the way athletic times for the half-mile might be discussed by runners. A jovial former seminary buffoon named Tim Murphy boasted that he could manage the whole thing in thirty-four minutes. If so, it showed a remarkable facility Frank Darragh couldn't match—the Latin seemed to him to demand a slower enunciation. Verses such as '*Undique circumvenerunt me sicut apes; adusserunt sicut ignis spinas: in nomine Domini contrivi eos*' did not rattle off the tongue. Neither did they roll off the mind, in their significance. 'They surround me like bees; they engulf me like tongues of fire . . .' He had got to say Matins and Lauds the evening before, as was customary, and Prime and Terce and Sext between his two Masses, and now on the tram he recited None from his breviary, his lips moving, as required by canon law, to pronounce the Latin hymns and psalms and versicles.

The purpose of requiring priests to recite the office the world over, from Nazi-occupied Belgium, where his breviary had been published by the Benziger Brothers, to the southernmost priest in New Zealand or Argentina, was to remind the individual cleric that whatever business the rest of mankind might be engaged in—invention, invasion, impregnation—his job and caution, his only possible joy, was in pursuing the divine order. It was there in the vulgate Latin version of the psalm he read with a slight, unobtrusive flutter of his lips, as he hung from a strap, expelling the words in minor whisper which the tram-clang drowned. '*And I shall walk on a spacious road because I follow all your precepts . . . I am reminded by light of your name, oh Lord, and I guard your law . . . I shall take delight in your mandates, which I guard.*'

He was towards the end of None, of the versicle and response, Darragh doing both, unlike the monks with one side of the chapel uttering the versicle, and those on the other side singing the plainchant reply. He had got as far as the words '*Averte oculos meos, ne videant vanitatem*—Avert my eyes, that they should not see vanity,' when he felt in an instant cleft in two by the sharpest agony of loss. It arose from nothing, from a slight jolt of the tramlines, and carried not only the face of the young mother, but also the face of the boy generated from her, leaning confidently against her knees. Had he ever known such a woman? Had he leaned against his mother's knees with such casual confidence? He blinked and looked up. The eyes of a pro-portion of the tram-travellers, reverent and hostile, were on him. He felt certain they could see his extreme condition, the sudden axe which had divided him, shoulder to loins. How will I eat dinner with my mother? he wondered for a second, though he hoped the extremity of feeling would depart by then. The rest of the office remained to be said: Vespers, Compline. How could it be completed before midnight if he felt as distracted as this? His legs ached too, for no good reason, and he wished he had taken the schoolboy's offered seat.

As the tram began the climb to Edgecliff, however, the pain retracted to become a dull, habitual depression, and he began reciting the hymn of Vespers. 'Extinguish the flames of passion, draw off the heat of poison, grant the salvation of bodies and the true peace of hearts.' He feared, however, that for him an age of automatic grace had passed.

The bungalow of Darragh's childhood, approached with the new feeling of having somehow aged during a mere tram ride, and of being tested, stood on New South Head Road in Rose Bay. It was built of plum-coloured brick, and its street-facing windows had little segments of stained glass to relieve them of their banal transparency. His mother, a vigorous, lean woman in her early fifties, tended the rosebushes which marked the way to the verandah and the front door. His parents had bought the house in 1923 from an old Scot who had placed by the front door a framed glass sign in which the word *Arbroath* was marked out in gold tinsel. They had left it there. The child Darragh had not realised it was the name of a Scottish town, rather than a formula for the hearth. In his present mood of, at best, wistfulness, on this still Sunday suffused with the smell of legs of lamb baking in a thousand kitchens, it failed to evoke much in him.

One of the baking legs of lamb which, despite meat rationing, were still offered up as a matter of course to Australian Sabbath appetites was inside *Arbroath*, and Darragh paused at the closed front door and let its savour lead him back to a more grateful sense of who and where he was, and what was his destiny. An only child. A father always pleased for his son's academic success. Before his sudden death eight years past, Mr Darragh told Frank that though Mrs Darragh was shy and not a woman to make a display, she boasted about Frank to all the neighbours. If she showed wariness in her affection, it did not mean she was not as generous as the young mother he'd met on the train. 'Your

mother is a brick, a true rock,' his father had told him approv-
ingly. 'You know where you stand with her.' Young Frank was as
willing as his father to find her reticence endearing, and not to
mistake it for coolness. At the Christian Brothers' college at Rose
Bay, he had given his teachers similar cause for celebration. He
suffered from no learning problems or laziness, and so did not
need to be punished in the muscular way of the Brothers'
community, with leather straps and fleas in the ear. He was competent alike at such contrasting puzzles as cricket and algebra.
Nothing befell him, not even in adolescence, to drive him to
rebellion, or make him seek a world other than the one he
knew—unless it was the idea he had of his father's participation
in the ill-defined mysteries of war, that massive and risky secular
sacrament. He had been exactly the sort of unsullied, unworldly
yet not stupid young man the seminary sought.

At the door of *Arbroath*, he rang the bell and his aproned
mother opened the door. 'Frank,' she said with a careful smile.
Darragh had learned from childhood to read her small signs, as
now, when with her eyes modestly gleaming she led him through
to the dining room and his Aunt Madge. Madge, his maiden
aunt, came through the curtain from the kitchen where she had
obviously been assisting his mother with the bake. His late
father's sister was a fuller and less restrained woman with a
plump, pleasant face and brown hair. She believed in rouge, and
her cheeks gleamed with that and with the sherry she always
drank before Sunday dinner. While he admired his mother for
taking quiet delight in things, Aunt Madge was rowdier. Her
story, however, like her parents', had been shaped by the Great
War. The family story was that her boyfriend from the Illawarra
had been killed in France on some muddy, indiscriminate
patrol—he had been a mere eighteen years old.

Madge had spent her adult life as buyer for the millinery department of a store in the city—the highly trusted Miss Darragh who would have made a wonderful wife. For a time about 1934 when Mr Darragh lost his job at Hawley and Ledger, the importing company at which he had worked for thirteen years, Aunt Madge had moved in with her brother and sister-in-law as a minister of mercy to help them pay the mortgage. But most of the time she liked to live alone, in a flat at Dover Heights.

When she loudly kissed him now, Darragh could smell the pleasant blush of sweet wine on her breath. Past her, he saw the table set with white linen on which cruets sparkled, and was fully absorbed and consoled by the intense and encompassing smells of roast potato and moist lamb.

'We'll sit down in five minutes,' said his mother. 'I have beer if you would like it.'

After the long tram journey, he chose to have a glass. 'An aperitif,' said Aunty Madge, for the sake of elegance or of what his father called 'bush flashness'. While his mother went to get it, Darragh took off his jacket and went to the room he had occupied as a boy to hang it up. He also undid the press-stud at the back of his neck, and released the Roman collar and stock he had worn all the way from Strathfield. The underside of the stock was sodden with his sweat. So now he became an ordinary fellow in black pants and white shirt, about to eat spud and carrot, baked onion and lamb, with mint jelly taken from a cutglass bowl.

With the heaped plates before the three of them, Mrs Darragh asked her son to intone grace. He did so, and after a perfunctory sign of the cross as habitual as a kiss between spouses, Aunty Madge looked at her plate and said with an augustness of elocution which was her style, 'Who would believe there was rationing?'

'I would,' said Mrs Darragh, and risked a smile at her son.

Aunt Madge had extracted a price for helping out the family during Mr Darragh's unemployment, which had barely ended six months before he died. She had a habit of inviting herself to all occasional meals—Sunday, Easter, Christmas—and even many evening meals at *Arbroath*. Her company was welcome to Mrs Darragh, and Aunt Madge disliked the fuss of shopping and dealing with books of ration coupons. She devoted a great deal of her free time to film-going, and could always tell Darragh which film to see on Monday nights after tennis. '*That Night in Rio* is a commonplace little thing, but if you happen to like Carmen Miranda . . . *Dive Bomber*'s not a bad war drama, a little unrealistic if that's what you're after. Errol Flynn, what a looker! They say he's an Australian. I met a fellow after Mass the other day who claimed to have shared a desk with him at Marist Brothers, Parramatta. I said to him, "Mr Henry,"—that's his name—"Mr Henry, I wouldn't believe you except I know a fellow like you wouldn't lie on the doorstep of the church." I'm not sure the beggar wouldn't though. *Blossoms in the Dust* . . . very touching. Handkerchief-soaker. Greer Garson looks like a saint but from what I've read may not be one. *Love on the Dole* . . . now that's a real film about real people.'

'I'm surprised,' said Mrs Darragh, with a half-smile which invited Frank into the cautious joke. 'A woman of your age going to see *Love on the Dole*.' It was said to be a notorious film. Priests and ministers who had not seen it had widely preached against it.

'Well, it's the way people live,' said Aunt Madge, her voice sweeping in its authority. 'If you treat people unjustly, they don't just offer it all up for the souls in Purgatory, you know. They try to find an outlet. Anyhow, where were all those priests who run it down when the working men and women were hard up during the Depression? They weren't to be seen then. But they're quick to blame the poor for living close to the bone.'

Frank Darragh was used to Aunty Madge being an anti-clerical but devout Catholic.

'The actors in *Love on the Dole*,' Mrs Darragh surprised Frank by saying, 'were never your poor working men and women, Madge. That Deborah Kerr. In real life she's got a plum in her mouth like the queen of England.'

'That's not what I read,' said Aunt Madge. 'In fact, I read that she had quite a hard upbringing as a shopkeeper's daughter. Anyhow, you'd approve of the newsreels.' Fork in one hand, Madge raised her other to trace phantom headlines in the air. 'Rommel's army on the run in Libya, and our dear boys having Christmas in Egypt. Poor things. They look so young. Will they last the year?'

'Will any of us?' asked Mrs Darragh, chewing her lamb resolutely.

Darragh felt a familiar spurt of concern and wondered whether she was really afraid, in the way the people in the confessional were afraid. She had never shown him any fear except when he was ill with whooping cough and pneumonia as a child. She looked levelly at her son.

'You should go and speak to Mr Regan.' Regan was the next-door neighbour, a thoughtful man, father of three daughters. Darragh had never seen him, even at the most casual moment, dressed in anything less than a shirt with detachable collar, a vest and watch chain, and well-pressed, well-tailored pants. 'Mr Regan has room for me, and for Madge if she chooses, in his air-raid shelter.'

Aunt Madge declared, 'I might come over here, but it is a mile.

Whereas there's a shelter in the park right next door to me. I have
a choice between being killed with the sight of Mr Regan's long,
droopy face, or among strangers at the park.' She laughed,
tickled, 'But, God's will be done . . .'

Mrs Darragh murmured, 'Nice talk for a socialist. And for a
friend of Deborah Kerr.'

'If you'd read *Rerum Novarum*,' said Aunt Madge, referring
to a famous social justice encyclical of Pope Leo XIII, 'you'd see
that there is no conflict between social democracy and faith.'
Aunt Madge had been a great supporter of the Labor premier of
New South Wales, Jack Lang, and had given out 'How to Vote'
cards in Rose Bay among what she called the 'silvertail' voters.
She was able to quote from the encyclical, as she did now, for it
was the holy text of progressive, political Catholics. ' "Hence by
degrees it has come to pass the working men have been surrendered, isolated and helpless, to the hardheartedness of employers
and the greed of unchecked competition . . ." No one with eyes
in his head would argue with that one.'

It was hard at that moment for Darragh to believe that all the
particularity of Aunt Madge and his mother could be wiped out
by a stray Japanese bomb. And Mrs Darragh had already told
him on previous visits that in the event of the invasion itself, she
and Madge had been invited to join the Sisters of the Sacred
Heart in their convent-fastness at Rose Bay. The nuns were confident that even the Japanese would not violate such an obviously
august cloister. Indeed, Frank Darragh could not think of a better
place for his mother to shelter should those terrible hosts that
had sacked Nanking improbably arrive in the suburbs of Sydney.
He feared he himself would be engaged with his congregation in
Homebush and Strathfield. What place, apart perhaps from the
abattoirs and the brickworks, Homebush and Strathfield could

play in the grand plan of a Japanese Greater East Asia Co-Prosperity Sphere was difficult to imagine, but that might add to the peril of the event. Somehow he could imagine the soldiers of the emperor becoming so enraged by the irrelevance of the suburb that they might be provoked to obliterate its people.

At his mother's urging, Frank Darragh went next door to see Mr Regan. Sweet-faced and slightly dazed, Mrs Regan sought to feed him another meal, and the Regan daughters, who had known him in his adolescence, quivered with excitement to have Frank Darragh, translated into priesthood, present in their home. The fact he was wearing shirtsleeves seemed to amuse them.

'I must talk to you, Father Frank,' said Mr Regan under his breath, and collected from his ice chest a bottle of Dinner Ale and led him out of the cooing and fluttering and teasing of the Regan girls into the back garden and down plank steps into the bomb shelter he had so industriously dug among his backyard shrubs. Frank felt already heavy with his meal, and hoped that Mr Regan, a man in his late fifties, was not about to embark on a moral and military weighing of this languid, humid hour in the world's plummet towards a resolution. In the centre of the damp-smelling air-raid shelter, amidst harsh-timbered bunks, stood a coarse-grained wooden table, and Mr Regan sat at it, inviting Frank to take a chair on the far side. The air was dimmest umber. Mr Regan uncapped the Dinner Ale and poured two glasses. Apparently, in his experience, few priests had ever rejected the offer of a drink.

'Well, Frank,' Mr Regan reflectively stated, 'everyone knows that if they land it will be in the Eastern Suburbs here.' Darragh had not known that *that* had been established as military reality. 'I'm sending the women to my brother-in-law's place in Cootamundra. At least there's room to hide out there.' He sighed. The chance of bloody chaos threatened the fine-sewn seams of his vest, the salt-and-pepper cloth of his pressed Sunday trousers. But he would not flee. The worst he could face was murder. What women faced was unspeakable. Besides, he was a real estate agent. As a member of St Vincent de Paul, he had frequently slotted poorer families in Christ's name into houses and flats which awaited occupation. The Japanese might spare him for his expertise in finding them billets.

Mr Regan took out a packet of Capstans from his vest and lit one sombrely and with a flourish, as if it would be the only cigarette he would smoke that day. 'Did you happen to read the *Telegraph* today, Father Frank? The front page is all cricket and racing. People dancing on the edge of the abyss. The Australia Hotel and the Trocadero crowded with revelry. The divorce courts full to the brim. I read a piece this morning about an air force officer who went to his wife and said that he was not made for marriage. Just like that. Without any apology. And as if he hadn't already married her. The judge ordered him to return to her within twenty-six days.' Mr Regan shook his head. He considered the judge ultimately impotent in these matters. 'This is the problem as I see it. That we're a race that deserves punishment.' He lowered his voice to a confessional hush, and the words caused him pain. 'Myself as much as anyone. I do not exclude myself.'

Darragh said, 'I doubt anyone really deserves bombing, Mr Regan.' He was embarrassed to see this man who had been one of his elders when he was a boy reduced by the times, and by Darragh's own dignity as a priest, to adopting a confessional tone. Mr Regan admitting guilt, regret and fear of unarguable doom. This man who had always been so certain and so venerable in the eyes of the fourteen, fifteen and sixteen-year-old Frank Darragh.

'Our god is a racehorse,' said Mr Regan, in explanation. 'Our god is a glass of beer. Our god is a dance or worse with a pretty girl. How can we complain if the true God shows us His harsher face? How can we argue if He chooses another power as His agent?'

Frank sipped his beer, which made him yawn. He changed the subject. 'It's very kind of you to have Mum and Aunt Madge in here.'

Mr Regan gave a concessive brief smile. 'Oh yes. But they should go to Cootamundra or some such place themselves, you know. Somewhere that's negligible, you know. But your mother and Madge are very stubborn.'

'They intend to shelter with you. And then with the nuns, if it comes to that.'

'Well, the nuns feel bound to protect the mother of a priest. And Madge.' Mr Regan laughed. Everyone seemed to have a wry affection for Madge. 'Madge comes along in her wake.'

Mr Regan himself took a mouthful of beer and peered into the mid-distance. 'I wanted to ask you . . . Pray for me, Frank.' Indeed the man had taken on what was to Darragh the now-familiar breathlessness of the penitent. 'I doubt my courage,' he said. Frank felt abashed—there was no wire screen between him and Mr Regan the patriarch, no curtain, no grille or sliding wooden shutter.

'If the Philippines fall to the Japanese,' murmured Mr Regan, 'and there seems nothing to prevent it, Sydney will be even fuller of Americans than ever. And, you know, they are a corrupting influence.'

'Perhaps we corrupt them just as much,' said Darragh, thinking of the young soldier who had insisted on offering too much for a Mass.

'No,' Mr Regan maintained. 'In my case it's the other way around. Look, I had an American colonel come to my office the other day. He had with him a young woman, an American—she was in uniform. What they call their Army Air Force. The man had a smooth look. Very different from us; they're not as dowdy. The colonel wanted me to show him a flat. I could tell it was for the young woman, yet they seemed just about as normal and confident as a married couple. And I was embarrassed, but I did it. I knew, you see, he was setting up a love nest. I've always discouraged that sort of thing—I know how to put off a fellow Australian. But there was just something about the easy attitude of this chap I went along with. Just glided along. Like a weakling.'

He looked up with eyes in which shame and confusion were too naked. 'Sometimes,' Mr Regan continued, 'I think Christ put the Church into the hands of the wrong people. The Europeans, the Americans. Us. What's happening is a judgement of our easy ways. The races at Randwick while men die. Our general lack of fibre. I felt that I must confess it to you too, even though I knew you as a little kid. Just to show you there are old fools as well as young.' He refilled his own glass, and Darragh's. 'I got a good rent, needless to say.'

The man hung his head, his informal confession concluded. The self-imposed test of telling it to a young priest who knew him as a pillar had been passed, but seemed to have exhausted the man. Darragh felt bound to attempt to comfort him. 'You have to do your job, Mr Regan,' he said. 'It's not your job to force a confession from this colonel. The woman might have been his daughter.'

Mr Regan shook his head.

'If anything,' Darragh persisted, 'it's the colonel who is the sinner. You have no certain knowledge that he wanted the flat for a bad purpose.' He was arguing like a Jesuit.

Mr Regan said, like a theologian, 'The worst sins are the most excusable. They're the ones that get us damned.'

Frank saw that the man was burdened with something he'd done, probably a long time ago, for which he'd never forgiven himself. 'I wouldn't say that, Mr Regan. You seem to be pretty hard on yourself.' He forced a smile. 'On all of us.'

Mr Regan shook his head and seemed suddenly, but too late, interested in his seniority. 'You may not understand what I'm getting at, Father Frank. You're young. What concerns me is this. Will I in a year's time happily be renting flats to the Japanese? For the same reason I did to the American? For that's what my office door says I do, and it's what I do by habit. Will their strangeness make me say, "All right, cripes, I might as well." '

'I'm sure you'll behave like an Australian patriot, Mr Regan.'

'I've been a real estate agent thirty-seven years.'

Eyes averted from this neighbour tormented by scruples, Frank began to advise him that one of the great human errors was to decide beforehand how we would behave in a given situation. We could not predict what divine grace, appropriate to the moment, would flow our way. This seemed to give Mr Regan little comfort, and Frank Darragh was happy in the end to be told he ought to go and see his mother and aunt again. Mr Regan himself stayed on in his bomb shelter to finish his bottle of beer, and Frank passed through the household of lithe, Cootamundra-bound Regan women, so that he could go on his way to say goodbye to his mother and Aunt Madge.

CHAPTER THREE

LATER, DARRAGH WOULD see Mr Regan's over-frank and unsacramental confession as the beginning of a phase of exceptional confessions cast up—so Mr Regan would have it, and so Darragh himself saw it—by the corrupting and perilous times. The following Saturday afternoon, for example, Darragh heard the confession of a young soldier—there was a dim glint of khaki shirt through the confessional screen, and Darragh thought he knew the penitent beyond, identifying him from voice and outline as a rather sensitive young militia sergeant whose parents lived in the parish, a man who had been involved in theatrical companies in the area, and whose angular, fine-cut features made him somehow an unlikely member of the sun-blasted, hard-handed Australian army.

The sin as confessed was this: the soldier had been invited to a smart party on the North Shore but was embarrassed to have found no girl to take. A neighbour of the soldier, a few years younger, who had gone to the same school as he and with whom he had a special friendship, offered to take part in a startling stratagem. This boy, seventeen and of delicate frame, had offered to dress as a woman, just as happened in Shakespeare and comedies, and accompany the soldier to the party, for the purposes of farce. This was innocence itself, for Darragh seemed to remember something along these lines in *Twelfth Night*, which he studied in boyhood. And the volunteering boy was used to doing this, apparently. It was somewhere between a frequent joke and a common performance. He had attended acting classes, said the sergeant, and knew all about theatrical make-up too.

On the day of the party the young soldier had sat with the boy as he made himself up at length, and by the time they went to the party together, the disguised young man looked more handsome to the militiaman than many a girl. The soldier had danced all night with the made-up boy, and then they had left and performed what the tormented soldier called 'an indecent act'. Now he found it very hard to stay away from his friend. He had realised that women did not count for him.

Darragh, of course, had heard of the existence of such sins, but to meet the proposition in the flesh raised something edgy in him not only in terms of moral outrage but because he felt inadequate to the task of counselling the militiaman. Yet he began, since it was his task to begin. The militiaman must realise, he said, that he had greatly imperilled himself—he had not merely outraged God but was tending in a direction which would make him an outcast. To Darragh, eternal priest and—he would himself admit—sheltered boy, there seemed to be a wilfulness in that. He wanted to be angry, but under the exorcist's burden of being a merciful confessor, he felt, too, that without the army and the heightened time, without the threat of dying too young in some horrifying tropic place, without all borders blurring or being borne away, this young man would not have behaved in this perverted manner. History had knocked the soldier out of his orbit, had confused the directions he should take. 'You must avoid this association,' said Frank firmly and with utter conviction, but fearing, as with Mr Regan, he might be out of his depth. For to the Frank Darragh who occupied the confessional that day, with the power to bind and loose humanity from its shame and moral wilfulness, woman constituted the ultimate temptation. The dream of closeness with a woman, of being party with her to the revelation of some unutterable mystery. The girl on the train was both noble soul and alluring creature. But not so a boy dressed as a pseudo-woman. Woman was so much the pole star that he could not imagine why this militiaman-navigator beyond the grille should be swayed by such false magnetism.

'I tell myself I'll avoid him, but I don't know how to,' the soldier admitted. 'I see him everywhere.'

'Everywhere. You mean, you run into him all the time.'

'Not all the time. But I see his face everywhere.'

'No,' said Darragh, deciding that severity would not serve and adopting a gentler tone. 'No, that's an indulgence. You shouldn't talk or think that way. You'll find that you will meet some girl—indeed, you should try to do that. That will put you back on your proper track. It is possible for a good person, and I know you are a good person, to be thrown sideways by some kink. But that's all this is. A kink.'

Darragh hoped his own revulsion had not emerged.

'Then I'll try,' said the soldier, more insistently. Darragh could not doubt the sincerity of that, and yet it seemed to him that a whiff of hopeless self-knowledge drifted through the screen. Darragh himself was infected by it, and struggled in its coils.

Darragh came clean. It was, an instinct told him, most fruitful. 'Look,' he said, 'I'm only a young man, like you. As man, I know no more than you know. Possibly less. As priest I know the sacramental power of absolution, and I know too the power and mercy of the Virgin Mary, the ultimate woman, the Tower of Ivory, the Star of the Sea. She will not let you be lost. I promise you. She will not let you.'

The soldier said nothing.

'Do you understand?' asked Darragh, more in hope than in authority.

When the soldier said he did, Darragh absolved him. But strangeness had entered Father Darragh's moral atlas.

His Tuesdays were devoted to visitations. He had divided the streets of Homebush and Strathfield and, with the help of the parish rolls, set forth systematically to visit the faithful on foot. When he took his black felt hat off at their doors, his straight brown hair, assiduously parted, itched with sweat. He was careful not to enter households where young women were on their own, chatting to them instead at their doorways, touching, with the implied beneficence of his office, the heads of their children who gazed up snuffling at him. Sometimes a parishioner's son or husband was home on leave, and Darragh was brought inside to drink tea from the best cups and had fruit cake forced upon him.

The near sixty-year-old Clancy sisters lived together in Beresford Road, and in particular fed him. Occasionally he visited them out of pure hunger. He knew them to be penitents of his, that they confessed their non-sins to him once a month at least. 'I was snippy with my sister.' They were stoutish, forthright women who at some stage had sold up their late father's pub in Narromine and moved to the city to live comfortably ever after on the proceeds. They wore support hose under their big tents of floral dresses, and their thickening ankles put stress upon the

leather bulwarks of their plain shoes. But he had no doubt that
they were among the beloved of Christ. They lived virtuously but
without fuss, they were frank to a fault, and they gave amply to
the monsignor's building fund. The elder Clancy told him once,
'I'm pleased to have escaped all the fuss of marriage. Children
would be nice—our brother has the two. But marriage is a
torment, Father, for many women.' And she would draw herself
up in all the certainty of her lucky escape. Who was he, a celi-
bate, to disagree with her?

He was drinking tea with them on the Tuesday following the
soldier's confession. It was nearly noon, and he had at least six
and a half cups in him from various households, and his bladder
ached. They were the sort of people, the Clancy sisters, one could
ask for the use of their lavatory. They had no illusions that priests
lacked bladders. Their bathroom was always set up in taste, with
a special towel laid by for his use, and a fresh bar of Cashmere
Bouquet. They always presumed, too, he was there for a dona-
tion. They did not resent it, but offered him money to take back
to the parish—generally, as now, £10 in a white envelope.

'But I didn't come for that,' he said.

'Well, if you're to be a parish priest you must get used to
asking for money.'

The Clancy sisters were also astounding informants. They did
not seem to be shocked at all by scandalous behaviour in the
Strathfield–Homebush area. Nor did they adopt any pharisee
airs—they were honestly enthralled by gossip, a generally minor
sin they might, for all Darragh remembered, have mentioned in
the confessional. They knew which absent soldiers' wives were
behaving badly. They had, perhaps from their pub-owning papa,
such a normal air of knowing all about the debased nature of the
human heart, even of their own hearts, that it was hard to see

them as narrow carping gossipers, as whitened sepulchres while within everything was rotten.

'Mrs Flood,' said the elder Miss Clancy, while the other shuttled about their kitchen, 'her mother was such a good Catholic. Her father was rough as anything, they said he was a Communist at the saleyards. She rents a room to a young fellow from the brickworks. Strapping young bloke, but they tell us 4F, unfit to serve.' Miss Clancy tossed her head in the baldest disbelief. 'He seems to serve the Flood household all right.'

The other Miss Clancy came from the kitchen with fresh hot water.

'Mrs Flood,' she sharply informed Darragh, 'now shares bed and board with the young fellow, and the husband resides on the back verandah!'

They both shook their heads, though they did not seem as shaken as Darragh by this degree of lasciviousness in a prosaic suburb.

'You should go and see her, Father,' said the bossier of the Clancys. The command made him uneasy. Another dictum of his old spiritual director: 'People don't come around by being harangued. They respond to example.' He would need to think about what example he could set Mrs Flood.

'Thing is,' said the older sister, 'she has this very bad consumption. Coughing all the time. Bloody handkerchiefs. She's been in a sanatorium . . .'

'Boddington,' said the younger Miss Clancy. 'In the Blue Mountains.'

'You'd wonder where she'd get the energy. And for the young fellow . . . well, you'd wonder what the attraction is.'

'Red hair,' said the younger sister, offering Darragh more Scotch Fingers. 'Some men are crazy for it.'

Darragh supposed he should visit Mrs Flood sometime in the near future in view of her medical condition alone. It would be a difficult business if the brickworker and the husband were both at home at the time. What could be said? Perhaps the Clancy sisters were wrong about the boarder. But they had an aura of great certainty.

When Darragh asked them, before leaving, if they had an air-raid shelter to go to, they told him of course they did, only two doors up. As for their ever fleeing, 'No Jap would dare put a foot in our front door,' said the eldest. Darragh hoped she would not be disabused of that proposition.

He returned from the Clancy sisters with that unaccustomed sense of oppression recurring. He felt he needed what he rarely needed: not a mere afternoon nap, but a few profound hours of sleep. It was as if to the scales of sin the Clancy sisters had added that one backbreaking straw—the sexual villainy of mortally ill Mrs Flood. This tattle about the red-headed adulterer seemed connected in its high colour with the confession of the soldier about the boy seductress. He knew his father must have seen fantastical things in Paris and London, where soldiers sought in viciousness a model of the horror they were on leave from. But the younger Darragh's boyhood had been sheltered from the concrete evidence of human desire which many of his fellow seminarians brought from their childhood farms and raw inner suburbs to their studies. He was prepared for the sins which occupied the major headings in Noldin's *Summa Theologiae Moralis*; he had not expected to face in Strathfield the *danse macabre* of Noldin's more fanciful footnotes. Surely, the footnotes of extreme perversion belonged to Europe, to France, say, with its world-weariness and its ancient record of sin, which God had punished in 1940 by letting the French army collapse.

The reliable springs of divine wisdom on which he drew confidently in the confessional and in daily life to deal with normal sin now seemed more remote from him. There was as well a stupefying sense that further shocks awaited before the Japanese Empire finally lapped up against the Clancy sisters' doorstep.

In an attempt to ward off the itch for oblivion, to achieve a sense of the normal, a sense of being held in position by wisdom incarnate, Darragh read what was left of his office—Vespers and Compline. Psalm 139, now that he looked at it, was full of warnings about the fallibility and ill will of humanity. '*Acuunt linguas suas ut serpens; venonum aspidum sub labias eorum.* Their tongues are as sharp as those of serpents; the venom of asps lies under their lips.' So far from redemption, this creeping, serpentine species of which he was a member.

Mrs Flannery cooked an entire dreary lunchtime meal for him that day. The monsignor was not in, and so Darragh was able to read the *Herald* as, in his sudden spiritual weariness, he devoured Mrs Flannery's floury cooking, aware that on this poisonous earth he was fortunate to be fed, but incapable, for once, of a sense of gracious thanksgiving.

The *Herald* ('Protestant rag that it is,' said the monsignor as he thoroughly read it) had predictable tidings. A surrounded Australian battalion had successfully fought its way back to the British lines in Malaya, but the mark of the Japanese advance was further down the Malay Peninsula than it had been the last time the *Herald* published its dispiriting map. The government was already discussing plans for the evacuation of children from Brisbane and Sydney should the Japanese capture fields which put those targets in range. Children had already been moved from the tropical port of Darwin. But framing the news of military catastrophe and the coming bewilderment of children were

the graphic advertisements in which Pepsodent toothpaste promised the young success in their social life at their local tennis
club—'Shirley's teeth are so much whiter!' In Capstan and Turf
and 33 advertisements, the faces of confident smokers too,
hemmed in the columns of bad news. Salvital promised the
threatened populace of the Commonwealth of Australia, no
matter what, a settled digestion, and Solvol assured them they
would meet every emergency with immaculate hands.

A chastening statement from the prime minister, Mr Curtin:
'The Spearhead reaches South—Always South'. Mr Curtin suggested that the whole future of 'our race' was at stake. At
Leichhardt Stadium, Billy Britt had fought an American soldier
named the Alabama Kid. Britt, a Catholic Youth Organisation
boxer of some renown, had been flattened in the eighth round by
said Kid.

Darragh took his plate to the kitchen to thank Mrs Flannery.
She had tapioca pudding for him, but he suggested that as much
as he liked tapioca, he might have it that night. He heard his own
voice and feared it sounded sullen. He hated to sound that way.
It had been part of his self-respect as a youth to overcome the
natural surliness of boyhood. But here it was, asserting itself at
his age, in the presbytery kitchen.

By the time he reached his room, which blessedly pointed
towards the quiet, tree-lined street rather than towards the
convent school, he was staggering with exhaustion, and broke
the rule of neatness by lying on the bed in his black trousers. His
chances of surreptitiously ironing them later, without Mrs
Flannery's knowledge, were non-existent, since in domestic
affairs she was all-knowing. But he would deal with that question
later. He was instantly asleep, with the sort of tiredness which
induces vivid dreams.

He saw very clearly in the brassy afternoon light that came from his window and penetrated his sleep the striped awnings which Australians used to transform back verandahs into bedrooms. Millions of Australians, adolescents or inconvenient uncles, lived verandah lives and dreamed verandah dreams, sheltered by such awnings. Hundreds of thousands, anyhow. The canvas always patterned in yellow and browny-orange—very nearly the same colour as the flags which were put up on beaches to mark safe swimming spots. By the awning of Darragh's dream sat a grey-faced, thin man, wearing a satin-backed vest, a collarless shirt, undistinguished pants, smoking a thin, self-made cigarette. He seemed the loneliest man in that plain void enclosed by orange and yellow sun-blasted awning. Occupying in his own household the space reserved for the visitor, the child, the over-staying, under-paying guest. Darragh approached him and asked, 'What have you done?' For though the man's demeanour was humble, there was no doubt that he had achieved something worthy of a mad emperor. The man was philosophically inhaling the smoke from his little glowing cigarette and had his eye on the middle distance. 'What have you done?'

The man rose like a night porter or watchman roused by an unexpected demand or question. The fag-end dangling from his thin creased, yellowed fingers, he moved from his chair to lead Darragh on a tour of the atrocity.

There are some dreams, particularly the dreams of exhausted afternoons, in which your sense of movement seems very close to movement in the waking world. There are corridors to be traversed, and doors to be opened, and the weary pale man, leading him and opening the way, performed those services for Darragh. He opened the bedroom door and entered into a wired, room-sized meat closet where immaculate sides of lamb hung from hooks. He picked up from the floor some sharp implements which might stand in the way of Frank Darragh's thorough inspection. On a couch by the meat closet's window sat a blood-ied handkerchief. Darragh looked at it and rage filled him. The man nudged the floor and inhaled his narrow-gutted cigarette and, forcing a joyless cloud of smoke, hissing, between his teeth. 'We were expecting you earlier,' he said.

If the clean-slaughtered sheep of this dream were calculated to wake Father Darragh, they did not. But they flavoured his ongoing sleep with that particularly acrid fear peculiar to dreams. Even his unconscious mind was aware of his limbs fibrillating and turning chill, the sort of coldness that comes, say, from standing too close to some edge. *I come to bring you a clean sacrifice . . .*

He was also somehow aware of the afternoon advancing, and was pleased at that, so that any new, conscious-stricken require-ments of the day would need to be postponed. Sometimes, if he was about at the right hour, he went over to greet the children as they left school. But that hour of promise and innocence and blessing slipped away beneath the umber tide of his sleep. It was five past five when he woke, his body sweaty because of the ill-considered amount of clothing in which he'd fallen asleep. At seven o'clock he was to conduct the Benediction of the Blessed Sacrament, singing the hymns with the congregation, raising the monstrance with the Divine Host within it to bless the faithful petitioners, each one of them with their heads bowed in pre-dictable ways: Dear God, save my boy, stop the Japanese, make my husband kinder, aid me as the other man charms me, give me a happy death, ease my pain, assuage my doubt!

As he went to the bathroom to rinse his neck and upper body, he could hear Monsignor Carolan's voice raised in conversation in the lounge room downstairs. Tuesday. The monsignor always had lunch with his classmate Monsignor Plunkett on Tuesdays. Monsignor Carolan had once told Darragh, 'Plunkett knows every rich Catholic between here and Bourke, and knows how to talk to them, too.' Darragh decided that when he had washed and changed his shirt, he would go—as a polite curate should— and pay his respects to eminent Monsignor Plunkett. So ten minutes later, in the sort of collarless shirt to which priests attached their stocks by means of a stud, he made his way down the stairs. Halfway down, it became clear to him that the monsignor believed him to be out of the house. He was speaking in that full-blast voice which powerful men develop in their middle age, and he was discussing Darragh.

'He hears bucketloads of confessions,' the monsignor was saying. 'That seems to be his chief definition of what a priest does.'

'Sounds morbid,' suggested Plunkett. 'I hope not, Vince.'

'No. A happy soul. If anything innocent as a lamb. See, an only child, elderly and protective parents. The father's dead. Poor young Frank knows nothing of the world. He also knows nothing about the eleventh commandment, the sacrament without which nothing gets done. Thou shalt raise plenteous finance. I don't think he'll ever be any good at that one. Parishioners tell me he visits them and asks them *not* to give him money.'

'Some sort of a zealot then?'

'No. Too earnest, that's all. You see, everything he does flows out of his innocence. What's going to become of him if events shake him up?'

'What sort of events do you mean?' asked Plunkett.

'Well, he's the hero of silly pious women and pale self-abusers. What'll happen when he meets real people?'

Darragh would have hated to be caught on the stairs, listening, his face full of blood. He eased his way upwards again. Knowing it was vanity, he was nonetheless sharply affronted to hear his parish priest's assessment of him. He had been attracted to the Church by the certainty priests could enjoy that the orders and opinions of their superiors, their parish priests and bishops, must be accommodated and accepted as God's will. He had had no trouble with that proposition till this afternoon. Why couldn't he just accept the monsignor's unflattering report? He could not, and although he knew it was futile, he felt anger as well. The monsignor was pleased enough with his innocence to exploit it to have early Masses said! To have him take Benedictions, and double shifts in the confessional! Darragh would tell him too, but not yet; in robust anger, but not while this stupid state of pique was on him.

Walking in his room, he struggled through the last of Compline, and then said the next day's Matins and Lauds, thus completing his daily duty. He was distracted throughout by rage and shame, by the question of which he should be, angry or self-questioning. His lips still enunciated the Latin in the rounded Italian style he had cultivated before his ordination. *'Fratres: Sobrii estote, et vigilate* . . . Brothers, be sober and keep watch, because your adversary the Devil, like a raging lion, goes about seeking whom he might devour . . .' As these words fell from his tongue like unregarded pebbles dropped by a negligent hand, he rehearsed the furious speeches he would never make to the monsignor.

Even for a man who was instructed to rejoice when criticised, it was too grave a night, given what he had overheard on the stairs, given, as well, boys in make-up and 4F interlopers from the brickworks, to sit down and eat a salad with the monsignor.

The living room was empty now, and Darragh went to the kitchen and found Mrs Flannery at her work, slicing the previous Sunday's lamb from which the summer air seemed to have drawn all succulence.

'If you'd excuse me from being at tea, Mrs Flannery,' Darragh told her.

Mrs Flannery said, 'But you can't give Benediction on an empty stomach, Father.'

Darragh held up an apologetic hand. He could see its dishonesty before his face. 'Please—I'll make myself some toast and tea afterwards. That will do me.'

'Go to the ice chest when you're finished Benediction. You'll find I've left you something under a beaded cover.'

Darragh foresaw greasy slabs of cold mutton, with sliced beetroot and lettuce, and a jug of condensed milk mayonnaise, the latter covered with its own little beaded doily. What sort of man despised such niceties, such marks of regard, he wondered. But in his present state, he did.

For all he could imagine doing after Benediction was to sink again into torpor, in which all questions would be for the moment suspended. He had heard of priests experiencing these phases of despair, when the tide of grace ran out, when the performance of duty seemed arid. He was concerned it had happened to him now, when he was barely three years ordained, when there was so far to go, and such great changes to be accommodated. And not over time either, but this year. This half-year.

When he got to the sacristy door at five to seven, the altar boys were standing there in the last of the light, gazing out for his arrival. They knew he was generally conscientious enough to get there early. Due to an edict of the monsignor, the boys were forbidden from lighting the charcoal for the incense until a priest was present, for fear that in their brio they would burn the church down. Now they set to work on igniting the beads of charcoal, and they looked sideways at the robing Darragh as they did so. Altar boys had an infallible nose for the mental state of a priest. This was the first time, Darragh knew, they had seen him so beset.

It was five minutes past seven before Father Darragh, phenomenally late by his own standards, followed the boy carrying the incense, and the other with the brass thurible with its small load of glowing charcoals, to the altar, and the organist began playing that resounding Benediction hymn '*Tantum Ergo Sacramentum*'. The congregation, the taste of their evening meals on their tongues, having rushed along Homebush Road in the certain knowledge that he always began Benediction on time, might themselves have been a little bemused by the late start. The golden cope hanging from his shoulders, Darragh ascended the altar, unlocked the tabernacle with its brass key, and extracted the large consecrated host, the body and blood of Christ, and inserted it in the great brass and golden sunspray of the monstrance. Leaving it on the altar in its place of honour, he descended the steps, a ritual recognition of the supremacy of Christ's Eucharist. This descent had until the last few days enriched him, but now it was just taking carpeted steps and trying not to trip on his long white alb. Feeding incense into the thurible, he swung the smoking metal bulb in the direction of the sacrament, while the congregation bowed profoundly behind him. But the task of holding the chains and directing the thurible was best achieved by him with eyes raised to Christ his brother, hidden behind the banal species of a white disc of unleavened bread. 'Help me,' he begged fraternally.

CHAPTER FOUR

MRS FLANNERY SEEMED as innocent of slumber as of girlish-ness. The concept of her rest somewhere in the presbytery, in a specific housekeeper's room on the ground floor, defeated the imagination. She was always in full, wakeful throat when she woke Darragh at a quarter to five. Instantly awake, instantly uneasy, remembering all, he still knew exactly his program for that morning. He was to hear the confessions of the brothers, and say Mass for them in their tiny chapel a mile west from St Margaret's. The monsignor sometimes even asked him to hear the muttered lapses of the Dominican nuns one mile east, generously offering Darragh the use of his Buick for the visits, forgetting that Darragh had not yet finished his education as a driver, and was likely to clash the Buick's silky gears and use up too much of the petrol ration, generous as it was for ministers of religion.

He was always humbled to hear the confessions of the Christian Brothers, some of them middle-aged. Barely ten years before, he had been taught by such men. They were fellows whose vows of poverty left them with very little except the charity of the parents of the boys they taught. They lacked a car between the lot of them. If they went to the dentist or the doctor, their superior, Brother Keogh, gave them a few pence for the bus. Darragh realised that he did not have the humility to become one of them. These were monks who had none of the powers of the priesthood. They had no altar or pulpit. Whereas with a sacred thirst, he had desired the power he had—the power to bind and loose.

He pleaded with the Virgin Mother, the Mother of the Universe, to help him find meaning in shaving. To the monsignor's amusement he used the modern kind of shaver with its detachable blade. The Ingram's Shaving Cream jar was as rich a blue as the mantle of the Virgin. But he experienced no revival of spirit.

Walking the mile in the quiet morning, a dawn which seemed safe beyond war and the hot breath of history, his throat was full of dust-dry yearning for the right kind of cleverness, the appointed mix. The Brothers' small chapel, when he entered it, was full of blue-grey humidity and the cold tallowy smell of candles. In the little room adjoining it, which served as sacristy there, stood a small confessional stall—a chair and a kneeler facing each other and, above and between them, a red drape which protected the face of the penitent brother from the gaze of the confessor. By virtue of his having been chosen for the task of absolving them, he encountered aspects of these brothers of the teaching orders which he had never suspected when he was a child under their tutelage. So many of them pleaded to unkindly and demeaning words, and the ones who did seemed to be the men least likely to have uttered them, and thus were those most awake to a child's feelings.

He was surprised, not at the level of his reason, but in that part of his soul where he was still a boy, to find some older brothers, advanced in their careers, still troubled by the flesh, by disbelief in what they were doing, and in the case of one brother, by the death in the crash of a bomber of twins he had taught. It was clear to Darragh that the brother felt for these two the way a father would for his sons—that in another time and place, he believed he might have fathered two such boys. The horror of their blazing deaths had altered the maps for this good, honest, unambitious man.

Some of the older brothers suffered what he now knew to be the standard feelings of loss of faith, of having been abandoned by God. Men who had felt themselves to be intimates of Christ and His Mother had lost that familiarity. This, Darragh told them as he had been taught to tell them, was the pain which arose from the end of one form of closeness and the testing beginning of another, less obvious nearness. He knew this because he hoped it was true; a mere endurance trial, and happy revelations soon to come.

One monk confessed to being attracted to the mother of a pupil. He had received kind words from her, and they had tormented and exhilarated him.

And now, on a morning when he was least prepared for it and had thought he had already heard the chief sins of the community, there came another extraordinary confession, a further blow to that innocence of which the monsignor accused him. It was a youngish voice Darragh recognised, the voice of a contemporary, from beyond the curtain. After asking for Darragh's blessing and announcing that his last confession had been a week previously, the brother said, 'I do not want to become a man who makes bad confessions, or goes to communion in sin.'

'No, my son,' said Darragh, in a voice which fraudulently implied that he had heard everything that could possibly be confessed.

'I had no intention of doing this, Father. I've struggled with it six months. I took a boy, one of our favourites, to a private place, and I touched him, and he touched me.'

Darragh had never expected to find such vipers sliding under the confessional veil. It was now he knew for certain that every strange extremity of guilt was determined to beat its way to his ear. For a time Darragh found it a test to articulate. He had no idea why a young man, a contemporary, would harbour *that* desire, and then honour it in practice. For it destroyed the core of his vocation; the shepherd became the wolf.

'Father . . .?' asked the young man's voice from beyond the dense velvet curtain. He seemed to fear that the scale of his sin had incapacitated his confessor. He was nearly correct about that.

Darragh struggled forth a broken-backed question. Was there, he asked, what could be called full indecency?

'On my part,' confessed the young man. He sounded almost confident now he had transferred his shame and his bewilderment to Darragh. He was full of breathy resolution. 'I'll never do it again, Father.'

Darragh said urgently, 'You *must* never do it again.'

The young man beyond the velvet seemed aghast at the whispering fury in Darragh, and shocked to muteness.

'I tell you, you must never do it again. The child was put into your care by God. And you have done this to him! Do you think he will ever forget? Do you think you can ever restore his innocence?'

'No, I can't. All I can do is to try to make amends to him.'

In fact, the young brother sounded crazily confident he could do so.

'You shouldn't try to do anything without speaking to your superior.'

There was a silence beyond the curtain. Darragh could guess that the young brother was most fearful of being made to do that; to admit to such a crime in front of the head of his community. He had hoped that what he had done to the boy was now walled up forever in Darragh's brain, bound never to emerge. But if a condition of being absolved was that the young man tell Brother Keogh, there would be no red-velvet secrecy. He would be required to go on retreat, a time of withdrawal and reflection at a monastery. He would be sent to another school with a cloud over his name. The most senior men in the order might be warned of him, and the chief sin of his life.

'Has this ever happened in the past?' asked Darragh.

'No,' said the stricken brother. 'No. I have had temptations . . . This is . . .'

Darragh sat back in his chair, and could understand why the ancient monsignor at Manly should move slowly beneath the wake of the demons he had taken on in China.

'You must not try to make amends in your own right. You need to speak to your superior and also to a more senior priest, a spiritual adviser. I can advise you only to pray to the Virgin Mary who is the mother of you and this boy both. And I must ask you to pledge before God that you will never do this obscene thing again.' Mercy was slipping from Darragh. Abhorrence and severity reigned in his heart.

'I pledge,' said the young brother. 'I do, Father.'

'You must see a more senior and experienced confessor as soon as possible. And though you are absolved of this sin, you must tell him about it.'

'I will.'

'*Urgently*,' said Darragh, with the urgency of his own abhorrence.

He gave the young man the Sorrowful Mysteries for his penance. Parents should be warned, but they could not be, not by Darragh. 'I will pray for you,' he told the brother after he'd spoken the formula of absolution.

The assurance sat in his mouth like a stone.

And even so, that morning, the duty of visiting Mrs Flood, and drawing off the venom of that dream of a husband exiled to awninged verandahs, remained. Back at the presbytery, he ate hard-boiled eggs—he had to drink tea on top of them to wash them down, and found the combination repellent. The reflection that for thousands of miles northwards, from the Dutch East Indies to the north of China, all hens had fallen under the requisition of the Japanese army had no effect in evoking a normal, banal sense of gratitude in him. From the living room could be heard the portentous anthem of the 'ABC News', and a well-modulated voice reciting—unsurprisingly after the confession he had heard—the signs of the last days of Western Christian civilisation, but particularly the earth blessed by the Southern Cross, the Land of the Holy Spirit, as a few Portuguese navigators had called it. He feared the Spirit would not stir the air of this dull, humid morning.

Monsignor Carolan came in, lifted the teapot off the table and shook it. Reassured that there was tea inside, he poured a cup.

'How is it going there, Frank?'

'It's going well,' lied Frank, now that the monsignor could not quite be trusted.

'I was hoping, since there's a finance committee get-together at Mr Gaffney's on Thursday night, you might be able to take Benediction for me that night too.'

'All right,' said Frank, but not before an instant of consideration.

'I don't want to work you to death, old son,' said the monsignor, beaming with his characteristic Australian bonhomie. He might have been a successful farmer from the bush, a suburban real estate agent. The filament between him and his brethren working in earthly occupations seemed thin at such moments. The weight of his priesthood could seem to rest lightly on him. Yet he was the monsignor. He kept God's bank passbooks too. All the elite of the archdiocese of Sydney were such men. The alternative, when it came to parish priests, seemed to be isolated, cranky, semi-hermitic and misanthropic old coots in faded, scurfy soutanes and run-down presbyteries.

'You just tell me if you need a break,' said the monsignor. 'You could go up and stay a few days with Father Roberts at Katoomba.'

'I don't think I need a holiday yet, Monsignor.'

'Okay.' The monsignor ingested his tea in one long draught. 'Did you hear the Japanese bombed Derby?' Derby was an improbably remote place in Western Australia. But they were citizens of the Commonwealth there!

Darragh asked, 'What will happen to finance committee meetings at Mr Gaffney's when the Japanese come sailing up the Parramatta River?'

The monsignor frowned. 'That's a pretty strange question, Frank. I suppose the answer is, we'll do what we can.'

At this opening, Darragh trembled on the edge of losing his temper, and knew he could not win the argument in his present state. He looked full in the monsignor's eyes, daring him to see the change in his curate. The monsignor looked away, and shrugged, and left the room. 'Look after yourself, Frank,' he called over his shoulder. That was the problem—how to answer the monsignor in a way which did not concede the point?

Now Darragh walked Homebush Road on his way to Mrs Flood's address as it appeared in the parish records. Christ had amazed a woman He met by the road in Palestine, a region to which the British and Australians now grimly clung. 'I am not married,' the woman had told Christ. And He said to her that indeed she wasn't, that the man with whom she lived was not her husband. Her imagination had been at once captivated, her morality revived. Darragh said a hopeless prayer to the effect that he might have a similarly kindly impact.

Thin beneath his black serge suit and clerical stock and collar, he did not sweat much, which was welcome, since on days of high heat, sweaty priests glistened within their stoles, their encrusted chasubles. Women like the Clancy sisters and others of their age were always asking him did Mrs Flannery feed him enough, as if they wanted him to turn into a fat, companionable, sweaty parish priest of the kind he precisely did not seek to be.

Today he was bound north towards the railway line, and the road called The Crescent, which wasn't a crescent at all but a straight street, where Mrs Flood awaited the conclusion of her tuberculosis in the company of her two men. He would have felt himself a ghost, and possibly would have liked that, had not he encountered mothers walking their children to St Margaret's. They exuded huge smiles in his direction, and he bleakly prayed that none of the boys would meet a pernicious brother. If Mr Regan was correct in his idea that the Japanese were God's mechanism to erase a godless generation, the only trouble was that the inviolate children had to suffer the correction as well.

A military transport train ran along the embankment above The Crescent, and soldiers whistled from its windows at two girls emerging from Pedderick the chemist's. Boys whistling their way through every suburb and township between Sydney and some camp in the bush. The war did not seem to suppress them. Maybe they found the imminent prospect of the enemy as hard to believe in at this moment as did Darragh himself.

Beyond a garden of lank grass, the front windows of Mrs Flood's low-slung house were open. Thus Darragh surmised she must be in. The doorbell, the kind you cranked, was answered by a tall man. He wore grey pants, grey vest, white collarless shirt—very much like the abused husband in his dream except that he was fuller in the body. The man's stoutness saved Darragh from perceiving the dream which had motivated him to come here as too prophetic. As well, the fellow showed a normal secular shock at seeing him.

'Aw yes,' he said, as if he knew this awkward day would arrive; and here it was.

Darragh said he was the curate from St Margaret's. 'Is Mrs Flood in?' he asked. 'I believe she's been fairly sick.'

'Yeah,' said the man, rubbing his overnight beard. 'Yeah, she's been a bit up and down lately. It's her condition.'

'Is she at home?'

The man stood back, reluctantly permitting Darragh to enter. The hallway had an odour of dust spiked with the bitter scent of invalid tonics and tinctures. 'We're out in the kitchen,' said the man in the vest, directing him up the hallway. Darragh turned. 'You're Mr Flood?'

'That's right. Bert.'

'Father Frank Darragh,' said Frank, offering his hand. But the mutual clench was full of doubt. After all, how could you achieve the normal electricity of mateship between hand and hand if you introduced yourself as 'Father Frank Darragh'? What other description could Frank give himself though? They would suspect him more if he did not introduce himself in those terms, which nonetheless created an instant space about the priest, across which the sacramental mercies might or might not operate. Mr Flood retrieved his unwilling hand, and led Darragh up the hallway.

In the sunny kitchen, at the head of a scrubbed table with the well-intended remnants of sandsoap embedded in its grain, Mrs Flood, in light from the window behind her, sat in a wicker chair buttressed by pillows. She made a splendid invalid, possessed of a strange beauty. Seated beside her on a plain kitchen chair was a lean but muscular young man, fair-headed, drinking tea and holding in one hand, folded for reading, a newspaper entitled *The Worker*. Seeing Bert Flood and Darragh arrive, he creased it exactly to the size of a legal deed and laid it on the table like an opening bid. His left hand was heavily bandaged.

'Rosie,' said Mr Flood, gesturing with embarrassment towards Darragh, 'this is the priest from up the road.' There was a clear, pleading message: *you* deal with him. *You* send him on his way with a flea in his ear. There was no doubt Mrs Flood had the presence for such a task. She and the young man studied him in committee. Mrs Flood's red hair had sinuous curls, apparently of its own volition, without the intervention of beauty parlours. Her eyes glittered. She wore a generous trace of smile that gave Darragh hope of a welcome.

He heard himself repeat his name and tell her he'd heard she wasn't well. Breathing harshly, and her eyes glimmering in some kind of appreciation, Mrs Flood rubbed her lips with an immaculate handkerchief. She said, 'Sit down, Father Frank.' Generally only the close friends of priests had the liberty of calling them by their first names. She was, of course, aware of this, and was possibly sending him a signal—he would not be getting conventional reverence in this kitchen, but then he would not get typical denial either. And perhaps, in her voice crimped by her disease, with the second syllable of 'Father' reduced to a wheeze, she was presuming on the authority of her illness to help her through this meeting.

'It's years since we've had a priest here,' she told him from her chair.

'But you're on the parish roll,' said Frank.

'Yes,' she admitted. 'I used to go up there sometimes for Mass. But that monsignor of yours, he's money-crazy.'

'Not for his own sake,' said Frank.

'Oh, Father Frank, he used to drive a pretty nice car. You met Bert, did you? And this is our friend, Ross Trumble. Ross crushed a finger at the brickworks. He's off on compo.' Darragh exchanged nods with blue-eyed Mr Trumble.

'Get us some tea, eh, Bert?' suggested Mrs Flood. Bert went to the stove willingly to check on the state of the kettle, which was close to boiling.

'Sit down, Father Frank. Take that chair, that's right. I bet those old biddies the Clancys told you to come and try to improve me. Did you drive down yourself?'

'Walked,' said Frank.

'Good for you, young feller,' said Mrs Flood. She called to her husband, 'See, Bert, not all of them have cars.' It sounded as if they had once had a bet on the matter.

Ross Trumble still considered him, and the man's cheeks had become flushed from mounting discomfort or hostility. It was clear from these signs he had not met many priests, had preconceptions about them, and waited in uneasy certainty for Darragh to manifest himself.

As Bert came to the table with the replenished teapot, and a fresh cup and saucer for Darragh, Mrs Flood asked, 'What can we do for you, Father?'

'Well,' said Frank, 'since you're ill, and no doubt you find it hard to get to Mass, I thought you might welcome the chance for me to hear your confession and bring you communion occasionally.' The young man was looking utterly away now, not willing to share his gaze with Darragh. He knew it wasn't his place to say yes or no, however.

Mrs Flood was overtaken by an authentic tubercular coughing fit. It was not opportunistic, a disguised answer to Darragh's offer. Mrs Flood did not need to disguise anything. The young man, Trumble, rose, turned his back to the company, and went to a bench and poured a brown liquid into a glass. He brought it back and put it down in front of Mrs Flood who, gasping and signalling with eyes and small gestures of her hands that she would soon be well, reached for it and swallowed it at a gulp, right on top of her still active, gasping cough.

'Thanks, Rossy,' she said in a choked voice, as serenity re-entered her eyes.

She smiled, and Trumble gave the briefest grin of gratification.

'Kind of you, young Father Frank,' she said at last. 'But I don't think it's come to that yet. I've got a fair way to go, I hope. Rossy and Bert look after me well.' She reached out and gently patted the young man's bound hand. 'Sinner I am, but I'm not ready for the big last confession.'

There was an implicit wink in the way she spoke. She was not vicious, yet Darragh would not have been surprised to see her flutter her eyelids in attentive Ross Trumble's direction. She managed with ease this company of three men, two of them rendered uneasy by the presence of the third.

With her polite refusal, what could Darragh do, having chosen the subtle rather than the didactic line? He said gamely, 'I wasn't trying to imply that you needed the last rites, Mrs Flood. But every Catholic is supposed to make his Easter duty, to go to confession and take communion before Easter. Would you like me to visit you before Easter?

He looked at Bert. Bert must understand that an Easter confession could restore his marriage. You would expect a husband to hang on the wife's reply to such an idea, but Bert did not seem to hang on anything or see significance in much. He remained a mildly friendly presence, and distractedly smoked his thin cigarette. His mind was not so much elsewhere, but had long moved away from here, from the triangle around the table and the priest who could amend it.

Mrs Flood seemed to pity him in his bemusement. 'Look,' she said, 'you're a nice young fellow, Father Frank. But neither of these boys here are Tykes. And I think I'm going to have to wait for them to get more used to the idea of you calling in like this. How about if I get them to give you a call if I need anything? Anything along the lines of communion, or eternal salvation. What do you say, eh?'

She beamed, offering her small concession, having thoroughly won this encounter.

Darragh could merely utter the official line. As much as he believed it he sounded like a cop reducing some complicated statute to plainest English. 'I do urge you to think about doing your Easter duty, Mrs Flood. It's a requisite placed by the Pope on all Catholics.'

'I'll certainly think about it, Father Frank,' she told him, but with a sudden sisterly frown which warned him not to try his luck further; not if he wanted to be welcome.

Darragh finished his tea. To try to elicit something from the men—he was not sure what—but to try to engage them, he began to talk of the war.

Mrs Flood explained, with a heightened colour in her cheeks

for which Darragh hoped she might not have to pay later, 'Rossy here's a bit of a Red, you see, Father Frank. He thinks the most important thing is the battle in Russia, because if Hitler wins, that's the end of the revolution. But God, I have to say I'd hate it if the Nips came. I'd have to call on you then for sure, Frank.'

Frank?

'Well, perhaps we could meet a little earlier than that,' said Darragh.

He saw Bert rolling a further, conclusive cigarette, and maintaining the composure of those who survive by being beneath notice. A verandah-dweller to a T. Bert and Trumble and Mrs Flood knew it was time for him to go. Supporting his bound hand a little, Ross Trumble stood up. 'I'll see him out,' he insisted.

'May I give you a blessing before I go?' asked Frank of Mrs Flood.

'Don't see what harm it can do.'

Trumble averted his eyes during the small rite.

'*Benedicat vos . . .*' He used the plural, so that even torpid Bert and hostile Ross, without their knowledge, were encompassed in the rite. '*Benedicat vos omnipotens Deus, Pater et Filius et Spiritus Sanctus.*'

'Feel better already,' said Mrs Flood, opening the bright eyes she had kept closed for this prayer, her marvellous smile in place. 'Thank you, Father Frank.' With the generosity of that smile she had beguiled first Bert, and then lean Ross Trumble. She who had the power to leave them with nowhere else to go, exactly as she had left Darragh with nothing else to do except depart.

He told all of them it had been a pleasure to meet them, that he would remember Mrs Flood at Mass, and then Ross Trumble was solemnly leading him back up the hall. The tall, fair-haired brick worker opened the door with his undamaged hand and then blocked the exit.

'Look,' he said, 'I can't call you *"Father"*, so don't expect it.' He waited a while as if he half-hoped for a strong chastisement from Darragh.

'I can't make you do anything, Mr Trumble.'

'Okay, Frank, listen. You're just another feller to me, you see. You seem a fair enough bloke which makes it all the more bloody outrageous that you should come here with your "I'm Father Darragh" and your "Let me give you a blessing", and all the rest of the bag of tricks.'

'It's what I was put on earth to do,' Frank asserted. He still hoped it was true.

'Yeah, and you might be sincere about it. But I bet you live pretty well. Better than us.'

Darragh could do nothing but fall back on his common malehood and shrug. 'I get paid barely thirty shillings a week.'

'Yeah. But all's found for you by the believers, isn't it? And you whack on about God and redemption, but really you're put here on earth to keep the workers in their place. To offer them heaven instead of justice.'

'I've heard all those arguments, Mr Trumble.'

'I think they're pretty good arguments, Frankie boy.' He was breathless with anger, Darragh noticed. 'I mean, God doesn't need marriage, but the banks certainly do. One little two-person mortgage after another. Do not fornicate outside the marriage because you'll buy the second woman a dress or a jewel, and that'll get in the way of bank repayments!'

Frank said with an ironic smile which invited Trumble into the joke as well, 'I never knew that. That I was a bank employee.'

Trumble wouldn't concede. 'You're as much a bank's man as any copper. Look, I know what you're here for. You've heard the gossip and you're chasing us up. You think if you hear her confession you can make her split up with me. All of us out in the kitchen knew what this was about. So to me you're just a bloke who tries to stand between a man and his woman. And according to tradition, that's a bloody dangerous place to stand.'

Darragh, edgy with anger, nonetheless decided to resort to equivalent frankness. 'Come on, Ross. The way you're living isn't natural.'

'It's natural as hell to me. I'm warning you, you've got no special protection just because you happen to wear a dog collar. You ought to wake up to yourself!'

Darragh had always surmised that one day there would be threats of this nature. He had imagined that they would be easier to brush off than this one was. His arms and legs, ready to fight if needed, felt heavy with alarmed blood. His mouth was dry, and he felt foolish and negligible.

'Are you going to let me out of the door?' he asked Trumble. 'I've got other duties today.'

'You poor young bastard,' said Trumble, and stepped aside at last.

Darragh walked out, down the steps, across the garden, and took exact care closing the wire gate, as if that might earn him some credibility from Trumble.

CHAPTER FIVE

BACK IN THE presbytery, Frank Darragh ate his lunch with a wooden but profound appetite. In the face of Mrs Flood's charming refusals, of Trumble's hostility, he urged himself to greater firmness and self-respect. It was not as if this fallow season of the soul was unexpected, and its feelings of leadenness and futility. Every authority spoke of the onset of the disease called accidie, a sort of religious version of profound boredom, a sense of the withdrawal of grace when no notable sin has been committed to explain it. Mystics—St John of the Cross, St Teresa of Avila, as well as Thomas à Kempis in *The Imitation of Christ*—all wrote of this sudden absence. It could last for years, and the traveller had numbly to seek his way, in the certainty that illumination lay at the end of the track. He had had it easy until now, yet who was he to expect it would be joyous all along, when even St John of the Cross had walked the path of ashes? Still, with this deadness in them, it was not to be wondered that some priests preferred playing golf to hearing confession, or that they consoled themselves with food or drink or gambling. And with oblivious sleep. Manoeuvring other, younger priests into doing the early Masses.

The idea he had been so free with when hearing the brothers' confessions, that this was a test, brought him only the dimmest sense of consolation. For the first time he was not intent to finish the residue of his office, of which so far he had recited only Prime. Nonetheless, he walked up and down behind the church, yawning occasionally, beating his way through the hours, muttering, speeding through the '*Veni Creator*'. He could hear a chant of times-tables from the school behind the church. Because it was the sort of thing curates did when he was a kid, he went to his room, put on his collar and coat and then walked across to the school, where the children were about to emerge from the classrooms to start their walk home, in convoy for fear of the more robust stone-throwing children of the state school, or to board the 413 and 414 buses. In the meantime the real enemy had come closer. A long way off, but closer than that in the geography of dread.

St Margaret's Primary School was a succession of four sunny red-brick rooms connected by a corridor. On the tarred playground, hopscotch lines had been painted by some enterprising nun or parent. A toilet block of brick and lattice work completed the quadrangle, the campus, at the as-yet humble but serviceable St Margaret's Primary. It was staffed by the nuns from the Dominican convent, who were driven each morning from the Boulevarde, where their splendid high school was located, to St Margaret's by a pious old man named Dyer, and driven back to their convent again after school. As Darragh waited on the edge of the playground, one freckled boy of about ten years emerged on the steps outside the classroom corridor, holding a school bell. The boy was about to clang it to signal the end of a day's education at the hands of the Dominican sisters when he saw Darragh in the yard. He straightened his fairly languid stance, paused, and rang the bell with a severity which such a sighting warranted.

Sister Felicitas, the principal, emerged. Sister Happiness. But she had a splendid hard-headedness like the monsignor's. Her spirituality seemed of a functional, sane, confident nature. A youngish woman, she was perhaps ten years older than Darragh, perhaps less, and was clearly being groomed by her order for high office, headmistress-ship and mother superior-hood of one of the posher convents the Dominicans ran. She was quite a good-looking woman in a sharp-featured way, Darragh abstractly thought.

Now a jostling queue of children built behind Sister Felicitas in the windowed corridor. The rowdy boys, the prim girls, the junior wide-eyed children of both sexes. He could all but hear their whispers, 'There's Father. Shut up, there's Father.' The presence of a priest in the schoolyard had always lent a sacramental weight to his own childhood home-goings.

Mothers were beginning to mill in the bitumened laneway between church and school, and saw him.

Felicitas called to her students, 'Father Darragh is here. You must all say good afternoon to Father Darragh. Silence. Silence there, you ruffian. All say, "Good afternoon, Father Darragh."'

From within the corridor came the tremolo greeting. 'Good afternoooon, Faaather Darraaagh.'

'Now don't run,' the nun ordered. The children descended, two by two, the short stairway to the playground. Small girls held hands. Boys seemed about to explode from the pressure of their own seemliness. Around the corner of the school, mothers marshalled children for their convoys down Homebush Road. A few dozen students crowded for a while around Darragh, who wore as innocent a smile as he could for them, and told them they had better get on home. A girl showed him an essay with a little gilt star and a holy picture of Our Lady of Succour attached to it—marks of high academic achievement. When he said it was all very good, she ran off, high-stepping with delight.

As the crowd began to clear, Darragh saw, standing by the school corner, the young woman and the boy he had met on the train a few weeks before, on the way to his mother's. He could also see, absolutely obvious in her, the impulse to speak to him. For a second he felt reinvigorated. A merciful God had sent her up Homebush Road to renew his soul by making some small demand on him. Even so he did not move. He waited confidently for the matter to resolve itself in her. At last she came towards him across the hopscotch lines, her eyes wide and full of doubt behind her auburn fringe, her long lips engaged in her internal dispute about the wisdom of approaching him, her son by the hand.

'Father Darragh,' she said, arriving. 'We met on the train once. Anthony, you go and play.' She released her son's hand, and the little boy went hopping across the playground, relishing its sudden, uncommon vacancy.

'I didn't introduce myself then. I'm Mrs Heggarty. Mrs Kate Heggarty.' As if the name itself were a burden, tears rose in her vast eyes. She did not look like a Mrs. She was too young, and had an unsullied air.

'Oh yes,' said Darragh. 'And your boy goes here to St Margaret's. Anthony.'

'That's it,' she said.

'Your husband will be home soon. Isn't the prime minister

going to bring all the troops back here? To face the Japanese?'

'My husband has been taken prisoner. Not dead. *Captured.*'
She put the slightest, frantic stress on the word, and the weight
of her green eyes upon him.

There was a time before, and recently, when he believed the
world simple and had confidence in the automatic comfort of
soul which he represented simply by being a priest. He could say
something blithe and plain, and people in grief nonetheless considered them an utterly original set of words particular to their
sorrow, and dedicated to it. 'He led a decent Catholic life,' for
example, or 'She was well prepared for death.' Now, though, the
oft-uttered and reliable clichés evaded him. He could only reproduce some parboiled idea picked up from newspapers. 'I believe
the Germans treat prisoners better than the Japanese do.' Since
this gave Mrs Heggarty nothing, and far from easing the tension
in her face caused her brow to knot, he struggled, a mere secular
fool, graceless and floundering. 'Of course, despite Hitler, they
come from the Christian tradition,' he said.

He wondered did the government go on paying her husband's
wages during his captivity. Lord knew how long that would be.
The war in the northern hemisphere seemed endless, fought
at one end on unimaginable reaches of the Sahara, and at the
other on the equally immense steppes of Russia. Only in the
southern world, increasingly Japanese, were the fronts fluid
and daily altering.

Mrs Heggarty blinked and shook her head free of his in-
anities. She murmured, 'You know, it's cold, he said in all his
letters. My husband. He said I wouldn't believe how cold the
desert could get. I hope the Germans give him a blanket.'

'Of course they will,' said Darragh, but he was blindly hoping
too, and she could tell that. He had the purest impulse to take

her by the shoulder, to place some reassuring pressure there. A fraternal thing. That sort of innocent vernacular gesture was forbidden to him, though. He saw with a particular resentment he had never until now experienced that he must operate on a bloodless and austere level. Ah, he remembered—there had been a piece in the *Herald* about a Rommel offensive. Towards Benghazi in North Africa. 'I shall remember you and your husband in my Masses,' he assured her.

He could see that this had at least some meaning for her, she did not consider it nothing; she considered it part of what she had come for.

'You must do that,' she told him. 'We need it. Things weigh heavily . . .'

He had feared that Mrs Flood had so diminished him with her twinkling irony that all his offices might seem negligible to the daughters of Eve, to every single one of them. But it was delightful that it weighed with her, his intention to pray. She was clearly from a tradition of observance. On little evidence he surmised her parents: a working man but nobody's fool. An Aunt-Madge-like, Lang-voting mother. Faith and social justice! For Mrs Heggarty was no supine soul. She had an air of independent thought—or so he believed on the slim evidence of their two brief meetings. She was the sort of person about whom he was willing to make fairly early and positive judgements. The forth-rightness with which she'd spoken to him on the train, that was his guide. So he stood constructing a history and a soul for her, out of the few scraps of what he actually knew.

'This is his last letter,' she said, extending a small, square, stiff letter. The army photographed the letters of soldiers and sent them off to families in this form, a card, the writing sharp but reduced. 'His job was towing an anti-tank gun around the desert,' she said, surrendering the letter now with a small shrug, as if to say: He only drove a truck . . . why did the Germans bother taking him?

Darragh looked at the letter. 'Dearest Sweetheart and Tiger,' it was addressed. Mrs Heggarty pointed to a passage which read, 'You wouldn't believe how cold it is at night. Even in Alexandria—what we call Alex—it can get colder and foggier than you'd think was likely. I thought this was supposed to be Africa, eh? Not like at the pictures though. Not like *Tarzan*.'

Having proved the assertion that her husband found the desert cold, she emitted a sound like creaking. A tear or two appeared on her cheek. But Darragh felt that she had then sternly cut off the subtle machinery which produced them.

Sister Felicitas and her small group of nuns had emerged from the school building and moved away, carrying their satchels to where Mr Dyer's car waited for them beyond the gate, ready to return them to the bosom of their community. There was a small flavour of starch in the way Felicitas called, 'Good afternoon, Father Darragh. Good afternoon, Mrs Heggarty.' It was as if she was in her way jealous of this close discourse, the chance of tears and anguish which hung over it.

When the nuns vanished up the laneway, there were only lolloping Anthony and this married girl and Darragh in all the reaches of tar.

'Could I come and talk to you at the presbytery, Father?' Mrs Kate Heggarty asked.

'Certainly,' said Darragh.

The presbytery's severe parlour was indeed designed for meetings with the laity. They took place beneath the tranquillity of the Virgin's gaze from a statue placed on a plinth above the table, beneath the authority of the picture of Pius XII on the

wall, and the glow of Christ's suffering heart above a credenza.
And under the strict but oblique observance of Mrs Flannery,
too, who suspected that any layman or woman not connected to
fundraising or prospective marriage was somehow engaged in
trickery and special pleading when they came to an appointment
in the parlour. Indeed, she felt that the monsignor and Darragh
had better things to do than look after the obscure wants of the
laity. That's what confession was for!

Darragh was so aware, however, of the pressure of despera-
tion in Mrs Heggarty that he would have been willing to hold
such a meeting this afternoon, while her son Anthony zoomed
unheeded around the playground. Indeed, on a selfish level, he
sought to continue this dialogue, for it was a solace to him as
well. Her offer of the letter was a solace. She had thought him
to have potential influence over her husband's plain words sent
such an exorbitant distance. Poor Private—or was it Trooper or
Gunner?—Heggarty's capture and its impact on Mrs Heggarty
had brought Darragh a purpose in the midst of a vacant day. The
still-receding backs of St Margaret's four black-and-cream-
habited nuns, making for the street and Mr Dyer's big old car,
inhibited him though. He was reminded that he should perhaps
be less impetuous.

'I could see you tomorrow,' he said. 'At four o'clock. Could
someone mind Anthony for you?'

'Yes. I'll arrange it.'

She had regained her composure, her cheeks were drying.
This admirable soul.

'But are you sure,' he asked, taking the part of the monsignor
and Mrs Flannery, 'that your problems could not be better dealt
with in the confessional?'

She thought and then shook her head. Again, poor Private

Heggarty. To be separated from such a tower by the chances of battle.

He said, 'Look, your husband *will* return, with a smile on his face. One of these days soon. The war seems endless. But I'm sure it will end.'

What a silly utterance, he chided himself. For it was, of course, the intervening days which weighed on Kate Heggarty's spirit.

When Darragh came to breakfast after early Mass the next day, he found Monsignor Carolan eating boiled eggs in the presbytery dining room. From his face, Darragh could tell the world had changed further, even since yesterday's bombing. 'Well, it's happened, Frank. That *ee-jit* General Percival has surrendered Singapore.' Monsignor Carolan, influenced by the Irish nuns who had taught him in his childhood forty years past, called anyone he didn't like by that Irish version of idiot. And General Percival, British commander in Singapore, had been an ee-jit he'd inveighed against regularly.

'Our Australian boys were more than willing to fight on,' said the monsignor, the livid white of egg showing momentarily on his tongue. 'But Percival's shown that as good as he is at burning people's houses, he's no good at dealing with true warriors.'

Monsignor Carolan's father had come to Sydney from County Cork, and as every Cork man knew, General Percival, as a young officer, had burned down the family house of Michael Collins, Irish Free State hero. Pro-Free Staters had been waiting ever since for God and history to punish Percival.

'All those poor boys,' said the monsignor, reaching for the toast rack. 'Prisoners now because of that fool, that gormless coward. It's just like the last business—lions led by donkeys. Fine intellects left in a hole by ee-jits. And we'll know about it, Frank. There'll be desperate women around now. Their husbands prisoners of war.'

'I've met one already,' Frank said. 'But her husband was captured in Libya. By the Germans.'

The monsignor shook his head. 'You're young, Frank. You should watch out for women who have nothing to lose. They're not quite responsible for themselves at a time like this. Don't be too open to them.'

In a pitiful try at proving his worldliness, Darragh said, 'The woman I spoke to yesterday has asked to see me in the parlour. I suggested the confessional, but she insisted on seeing me for counsel.'

The monsignor turned ruminative. 'Fair enough, Frank. I leave it to you. Though I'd suggest it's always good to keep the parlour door open during talks like that. It helps moderate behaviour.' Even in the seminary Darragh had heard speeches like this—advice about managing women, who were of their nature a volatile and perilous quantity.

The monsignor finished his toast.

There did seem to Darragh to be an altered air that day, even in quiet Homebush Road. The world had changed. It had been axiomatic that Singapore could not fall. The Japanese, makers of laughable prewar junk products—inferior toys, unreliable clocks—had altered the universe by taking the untakeable port. His father had sometimes, influenced by Irish forebears, mocked the concept of the British Empire, for which of course he had been a Great War warrior. But there had been a profound comfort in its being there, to be lauded or sneered at. Now the exclamation mark of that empire, the long shaft of Malaya, the plump point of Singapore, was borne away, all in a little more than three months.

He owed it to the Eternal Church and the Communion of Saints to spend the morning visiting the elderly sick of the parish. When Darragh called into Pedderick the Chemist's to buy shaving cream and razor blades, three women were already there, one talking to Mr Pedderick and two others discussing Singapore by the door. Words such as 'disaster' and 'poor Mrs Thorpe' filled the shop. His entry caused the conversation to mute itself, except that Mr Pedderick said, like an accusation, though Darragh could not be totally sure, 'Fifteen thousand Australian prisoners!' Darragh felt an urge to say that all things being equal he was willing to place himself in the way of the Japanese tide. But that would have brought conversation at Pedderick's to a total halt.

It was good to enter homes where his motives were not judged. To stand before people weak from the pressure of the earth's calamities, but now immune from them too, since they were about to broach eternity. The Japanese would not arrive in time to enslave them. For their journey, they lay in beds beneath pictures of the Sacred Heart. Brown scapulars devoted to St Anthony were twisted around the bedposts, missals brimmed with holy cards at the side of the bed, and the odour of devout candles on the sideboard contested the thinner smell of pre-decomposition, the traces of urine and excreta which announced the decline of the human system. It was possible to believe but impossible to imagine, when he thought about it, that Mrs Heggarty could reach this stage. She would exhale her soul, he was sure, in mid-splendour.

Before and after a light lunch he said his office with an energy and freshness which had been lacking on other days, and then realised that it was his coming pastoral meeting with Mrs Heggarty, who had in her extreme hour, revived his zeal. From his room, he remotely heard the quarter past three bell rung by the freckled child on Sister Felicitas's steps. He read that morning's paper which Mrs Flannery had brought him, and all was reverses: Singapore gone, along with Hong Kong, whose British garrison was swamped so quickly and who with their wives and families lay now in the hands of the newcomers, the punishers. The Dutch in the Dutch East Indies overwhelmed— Sumatra reeling, Java quaking. Photographs of American flight crews with unconscionable smiles spiced the newsprint with hope. It seemed essential that he occupy himself thus, with sombre issues, until Mrs Heggarty arrived downstairs, and Mrs Flannery answered the door, admitted her, summoned him. Until then, he tried with some success to suppress daydreams, especially those involving fraught and beautiful women.

To fill in the time further he began reading a detective novel about one Lord Peter Wimsey, who lived in a world unidentifiable to those who inhabited Australian suburbs, to those who ministered to the sins of such as the pernicious brother of the Strathfield community, or Mrs Flood. Even the suspicious characters did not speak to Lord Peter with the particular working-class directness of Mrs Flood's lodger and lover, Ross Trumble.

Remotely, he heard the large knocker at the front door sound. He rose and put on his black serge coat. He picked up his breviary, as if it was the natural armour to take him to such a confrontation as that about to occur. He paused to take in a breath, but did not look at himself in the mirror behind his door for fear that he would spot the hollow man he had been for the past week. Mrs Flannery could be heard making her brisk way to his door, and then knocking. 'Father? Mrs Heggarty is waiting for you in the parlour.'

'Tell her I'll be just a moment,' called Darragh in the voice of preoccupation. He gauged the passage of a minute. He'd always hoped he would never spend a minute in this way, for vanity's sake, letting fallow, godless seconds evaporate. Then, full of a kind of terror and indefinable hope, he opened the door and heard his own steps like those of another person in the corridor and on the staircase. The door to the parlour was open, and pushing it further aside, he saw her seated in a chair at the far end, with the window behind her. She had dressed as if for Mass in a fawn suit, and a little slanting domed hat with a feather at the brim. Her hands were joined nervously at the table, but now she stood up, as she had stood up all her life for the entry of priests. *Introibo altare dei.* The emergence of the vestmented priest from the sacristy onto the altar steps, of the school-visiting priest in a classroom, had been bringing her to her feet since babyhood. You could tell these things by instinct.

'Hello, Mrs Heggarty,' he heard himself say, like a kindly grocer.

Frowning most frankly, she told him good afternoon.

'Take a seat,' he said, sitting under the picture of Pius XII, the former Father Pacelli. His Vatican lay deep in the fascist state of Italy, whose German brethren had captured Mr Heggarty. Yet the Vatican's eternal *magisterium* rose above such temporary political facts.

'Have you heard anything at all about your husband?' he asked.

'I spoke to another woman,' said Mrs Heggarty, not quite engaging him with her green eyes. 'Her husband was captured last year. She said it took at least six months for the Red Cross to find him and for her to get a letter.' The pressure of such a wait brought the possibility of tears to her face again, but they were suppressed. 'The Department of Defence said they'll send me his wages direct. But he was only a lance bombardier.'

So . . . Lance Bombardier Heggarty.

'Soldier's pay,' murmured Darragh. He had heard her say that, in the playground.

'That's right, Father,' Mrs Heggarty asserted. 'Nothing to write home about.'

'Does Anthony know what's happening?'

This was progressing well, he believed, for Mrs Heggarty seemed to be aided by his questions, not that they showed any superior skill.

'I'm still trying to choose the moment.'

Darragh nodded.

'We don't know when the war will end, do we?' she said, lifting her eyes, like a woman closing with the chief point of debate. 'We don't know whether it will end at all. And if it'll end our way. Do we?' The tears gamely repressed behind her features gave her questions an enhanced authority. He knew at once she had lived in a harder world than he had.

'Surely Western Christianity will succeed in the end,' said Darragh, 'even though it's hard to believe from the papers.'

'But the Nazis are Christians, as you told me. And they're doing pretty well, aren't they?' asked Mrs Heggarty with a touch of aggression. 'Every time we set out into Libya, they drive us back. Don't they? These Christians. And a lot of them are Catholics.'

Darragh blinked. He did not want to think too much about the Nazi Catholics. He had enough conundrums already. 'Let me say this, Mrs Heggarty. Sometimes I think there will be suffering before there's deliverance. You're part of the suffering now, and I sympathise with you.'

'I know you do,' she said. 'But I'm the one who has to go through it.' Was there a further hint of aggression in her voice?

'Perhaps I could speak to the gentlemen in the St Vincent de Paul's?' he suggested. 'In case there's anything you need . . .'

'I wouldn't want charity,' she said, a leaden working-class pride at once apparent in her. 'We've lived our lives avoiding anyone's charity.'

'Well, there's a place in the city—CUSA—it helps out soldiers' wives.'

'Yes,' she said. 'Charity.'

Darragh said, 'I know you're a proud woman. But sometimes we all need——' She cut him off again, more briskly.

'We all need . . .' she said with a nod.

He could not make up his mind now how things were going. One thing he knew: he could not imagine the monsignor accepting so many interruptions.

She settled herself in her chair. 'Sorry, it's not your fault. I get this anger, and sometimes it doesn't fit inside a room, even a big one like this.'

'You can't help feeling some anger,' he said.

She shook her head. 'Do you know my chief reason for coming here? I don't want to be one of those Catholics who creeps away from the confessional and never speaks to a priest again.' She talked like someone contemplating apostasy. 'That's why I'm speaking to you face-to-face, like an honourable person. There is a man . . . that's all I'll say. No more and no less. A visitor. Nothing else.'

Remembering Mr Regan's moral outrage, Darragh nearly

asked without thinking, 'An American?' But that was the height of irrelevance. The question of nationalities had no place in the moral counsels of the Universal Church. He was aware of some ridiculous serpent of vanity in him. It was almost as if he felt entitled as her priest to approve her connections with other people, and she had neglected to let him.

'This man isn't like other men,' she said. 'He's patient and courteous. He demands nothing, and I do not choose to offer anything but tea and conversation.' She had grown flushed, as if she had surprised herself with her own forthrightness. 'But he's there, of course, at least now and then. He's careful how he comes in, so that I'm not embarrassed with the neighbours. But he's willing to provide my son and myself with a few things which make life decent. A pound or two more of meat, a half-pound of butter, an orange. Chocolate . . .'

She shrugged, and brought her hands together. She had been opening them as she spoke, to indicate spaciousness. You could tell she was disappointed in herself for mentioning chocolate by name.

She said, 'There's no glory in rickets, Father. God doesn't want scrawny ribs.'

Darragh could feel himself flushing too. 'I understand exactly what you're saying. But I doubt this fellow does it all from the pure kindness of his heart. Are you telling me that he wants nothing?'

Darragh was voicing the concern not of his own worldly wisdom, but of the sexual scepticism Noldin and other moral theologians passed on to all their students. Even innocents.

'There *is* pure goodness of heart,' she told him directly. 'Surely a priest would take that for granted. But there are also mixed motives, and we live with them all the time. Especially if they favour us.'

'Do you realise . . .' he asked her in a voice he did not want Mrs Flannery—should she be ensconced somewhere supervising their dialogue—to hear, 'do you realise this is a proximate occasion of sin?'

She leaned her head to one side and spread her hands again. 'It hasn't proven to be,' she said, like a challenge.

Darragh could say only, 'Well . . .'

Mrs Heggarty relented. 'It has *not* proven to be. But I don't want you to think I came down in the last shower either.'

Darragh still kept his voice low and fraternal, but something had shifted in him, something unpredicted. Noldin and all the parish priests of history had put their words unbidden in his mouth. 'So this is what you'll do?' he murmured. 'Sell your soul for items of groceries?'

He wished the words unsaid. Indeed, she seemed disappointed. 'Father,' she said, shaking her head, 'you said you understood exactly what I meant. I'd sacrifice my soul for dignity, because people without dignity have no soul to save anyhow. For the dignity of my boy. So that he doesn't grow up as a bony, miserable little working-class brat.'

Even in his self-disappointment, Darragh was still wary of eavesdroppers. 'You're talking like a Marxist,' he murmured. 'What about the dignity of suffering?'

'Well,' she said in her level way, as if being gentle with him, 'you'll have to forgive me, Father, but I don't see too much dignity of suffering here at the presbytery.'

'How can you consider what you're telling me, though? And how can you talk this way when your husband has just been captured?'

She still refused to be easily cowed—her assertions, which she'd obviously kept secret till today, ran confidently in the parlour. She had all the pride and skill of a confident heretic.

'I talk this way *because* my husband has been captured. The fellow I speak of, the visitor, is a decent fellow, but he is a fellow after all. I was intending . . . well, let me say, not to give him any encouragement. I *am* a married woman. But I need to take the risk of those occasions of sin you speak of, for my sake and Anthony's.' She shrugged and composed her breathing. 'I'm sorry,' she said, almost with a fondness. 'None of this is your fault, Father Darragh.'

Through an over-striving of which he could not cure himself, he was failing this hard, bright, pragmatic soul. Are the best damned? he wondered for a second.

'Why do you come to me, then?' Darragh challenged her. 'I don't want to offer you counsel when everything I say is rebuffed.'

'But,' she said, 'I feel I owe it to the Church to explain myself.' She lowered her voice further still. 'And if I'd gone to some old monsignor, he wouldn't have let me do it. He would have roared at me and told me to be gone and say the rosary.'

'Oh yes, but I'm soft enough to listen to all your ranting. You are married! That is the reality. And your husband is a hero.'

'An ordinary man, but a hero. I hope they are kind, those Germans.'

'And what will he say when he comes back, and all the gossip rises up around him?'

'I must hope he'll be understanding. Of the fix his capture put me and Anthony in. Look, I *do* intend to remain innocent——'

'And create scandal,' said Darragh.

'Let the old scandalmongers have their field day. If they're so keen on virtue, let those old biddies live off lance bombardier's pay.'

So, another argument dispensed with, he scrabbled for what was left in the arsenal of his moral theology. Later, he would realise that he should have been calm, rather than try to win the argument, but he could not see that at the moment.

'One day you will be a grandmother,' he now argued, fumbling away, a losing debater, 'and your son . . . Anthony . . . he will understand the truth.'

'He'll understand by then what poverty does to people,' she told him, her face wan, this confrontation costing her, Darragh was happy to see, all the resources of her spirit. 'I'll raise him to understand. You speak of the sin against the Holy Spirit. Poverty is the sin against the Holy Spirit. It debases people to a state where they have no virtues because they're at an animal level. If they're put there by capital, then capital goes to Mass and communion, and the poor go to hell.'

'How can you believe this and still be a good Catholic woman?' asked Darragh unwisely, letting his confusion turn him into automaton priest.

'I think I might believe it because I *am* a good Catholic woman. Have you read *Rerum Novarum* by His Holiness Pope Leo XIII? My father said it was the Church's answer to Karl Marx.'

Ah! thought Darragh. An Aunt Madge woman after all. She came from a political household.

'*Rerum Novarum* never told you to put yourself in the power of men.'

She performed a particularly authoritative and ironic shake of the head. 'I think . . . in telling you all this . . . I'm putting myself under the power of a man now.'

Darragh was intoxicated at once with horror and hope.

'But I'm a priest.'

'Like Christ,' she suggested, shocked with the energy of her own argument. 'Christ was a man, too. That was the whole point.'

He could imagine her family more particularly now. Lang Labor voters, for sure. The mother a believer in earthly justice from the Prince of Peace instead of Lenin and Stalin. The father a book-reader. Passing on the daily bread of such ideas as the one she'd uttered: poverty debases people to a state where they have no virtues, because they have no soul.

Darragh urged, 'Tell me what I can do for you, Mrs Heggarty. I can speak discreet words to people who could help you. Please, let me do that much. Our charity may be kinder than that of this visitor.'

She frowned. 'You've got good intentions,' she told him. 'I hope you don't get spoiled in some way.'

'How could I be spoiled?' he asked. 'You're the one about to go into danger.'

'Well, it strikes me the Church isn't always kind to its angelic brethren.'

'Angelic brethren?'

'Yes. You're sort of unspoiled. You don't get cranky with me, you don't rouse. You don't get outraged at my cheek. You tolerate everything and offer answers. You haven't got any of the normal airs. Except . . . your answers. Really, they're the usual little answers. They're simple answers. They'd be all right if the world was run by fellows like you, but . . .'

He didn't like his less than influential nature and future announced to him like this. It made him vengeful for a moment. 'You may take this man's help and it could avail you nothing—the Japanese might come . . .'

'And bayonet all fallen women, I suppose. Or worse. You're

right. People like my son and me . . . we have to survive for the week. We have to have our dignity in the hour and the day.'

'Who talked to you about this ridiculous dignity business?' he asked, nearly enraged. 'Is it one of the lines your kind man tries out on you?'

She waved her hand to dismiss this. 'I have my own ideas,' she assured him.

'The idea of redemption as an economic matter—it's one dear to the Marxists. It's the only redemption they have.'

'Would redemption on this earth be such a terrible thing?'

Ross Trumble lived in The Crescent that wasn't a crescent. So did Mrs Heggarty, as the parish records showed. Had they talked? Surely Ross Trumble wasn't the so-called kind man? For a moment, though, before he decided not to, it seemed nearly a reasonable thing to ask her did she know Mrs Flood's lodger.

Instead he told her, 'Until Hitler invaded Russia, the communists wanted no part of your husand's war. They went on strike to keep food and uniforms and weapons away from your husband.'

She was mildly unimpressed, and he reduced her to combativeness rather than thought. 'Do you think that's why we're losing the war? Look, I just wanted to be an honest woman with you, Father Darragh, and that's all. I'm determined on my way.'

Darragh, struggling, tried out the idea that he and she were not Protestants. 'In the end, we submit our consciences humbly to authority.'

But Mrs Heggarty said, almost with apology, that she was guided by authority but was not its mindless slave.

So he was forced at last to sit awhile in silence, having used every available argument he had at his conscious disposal. Her ideas might be heterodox, but he felt he could not match her strength. He had thought that this could never happen—he had gone forth to Strathfield, New South Wales, believing that he was fully equipped for every earthly argument and half of heaven's. And now, her ideas seemed even to him to shine with a certain sad and plausible wisdom.

Having come here to tell him in her genial but egregious pride that she would not creep away, and having now imparted that, she began to stand up and then to advance past the polished table to the door. The reproduction of Raphael's Virgin smiled down on her, the Sacred Heart blazed. Darragh rose as she approached the half-open door. He stepped forward and touched her elbow. 'Please wait.' But he saw then that Mrs Flannery was arranging some flowers on a hallstand by the beaded-glass front door, and had turned her full gaze towards him and Mrs Heggarty.

'Thank you for all your advice, Father,' said Mrs Heggarty, and nodded and left.

CHAPTER SIX

AS IF TO CHASTEN people and put them in a mood for the penitential season, Singapore had fallen the weekend before Ash Wednesday. Frank Darragh celebrated Shrove Tuesday on the steps in front of the sacristy by stacking the leftover palms of 1941's Palm Sunday into an open tin tray, in which he had already lit some charcoal. The palms from April 1941 had dried out—the last terrible year had desiccated them and they burned quite easily, the little bit of charcoal barely adding to their dusty mass.

He had spent a dreadful night, because his sense of loss, of having been given Mrs Heggarty for rescue and having failed in the task, could not be absorbed into the allocated hours of rest. He felt grainy with sleeplessness. He believed that a sort of grit had entered the soul, lay on the face of all leaves, and dimmed every bloom. How could he live to be a priest as long as Carolan had, when he could not convince a young wife, this young wife in particular, towards wisdom? When she uttered her reasons for what she did with such philosophic flagrancy! The Japanese might save him the trouble of a long priestly career, of course, but he did not want them to.

What galled was that he had no weight with the woman, no gravity to alter her path, to stop her in her purposeful flight. She had chosen to speak to him because she could say what she could not to more austere men. The interview had left her without a burden. She could tell herself she had been honest with the priests, and no hypocrite, and she had won her argument, strongly made her point. She did not leave stinging with shame at her apostasy, as the powerful of the Church would have made her do. She left saying a pleasant good afternoon.

So it was as Monsignor Carolan had said to Monsignor Plunkett—he was an easy target—and his anger at the monsignor was unjustified. No doubt his visit to Mrs Flood produced in The Crescent, after he left, tinkling, wheezing hilarity from the lady herself and the darkest, most dismissive curses from the men at the kitchen table. So his role was to be God's fool, and he must be happy to be if necessary. Except, with all of that, his connection to the God of his joy seemed to have been cut. At Mass that morning the Latin had fled undervalued from his lips.

There was a worm in his mind, too, an obsessive little creature which tried to convince him that the Communion of Saints, the body of the faithful, was stripped of a large part of its meaning should Mrs Heggarty defect from it. In the state he was in, he hungered for the salvation above all of that one soul. It was as if all other souls could go to ashy oblivion. His own, his mother's, Aunt Madge's, Mr Regan's. This little job with the palms seemed appropriate to his present state: reducing last year's green life to ashes. But it was a toxic vanity, he knew, to think in that way, that the ashes in the metal pan answered to the ashes within the soul. Vanity to think, too, that Carolan always permitted or persuaded him to do these jobs, the jobs of a sacristan, and he had done them for two years now with dog-like eagerness. While the monsignor and his beloved finance committee occupied a higher level, above such banal, pietistic tasks.

Tomorrow morning, for Ash Wednesday Mass, said in black vestments, the church would be packed. Those whom piety did not bring there, the anxiety of the times would. The captured cities of Asia would add their embers to the event. Darragh and the monsignor would both need to be on the altar, and as the faithful knelt, would each proceed along the altar rail from different directions, planting the mark of these very ashes on the foreheads of the faithful. Darragh, dipping his right thumb in the brass pot carried for him by an altar boy, would make a small smudged cross on each brow. He would intone, '*Memento homo quia cines es, et ad cinerem reverteris*—Remember, man, that thou art dust, and unto dust thou shalt return.' Or as the seminary wits had it, 'Remember, squirt, that thou art dirt, and unto dirt thou shalt revert.'

A large black car had stopped by the gate in line with St Margaret's long wall. Atop this car, in a wooden bracket, lay the great black bladder which, by technological means Darragh did not understand, fuelled cars now, supplementing petrol with coal gas and saving fuel for the machines of war. A pear-shaped man in a well-cut grey suit and vest, his face shaded by the brim of a felt hat, came walking into the church grounds. Another, similarly dressed man remained in the vehicle. As the man got closer, Darragh took in his broad jaws, the way the breadth of his face diminished as it got closer to the brim of the hat. He wasn't a handsome fellow, but he was strongly built beneath his inherited body shape. And there was an amusing glitter in his eye.

'Good morning, Father Darragh,' he said, with the confidence Darragh associated with regular Mass-goers.

Darragh brushed his hands and said hello.

The man introduced himself. He was an inspector from the CIB. Darragh was not absolutely sure what these initials stood for, but thought the C might stand for Criminal. The man's name was Kearney, a name which somehow sat well with his earthy Irish face. It was a name Darragh had often seen in newspapers, and heard invoked by priests as that of a no-nonsense, skilled policeman and utterly faithful Catholic. Despite the influence of the Masons in the New South Wales police force, he had got to the rank of inspector. He might, they said, become the first Catholic commissioner.

'I'm in Concord parish,' said the policeman, 'so we've never met.' It still seemed that it was on the strength of that parish affiliation, rather than as a policeman, that the inspector now extended his hand for shaking. 'I went to school at the Brothers' up the road,' he said. 'Brother Keogh called me. He's frantic, poor fellow. One of his men has just walked out. A young bloke, Brother Howley. Like that. Packed a bag and fled.'

The brothers liked to call each other 'the men'. With some justice, as Darragh was the first to admit. They expected each other to be men, and told the boys they expected them to be too. Their hard disciplines were not designed for what Darragh's father used to call 'lily-farts'. To be a man meant possessing something like sturdiness of soul, and an ability to play rugged football. And Darragh knew exactly the 'man' who had walked out. Rather than stay and sin again. Or rather than face his superiors, or an older, more severe confessor. Or another potential motive willing to risk damnation as his punishment.

'The fellow didn't talk to Keogh or to anyone,' said Inspector

Kearney. 'Didn't apply for a dispensation of his vows, which in his case is quite possible, since they're simple vows and a dispensation would come through in a few months. But no. Just caught a bus, the day before yesterday, and hasn't been seen. You hear confessions over there, I believe. Now I know you can't break the confessional seal, Father, and I wouldn't want you to. But Brother Keogh thought—you being the same age as the young bloke—you might have had some informal chats with him. Something to give you sort of an inkling.'

'I'm sorry, he didn't talk to me, more than a good morning here and there. I got no impression he would leave like this,' said Darragh. He was, at the same time, amazed at himself that he was not more shocked. The inspector's knowing eyes weighed him—to the nearest ounce of reticence. Or of frankness.

'I wouldn't be doing this, Father, except poor old Keogh's so distressed. We're up to our eyeballs with all the Yanks in town, and there's a lot of wartime nonsense between men and women.' He shook his head in a women-will-never-cease-to-surprise way. 'But I felt I'd better take the time to make Brother Keogh happy. It's a serious business to him, this vanishing act. The young bloke had his eye on the army. Did you hear anything about that?'

'No, I didn't have any clue that this was going to happen,' said Frank, deliberately choosing a demi-slang, motion picture-derived word like 'clue' instead of something more elevated—'perception', for example. Perception was the sort of word used by innocents.

'One of his mates up there, Brother August . . . he said the fellow was talking about joining the army. He thought Howley was just speculating. Just daydream stuff.'

'In the army,' said Frank, regretting it as soon as it was out of his mouth, 'on the battlefield, chaplains are empowered to give a general absolution. Without confession.'

The policeman's eyes blazed with an appetite for connections. He was, Darragh saw, no flatfoot, no mere New South Wales walloper. 'So you're saying that maybe this youngster ran away and joined the army. Just so he didn't have to confess some sin?'

'I . . . I'm sorry to say I had little contact with the young brother separately from the sacraments. If he had spoken casually to me . . .'

The inspector nodded, but knowledge did not leave his eyes. 'Well, we've asked at every recruiting station in Sydney. Shown his picture. Navy, army, Royal Australian Air Force. Militia. He never mentioned relatives to you, did he? During chats, I mean. I just thought he might have had doubts and he'd talked to you outside the confessional. When young men leave the Brothers, they often go to relatives.'

'What could you do if you found him?' Darragh asked.

'Well,' said Inspector Kearney, 'I couldn't arrest him, could I? But I could ask him to come back to Keogh, for a bit of wise counsel, you know. A bit of spiritual guidance. The young fellow may have something he's made into a big problem, but it's not. In any case, if he wants to go, if he still wants to join the forces, it looks like there'll be enough war left for him to get his fill. I had a bit of time in the last one, and let me tell you, it doesn't take much of it before you start wishing you weren't there.'

The newspapers said that the Japanese in Singapore had left some British officials in place, to run the water and electricity, and even to do policing. Kearney had the flexibility, the worldliness, to be left in place after an invasion and fall. In a way, Darragh admired this great gift, this easy aura of capacity, of usefulness.

'I'm only doing this as an old boy of the place,' Kearney reasserted.

'Yes,' Darragh acknowledged, 'it's very good of you.' He could see the inspector thinking: This fellow's not my kind of priest. Not a man's man.

There was not much more Darragh could say, since when a man achieved the power to bind and loose sins in the confessional, he lost the power to be an actor on any matter revealed therein. Darragh would willingly have travelled with Inspector Kearney to recruiting stations, but by the highest possible ordinance was not permitted.

'By the way, Father,' Kearney said, that bargaining irony in his eye. 'I haven't been able to see my parish priest. I can promise you I'm working very hard hours. I wondered if you could give me a Lenten indulgence?'

A release from having to fast in Lent—that's what he was asking. The inspector's sturdiness was wrapped in a degree of flab, but public officials working long hours could be absolved from a literal observance of the fast. People like Mrs Darragh and Mr Regan went meatless on many days of Lent, but the burden on them might not be as great as it was on a member of the CIB, pursuing human viciousness beyond imagining.

'You can certainly be exempt from the fast,' said Darragh. 'But there may be something you could sacrifice. Perhaps you could go off beer.'

For the inspector had the look of yeasty appetite some beer-drinkers acquire.

'Well, you see. Beer's my only ease from work.'

The man was trying to settle a contract, via Darragh, with the Unutterable, who could not be bargained with.

'That's something you must decide about then,' Darragh told

him, and the trace of a triumphant smile appeared on Kearney's face.

'I don't want to make a special case for myself, Father,' said Kearney, making, for the sake of it, a special case. 'But I do have to deal with hard things. I was on the Shark Arm case, for instance.' Darragh remembered it: a shark caught in the harbour had disgorged a human arm. Everyone in Sydney knew how, due to the shark's disgusting retch, a murderer had been caught. Darragh had been haunted in his youth by an image of the white putrid limb lying on the slick boards of the aquarium at Coogee. 'I worked on that Pyjama Girl case, too,' said the inspector. Again a famous case—how could it not be?—the mouldering body of a girl in pyjamas. The inspector stepped close to him. 'You can be sure by the end of this week if not this day, I'll be standing over some bloody mess. The violently dead give a fellow a thirst and an appetite, you know, Father. This case of the young brother, it's the cleanest thing I've had to do in years.'

For the sake of not letting Kearney get clean away, Darragh said, 'Then as I say—perhaps something else. Tobacco, sweets. A gesture. But as for the general indulgence from fasting, you have it.'

'He might have enlisted in the army under another name,' said the non-fasting Kearney suddenly. 'In which case . . .' He opened his hands, palm up to the sky. It indicated even Brother Howley, fled and perhaps under an alias, justified his exemption.

The inspector and Darragh shook hands, and the inspector went back to his car, where the other policeman waited.

Darragh himself went to the sacristy and brought out the two cineria, the long-handled urns. As he shovelled ashes into them with a little green garden spade, it struck him that he was not bound by any confessional discretion in Mrs Heggarty's case. She had come to the parlour and given him thereby the power to discuss her situation with her at further reasonable times. He had an impulse—which he hoped he would have felt for any threatened soul—to write to her and arrange another meeting. He could send a note home with her boy, Anthony, from the school. All advice was contrary to such a practice. All the axioms of wisdom. The priest who follows a woman into the pit is in the pit with the woman!

There was a famous case to prove the point, too, a case recited at every seminary in the Pacific region. Every priest in Australia and New Zealand and in the islands of Oceania, including Frank Darragh, had been raised on this cautionary tale of how perilous it was to become close friends with a handsome woman penitent. Fifty years past, in days when most priests were Irish-born, the Irishman Dean O'Haran of St Mary's Cathedral had been such a popular preacher and confessor that photographs of him were sold at church fêtes, and in his human vanity he had given copies to those who sought his spiritual advice. One of these had been the pretty wife of a famous Australian test cricketer, Conyngham, who sued the dean as co-respondent in a divorce, claiming that O'Haran and his wife had committed adultery in the confessional and crypt of the cathedral. It had become the supreme scandal; the bigots and the prurient of the day were delighted, and though the court proclaimed Dean O'Haran's innocence, it was claimed that some heavy-handed Irish, men like Kearney perhaps, had intimidated witnesses.

Appropriately, in his desire not to become the dazzling and bedazzled O'Haran, it could now be his interminable and barely endurable Lenten sacrifice not to contact Mrs Heggarty. But that was narrow piety. Kate Heggarty's state might alter perilously during the penitential season. To keep aloof might be misguided and another form of that most pervasive of sins, vanity.

CHAPTER SEVEN

L ENT BEGAN. DARRAGH had nearly done Lauds for the next day in his pacing place between sacristy and presbytery when Mrs Flannery emerged from the presbytery door waving the evening *Sun*. For her to be flapping at the air with it like a frantic newsboy was exceptional. The *Sun* was the monsignor's afternoon paper, the better of Sydney's two poor evening rags. When it was delivered to the presbytery, Mrs Flannery read it first, turning the pages with such care the paper looked utterly pristine, and a few times she had offered it to Darragh, but on the proviso that he treat it with the same archival care, for the monsignor himself would be reading it later that evening.

'You wouldn't believe it, Father,' said Mrs Flannery with a kind of ferocious satisfaction. 'Those little yellow beasts have bombed Darwin. There are dead Australians everywhere.' Her eye showed an enraged Irish glint. Like the Clancy sisters, she had a grim confidence that the Japanese would get what-for from her, if ever they dared turn up on Homebush Road.

The front page showed a radio-photograph of a destroyed

post office, and half-naked gun crews firing at the sky. This had all been forecast, but there was an awe to it now that it had happened, a peculiar feeling of belief being expanded to accommodate the new flavour of this damage.

She did not let him hold the paper, and having imparted the news, returned the *Sun* to the presbytery. This gravest of tidings had to be reserved for Monsignor Carolan's gaze.

He did what a priest should. He prayed for the dead.

Mr Conover, the air-warden parishioner, along with his colleagues, had been busy through Strathfield and Homebush. The schoolchildren at St Margaret's and at the state school near Mrs Flood's home now carried with them as they transited Homebush Road, north or south, a little linen bag. In it lay the basic equipment needed for enduring air raids: two tennis-ball halves to place over the ears, a wooden wedge to put between the teeth, a whistle to blow beneath the rubble, a tin container of burn salve and a safety-pinned roll of lint bandage. Adults were advised also to travel with a first-aid kit on their persons, and Mr Conover dropped three such small tin boxes into the presbytery. Though Darragh tried for a few days, when going out, to force his kit into his side pocket, Monsignor Carolan seemed to think it would push summer-weight black fabric out of shape, and put the kit in his vehicle, unwilling to sacrifice his tailored alpaca neatness until the moment some sort of bombardment actually occurred.

Mr Conover also gave Monsignor Carolan a personal tour of local air-raid arrangements, so that once again the monsignor would be saved from the inconvenience of air-raid practices until the dreadful day arrived, and Sydney suffered the destiny of Antwerp, Rotterdam and Singapore.

The chief air-raid shelter for St Margaret's, both the church and the school, was the dark place beneath the altar, a sort of crypt in which no one had been entombed and which served more as a place where old trestle tables were stacked, and even an ancient, blunt-bladed parish lawnmower had found its retirement. There was barely room for an adult to stand upright in there, but given that the architect's plans showed that St Margaret's altar was supported by a reinforced floor and by steel columns, some of whose dark uprights could be seen iron-black within the crypt-cellar, it was an appropriate shelter for the brunt of modern aerial bombardments.

A note to that effect was sent to all the parents of St Margaret's children. The infants would be safe beneath the steel-braced, sacred vault of the high altar. Sister Felicitas told Darragh one afternoon that she knew God would not let the high altar be destroyed, but Darragh thought God's will was more mysterious. Catholic beachheads of stone and steeple, of marble and tabernacle, had been consumed in Shanghai, Hong Kong, Singapore. The sword of Shinto rage had been permitted to bear them away.

His late father had frequently shown him the pictures, in Bean's *Official History of Australia in the War of 1914–18*, of the destroyed church in Albert, with its steeple full of holes, its sanctuary in ruins, and the Madonna at its apogee tilting towards Germany. From within that Virgin's shadow, the Australian Corps had repulsed Ludendorff's men, but the church, and anyone depending upon its structural strength, had been desolated. Darragh, since his misery and doubt had begun, had started to consider whether sometimes God showed His presence in the midst of horror by pretending not to be there.

On an arranged morning in Lent, Mr Conover, who looked like the all-wise Lionel Barrymore from an Andy Hardy picture, came to collect Father Darragh from the presbytery for air-raid practice. They walked together to the school, where Felicitas and the nuns had assembled all the children on the tarred playground. Some of these latter were babes—five-year-olds, even an occasional bright under-five. No amount of assumed brashness on the faces of the third graders could wipe out a pervasive quality of wide-eyed uncertainty in the mass of children. One of the younger nuns, parading the senior ranks with a hand-clapper device which warned children to behave, seemed herself restive and fearful. The jaws of the clapper, audible to Darragh, seemed determined to eat away all bravado, to summon an appropriate fear to the place.

Sister Felicitas beckoned the distinguished air-raid warden and Darragh forward, introduced them again to her charges, and invited Mr Conover to address the children.

'Children,' said Mr Conover, like a kindly bishop, 'have you ever heard the air-raid siren sounding from outside the council chambers, just up there, a block and a half away?'

The children, used to pacing their chanted responses to adult authorities, cried, 'Yes, Mis–ter Con–ov–er!'

'Today we will practise what will happen if the air-raid siren sounds to announce a real air raid. Now, there were enemy bombers which bombed Darwin, and children there went safely to shelters when the siren went, and came out safely afterwards. Do you understand?'

They told him in their school plainchant that they did. Mr Conover turned to Darragh, 'Father, if you could go into the shelter first, so the children who come in can see you as they enter . . .' Darragh agreed. He hoped that on the day, in the instant before some terrible impact of war, he would be able to console these innocents, cast over them the mantle of the sacraments. What he did not want to think of, what he knew would be easy to think of in a vulnerable shelter, was their being lifted by the hand of detonation, and pounded to dust.

'Father Darragh will be in the shelter first, so there will be nothing to worry about. God and Father Darragh will mind you.'

All eyes turned to Darragh, and they believed. On Conover's glib tongue, he had become the parent of parents. Now that they had invested their faith in him, the young nun's wooden clapper could afford to turn silent.

'So let us imagine that Japanese bombers have appeared over Sydney. The siren at the council chambers has sounded, and you come out here, obeying the nuns. No pushing, children, for the siren will sound in good time to allow everybody to get to the safe place. Now, Sister Felicitas, which children go first?'

Felicitas knew. Third graders, girls first, were already moving in orderly pairs. The little girls of St Margaret's affected a solemnity which only a few of the larger, freckled boys, muttering, tried to bear away.

'Father,' said Mr Conover. Thumb in vest pocket, he gestured to Darragh with his free hand to take the lead of the marching children. As he reached his place at the column's head, Darragh could hear the girls' voices behind him, whispering and clicking away, a knitting-needles sound as they sewed together their mysterious discourse. 'Father . . .' he could overhear them say now and then. They were not fully at ease but had been told to be brave for the sake of the youngsters. 'Father . . .' Their reliance on him gave him back a purpose. He reached a low green door in the church wall, a door of tongue-and-groove planking. Apparently Mr Conover considered it up to strength in the event of dive-bombers. Darragh wriggled at its painted latch and opened it. 'Very well, children,' he said over his shoulder, and stooped and entered a dark place which exuded the smell of clay and abiding moisture. He lit the torch with which Conover had provided him and guided the children to benches which lay all around the edges of this extensive cavern. The girls hurriedly sat, anxious to find a place beside best friends and face the unimaginable peril hand in hand. Encouraged by the entry of the older children, the five and six-year-olds followed, many of them surprisingly composed, like people performing a practised rite. It was then that he saw, among the dimly lit infant faces, that of Anthony Heggarty, the son of Hitler's prisoner.

The light of unwitting victimhood which shone on so many young faces seemed to Darragh to mark out the young Anthony Heggarty's features in particular. The child had taken up his place on one of the benches yards from Darragh. Suddenly all the children, more than a hundred and twenty of them, had found seats under the instruction of those excellent marshals, the Dominican nuns.

Mr Conover himself entered, stooping in his suit, and closed and latched the green door from the inside. A new order of murk prevailed and the earthen smell dragged at young nostrils. There was an unconscious bout of anxious sniffing, until the children became accustomed to the air of the place. The light of the nuns' and Darragh's torches was rendered intense but narrow.

'Now,' said Mr Conover. 'You all have your linen bags. Say the bombing becomes heavy. Take out your little halves of tennis ball and put them over your ears.'

There was a rustling of linen and fingers, and soon all the children had a demi-globe of tennis ball attached to either ear.

'Now your ears are protected,' said Conover, 'but you can still hear Sister, can't you? And you can still hear Father Darragh.'

Although he wondered how either Felicitas or himself could be heard during a bombing raid, Darragh was delighted for the children's sake to play along, and do a voice test, as did Felicitas, and all the children as a mass, including the fourth class tough guys by the door, chanted in unison that indeed both could be heard. The noise of their answer surprised them a bit, for it zipped around the steel columns and returned quickly to them from the buttressed under-floor of the altar.

Sister Felicitas took over. 'So Mr Conover would like you to keep those halves of tennis ball on your ears for five minutes now, for bombing can last that long or even longer. If the noise is so loud that you might be tempted to bite your tongue, you'll be told to take out the plugs you have in your linen bags and bite them with your teeth—isn't that so, Mr Conover?'

'That's exactly right, Sister Felicitas,' Mr Conover agreed, maintaining the myth of leisurely bombardment, of explosions which left space for leisurely decisions.

So the children were told to remove one tennis-ball half, get the plug from their bags, bite it, and then replace the temporarily removed earguard. A nation of tennis players, going to war with hemispheres of rubber to protect their eardrums.

The children bit away at their mouthguards for a minute, some too avidly and with exaggerated tooth-display. 'Firmly but gently,' Sister Felicitas told them. An older boy dropped his in the dirt and others spat out theirs to laugh at him. 'Take those boys' names, Sister,' cried Felicitas, and the one with the clapper hastened to do so.

The same nun, having taken the names of the miscreants, wielded her clapper at a nod from Felicitas, and the children were asked to return their mouthplugs but not their earguards to their pouches.

'So,' said Felicitas, 'we shall ask Father Darragh to lead us in the singing of "Hail, Queen of Heaven", keeping the tennis ball halves over your ears while you sing.'

Darragh counted to three and then swung his hand, and the children burst forth, their voices sharpened, exalted by where they were.

> *Hail, Queen of Heaven, the ocean star,*
> *Guide of the wanderer here below,*
> *Thrown on life's surge we claim thy care,*
> *Save us from peril and from woe . . .*

Young Heggarty, eyes fixed, sang the words off distractedly into a void. Darragh liked the hymn, and belted it forth with an automatic joy, the enthusiasm which had been his entire life until recently. He had always presumed himself as close to the Virgin Mary as to his earthly mother in Rose Bay. He could not envisage the features, though. The standard statues of the Madonna, the lady in blue and white, with her foot upon the serpent's head, had derived in considerable part from the visions of St Bernadette of Lourdes eighty or so years past. A biblical-scholar priest at Manly, however, had once remarked that every racial group made statues of its divinities and saints in their own likeness, and that although statuary provided a fair spiritual focus between the faithful and their saintly intercessors, the features were not meant to be taken literally but, like an illustration in a book, as an aid to imagination. The professor then surprised Darragh by suggesting that Christ and His Mother, as Aramaic-speakers and inhabitants of Galilee, must have been Bedouin-brown. The Virgin Mary was unlikely to have exceeded five feet three inches in height, the scholar said, and Christ Himself unlikely to be more than five feet seven.

The Heggarty boy was dreaming, the familiar words slipping half-formed from his lips. Another hymn, 'Faith of Our Fathers', was proposed by Sister Felicitas, and Darragh again acted as choirmaster. The small, well-schooled voices sawed their way up and down the complicated verse:

> *Our fathers chained in prisons dark,*
> *Were still in heart and conscience free.*
> *How sweet their children's fate would be–ee,*
> *If they like them could die for Thee–ee . . .*

Five minutes of protected eardrum practice passed. Via his sighting of Anthony Heggarty, the worrying images of Mrs Heggarty and the stranger, generous for a purpose, replaced the idea of Japanese bombardment and of the dimensions and appearance of the Holy Family in Darragh's mind. The urgency had re-arisen in him to write to Mrs Heggarty, to send a note home with Anthony. After this air-raid practice he would examine his conscience perhaps, and if there were to be a letter, it would be based on an honest exercise of piety, not on the basis of pride, or of any other desire his instincts told him it was better not to name.

Sister Felicitas called on him, now that the tennis ball halves were back in the linen bags and the children had had as much practice as their years could stand, to bless the entire group. '*Benedicat vos omnipotens Deus . . .*' The littlest ones were allowed into the open air first, and crouching under the low roof still, Darragh heard how the sunlight outside gave them back their voices and called out all the laughter which, in the bomb shelter, had lain buried.

Back in his room and at his prie-dieu, its kneeler buffed by the knees of a number of former St Margaret's curates, Darragh attempted his examination of conscience. He began with formal prayers—the 'Our Father' the '*Ave*', the '*Confiteor*'. Then he tried in their residual light to organise his motives, to place them in line with absolute principles rather than with thoughts about how eminently, touchingly, beautifully ripe for salvation Mrs Heggarty was. Her honesty, for one thing. It seemed to give her a special strength of claim. He put in a quarter of an hour, recited some more prayers in conclusion, rose with the matter unresolved, and went straight to his desk and wrote the note to her, as he had really known from the start he would. He had been concerned, he said, by their conference. If she would like to speak again, she must feel free . . .

He waited in the playground, intercepted Anthony Heggarty, placed the letter in his satchel and told him to be sure to give it to his mother. He did not care, nor should he have, if Sister Felicitas saw this transaction from her dominant place on the school steps.

CHAPTER EIGHT

I
T WAS THE kind of late summer day in which, if possible,
people stayed indoors. The air blazed beyond the windows,
and was rendered dense with smoke from a bushfire in the Blue
Mountains. Saying his office in the corner of the living room,
Darragh was interrupted by Mrs Flannery, tentative because she
knew the importance of the hours. There was an American
soldier at the door.

'Oh,' Darragh commented. 'I didn't hear the bell.'

'No,' said Mrs Flannery. 'He sort of appeared. He looks very
impressive.'

Mrs Flannery might have made an Australian soldier wait
until Darragh had finished the office. But the Americans had the
authority of their strangeness and their air of confidence.

The soldier in the hall, Darragh noticed in the small time
before the conversation began, was a large, well-made man, but
did not stand with the typical jauntiness Sydneysiders associated
with his type of particularly well-cut uniform. He held his cap at
his side, and his smoothly combed brown hair did not seem much

brilliantined. The stripes on his sleeve were worn, as Americans wore them, the reverse way to Australian chevrons—pointing to the shoulder, ascendant. Beneath this man's three stripes were further semi-rondels. The man stood peering up at a painting of St Jerome, translator of the Bible into vulgate Latin, who knelt in umber oils amidst the scrolls of his own and others' scholarship, bare-breasted, a stone nearby for penitential beating of his breast. He withdrew his gaze from it dazedly as Darragh appeared before him, and blinked. He had extraordinary almond eyes, as fascinating, Darragh thought at once, as those of a knight or courtier or angel in a Renaissance altar piece.

'Father,' the soldier said, 'am I disturbing you?' He was perhaps a year older than Darragh, and his particular mixture of forwardness and courtesy was refreshing on a dull morning in Lent. Darragh said not at all, and marked his place in Vespers with one of the coloured in-sewn tassels of his breviary.

'My aunt's died back home,' said the soldier, fixing him with the almond eyes.

'Ant?' asked Darragh, thinking this an insect joke.

'No,' said the soldier, shaking his head, self-reproving. 'I forgot you guys pronounce it different. My A–U–N–T. She's a widow. And not so old. I was wondering if you could say a Mass for her.' He pulled from his trouser pocket a folded envelope. He knew the protocol for offering a priest a stipend for saying a Mass for the dead.

'My father's sister-in-law, see. Louisa Fratelli. More or less raised me, with my parents being so busy with the market garden. I've written her name on the envelope.'

Darragh accepted the envelope and considered it. He looked inside. There was, as the last time an American had asked him to say Mass, a full pound note. But this was to be a Mass for the dead. To be asked to say Mass for a person who had died so far-off—that was a new experience.

Darragh said, 'I should tell you . . . the normal stipend for a Mass is as little as five shillings and never more than ten.'

'Please, Father. Take it. Put the rest in the poor box.'

Darragh said, 'Thank you. I will. We have a very active St Vincent de Paul branch here, and soldiers' families to look after, Sergeant . . .'

'Sorry. I'm Master Sergeant Gene Fratelli. G–E–N–E, as in Gene Kelly. Eugenio, I was baptised. I'm an MP, but I take my armband off in places like this.'

Darragh introduced himself and asked, 'Where did your aunt die?'

'Next door my parents. Place called Stratford. In California. The Central Valley. Lots of Italians. Some Portuguese. You know. The Portuguese and Mexicans do the picking.'

'Why did you come to St Margaret's, Sergeant?' Darragh wanted to know. 'Not that you aren't entirely welcome.'

'I've been to Mass here once or twice.' Darragh was surprised. He would surely have noticed such a striking face from the pulpit.

Darragh suggested, 'There's a dance club at Flemington—a lot of American soldiers go there.'

'I don't hang round those places, Father. I like quieter people. Someone to take a poor GI in and give him dinner.'

So, someone in the area had kindly fed Sergeant Fratelli, Darragh concluded. He could not quite defeat in himself the idea that there was something odd about a man wanting a Mass said in Australia for a woman who had died in California. But there was no reason why such an arrangement was not entirely proper. The Communion of Saints transcended all borders and traversed an ocean with ease.

'I'll announce your aunt's name at the Masses on Sunday,' said Darragh.

'Louisa Fratelli,' insisted Darragh, for verification.

'You know, that would have tickled her,' Sergeant Fratelli told him with a sudden smile which reached up and nicely kindled the almond eyes. 'I'll try to be here for it, unless I'm on duty of course. I'm running Suspects Squad at the moment.' Darragh did not know what that meant, and did not ask.

'Who's this guy again?' asked Fratelli, nodding towards the painting.

'St Jerome. Fourth or fifth century. I don't know the exact dates, Sergeant. He came from North Africa and translated the Bible into Latin. He's the patron saint of librarians, and he was secretary to a Pope, but he often lived in desert caves.'

'He was an Arab?'

'Egyptian, I believe.' Darragh was not utterly sure.

'And the stone in his hand, Father?'

'He was penitential. He beat his breast with desert rocks.'

'Wow,' said Fratelli. 'That's what I like. I like saints' stories. Because I'm not one myself.'

He smiled, his lips folding gently. 'Are you and the head priest fixed for groceries, Father?'

'Yes, thanks, we're well off.'

'You'd say that,' Fratelli asserted, as if he knew Darragh well. 'I can get stuff easy. The PX at the Showgrounds.'

'Please, don't go to the trouble . . .'

'Okay. But you guys have rationing and all . . .'

'You're a generous man. But we're well looked after, thank you.'

The man saluted casually, without that British snappiness the Australians were taught to affect but rarely managed. With a last

look at St Jerome, he let himself out of the door. He had fascinated Darragh with his casual courtesies, which were stylistically
different from those of young Australian men. Darragh had
noticed that in addition to his stripes, he wore three white service
bars on his lower sleeve, which meant he had served in the army
for some years, probably since he was eighteen, and thus—as
Kearney had in Sydney—had beheld mayhem. That reality made
it harder for Darragh to define the man Fratelli was. But that was
merely one small mystery cast up by the new order of the world,
when to defeat the risk of terrible Japanese strangeness, one
needed to invite some relative strangeness within the walls.

CHAPTER NINE

THIS BLAZING DAY proved itself to be one ripe with incident when, having returned to the recitation of his office, he heard the telephone ring.

'I'm so sorry, Father,' said Mrs Flannery. 'There's a Mr Flood on the telephone for you.' He closed his breviary again, his heart pumping at the unexpectedness of this summons.

It was indeed Mr Bert Flood, speaking loudly but in his normal neutral tone. 'Father Darragh. Ross is off to a trade union meeting in Lithgow. The missus wondered could you call in today?'

Darragh said that of course he could.

'She's not up to much anymore. The smoke's bad for her. The doc gives her a month or two.' In his way Bert was saying, she's not capable of sinning now—only of suffering. 'This is a chance for those last rites, you know, if you want . . .'

Ross Trumble was away, and so Mrs Flood was willing to die as a secret penitent. It seemed she did not intend to tell her lover. This was a very pragmatic use of Christ's sacraments. The absolutism of Darragh's nature until recently would have frowned on such a dodge. But now that the world had grown complicated, he was willing to be of service to Mrs Flood on any terms. He felt a light-heartedness at last descend on him as he put on his clerical stock and collar, and crossed through the particled air to the sacristy, which the thick bricks of the church had kept cool. He put on his stole and white thigh-length surplice, fetched the small black bag in which he would carry all that Mrs Flood needed, retrieved the keys to both the tabernacle and the locked box on the sanctuary wall where the holy oils were kept, and walked out onto the altar steps, feeling once more the excitement of the complex duties ahead of him. The altar had been clothed by the women of the altar society in the violet altar facings of Lent. He ascended the steps after genuflecting, moved aside the altar card in front of the tabernacle, the one with the prayers for the Offertory and Canon of the Mass, which he knew by heart. He pushed aside the violet tabernacle cloth, feeling again grate-fully fed by these ritual movements, and with the key opened the bronze tabernacle, the strongbox of the Divine. Here, along with a large, full-bodied and lidded silver cup named the *ciborium*, the feeder, containing altar breads which would be transmuted into the body and blood of Christ at Mass tomorrow morning, was a further such vessel, veiled in violet, containing some communion hosts consecrated by himself at that morning's Mass and left there for emergencies such as a call from Bert Flood. He removed the veil and lid of this one and placed two hosts in the disc-like metal container, the pyx, from the silk-lined bag he had brought from the sacristy. He made sure the clasp on this disc clicked tight shut, preserving the body of Christ from contamination until it deigned to rest on Mrs Flood's capricious tongue.

Having locked the tabernacle and adjusted its veil and again genuflected, he moved down the steps to the left side of the altar. Here another but less ornate metal box was attached to the wall. He unlocked it and saw before him three metal canisters, tubular urns, on a shelf. The holy oils. The oil, consecrated by the arch-bishop at the cathedral in Sydney each Easter Thursday morning, was fetched out to every suburb by the parish priest or the curate. Again, Monsignor Carolan always sent him, Darragh, to attend the ceremony in an alb and stole to bring back a year's supply of the three species of oil. Yet it was the allure of these mysteries which had brought him to the priesthood. Although he was attached to his parents by an intense love of the kind which pre-empted any questioning, he had seen nothing in their marriage to attract him to the state. Marriage—both their faces said it at different times—was hard, and uncertain. Fred Astaire might dance in tails with Ginger Rogers, but real life, and dogged love, seemed noble yet squalid. The memory of physical love, of what people called sex, seemed to tease people with wistful memory rather than make them happy. The priesthood, with its arcane knowledge, the drama of the rites, rose above the doubt and the ordinariness of the moment. It had a vestment, an incantation and a soothing code only its priests understood. Who would not want to become a priest, and consider it an honour?

Each canister before Darragh carried engraved letters to iden-tify its separate use. O. C. for baptisms; O. S. for confirmations; O.I., *oleum infirmorum*, for the anointing of the ill. He added this latter canister to a metal bracket fitted into his black bag. Vanity again arose—the idea that Mrs Heggarty might respect him better if she saw his competence among these symbols and substances. But he shook it away. The memory of cautionary tales about fallen priests recurred. The alcoholic priest who had left the priesthood, mixed with prostitutes, and one night, crazy for drink and in pure malice, consecrated the entire contents of a bread shop window. Once a priest and always a priest, he had transformed the bread into Christ's body, making his Saviour hostage to whatever customer, pure or impure, Catholic or Protestant, ate of the contents of the shop. And a companion tale: the same kind of priest, lying with a fallen woman who suddenly goes into the throes of death. She pleads for the last rites, the *oleum infirmorum*, and he goes to the kitchen and, purely to appease this dying woman, fetches butter and anoints her. These tales indicated that a fallen priest was a dangerous man, an assassin, a mocker. He was not yet such a man, but to think of Mrs Heggarty so compulsively was to reach the first station on a very long line which led to a version of the priesthood which exploded inwards on itself.

There were some four or five hours of sunlight left as he took to Homebush Road and its bubbling tar, now carrying his surplice and stole and two candlesticks in a bag somewhat like a workman's, and also within it the small black box containing not only the pyx and hosts and oil, but wads of cotton to apply the unguent to Mrs Flood's organs of sense. A professional pride helped him deal with the bullying heat and the stained air. Extreme unction. An anointment at the last. A smearing of those human extremities which had walked into, sniffed, eyed or tasted wrong. In the Eastern Orthodox Church priests anointed the loins, the region of so much lethal peril, but fortunately that was not the custom with the Roman Church.

Bert Flood, opening the door of the little house with a greater speed than last time, wore what looked like the same vest and pants and collarless shirt as before. 'Oh yairs,' he said, as if he had forgotten he had called Darragh. 'The missus is in the bedroom.'

He was one of those Australians who confused Darragh. Bert Flood's demeanour bore out the description given by one of the bush poets: 'Hadn't any opinions, hadn't any ideas.' He appeared as if he had leached all anger, enthusiasm and purpose out of his soul, to the extent Darragh wondered how he ever got himself to the intense point of proposing marriage to Mrs Flood, and what she thought of him when she agreed. But in his way, he had achieved a dramatic point now by opening the door to Darragh.

Bert led him to the first room off the corridor. Darragh noticed a pleasant smell of menthol and camphor in Mrs Flood's bedroom. The woman herself lay diminished in the middle of the bed, buttressed with pillows, and there was a hectic redness to her cheeks. Beside her on a wicker table lay various brown bottles, and a glass with the dregs of some fluid still in it. A picture of a sylvan arbour, bearing no resemblance at all to the landscapes in which Mr and Mrs Flood had conducted their marriage, sat over the bed, in its way like a prayer for Eden, or for a cleansed earth in which all growth and all manners were orderly. Both partners had failed the idyll.

It seemed to Darragh that in aging by ten years since he had last seen her, Mrs Flood had managed to become more ageless. Wastage was visible, however, in the way her facial bones made claim upon the rosy filament of flesh laid over them. The death's head was threatening to emerge. The humming rattle of her breath was a permanent sound. There was no tubercular charm to it today. It sounded frankly like the clatter of some failed mechanism.

'She's not too flash at talking for long,' said Bert. But her eyes were alight as they picked up Darragh's arrival. In the context of her decline, her smile seemed more childlike than girlish. But at least she was not one of those of whom Christ said, 'I wish you were either hot or cold, but since you are neither, I shall spit you out of my mouth.'

Darragh asked, 'Could I put the pyx and the oil on the table here?' Bert nodded, bustled past, and rearranged the bottles of medicine and tonic to make room for Darragh. Then he touched Darragh on the elbow and gave him a solemn wink. 'I'll leave you to it, Father. I'll get the kettle on.'

'You're welcome to stay, Bert. It's your house.'

The idea seemed to panic Bert.

'No. I'll get the kettle on.'

For that was the great secular sacrament—tea. Before Bert had even left, Mrs Flood reached out and grasped the hem of Darragh's coat, dragging him closer. 'Don't make Ross clear out. We met in the sanitarium. He had this curse too. He's a good fellow. And I'm past it all now. Past every crime, eh? If you come on heavy, it'll only make trouble for poor old Bert. All right?'

It was apparent from the effort this took that she could not make a detailed confession.

'Don't talk,' he said, in command with the dying. 'You can nod, Mrs Flood.'

She nodded to show she could. A new submission had entered her.

He unpacked his bag, placed the two candlesticks from his small black case on the table, lit them, put on his surplice and stole, while Mrs Flood's eyes glittered with a kind of hunger at all these activities. He instructed her to pray mentally with him while he recited the Act of Contrition.

'Oh my God,' he intoned, 'I am heartily sorry and beg pardon for all my sins . . .'

She said arduously, 'There's one thing, Father. You know why I married Bert. He didn't make a fuss of me. I was impressed. We worked for this store in Cobar, and Bert was a warehouseman, and I sold frocks. The boss was always grabbing for me. But Bert didn't make a fuss. It turned out he couldn't make a fuss of anything, poor old dear.'

'Don't talk, Mrs Flood. You don't need to.'

'These . . . what you call, sins of the flesh.'

'It's all right.'

'They're not so bad. They're just silly little things half full of dark. But there's light and heat too . . .'

'Yes, but you repent of them?'

'Look at what the Japs did in Hong Kong . . . and the Black and Tans in Ireland . . . They *were* sins!'

'But the people who committed them don't have the benefit of our beliefs,' he said, entering into the debate despite himself. 'Leave it all to God and repent.'

'All right,' she gasped. 'I do.'

'Please, you don't have to talk. Just nod.'

Indeed she nodded with a poignant urgency. Confession was easy for the sinner of limited breath. Mrs Flood continued to nod her affirmation of repentance as Darragh recited. Her lips throughout worked dryly on the sentiments she lacked the breath to state. She said ambiguously, 'I'm sorry for Bert,' as he absolved her.

Then he took the small white host out of the pyx, and she opened her mouth as taught in childhood, and he placed it on her tongue. 'Now, Mrs Flood, you'll understand I must wash my hands before I open the holy oil. Is that all right?'

'Don't be delicate on my account,' she instructed him, pointing with her right hand in the bathroom's direction.

He went and found it, scrubbing himself at the basin from which hung an old razor strop, possibly Bert's. Bert had laid out a clean towel. In his way the fellow was astonishing. Darragh went to find him to ask him would he help with the bedclothes, since they would need to be moved back for the anointing. But Bert was not in the kitchen, or on the awninged verandah which was his isolation ward from both marriage and the disease.

Returned to Mrs Flood's room, Darragh took up the container of oil from its bracket in the black case and, with the appropriate words, absolved with this holy chrism her eyes for all the wrong they had seen, her ears for the burden of what they had heard, her nostrils for having drawn the breath of sin, her hands for their ill-considered caresses, her mouth for its mortal appetites, and finally, the sheets drawn back, her feet, pink and delicate and not like normal suburban feet, for walking in dangerous paths. '*Per istam Sanctam Unctionem indulgeat tibi Dominus quidquid deliquisti*—Through this blessed oil may the Lord forgive whatever ill you did.'

The passive effort involved in having the sheets pulled up to her chest again by Darragh seemed to exhaust her. Darragh ate the second host himself, and stood in prayer a moment.

'I'll try to find Bert,' he said.

This time Bert was in the kitchen, unpacking a brown bag. 'I ducked round to Moran and Cato's for some biscuits,' he said in his voice of flat melancholy, yet it was touching to find that he considered Darragh's being there an event, a significant passage, worthy of the good cups and a few Arnott's shortbreads.

'Mrs Flood is finished,' said Darragh. 'I mean, she's been anointed, and the rest.'

'Righto,' said Bert. 'She'll be happy. And Ross will be sweet. His bark's worse than his bite. He feels he has to be rude to you. Union rules.'

The *Daily Mirror* was on the table with its predictable stories of Allied progress in Africa and Allied devastation in Asia. All the military success was in the wrong place for Bert and Darragh, and came at the cost of Lance Bombardier Heggarty's capture and Mrs Heggarty's endangered soul.

Darragh said, 'Mrs Flood will be safe now from all this.' He waved his hand at the headlines. As soon as he said it, he thought he might have uttered the wrong sentiment.

'She'll be missed,' said Bert. 'She was a lovely girl. She was an usherette at the State when we came down to Sydney, believe it or not. Don't know what she was doing with an ugly bugger like me. Pardon the French, Father.'

'French?'

'My swear words. Pardon them.'

'Of course.'

A half-grin came to Bert's face. 'Not that I'm likely to give them up, you know. I hope Ross didn't say anything too nasty to you last time you were here?'

'No,' Darragh lied.

'See, he can be an angry mad bugger. Make a good soldier if he hadn't had the crook lungs himself. An orphan, you know— at least his mother died young and he was on his own. Most orphans are angry buggers because they feel they didn't get a fair shake. Toys at Christmas and all that stuff. Had a hard life, of course. But no sooner does the party say we need you somewhere than he's there. Works like a Trojan, that feller.'

Darragh wondered what a priest could say when the wronged husband clicked his tongue over the well-known and affection-ately recorded traits of the lover.

Tea finished, Bert led him up the hallway and paused at the bedroom door to allow Darragh to say goodbye to Mrs Flood. But the woman was noisily yet delicately sleeping. Raised and redeemed on her pillows, she wore the same gracefully amused smile she had before he had laid the oil upon her extremities.

'Call on me again, Bert. Whenever Mrs Flood wishes.'

He was no longer frightened of Trumble, knowing him to be himself a frightened, fatherless child helped reduce his Marxist ardour to size.

CHAPTER TEN

OVER THE PAST few days, the smoke had been dissipated by rain and cold southerlies, and Darragh had begun to wonder if Anthony Heggarty had remembered to pass the letter to his mother. It seemed to him to justify the monsignor's low estimation of him that he had entrusted such an important document to a first-grade child.

Darragh consoled himself during downfalls with a book of Monsignor Knox's witty essays, *The Mass in Slow Motion*, in the parlour. Now that the first breath of winter had struck, it provided a congenial corner. Looking through the parlour's side window, he saw the child, Anthony, standing at the door, gathering himself to knock, water in his hair. Darragh moved quickly, to get to the door before the bell alerted Mrs Flannery.

Seeing him, Anthony extended his hand, an envelope in it, spotted with warm rain. 'Thank you, Anthony,' said Darragh. 'Are you well?'

'The Nazis have my father,' said the boy. This seemed to be

obviously a quotation from Kate Heggarty. 'But it means he'll come home safe.'

'Yes,' said Darragh. 'And I pray that it's soon.' And he did. He wanted Mrs Heggarty's soul. He wanted her submission as he'd wanted Mrs Flood's.

The boy seemed happy and went away across the wet gravel towards the school. Darragh took the plain white envelope inside. The writing on it was in parish convent copperplate. *Thou shalt know them by their hand* . . . Under her address in The Crescent she had carefully written the date, and the letter was rather touchingly set out in a manner not unlike a school essay. 'Go home, girls,' you could virtually hear a nun in Kate Heggarty's girlhood say, 'and for your homework write the sort of letter you would write to a priest if you wanted spiritual advice.'

> *Dear Father Darragh,*
>
> *It is very kind of you to take an interest in our welfare. We would be honoured to have the blessing of your visit on our house at this troubled time. Except that I do not want to argue the matter with you again. I feel we argued the matter enough last time.*
>
> *I am now working every day until three o'clock, so that it would be better if you were to visit Anthony and me. It would need to be in the later afternoon about four.*
>
> > *Yours sincerely*
> > *Kate Heggarty (Mrs)*

She said *no arguments*, but she wanted to see a priest, and that was the first step, Darragh believed. A more critical voice within asked who she thought she was to put limits on a priest? She had no right to expect an easy visitation, not after her forthrightness in the presbytery parlour. Besides, she might simply relish playing with him, flexing her power over him by making him desire her salvation. So, for his own part, he intended to consider and not to rush.

By next morning he had convinced himself that some speed was advisable. He believed that an instinct or a revelation—one or the other—told him that he lived on a temporal plane, and that human souls are redeemed in time.

The Heggarty house when he arrived at it at four o'clock that afternoon was the kind that people called a duplex, a word which seemed to offer more than the narrow-fronted dimensions which now faced him. Mrs Heggarty lived in one of two adjoining dark brick little dwellings, both of them with the random air of being rented out rather than owned. But the Heggartys' place had its front gate and its little garden, and a side gate with a narrow laneway which led to the backyard where Kate Heggarty could hang the washing and Anthony romp.

Darragh's ringing at the door was answered by Kate Heggarty herself, who seemed flustered and out of breath, her hair done up in the sort of scarf factory workers wore, as if she had arrived home a few seconds before. She had the busy appearance of a woman who had a pot on the stove in one room, and ironing to do in another. But at the sight of Darragh she gave in to events and composed herself.

'Father,' she said. She seemed very solemn and a little confused. His earlier suspicion, that she wanted him here as a sop to her vanity, evaporated. She asked him please to come in.

She still had an air of bewilderment as she closed the door behind him, and in the dark hallway talked for reassurance, 'Gosh, my mother would be pretty upset with me for having a priest in the house when it's so messy.' But as they passed two shut bedroom doors and came into the lounge room, mess did not seem to prevail. Darragh was somehow delighted that she had here all the standard treasures of womanhood, including the china cabinet with a good tea set. A small statue of the Virgin Mary sat beside the mantel clock, to show that she had not definitely decided against that part of her being. On a lacquered rattan table stood the picture of her husband, Heggarty, in his dark serge, hopeful beneath a jaunty hat, and herself in a calf-length wedding dress. The marriage day. The picture established an authority in the room. The sight of the soldier's definite features brought to Darragh a sense of the filament of marriage pulled wire-thin by the distance between Heggarty and his wife, but still honoured here on a rattan table. In The Crescent.

'Please sit there, Father, and I'll go and get tea.'

Darragh smiled. 'I don't think I want to sit here in style alone. The kitchen's good by me.'

'Oh,' she murmured, gravely considering the issue. 'Gee. I suppose that's okay.'

She spoke like a woman trying to hide blemishes when there were no blemishes to hide. Nor did she place any stipulation, as she had by letter, on what might be said. Only that he would forgive the housekeeping. Yet the kitchen he entered with her was swept clean, the yellow linoleum polished to a well-worn sheen. The coloured glass in the windows of her deal dresser shone. Who am I, he wondered, to expect a perfect kitchen, and to accept it as a token of grace in its owner? Yet he had already done so.

'Please,' she said, 'sit down.' She pulled out a chair by her small, varnished kitchen table. These were, Darragh knew, the founding pieces of furniture of a hard-up marriage. And then it occurred to him that that was what embarrassed her—that she expended her life on the obscure maintenance of these few things bought on instalment payments from Mark Foy's or Grace Brothers. She would have liked to have the luxury of treating them negligently, but she could not afford it. Because of her poverty, she must maintain these sticks and laths as if they were museum pieces, and part of her resented the fact and longed to be able, for once, to be a bit negligent.

'Please sit,' she repeated with a breathless desire that things should go well. 'I'll boil the kettle.'

Darragh said, 'This house does you honour, Kate.'

She paused in lighting gas under her full kettle. She was as taken by surprise, as he was, that he had used her first name. 'Yes, but I just wish the maid hadn't taken the day off.'

All her movements fascinated him. It was a great temptation to dream oneself the possessor of this house, particularly this humble kitchen which so frustrated her pride. 'I don't want to break the terms of your letter,' he said. 'Not that I necessarily accept them, but we'll let that side of the argument rest. But I *have* remembered you. In the Mass and the office . . .'

She coughed. 'Yes,' she said. 'I'm pleased . . . No, that's silly, Father. I'm grateful.'

'And no news of your husband?'

'Except that I called the Department of Defence. They think his group has been moved to Tunisia, and that in time they'll be sent to Germany or somewhere else in Europe. They said they'd write when they know more. Poor fellow, he'll be bored stiff.'

If she considered boredom the extent of his sufferings, Darragh thought, then it was a good thing.

The tea was ready. She went to the ice chest and took out a lump of fruit cake.

'You can't make it properly, under rationing,' she told him. 'You have to skimp on the eggs and butter.'

'I can't,' said Darragh. 'Lenten fast.'

'What if I cut just a small cube? You could have that.'

He consented. 'A very small cube.' And sipping his tea he tasted the mouthful of cake she had cut for him and declared it superb. Perhaps, despite her disclaimer about the cake, the kind man's eggs and butter were in this recipe. And with the sweetness in his mouth, he began to ask himself what he was doing there. Shorn of all power except the power of his eunuch example. Did she like the idea, after all and despite herself, of a tongue-tied priest dancing attendance on her?

He was distracted by Anthony running in flushed from the backyard, followed by a neighbours' kids all demanding their slice of cake. Anthony with an only child's resolve swamped by the clamant, rough-elbowed children of her neighbour. To those children, Darragh was barely a presence, while Anthony was made to stand still and greet him. Then, with the fruit, flour and sugar in their blood, they raged out again without spoken intent, in a tight formation like migrating birds. They *knew* what they were about.

'Thalia Stevens's kids are a bit rowdy,' Mrs Heggarty explained with a faint smile. 'She's got too many of them to polish them. But she's the best neighbour I have. No pretensions.'

But was Thalia Stevens the source of some of her ideas, Darragh wondered.

There was now another rattle at the back screen door. Darragh thought it must be a late-arriving child. From his place at the table, however, he saw the stooped blond figure of Ross Trumble, leaning there, peering in. His face was weirdly bloated—he had either been in a fight or got a skinful of beer somewhere. He carried a heavily wrapped packet in his hands.

'Ross,' called Mrs Heggarty. 'What in heaven's name are you doing here?'

'I,' said Trumble. For a time, he considered the proposed shape of his intended sentence. 'I have had the afternoon off from the sick room,' he said. 'Been to town. The Journalists' Club. I have a friend . . .'

'The bar's open there, obviously.'

Heartburn made Trumble's mouth form into a rictus. When the spasm had passed, he said, 'You could say that, Katie. But I've got some chops for you too. From another friend. At the abattoirs.'

'Another Commo, I suppose?'

'Well, Katie, you don't need to take them.'

'I don't want them if they're stolen goods.'

'No, they're part of his meat quota, for Christ's sake.'

'No blasphemy, Ross. Come in then. Have some tea.'

Trumble opened the screen door and stepped in. As he put down the bundle of meat on the sink, his eyes took in the room, with Darragh at the table.

'Oh, Jesus,' he said. 'Father Death himself.'

'Father Darragh,' said Kate. 'And you be polite! Sit down here.' She organised a chair for him, back on to the sink, and picked up the parcel and transferred it deftly to her ice chest. She seemed to Darragh to be habituated to this movement—Trumble called in regularly, and brought gifts of meat. Surely she was not risking damnation for the sake of such prosaic parcels?

Today, however, Trumble found the business of sitting occupied all his mental and physical powers. Watching him, Darragh's own mental powers were centred on whether to stay or go. Why was it his kind of priest, and not the monsignor's kind, who sat at a tea party with a would-be apostate and a Communist?

'How is Mrs Flood?' Darragh asked Trumble.

'How's Mrs Flood?' Trumble repeated, but—it seemed—with not too much viciousness. 'Not too bloody flash is the answer. I ought to be there but I needed to have a break. I don't know. The sick room gets me down. I spent long enough sick myself . . .'

'You devote a great deal of time to her, Ross,' Kate Heggarty reminded him. The proposition that hung in the air was that he was a fine and considerate adulterer. The scales of virtue were shifting in this kitchen, and the standard weights no longer applied. Even Darragh felt the shift. The idea that there could be virtue at the heart of sin seemed not as outrageous an argument as it should. And this was the problem with Kate Heggarty, he saw. She was a Catholic, but within a world of Stevenses and Floods and Trumbles, whose codes of conduct had not been laid down in any Thomistic code, and whose ethics were not mediated by the Holy, Catholic and Apostolic Church.

Trumble drank his tea hungrily. It brought sweat out on his forehead. When he was finished, he looked up at Darragh. 'You know, I'm trying to be polite. But I don't like you breathing around Kate.'

'Shut up, Rossy,' said Kate Heggarty, a sudden and easy severity in her eye which showed she knew how to manage rough trade.

'You like sick women, don't you?' Trumble asked Darragh. 'You've got 'em where you want them. They can't do anything except say sorry. But Kate's not sick, is she?'

'Drink up,' Kate ordered Trumble. 'You're out of here, son!'

He looked up leadenly. 'It's the truth,' he said.

'You know I'm a Catholic. Don't even begin it, Ross! Drink up and get out.'

'Oh jeez!' said Trumble, but he drank and—to Darragh's amazement—rose, belched, said a polite general good afternoon, and vanished by the back door.

'Thanks for the chops,' she called after him. And then to Darragh, 'I'm sorry.'

Darragh smiled, but wondered whether he should question her about Trumble. For reasons he could not define, he didn't want to. He did not want to find out she had stooped to Trumble. He might turn into an automatic priest again and say something to drive her away. 'Don't worry,' said Darragh. 'I've been told off by Mr Trumble in the past.'

But he was delighted the man had gone. Now a conversation between a parishioner and a curate could develop. But Mrs Heggarty did not want it to, or had other matters more important to her.

'See, Ross never knew his mother,' said Kate Heggarty, anxious to explain Trumble's behaviour. Bert had been the same way. There was something about Trumble which made people enumerate the reasons for his blunt rhetoric and hostility. 'Rosie Flood was like his mother and his girlfriend all in one. And Rosie's dying, so he comes sniffing round other kitchens, looking for a future home.' And she smiled broadly at this; the pre-dictable brashness of it had endeared Trumble to her. 'He doesn't mean any of that stuff he says,' she continued. 'It's just he gets scared if he doesn't fill the air with it, he'll have to explain himself. He thinks everyone has to be told about the whole caboodle—history, society, religion, the world. He's easier with all that than he is saying hello like a normal person.'

Darragh could tell from the fading light beyond the screen door that soon he must go. He could not sit on in this quiet hour, drinking tea to no purpose.

'Look,' he said, feeling more her brother than her priest, 'I know you can't be harangued, Kate. And I don't want to . . .' He began again. 'To be honest, I can't see much benefit here, in these walls, from that fellow, whoever he is. I can't see anything notable enough to risk a marriage over. That's what puzzles me.'

Her face flushed, but only mildly. 'I think, living in the presbytery, it's hard for you to tell, Father.'

'Is there nothing to be said then?' he asked her. He knew traditional priests would scorn the asking of such a question. They would have walked out the door, warning her emphatically of hell. But that would not have been of any service to her.

'You know what I'll say,' she said, suddenly straining for breath. 'I know what you'll say. Have more tea though. Don't give me up for another five mintues.'

So he drank more tea and there was minor conversation but little to say. He rose at last, and thanked her and left fairly briskly, not to string out the futility. He was aware too that there was no basis for future meetings, unless like Mrs Flood she should unexpectedly summon him to bring the sacraments or other comfort. Walking home in a light shower, he felt depressed that the contact had ended. Was Catholicism and its orthodoxy sometimes better designed for the timid, for twitching souls who came too often to confession, for the scrupulous so hungry for absolution at every hour? That was a mystery. A mystery so great that, although not short of breath, he found himself pausing, like an asthmatic gathering strength for the next stride. Like the old monsignor creeping up the seminary driveway.

CHAPTER ELEVEN

As Darragh ate toast with nothing but a thin film of butter one Lenten morning, the monsignor, wearing his usual indoors clothing of white shirt and black trousers, came into the dining room, a long, knowing smile on his face. It was of a nature to make Darragh suspect that the man indulgently knew of his letter and visit to Mrs Heggarty, and would want to argue about it and offer a tolerant rebuke of the kind Darragh found harder to answer than screaming outrage. But it was some other mystery of human behaviour and divine will he wished to bring to Darragh's attention.

'A fine Catholic, that Inspector Kearney,' said the monsignor. 'Here is a man who must run the investigation of every notable crime in New South Wales. Yet he still has time for the faith of his childhood. He's tracked down your young man, Howley, the missing brother. This Howley's been working on a transport ship, taking supplies to Queensland. Good way to vanish from a community, eh? At least for a time.'

'Is he well?' asked Darragh.

The monsignor pulled the lower part of his face sideways and assessed his whiskers with the back of his palm. 'Brother Keogh went to see him at some seamen's canteen in town. The young bloke fobbed him off. By now he's no doubt been around the fleshpots of Townsville, which they say is full of Yanks.'

As for Mr Regan, Darragh's mother's neighbour, so for the monsignor: the Yanks and fleshpots went hand in hand.

'I suggested to Keogh you might want to go along next time, to confess the boy. And advise him.'

Darragh could not say anything of that. 'If Brother Keogh wants me to. Yes.' But what an awkward meeting it would be, over mugs of tea in some sailor-frequented place.

'The bugger's situation needs to be made regular,' declared the monsignor.

Darragh hoped that Brother Howley would both remain on coastal steamers and seek dispensation from his vows. Yet Darragh thought his case too complex for his talents. It was not normal in the way Mrs Heggarty's case was normal.

In the gravel walk between the presbytery and church Darragh paced and recited the office, the crunch of his boots pleasantly syncopating the utterance of the Latin psalms and hymns. This was near the place where he had spoken earlier to the formidable Inspector Kearney, who put murdered spirits to rest and thus needed his beer. As Darragh recited, he frequently had to repress the dangerous images of Mrs Heggarty's honest and lovely fury as she ordered Trumble from her kitchen. And even more fatuously, the silly daydream that he would look up to see her standing by the gateway into the street, tired now of apostasy, a sister in Christ. Her lack of so doing had him restive, and the Latin he recited had a strange feel of being tedious not so much to himself as to God. The *Cantate Domino* passed from his lips more as sigh than urgent whisper of exultation. '*Quemadmodum desiderat cervus ad fontes rivos aquarum*—As the hart yearns for the water of the brooks, so does my soul desire Thee,' felt like an utterance of pale hope rather than accomplished reality. How could it be the established truth of his soul when his eyes kept being drawn towards the street gate?

The gate to the street did creak in answer to his fantasy, and he looked up to see Master Sergeant Fratelli wearing a shining helmet, as if posing for St Gabriel in Raphael's *The Annunciation*. The letters MP on his sleeve showed he was on duty, or close to it. A large camouflaged car stood parked behind him as if, in the best police tradition, sealing an exit. Another soldier was at the wheel.

'Hello, Father,' called Fratelli. 'I said I'd be round. I got something you might need. Just a moment.'

He walked to the car, opened its back door and extracted a cardboard box. As he approached again through the gate, Darragh could see the box was laden with groceries, lustrously packaged. Even as America hung on for survival, it had the thoroughness to send its glittering products everywhere with its troops. Perhaps the images on the tins of Spam and peanut butter gave the American warrior a vivid sense of the preciousness of what he fought for. 'I thought that with rationing and all,' said Fratelli, 'you and the monsignor might need a little of something extra.'

'You mustn't put yourself out,' Darragh protested. 'After all, it's still Lent.'

'No, I can get this stuff easy, Father. Anyone of my rank can. It's nothing.'

Indeed, Darragh felt an automatic gratitude rise in him. This package would have great potency with Mrs Flannery, who was

always talking abut the difficulties of shopping, and the niggard-
liness of certain Masonic shopkeepers who knew that she worked
for the priests.

'Well, it's extremely kind of you,' said Darragh, though an
instinct told him there was something in Fratelli which wasn't
kindness—a mute, jolly force, like that of an out-of-control dog
who jumped on everyone, to impose its affection. Darragh took
receipt of the box and placed it on the sacristy steps.

Master Sergeant Fratelli, the child of Mammon who had asked
for a Mass, said, 'I'd better get back to the car.'

But the sergeant had not entirely gone. Near the gate he turned
and was back with a lowered voice. 'Let me know if you guys
ever need any gas. Petroleum, you know. I could help you.'

Darragh was bewildered by the offer. 'I don't think we need
black market petrol.'

Fratelli inclined his head. The strange, compelling quality was
back. 'If Uncle Sam can't help out a few priests, it's a poor world.
Thanks again for the Mass.'

'You were there?' asked Darragh. He had not seen Fratelli in
the congregation.

'Father, I'm sorry. I was on duty.'

'That's a good reason,' said Darragh, who respected military
duty.

Fratelli saluted, and went back out again to his camouflage-
painted vehicle. Carrying the strangely labelled butter, canned
salmon, beef and condiments indoors, Darragh became an
instant hero to Mrs Flannery. 'Well,' she said, as if willing to
admit Darragh had secret gifts she had not until now seen. As
soon as Lent ended, these delicacies, these enhancements of
human existence, could be opened and lushly employed in her
cooking.

There were other surprises that week. Bert Flood turned up at the presbytery door, wearing a blue suit and a broad dun tie, with the news of his wife's death. She had gone quietly, said Bert. 'The doc kept the morphine up to her,' he explained. He asked Darragh would he consent to bury Mrs Flood. Then, in the corrugated desert of his face, tears broke forth.

'Yes,' said Darragh, taking Bert by the elbow into the parlour. 'She made her confession. There's no hindrance.'

Bert said, 'She was such a beautiful girl. This bloody TB robbed years off her.'

'Yes,' said Darragh. 'I'm sorry, Bert.'

'She'd be really pleased if you did it.'

'I just wondered about Ross Trumble. I'm not scared of him. But will he attend the funeral?'

'Well, look, he helped to nurse the missus, and he's got a lot of respect for what she wanted. He understands this is her show. But I'll sit on him, anyhow.'

'Yes,' said Darragh. 'If he's got any respect for Mrs Flood, he shouldn't turn her funeral into some sort of argument.'

Bert took hold of Darragh's elbow in fleeting reassurance. 'He knows that much, and if he doesn't, I'll soon tell him. But Rossy's all right, Father.'

The question of Trumble's behaviour had already partly preempted the event, the coming funeral. Trumble, for whom everyone made excuses, was a very selfish revolutionary, or so Darragh decided.

There was to be no Requiem Mass, since Darragh considered that to be inappropriate. If he said a Mass, it might prove that there was no one to take the consecrated host but himself. Yet when he entered from the sacristy for the funeral prayers and saw shrunken Mrs Flood's coffin in place, he observed in the body of the church a number of Catholics—the Clancy sisters and Kate Heggarty among them—who could be depended on to stand and kneel at the right times and to make the sign of the cross impeccably. Darragh described Mrs Flood as a beautiful woman with a winning smile who had travelled far and returned to the faith of her childhood, and even this brought no other response than a stupefied stare from Trumble, who stood in the foyer, beyond the holy water font, amidst the church notices.

Kate Heggarty and the Clancys, along with others were among those who piled into the cars Bert had hired and followed the coffin on the short journey to Rookwood Cemetery, where Darragh read the final burial service. Trumble and Bert stood woodenly yet solidly together at the graveside in Rookwood, Trumble frowning under the stern management of Bert and perhaps of Kate Heggarty, who stood beside him. It was as if Bert had him on drugs, or whisky, or both.

As everyone left the grave, one of the Clancy sisters said to Darragh, 'Father, she had as fine a service as a *good* Catholic.'

Darragh was trudging over the lumpy clay detritus of recent burials towards the undertaker's car, which would take him back to the presbytery, when he saw Mrs Heggarty at his side. He flinched at the suddenness of the apparition.

'You do the burial service well, Father.'

'Thank you.' But he frowned. If she wanted to extend the tricks she had already played on him, what sort of woman was she?

'You were patient with me, and here I am, hearing the beautiful words of the Church. *Requiem aeternum* . . .'

'Yes,' he told her warily.

'I have to thank you for your patience.'

'Patience is my job,' he said neutrally. 'Not all of it. Part of it.'

'I would be better in the end to make allies among women in my situation. Soldiers' wives . . .'

Hope surged in him. 'That sounds sensible to me, Kate.'

She made a conceding-the-point noise with her lips. 'You know it's hard to live without a man's company. But you see in the end that even the most kindly gifts are a form of keeping a woman in her place. Binding her to feel grateful for every crumb.'

'But I've already had that argument with you,' said Darragh, growing suspicious of her motives.

'I'm sorry you think I'm a vain and silly woman,' she told him.

'What sort of woman are you?'

'It doesn't matter. I certainly don't think I have a mortgage on your time. I'm nobody. But my father's daughter, I suppose. Rebellious and questioning. That's unlikely to change, either. People don't get set in faith, like you think . . . like a strawberry in a jelly. But I am very grateful to you, Father.'

She nodded, smiled without intent, and found a path different to his amidst the clumpy earth of the necropolis. Darragh watched her receding, losing herself among the knot of people making their way between the headstones to the cars, and tea at Bert's. He wanted to call her back, as if a chance had been lost.

CHAPTER TWELVE

IT WAS PALM SUNDAY. A week before his death, Christ entered Jerusalem, a rebel prophet, before the hooves of whose donkey the people strewed cloaks and palm leaves. Christ had a week to suffer, a week to live. To mark this civic triumph which would bring about Christ's death at the hands of jealous authorities, both Judean and Roman, the altar was dressed with palm leaves, and a pile of cut palms stood on a table at the side of the altar, to be blessed and distributed to Mass-goers.

These palms were cut each year by seminarians in the deep gullies of the Blue Mountains, and supplied the parishes of the archdiocese and of much of the palmless hinterland of New South Wales. Darragh, as a student, had traipsed down with others into the sunless, lush groins of earth to cut the native palms, to load the branches, fresh and moist, in sacks, and then to climb out of the valley with them to the escarpment, where a Carolan-like monsignor from Darlinghurst had braked a large truck borrowed from one of the faithful who ran a transport company. This monsignor, secure in his power, dispensed everyone from his Lenten fast, for the truck was loaded with good things—pastries, cakes, pies. Lent was suspended for one giddy, plump hour as custard tarts and those pink-and-brown delicacies named Neenish tarts were fed into mouths absolved by the monsignor of their own greed. Palms clipped by virgin youths were piled on the truck-bed.

The Lenten fast would end at noon on Easter Saturday. And then the Resurrection would bring joy. So Darragh hoped. He loved the liturgies of Holy Week, and looked to them to restore him to his former self by their manifold mysteries and wonderfully engrossing rites. Since it might be the last Easter of Christian Australia, Darragh had resolved to observe it thoroughly. On Wednesday night the Lamentations of Christ were sung in the cathedral, Darragh catching a train to take part. As each lamentation was concluded—*Oh, my people, why have you abandoned me?*—one more candle was doused, to leave the great nave of the cathedral in deeper darkness. Darragh was back at the cathedral on Thursday morning for the Mass at which the oils were consecrated by the archbishop, and took St Margaret's metal vials, filled with the next year's oils, back to Strathfield with him. On Thursday afternoon, after a Mass at which the monsignor enacted Christ's humility by washing the feet of some of the parish schoolchildren, the altar of St Margaret's was stripped to naked stone, and the tabernacle left as open as an empty tomb. The Eucharist was moved to a side altar, where the devout kept watch till a late hour, as if in response to Christ's complaint to the sleepy apostles in the Garden of Gethsemane, 'Couldst thou not watch one hour with me?'

On Good Friday, a further vigil, and the Mass of the Pre-Sanctified, that is the Eucharist consecrated the day before. The crucifix, and Christ's pierced feet, were venerated, the reading of the Passion of Christ by the monsignor, Darragh and Mr O'Toole of the finance committee was conducted and, later, the fourteen Stations of the Cross led by Darragh. Each of the episodes of the Passion and Death was honoured by a numbered depiction of the event attached to the church walls, seven on the west side, seven on the east. The same prayers were recited at each station, to celebrate the event illustrated: Jesus Is Flogged, Jesus Greets His Grieving Mother, Jesus Receives the Crown of Thorns, and all the other intimate tortures to which, for fallen humanity, the Son of God dedicated himself for love.

Then Easter Saturday, and the donning of the white vestments of Christ's imminent Resurrection, and at midnight Mass the lighting of the fire in the entryway of St Margaret's from which the ornate Paschal candle was lit and then carried to the sanctuary and installed in its place. *Christus surrexit hodie, alleluia!*

These demanding ceremonies, with attendant sessions to accommodate sinners making a late run to the confessional, lifted the priest out of his lethargies and routines, and Darragh did not think for many seconds of aridity, nor congratulate himself on the redemption of Mrs Flood or grieve the loss of Mrs Heggarty.

The monsignor was going away with Monsignor Plunkett for a two-day golfing holiday at Bowral, and would not be in the parish from Easter Sunday noon until very late on Tuesday evening. There was some financial trick to occur on the Tuesday, the rolling over of a money bill, but Mr Crotty, treasurer of the finance committee, would attend to it. All that the monsignor needed to do was sign two or three sheets of official parish paper in case the bank manager needed a formal letter from the parish priest of St Margaret's for his files. Mr Crotty knew what to put in the letter over the monsignor's signature.

So Darragh received the signed sheets with the illustration of the splendid church in the upper right-hand corner, and put them in his desk before going off to Rose Bay and lunch with his mother and Aunt Madge. At his mother's that Easter Sunday, he ate sumptuously of the traditional meal of lamb and drank sherry with Aunt Madge who intended, now that Lent was over, to really hit the pictures and catch up on films sacrificed in the penitential season.

On the second morning of the monsignor's absence, when Frank Darragh was eating a breakfast rather richer than normal, the butter plenteous for once on the table due to the American sergeant's generosity, Mrs Flannery went to answer the cranking sound of the bell-key. Having himself heard that noise from the front door, more a rasp than a ring, Darragh had hoped it was not a particular tormented young parishioner, a fellow about eighteen, who attended Mass each day, spending most of his time in his pew rocking on his knees, eyes shut, a sad case of excessive piety. He would frequently approach Frank and ask for an impromptu session in the confessional, at which he would confess some nuance of desire which he thought would damn him to the pit of hell if it were not instantly absolved. This poor, freckled fellow, who worked for the state government as a clerk and seemed to lack friends, was locked in such a relationship to his own sinfulness that no other events counted with him. Even a Japanese invasion would hardly shake his career as the Narcissus of guilt. He was the only person who was likely to interrupt breakfast to plead for absolution.

But it was not him at the door after all. Mrs Flannery came back to tell Frank, 'It's an American military gentleman.' She clearly approved of the visitor, and lowered her voice. 'I think it might be the one who brought us those nice things.' There was obvious hope for the arrival of further nice things. 'He's waiting in the hall.'

Darragh abandoned his breakfast, put his serviette in its silver ring and went out immediately to see Fratelli. The sergeant's fingers, Darragh noticed at first, were working away, moving nervously around the rim of the large white helmet he held in his hands. Looking at the painting of St Jerome, he was full of a restive energy which had not been there on his last visit. He wore a white webbing pistol belt and a baton in its leather sheath, and was white-gaitered as if for duty. The armband with the letters MP on it completed the effect. He looked quite heroic.

'Father, hi,' said Fratelli.

'Happy Easter, Sergeant,' said Darragh. 'If it's not too late.'

'It's not too late,' said Fratelli, rather distracted. He extended a hand lightly to Darragh's elbow. 'We have an AWOL situation. A coloured soldier who's been missing from his company these two weeks past. I suppose you'd call it desertion, technically. He's a Catholic. Louisiana. You speak French, Father?'

'Not much. Why do you ask?'

'Our boy speaks Creole, or Cajun or whatever. A French language anyhow. But he's got English too. Could you come and talk with him? Otherwise he's likely to get shot.'

Shot? Here on the Western Line of Sydney? It sounded like a film. Fratelli had over-stipended him for a Mass for the repose of a soul, and now he found himself in a film.

'See,' said Fratelli, laying on Darragh his ponderously earnest almond eyes, 'he's been hiding with this woman up in Lidcombe. A white woman! The neighbours spotted him and called us. Just like back home, no one likes that sort of thing. See, these guys run when cornered and some of the white MPs won't stand for that.' A wave of Raphaelite ruthlessness passed over Fratelli's eyes. The courtier or the angel in Fratelli was merciful but all the time held a sword behind his back. 'But you could talk to him, kind of tell him the Virgin wants him to give himself up, and so on. Maybe you ought to take one of those things you wear round your neck.'

'A stole?'

'Yeah, you better take one of those.'

'But Lidcombe isn't in my parish. Can you wait a moment?'

Fratelli grimaced. 'Ten minutes,' he suggested. 'See, I've got this squad waiting outside. I'm in some trouble if that boy skips before we get there.'

Darragh went to the Catholic Directory by the telephone and got the number for Lidcombe parish, Father Gerald Tuomey, P.P. He rang it and the housekeeper answered. He asked if Father Tuomey or his curate were in. The housekeeper said no. Both were out. He began to explain—the American MPs wanted him to go with them to Lidcombe to give spiritual guidance to an American soldier whom they intended to arrest.

'There's no American soldier here, Father,' the housekeeper assured him.

No, he explained. Within Lidcombe parish. He had hoped to get Father Tuomey's approval, and to inform him as a courtesy.

'Well, he isn't here, Father, I'm sorry.'

'Will you tell him I called?'

There was no real choice, he told himself, hanging up, panting as if he'd just run a sprint. Darragh put on his clerical stock to which the white celluloid collar was always affixed, tied its strings around his shirt and fetched his coat. A small stole, purple on one side, white on the other, was always in his pocket—the minimum vestment for solemn moments. Leaving the presbytery, he found that two military cars and a truck were parked near the school, and early arriving schoolchildren were being entertained by having the military police ask them their names, 'Michael, eh?

Does anyone call you Mickie?' One of the military police was Australian—he wore a slouch hat, though he too was armbanded, bore ammunition-pouch webbing and had a pistol at belt. Darragh was comforted to see him. Something recognisable in an impending alien scene. He stopped to tell the children to go to the playground.

The scale of this military party, the fact that it was made up of troops of two nations, allayed his earlier canonical fear that Lidcombe was beyond his parish. This was obviously an urgent foray which transcended narrow borders.

'We're going,' called Fratelli to those of his men who were on the pavement. Those who had been talking to the children climbed back into the truck. Darragh joined Fratelli in the front seat of the first car. The corporal driver and the master sergeant both turned to him. 'You're a local, Father. What's the best way to Bombay Street, Lidcombe? It's north of the railroad station.'

This seemed to Darragh an excessive demand, that he, the spiritual counsellor, should also be called on to navigate. 'Surely you know the way,' said Darragh. He saw himself for a second, in this heightened scene, like a nineteenth-century farmer suddenly reluctant to show the mounted traps the way a convict escapee had gone.

'Sure, we looked up the Parramatta Road route,' the driver said, 'but there might be a better one.'

It seemed to Darragh that Fratelli understood his reluctance. He lowered his voice.

'Look, Father, you're a decent guy. But we're coming back with this Negro whatever route we take.'

'Go up Barker Road,' said Darragh, 'and turn right at Flemington. Then you can take Parramatta Road.'

'Got that, Corporal?' asked Fratelli. Along Albert Street,

Darragh could see they were still in the known universe of ordinary bungalows, not unlike his mother's in Rose Bay, and the occasional slightly grander two-storey house with wrought-iron balconies. The earth reached under a giant sky which seemed a guarantee of tranquillity. It was not a sky in which black soldiers could conceivably be shot.

They swung across the bridge over the railway at Flemington and passed the saleyards where sheep came to await slaughter, and then leftwards into the main road. Across the yellow tiles of the Sheepyard Inn (locals called it the Sheep Shit), doors grimly shut now, offering no beer until the afternoon bacchanalian hour or two, fell the shadow of men on an ammunition-pouched mission. The sparse shops of Parramatta Road were passed— Italian greengrocers recently returned from internment, milk bars, butchers, an opaque-windowed wine bar with its purple-faced dipso sitting hunched outside it, waiting for it to open and serve him sweet muscat sherry. Garages, Moran and Cato's grocers, the accustomed sequence, over which glided the silhouette of Sergeant Fratelli's convoy.

Left into Bombay Street and a long, long straggle of low houses—two-storeyed pretension had never reached Lidcombe. This was what Aunt Madge called 'battler territory', some of the dispiriting aura of the late Depression still hung here. Every tide of event seemed to sweep over the people of such a suburb and recede, leaving them as they were, with the character of desert fruit. As they were, that is, except for the grace of God, abundantly available to them at St Joachim's, Lidcombe, from the hands of Father Tuomey and his curate. In one of these houses with corrugated iron roof and mute windows—Darragh was supposed to believe—hid a black deserter.

The second car pulled ahead of them and vanished far down

the road. The corporal murmured that they'd come in from the next street. 'You okay, Father?' asked Fratelli, frowning at him, the sergeant's huge eyes unreadable, full of mercy or bloodshed.

'Yes,' claimed Darragh.

'This should go well,' murmured Fratelli, and Darragh was reassured.

'Father,' he said, 'you wait in the car till I send for you. Okay?'

'There it is,' said the driver, pointing to a house. 'Forty-seven.' Fratelli's car creaked to the edge of the pavement. Darragh could see up the side of the house to an old-fashioned garden, the sort in which privet and rhododendrons grew among paspalum grass, and chickens ran wild and yielded up their lives for weddings and feast days.

'Okay, Father,' stated Fratelli. The corporal had jumped from the car, and Fratelli made ready to follow. Noisily enough to warn a suburb, the truck's brakes howled behind Darragh, and its tailboard crashed open. American soldiers and three Australians emerged. Fourteen men all told. The mystery of command, which Fratelli exercised so easily. And though aware of having been conscripted by Fratelli, Darragh felt an unfamiliar exhilaration at being part of his command. Some red bubble of sweet fear and significance swelled in his throat. Yes, it was apparent. He was willing to be a soldier. Several of Fratelli's men, advancing crouched and with their weapons across their bodies, made a squad across the mouth of the laneway to the back, and the other half of the force, led by Fratelli himself, went up three or four steps to the front door and hammered on it. Before anyone could respond, they began to force it open. From within the shrieks of women were heard, and the household became suddenly shrill and raucous. The screaming of women was joined by the barking and shouting of soldiers' voices, a pitiless sound.

Waiting in the car, Darragh saw a barefooted, black man in a white singlet and trousers sitting on the sash of one of the side windows. He seemed to be having trouble fitting his body through, and instantly and fluidly amended his posture. The upper body and its white singlet disappeared, and now, with more success, the bare-footed legs in fawn army pants appeared. The black soldier hit the ground as those military police to the side of the house noticed the fact. He disappeared into the vast, semi-rural backyard. Seeming so exorbitantly over-dressed for their prey and their banal surroundings, his chasers followed him, yelling. The front door swung blankly open, and the shouting and shrieking were more distant. At last a fine-featured young American emerged from the laneway and leaned, beneath a glistening helmet, to speak to Darragh.

'Master Sergeant Fratelli says come now, Father, quick.' The young man gently opened the door for him, waited for him to step on the pavement and then led him away at a fast-paced walk, crouching, up the side of the house. Darragh found himself crouching too, and reaching for the stole in his pocket. As Fratelli had foretold, this business seemed to Darragh to beg a sacramental resolution.

So they passed the side of the house and came into the arena of action—a wide tract of grass decorated with privet hedge borders, lovingly kept in order. By the back steps of the house, an older and a younger woman, mother in floury apron and daughter in headscarf, stood stricken-mouthed under the guard and restraint of two of Fratelli's Americans. The rest of Fratelli's force lay in a cordon around a brown-painted structure at the end of the yard, a building which seemed undecided whether it was shed, barn, garage or stables, and seemed to be fairly close to collapse under its uncertain identity. It was apparent that the deserter had gone to ground in there, was somewhere in its umber shadows. Was his heart racing as Darragh's was? At a nod from Fratelli, who stood by a privet bush, the corporal called languidly, 'Come out there, Gervaise. Come on, ole feller.' But the chief sound for the moment was the weeping women, the lenient mother who probably kept the privet hedges, and the daughter who had been seduced by the black man. Fratelli presented himself solemnly to Darragh.

'You ready, Father? Can you go in and talk with the boy?'

The alternative to such an intervention did not need to be stated—it was apparent to Darragh in the tensely held weaponry all around. Even the Australians with their heavy .303s, their corporal—an older man, perhaps a veteran of an earlier war—now holding a delicate Owen gun, seemed to Darragh to be set only for the poles of resolution: the deserter's surrender or his death. This is what the caressing of weapons, the wearing of uniforms, the shrieking of women brought out in men—a glinting grim intent.

Fratelli left Darragh's side to let him think for a second, went to the women and told them reasonably to hush now, that they weren't helping anything. Then he returned. 'Okay, Father?'

'Yes.'

'Come on then,' he said, leading Darragh towards the besieged structure. Near the door he held Darragh back a second.

'Gervaise!' he called. 'Private Aspillon! You're in some big trouble in there. We've got MPs all round you, they've even come in from the other street. White troops, Gervaise, and you're technically a deserter. I don't need to instruct you on your choices, do I?'

A voice Darragh had heard only in recorded songs, the voice of black America, emerged from the shed, deeply layered with Southern and what Darragh thought of, from the little he knew of films, as Creole tones. Darragh likewise knew of New Orleans, as rendered down to him by motion pictures, as a place where Mexico and the West Indies, Africa, France and America all abutted.

The voice said: 'I'm no deserter, sir. Don't go putting that label on me. I'm just late back, that's all.'

The 'just' went on endlessly, enhanced with diphthongs and the history of enslavement and under-rewarded labour.

The corporal seemed suddenly angry on Fratelli's patient behalf. 'Tell that to the boys on Bataan!' he yelled, and spat and shook his head.

'Now we know you're a Catholic, Gervaise,' called Fratelli. 'I respect that. I've got a priest here. He wants you to come out.'

Fratelli turned to Darragh. 'Tell him to come out, will you, Father?'

Darragh was tongue-tied.

'His name's Private Aspillon,' Fratelli prompted.

Darragh found his voice. 'Private Aspillon, I'm Father Darragh from St Margaret's. You should come out and surrender to these men, and I'll be here to see you're well treated.'

'God bless you, Father,' came the resonant voice. 'But you don't know about military police. You look, you'll see batons on their sides. Designed exactly for black heads. My poor suffering black head. You can't tell me, either, they don't have guns in their hands. And you don't know about their watch-houses and their compounds, and you don't want to know either.'

The slight on the Corps of Military Police seemed to arouse Fratelli's men to some cursing and spitting. Only the Australians, either wise or indifferent, weren't heard from.

'You're trying all our patience, Gervaise,' called Fratelli jovially.

'Father,' cried the deserter, 'you come in here and I'll walk out with you. You stick to me and I know no harm will come.'

Darragh turned, full of decision, to Fratelli. 'All right. I'll go in there.'

Fratelli nodded and called to his men, informing them that the priest was going to talk to Private Aspillon. Oddly, as it seemed for a second to Darragh, he did not use a name. Just *the priest*. Darragh went forward to the brown-painted door, sunk on its hinges and half-jammed in muddy soil. He was not afraid, but delighted despite himself. Real work, he thought. Real, classic and remediable sin— desertion, lechery, the potential cruelty of batons and firearms. In the midst of all the factors he was the mediator. And already enchanted by Gervaise's tiered voice. There seemed to be a palpable soul behind it. 'I would you were either hot or cold, but because you are lukewarm I will spit thee forth from my mouth . . .' Gervaise had not been lukewarm. 'I go to call not the just, but sinners.' Gervaise fitted the bill.

Darragh now stepped forward into the half-darkness of Gervaise's refuge. A fat guineafowl descended querulously from a bag of seed and went out into the yard through the door Darragh had left ajar. Many bags of bran and pollen and a wheelbarrow blocked Darragh's immediate path. A Model T Ford sat on bricks in further dimness, its rump to Darragh, and beyond its front fender Gervaise stood up. He was tall with blue-black skin.

'That's you, Father,' he said.

'Of course.'

'You sounded like a priest,' said Gervaise, flatteringly. 'You'd got a lamb in your voice.'

'I . . . don't understand, Gervaise,' said Darragh, though he understood precisely.

'There was the lamb in your voice, not the tiger,' said Gervaise,

'The tigers are out there, and I'll get thrown to them.'

'Not by me. The man in charge—he wants you safe. And surely, you have to go back.'

'I like the way you guys say that. *Surely.*' He did his failed best to reproduce the Australian accent. 'My girl Rosemary says it that way. I like that. It's better than our way. You've got a lot of things that are better than our way.'

Darragh had negotiated the bags of pollen, but some five or six yards still lay between him and the absconder.

'We ought to go out now, Gervaise.'

'I want to confess, first.'

'Why not after we've gone out?'

'No, I want to confess first. In here I'm a sinner. Once I step out I'm Jesus Christ on the cross.'

'I wouldn't say you'd lived like Jesus,' said Darragh.

'Every man who suffers on earth is joined to the suffering of Jesus Christ,' said Gervaise Aspillon, his eyes blazing. And such a proposition could not be faulted theologically.

'I should tell them,' said Darragh, and he turned and went to the door.

'He's coming out in a moment,' called Darragh through the aperture to the earnest beseiging line. 'He wants to talk for a moment first.' Darragh did not mention confession. He did not want to subject it to the derision which he suspected lay submerged in the MPs, other than Fratelli.

'A few minutes, Father,' called Fratelli. 'Don't let him hold you up. He'll be persuasive.'

Darragh advanced to the front fender of the Ford.

'Hello, Gervaise,' he murmured from his new closeness. He and Gervaise shook hands. The black deserter's hand was huge and knobby with calluses. Darragh took his purple stole out of his pocket, showed it to the black man, then kissed its golden cross and placed it round his neck. 'Let's begin.'

Gervaise advanced and stood towering above him with head bent.

Darragh uttered the opening words of the rite, 'The Lord be in thy heart and on thy lips . . .' as Private Aspillon crossed himself and murmured in his sweetly dolorous voice, 'Bless me Father for I have sinned. It is . . . oh . . . maybe ten months since my last confession. I have been guilty of sins of the flesh—it is not my girl's fault. She is generosity itself. I have been guilty of pride.'

In the circumstances, Darragh knew he was permitted not to enquire much into this broad and heartfelt statement of guilt.

'I,' Gervaise continued, 'have been guilty of the greatest folly in that I saw in this woman a life, and I coveted it. Whereas the dumbest man born would have told me it was not a life I could live, not even on the Western Line in Sydney with a white wife. Stupidity offends the Lord, and for His sake, I am heartily sorry. For all these sins of pride and of the flesh I am contrite.'

It struck Darragh that this man had a straightforward but thorough understanding of the theology of penance. He had touched all the crucial components of contrition. Except one. 'And you disobeyed lawful authority,' Darragh suggested.

'Father,' said Gervaise, 'for some men authority—he pronounced it something like *orthorty*—'is a kind mother, and they love her. For others, an axe! I find the army hard, Father, and it's hard on me. Now the axe is here. Outside. Believe me, I'll be sorry enough for it. For this and all my other sins I am heartily sorry.'

Darragh absolved him. As soon as Gervaise had finished muttering a well-schooled Act of Contrition, he straightened. He did not need Darragh to advise him. 'Out we go,' he said. The 'o' of go once more had layers of dolour and diphthong to it. It was not the plain Australian go. It was a long journey of a vowel.

At the instant its sound wavered away, the air was cracked open by a sound so substantial it assaulted the ear and the brain twice, as shocking in echo as in its first instant assault. Then a rage of sound came, both sharp and constant crackling and also a broader, symphonic racket which absorbed all the shed's available space and seemed to Darragh to jolt the Model T on its brick pylons. Gervaise grabbed Darragh, who had placed his hands to his ears and yearned for the moist dirt of the floor, and pushed him into the lee of the Model T. Smelling of vegetables and cinnamon, the soldier's crouching body encompassed prone Frank Darragh's. It came to Darragh: they were shooting at himself and Gervaise for inscrutable reasons. Their repressed intention to use their weapons had burst out in a storm and, even beneath Gervaise's body and widespread arms, Darragh felt himself as a leaf before its force. Huddled with and oppressed so intimately by Gervaise Aspillon, Darragh felt that having started, the noise would remain continuous. Through the slits of his eyes he could nonetheless see sunlight flash everywhere and without discrimination as boards were blown loose and pulped and shattered. Darragh longed for an unlikely stoppage to the tempest and yet was astonished at how calmly he and the deserter lay, brave absolved Gervaise with his back exposed to the fire. The truth was that since the tumult possessed everything, owned every bone, took cordite deep into the nostrils, and completely filled the heart, it left no room for fear, not even a niche for an insinuating shudder of terror. Then, having laid claim to everything, it departed. The air now was hollow and thin as an eggshell, and all sound was smudged and spidery. But he did hear the wailing of women from within the house, and Fratelli distantly screaming. 'What sonofabitch started that? For Christ's sake, what sonofabitch?'

A few men claimed it wasn't them. 'I thought it was you, Sarge,' said the corporal.

Fratelli was angry, and displayed the harshness of command. 'Don't be a dumb fuck, Corporal. One of you Aussies?'

An Australian soldier called, 'We've got more bloody discipline.'

'You didn't fire at all?'

'Well we did, when you blokes started.'

Fratelli asserted, 'It's that Owen gun you guys have. Goes off if you breathe on it.'

'It wasn't the bloody Owen gun,' insisted the Australian.

'This'll be sorted out,' said Fratelli darkly, but less angry now.

The voices were advancing towards Darragh and Gervaise, on their way to inspect damage. Gervaise shook himself like a dog and made a painful hawking sound as if to clear his mouth of the bitter chemical taste of gunfire, and his head of the recent fury. He made eye contact with stunned Darragh and grinned.

'See, Father, even priests get shot at if they mix with black men.'

The shed was skeletal now, Darragh saw, and gave the deserter no shelter at all. Soldiers in white helmets entered through its fragmented doorway and through new holes in its walls. One of them possessed the commanding solidity which marked him as Fratelli.

Darragh, watching him over Gervaise's shoulder, was distressed and surprised by his power, his double-edged capacity both to shatter this tottering building and now advance to reclaim its human contents. Gervaise stood up, like a man greeting an acquaintance.

'Come out from there, Gervaise, you motherfucker. Show us your hands.'

The corporal driver ran up and angrily felt all over Gervaise's body. 'I never had a weapon, Sergeant.'

Fratelli shook his head. 'Let poor Father Darragh out of there.'

Gervaise moved aside, and Darragh advanced on feet he couldn't yet feel.

'I'm sorry about this, Father, and I'm sorry about the profane talk. It was the Owen gun went off, as they always do. Your guy.' He nodded to the outer world of the yard, where apparently the Australians held their post and tried to pacify the women, who could be heard weeping in shock. 'I do hope you're okay, are you?' The apology did not seem to match the storm of peril in which he and Gervaise had been put. Fratelli leaned close and said, 'Next time, maybe we shouldn't delay for the sake of the seven sacraments, Father.'

Darragh's fury rose up his throat. 'We'll have as many sacraments as I judge.'

'Sorry,' said Fratelli. 'Of course. But when you keep jumpy guys waiting . . .' One of his men was shackling Private Aspillon's wrists.

'Where does he go?'

'The compound for now.'

'I'll go with him.'

'I'm sorry, you can't do that, Father. Maybe you can visit him there later.'

'Where later?'

'The compound at Ingleburn.'

They had marched Gervaise out. He called something forlorn to the women on the steps, but Fratelli had given the Australian provosts the task of pushing them indoors so that they could not touch or caress the prisoner. Gervaise was a sinner, yet this act of prevention seemed to Darragh, his head still full of thunder and echoes, to be harshest of all.

One of the Australian soldiers had gone to the trouble to make tea in the kitchen which belonged to those women Darragh had not met and somehow knew he would not be permitted to meet. Sitting on a tree stump among the privet bushes, Darragh drank a cup hungrily, as Fratelli frowned over him like a brother. Then on the way back to the car, Fratelli sombrely asked Darragh whether he wanted something medicinal for the shock of it all, and somehow Darragh felt a returning warmth towards this striking young man.

'You went through it,' Fratelli murmured. 'You certainly went through it, Father.' He confused Darragh further by saying, 'Now you know the size of things.'

CHAPTER THIRTEEN

ITH HIS HEAD still full of the reverberations of the morning's fusillade, Darragh went across to the school that afternoon, to, as he saw it, the comfort of children. He watched them emerge, and wondered whether some of them, despite their unseamed complexions and the transparencies of their souls, occupied some undefined furnace equivalent to the one he and Gervaise had shared. He was solaced by the sight of waiting mothers in the laneway between church and school. Mrs Heggarty was not there. Anthony Heggarty would be part of the convoy of Homebush-bound, mile-walking children conducted by other young mothers Darragh recognised but could not put a name to. He saw the boy run crookedly to his appropriate group and stand saying nothing, head down, earnest. Darragh felt a clot of anguish inside his ribcage, and was tempted to weep. He wanted to tell the boy, 'Don't be so willing.' The world used such willingness profligately. The world despised it as a mute, uncomplaining resource. And after all, it detracted from alertness when there could be large steel vehicles driven by white-helmeted corporals. Anthony must slot himself in among the mean intentions of the world and get safely to his mother's kitchen.

It struck Darragh then, a happy revelation. The Americans have chaplains. There must be a telephone number, there must be a chaplains' office. If he telephoned the cathedral, they would probably have the number. He could alert an American priest to the fact that Gervaise was an enlightened soul. He went across the tarred playground, making for the presbytery telephone above which the monsignor had pinned a typed list of crucial numbers including that of the chancellery at the cathedral. As he entered the hallway, and passed the painting of St Jerome which had so fascinated Fratelli, Monsignor Carolan, back a few hours early from his excursion, wearing a black cardigan over a singlet, black pants and carpet slippers, appeared at the door of his study.

'Frank, come in, come in,' he said, gesturing one-handedly, a man with a lesson to impart. Darragh went into the study, with its big desk tidily maintained, its photograph of an Irishman, Archbishop Kelly of Sydney, a prelate recently gone to God. The monsignor's library was displayed on a shelf behind the desk, characteristic priest's fare. The theological texts the monsignor had had since seminary days, solemn cloth encasing solemn Latin. The *Summa Theologica* of St Thomas Aquinas, multi-volumed, red-spined. This great work of Christian theology had the sort of presence on the shelf that keystone works of civilisation always exude—as if they can improve a person's life and mind purely through their mute presence. Beside devotional works such as *The Priest at His Prie-dieu*, there was the poetry of Francis Thompson, the saintly alcoholic, and various works of GK Chesterton and Hilaire Belloc, the great modern Catholic writers. These books stood for the fact that maligners spoke falsely when they said the Church crushed the creative spirit.

The hardcovers were stored for reverence on the more visible shelves but gave way lower down to detective stories and Zane Grey's western novels, which lacked the automatic power of St Thomas Aquinas, and thus actually needed to be read.

The monsignor lit a cigarette and offered one to Darragh, but Frank Darragh did not smoke, chiefly on the aesthetic grounds that it made most men ashy and sloppy, that the residue showed up too easily on black serge. The monsignor, of course, was an exception. He did all these things impeccably.

'Frank,' he said once his cigarette was alight and drawn on, 'you are a good fellow. But you're beginning to annoy me. You do erratic things. Things contrary to all the wise counsels which govern the behaviour of young priests. This thing I've just heard about from Father Tuomey at Lidcombe. What were you doing there? Playing heroics in another parish. He's really cranky about it, let me tell you.'

Darragh explained that he had called Father Tuomey's housekeeper, and both priests were out. Urgent with the truth of the proposition, Darragh said, 'There was no time to wait or for slowing things down. They fully intended to shoot the man if necessary.'

'I believe they did their best to anyhow, and to shoot you too, and then where would we be? Are you all right?'

'A bit shaken,' he conceded. But, he did not say, a bit exhilarated too. Particularly now he knew he might be able to keep track of Gervaise. But even before that, in various obscure ways, exhilarated.

'I suppose I'll have to stand by you this time,' said the monsignor. Frank wondered, with a residual acidic briskness, whether his willingness to say early morning Masses, to hear confessions, to take Benedictions, helped the monsignor to be lenient. 'But what you have to understand, you might see things as urgent when they're not. From what I hear this black man was cohabiting with a white woman. He was a deserter from his post. He doesn't sound like grounds for urgent attention. I mean, despite all these romantic ideas about a priest being put in situations where he saves the souls of unknown people, people outside his normal reach, in practice that might happen once or twice in a lifetime. A fellow is faced with a man dying of apoplexy in George Street, outside Hordern's store—that happened to me when I was young. Swallowed his tongue and no one knew how to save his life. But it seems to me there's a tendency in you, Frank, that seeks this sort of drama at every turn. Well, you ought to sit on that. Don't embarrass me with other parish priests. You understand? Let *me* know if you've got some extraordinary intention. And you're not in the American army. So they can't come here and make you do jobs for them.'

It was a consideration: If there were chaplains, why didn't Fratelli use one of them? But there might have been some official problem about doing that. Fratelli's summoning Darragh might thus have been a gracious, *ex tempore* gesture towards saving the prisoner. On the other hand, had Darragh not been there to hear Private Aspillon's confession, the MPs might not have begun to fire. Darragh did not have the energy left, in the fact of the monsignor's chastisement, to follow the reasoning further.

'Since I did go, Monsignor,' said Darragh, 'and since I heard the man's confession and gave him absolution, I want to contact the American chaplains to look after him.'

The monsignor groaned and said, 'American chaplains,' in rather the way a person would say, 'Bulgarians!'.

'I'll get the number from the chancellery. He's a remarkable soul, this black man . . .'

The monsignor tossed his head and stubbed his cigarette with emphasis. 'Residing with a slut in Lidcombe? It sounds like it. Call the chaplains if you must.'

'And I'll speak to Father Tuomey.'

'No, leave the old crank alone.'

The monsignor sat at his desk again and opened a ledger. The *Summa Theologica* shone down on his financial labours. 'One thing I will say for the American troops. They're very generous with the collection plate. But they can't buy redemption, can they?'

Now Darragh felt robust of soul. He still suffered an occasional brimstone whiff of futility from his contacts with Mrs Heggarty, her air of command and independence, her good heart and self-diagnosed rebelliousness—a combination of traits he considered, as the Church did, dangerous to her. But now his duties possessed some meaning, since Gervaise and he had been welded together under fire and in sacramental intent.

Calling the chancellery, he found that a young priest he had studied with answered the phone and was able to supply him with the number of the US Army Chaplains Corps. Ringing them in turn, he spoke to a soldier who described himself as the chaplains' assistant. He certainly sounded like a doorkeeper to eminent persons. He was unimpressed by the idea that this was an Australian diocesan priest calling. There was no rudeness, but merely a sense that Darragh lay beyond the man's universe and thus need not be treated with too much alacrity. 'All the chaplains are busy.'

'There's something called the compound.'

'Yeah,' said the man. 'That's out near the Aussie camp. In Ingleburn.'

'Does compound mean the same as prison?'

'If you like, Father,' the chaplains' assistant conceded. 'A more temporary structure, you'd find. A stockade. That's Captain O'Rourke's territory, anyhow.'

'And Captain O'Rourke is a chaplain?'

'Yessir, that's what he is.'

'So *Father* O'Rourke,' said Darragh, wanting to assert the essence of all this, that God and not the army, not the white centurion helmets of Fratelli's men, had the claim upon this unknown O'Rourke. 'I would like to ask Father O'Rourke to visit this soldier I know. When could I speak to him in person?'

'Well, he's after-dinner speaker at the officers' club tonight. You could try him in the morning.'

'Would you give him my number as well?'

'Sure, Father,' said the chaplains' assistant with the first note of willingness that had entered their dialogue.

'Please ask him. It's important. It's about one Private Aspillon.' Darragh spelled it.

'Private Aspillon. I'll tell him.' And then, 'Don't you worry about it at all, Father.'

But caught between the strictures of Monsignor Carolan and the explosive savagery of the American army, he did worry for the integrity of Gervaise's flesh.

On Saturday Father O'Rourke proved yet again not to be in when Darragh called, and failed to phone back as well. Darragh had spent the day expecting the call and, apart from confessions, prepared a questioning sermon for Sunday. Altogether, it was natural that his sermon should reflect the state of his soul and of his immediate world. The Dutch and Australians reinforced the text by failing to hold Sumatra. Rabaul was bombed, and its Australian garrison looked likely to follow that of Singapore into indefinite but terrible imprisonment. Soon there would be further

Mrs Heggartys scattered around the pews on Sunday mornings. And in a short time, for all they knew, their church might be a stable for the species of pack mules the Japanese army had been filmed using in China.

'My dear brethren,' said Darragh from the high pulpit on Sunday, 'we are in the time of joy following Easter, but even in this season of jubilation, in the forty days after Christ's resurrection, all is still threatened. Our food is rationed, our community endangered, we hear bad news every day on the wireless, while sons are separated from mothers and wives from husbands without any of us knowing how long this will go on. Some of us have the comfort of our faith, but for many good people there's a sense that God has turned His face away. Some wonder if even the armies of the just, the American army and our own, do not harbour some unjust men. Is God testing us, or—and I, like you, hope this is not the truth—does He intend to punish us? For still cricket and rugby league and horseracing from Randwick are front-page news. Still the cinemas hold out images of godless pleasure. Still the divorce courts are full.' He knew this from reading the court proceedings published in every weekend's *Telegraph*. He, who intended never to have a wife, was as fascinated by tales of divorce as most priests were. At tennis on Monday, his fellow curates recounted divorce cases they had read about over the weekend. They were somehow pleased to have their cynicism about marriage validated.

'And yet everywhere there is hope,' he said, as his brethren wanted him to. 'Even today. I take some of my hope from a soldier I spoke to this week. He was a foreign soldier, and he had behaved badly, and he had done wrong. But I found in him a clear sense of what contrition was, and for a moment we were brothers in the Catholic faith, in the way that MacArthur's

Americans and General Blamey's Australians are brothers in their crusade against the enemy. So, all can be taken from us. We can be the subject of every disgrace. Bombs might land among us, God forbid. Our young men might be captured or die in battle. There is one thing which cannot be taken from us. Our . . .'

He paused because the words 'our dignity' had by the force of Mrs Heggarty's sedition nearly risen to his lips. It was as if the woman and her phrase had lodged under his skin. 'Our faith,' he said instead. 'That cannot be taken by force. It can be surrendered only of our own volition. We know that whatever happens in the future, however battles fall out, resurrection in its most important form will come to us, and salvation in its most important form. As for the rest, for the battles which await, we join each other in our prayers for deliverance.'

Though it was early in April, the heavy, white, braid-encrusted chasuble felt hot, and temporarily removing it while waiting in the sacristy between the half-past-six and eight o'clock Masses, Darragh saw a somehow familiar soldier appear tentatively at the door.

'Hello there,' Darragh said with some enthusiasm. The Mass, and his own words of hope, had made the world more fraternal.

'It's me, Father. I was with the American MPs.'

Darragh saw the corporal's stripes on the man's arm. He was the Australian soldier who had had the look of having been a Great War digger. He also possessed the enduring, creased face of a fellow who'd known the humiliation and the hunger of the Depression.

'I had the Owen gun the Yanks said went off.'

Darragh unpinned the maniple from his wrist and stepped forward. 'Please come in,' he said. The man did so, looking in awe at the vestment benches and the little stained-glass window which featured St Brigid of Ireland. To Catholics, a sacristy was an august place, occupied chiefly by clerics and acolytes.

'I didn't like that the other day,' said the man. 'I didn't like what the Yank sergeant said. But they've had an enquiry and I got shouted down. I know how to use an Owen gun, and I didn't make any mistake. The sergeant started it off. With his bloody pistol, Father. Pardon my language.'

If this were the truth, there was part of him which would not have wanted to know. That the angelic courtier and warrior, Fratelli, could be so crafty. Could he also be vicious in his cunning?

Darragh said, like a military veteran, 'Well, I wouldn't hold it against any man if his gun misfired.'

'That's the whole thing, Father. I wouldn't have come here to see you—my parish is Stanmore. If I thought I'd done it, I'd just lie doggo and feel silly, like any other chap would. You know you said in your sermon that not all soldiers are just men. Well that bugger—I mean, that American—he isn't. He's a blame-shifter, that one.'

'He seemed sincere enough to me. What I mean is, he had the welfare of the Negro man at heart.'

'Well, he was more than willing to set his blokes off. And everyone knows the Yanks are trigger-happy. Australian armies, we were raised to be sparing with ammunition. But not *them*. They squander. That's why I think in the end they might do all right. Their soldiers aren't as good as ours. Full of cheek, absolute skites. But, crikey, they've got some gear.'

'So you think he blamed you to save his own embarrassment.'

'That'd be right. And we're handy too, for them to blame. They think we're hillbillies. Even *their* hillbillies think we're hillbillies. But I wanted to tell you, anyhow. It wasn't the Owen. The Owen is a gun a bloke can depend on.'

Frank thanked the corporal, wished him well and saw him vanish. The corporal's accusations against Fratelli would have been easier to dismiss had Darragh, in the ten minutes during which he waited to go out to the altar for the next Mass, not been able to review his brief but intense contacts with Fratelli and decide that they had, after all, displayed from the sergeant's side, among the decisiveness and goodwill, and perhaps because of them, the shadow of an indefinite excess. Diverting his convoy just to pick up a priest in Strathfield seemed part of it. And yet, how could the man be condemned? The fine-spirited Gervaise, the theologically accurate Private Aspillon, had been comprehensively saved by Fratelli's decision.

On a busy Sabbath it was easy to attribute what the corporal had told him to the rivalry between Americans and Australians, which, as everyone knew, lay beneath the surface of their brotherly cooperation in the cause of the Christian world.

CHAPTER FOURTEEN

THAT SUNDAY EVENING he got a call from the American chaplain. 'Captain O'Rourke,' the man announced himself, and Darragh explained that he was concerned for Gervaise Aspillon.

'Yeah, I know the case, Father,' said O'Rourke. He had a voice like James Cagney.

'Gervaise made a sincere confession to me. I'm concerned that he might not be well treated in the . . . the compound.'

'Well, the guy was AWOL three weeks. Sounds like desertion to me. Only stood out where he was hiding because he was a coloured.'

'I wondered would you visit him, Captain?' Darragh used the military title because he had a sense Father O'Rourke was flattered by it.

'Sure. I've already been round there. Said a decade of the rosary with him.'

'And was he well?'

He heard a sigh from Father O'Rourke. What business was it of this Australian curate?

'You see,' said Darragh, 'I was at the capture with him.'

'Yeah. I can't see why that Fratelli guy didn't ask one of us. Made my feelings known to him, too.'

So Father Tuomey's was not the only territory which had been violated.

'Look,' said the American priest, 'you can't pretend they won't be a bit hard on him. Not with all that's going on. He shouldn't have fornicated with a white woman either. That gets us in bad with the Australians. You guys don't like that any more than we do.'

'He has a genuine taste for the sacraments and a strong doctrinal sense.'

'I'll do what I can. I've got the compound, the hospital, the dental corps and the signals personnel to attend to. We're overstretched. I've got nothing against the man, but he doesn't stand for more than the others do. The truth is, the others do their duty better than he's done.'

'Would I be able to visit him?' asked Darragh. Let me know if you've got some extraordinary intention, the monsignor had told him. Was visiting Gervaise an extraordinary intention?

O'Rourke sighed yet again. 'Look, we can do the job with him. Guys like him love to get on the good side of a civilian.'

Darragh weighed this monsignor-like advice, and considered whether he needed to see Gervaise more than Gervaise needed to see him. 'He seemed concerned about his safety,' said Darragh.

'He'd say that.'

Darragh paused again, to think of more pretexts. 'I'd consider it a great favour. And I think he'd feel safer . . .'

To Darragh's surprise, O'Rourke relented. 'I'll have to check it out with the MPs, and then get back to you.'

As Darragh waited for O'Rourke to contact him again,

Monsignor Carolan pursued his career as a student of battles. He still conned the battle maps reproduced on the front page of the *Sydney Morning Herald* and matched them against the maps of his *Times Atlas* to give them an added dimension.

In the third week after Easter, the monsignor sat for periods by his cabinet radio, with the *Herald* and the atlas in his hands, studying maps which represented the great island-dotted blankness of the Southwest Pacific. Through this and other overheard news, Darragh became aware that a crucial confrontation was brewing in that theatre of lethal blue called the Coral Sea. This wing of the Pacific was hemmed in on three sides by the Solomons, Papua, and Australia's north coast. It was believed that the Japanese Admiral Inouye was on his way across the huge arena of the Coral Sea to capture Port Moresby in New Guinea. And as the monsignor told Frank at breakfast on May 7, if Moresby went, then Australia would in short order be invaded.

Over the next days, the monsignor kept track of the events in the Coral Sea with a military fervour rather than that of a potential martyr of the one true Church. He seemed bravely undisturbed about the possible impact of the battle upon his plans for paying off the church and expanding the school. He was passionately intrigued by the fact that this was the first battle in the history of humankind in which the sailors of both sides did not see each other's ships, but only each other's lethal planes. Japanese carrier planes tried to sink the American and the Australian flotillas in this new and fantastical warfare. The destiny of the Western and Christian world was to be decided in these bright, equatorial waters, and Darragh was surprised he felt so little urgency, alarmed at his wooden sense of separation from the God of history and of the immanent world. By the time he emerged from the confessional on Saturday evening, the flagship

Australia had valiantly saved itself from persistent attack. Two more American aircraft carriers had been damaged, but the Japanese flotillas were broken and Japanese aircraft carriers had been sent to the bottom. By the time Darragh met the monsignor in the sacristy, at the end of saying the eight o'clock Mass on Sunday, Darragh heard that it was official. The Japanese had been turned back for the moment. They would no doubt try again, but they need not succeed any better than they had this time.

'I intend to declare this a Mass of thanksgiving,' said the monsignor, robing for his nine o'clock, his face translucent with happiness.

The next day's tennis was in large part a farewell to a classmate of Darragh's who had had experience as a youth in the militia and who had been appointed a chaplain to units in northern New South Wales. There were rumours that these battalions were about to go to New Guinea, so the after-match beer was drunk to jokes about rank—the classmate would begin as a one-pip lieutenant, a 'second loo–ie' as Australian jargon had it—and about the comic likelihood that the young priest might need or be tempted to take up arms, and thus become a warrior priest, like Father Murphy of the Irish 1798 uprising, or the Irish monk who had won the Military Cross for killing Prussians in the Great War. Darragh kept the story of his sharing the siege with Gervaise to himself. He was pleased no rumour of it had reached his friends.

Darragh returned to St Margaret's about dusk, his mind flickering with daydreams about a martial career. If the Japanese succeeded in the end, how much preferable would it be for a man to be among fellow soldiers, to be a military prisoner if necessary rather than part of the great mass of hostages. His nature was not a rancorously envious one, however. The daydream was more pleasant than bitter. Yet it was in its way intense again, as it had been on the day four years earlier, when the exorcist had urged him to be a merciful confessor.

As he came in through the front door of the presbytery, he saw Mrs Flannery seated on the edge of the chair which stood beneath a print of Our Lady of Perpetual Succour. She looked like a woman in a doctor's waiting room, and stood upright as Frank appeared. She had an officious and chastising whisper, and that was what emerged from her lips now. 'The monsignor's been waiting for you. He's in his office with that policeman.'

Which policeman? Surely the Lidcombe affair was not a matter for the civil police.

'Go in, Father,' said Mrs Flannery, gesturing with one hand. 'Go in!'

Darragh did so. Monsignor Carolan and Detective Inspector Kearney were drinking whisky together, seated either side of the monsignor's desk.

'The man of the hour,' said Inspector Kearney, putting down his glass. His double-breasted coat was unbuttoned and the monsignor was in his customary autumn cardigan. They had an air of being at easy understanding with each other and with the whisky they shared. But the monsignor seemed embarrassed as he stood up.

'Well,' he said, and shook his head. 'Frank . . .'

The detective rose too, and began to button his suit coat. He said, 'We presume you don't know, Father Frank. Mrs Catherine Heggarty is dead.'

Darragh became instantly giddy and was jolted sideways a step. The world had become too fast in its malice. He leaned against the wall and was gratified in some minor key of his senses to assure himself that it, at least, was still solid. Somehow the detective inspector produced a third glass from the table and sloshed some whisky and soda into it. Looking keenly at Darragh, he said, 'You should have this, son.'

Rather than believe what had been said, he was willing to accept the monsignor and inspector had devised this chastising lie to save him from folly. But Monsignor Carolan still seemed more tremulous than Darragh might ever have imagined him to be. He said, 'Because you had your Monday off, I had to give the poor thing her last rites. Rigor hadn't set in. I hope her soul was still there. Because the circumstances . . . they weren't promising.'

It was good priestly practice to absolve bodies not utterly claimed by death's iciness, in the hope that a repentant soul lingered, awaiting the blessed word.

Breath returned to Darragh. 'She can't be . . . She was at Mrs Flood's burial. Just ten days or so ago.'

'Ten days is a long time, Father Frank.'

'Tell me,' said Darragh. 'Was she in an accident?'

His soul at a distance from the room, he observed Inspector Kearney inform the Monday tennis-playing dolt who had wandered into the monsignor's study. 'Misadventure,' said Kearney. She had been strangled early that morning. Did they, Darragh and the monsignor, really know what strangulation was? asked Kearney. It was harder than in the films to strangle any healthy soul; it took either great strength or great accidental bad luck on the part of the victim, and sometimes of the killer. This hadn't been bad luck. This had been strength. And it had not been done by someone who had forced his way in. There were no signs of that. Quite the contrary, Kearney asserted.

Darragh, in misery, returned to his body and heard the inspector's words as a distinct series of bricks, or stones, laid in place. 'It takes strength,' Kearney explained in a lowered voice, 'to close off the oesophagus of someone healthy, to crush the larynx. Then at the same time, this strangler of Mrs Heggarty's constricted the arteries carrying blood to the brain. That takes double strength. Neighbours haven't told the son yet, he's been staying with them overnight. They got him ready for school and he's over with the nuns now.'

'I must see to him,' said Darragh.

The monsignor shook his head. 'There'll be time, and there'll be others to do it too. Stand still for God's sake, Frank.'

'His father was taken prisoner,' explained Darragh, to justify going over there, extracting Anthony . . . And then what?

'It's probably a case for the sisters at Killcare,' the monsignor said. The Order of St Joseph ran an orphanage at Killcare, between surf and bush, north of Sydney.

Darragh still thought he could sidestep the evil rumour of strangulation, a phenomenon unknown among women in Homebush and Strathfield, suburbs which, whatever their ordinary and occasionally perverse sins, protected their citizens with the dome of their own blessed banality. It was a concept, too, which could not be fitted to what he knew of Mrs Heggarty. So for a time he concentrated his uncertain but awful grief on that orphanage some hours distant. Killcare, he knew by instinct, would be overcrowded because of war, and because of the Depression which only war had put pause to. It was not a homely institution. Anthony Heggarty, Darragh was sure, would prove an unsuitable orphan. He would prove short of the stoicism his situation asked of him.

'I can't accept what you're telling me. She was far too strong to be strangled.' The word itself invited incredulity.

'You'd better accept it,' said the monsignor, his face reddening. 'Do you think we'd say a thing like that just for the joy of uttering it?' The monsignor had a sourness in his mouth he would gladly have spat out, but could not do it here, in his orderly study.

'You knew her, didn't you?' asked Inspector Kearney. 'In your role as spiritual adviser.'

The mad idea came to Darragh that if Kearney had possessed the nobility to go off beer for Lent, Kate Heggarty would be alive. But she was not dead, he knew. It was still a tableau they'd devised to punish him for Lidcombe. And for having invited her into the presbytery. 'See, we warned you about women . . .' But the monsignor had talked about last rites and rigor mortis. He wouldn't do that. He wouldn't be such a ghoul.

'I'm her spiritual adviser,' said Darragh. 'As far as I know. I haven't made a lot of progress.'

The monsignor assured him, 'I checked with the diocesan canon lawyer, Dr Field. He advised me that in these circumstances you are able to tell the inspector anything likely to help, unless of course it's under the seal of the confessional. The poor thing will have few secrets anyhow, not now. Everything will become public property.'

'Did she ask you about anything you can tell me?' asked Kearney. He was not as on edge as the monsignor. His work had inured him. 'You see,' he said, 'I'm asking you the same question as I asked you about that young runaway brother.'

Darragh could not frame words. He did not want to have her decisions, her rebellion and apostasy even, interpreted away in the stock terms of monsignors and policemen. 'Well, I don't know . . .'

'But she came to the presbytery,' stated the monsignor, flushed and insistent. 'She had a conference with you as her spiritual director, didn't she? It's not as if Mr Kearney's asking you to spill the beans from the heart of the confessional.'

'Yes, but I don't know that she sought advice on anything that would lead to this terrible . . . this terrible result. She is strangled?'

'Yes,' said the inspector.

The monsignor, more frankly annoyed than Darragh had ever seen him, began to do the inspector's task. 'Men are stranglers, Frank. You've never read in any newspaper of a strangling woman. And men worry soldiers' wives. I'd say that she talked to you about men. Did she?'

Darragh felt that if he said as much they would nod like elders and write her off as a loose woman, a whore, asking for it. He believed more strongly in her honesty than he did in her murder, and felt a duty to protect it.

'Please, Frank,' said the inspector.

'She told me that she had problems of faith. Her husband had been taken prisoner and it made her doubt the Church's good-will.'

'We didn't take her husband prisoner,' the monsignor complained.

'I'd like to see her body before I tell her confidences.'

'What's wrong with you?' asked the monsignor. 'She's lost her right to confidences, poor thing.'

Inspector Kearney had lowered his eyes. 'It's not possible, Father Frank. The body's been moved to the morgue. Awaiting the coroner's inquest.'

He had half hoped that if she had been laid out in her house in The Crescent, he might be permitted to visit her.

Darragh began to weep for her now. She was far gone into the hands of strangers.

To preserve her some small dignity, he said, 'She told me nothing which explains *this*!' The *this* he had not quite yet managed to believe in.

'But you must want her killer found, Father?' Kearney suggested.

Of course Darragh did, though he could barely believe in the man's existence.

'She said she could not remain a practising Catholic. I was very distressed to hear it. She told me that she felt very bitterly the injustice that her husband was a prisoner. His soldier's pay was not enough for her and her son to live on in dignity, she said. I told her I'd contact St Vincent de Paul to see if they could help her, and she said she was too proud for that. She quoted *Rerum Novarum*.'

'The social justice encyclical,' the monsignor informed the inspector. 'I've heard a lot of troublemakers quote that one in my day.'

The monsignor had anointed her extremities and her fine mute eyes, yet she had affronted him by being found so unfortunately treated.

'Did she mention a man?' asked the inspector. 'Her neighbours mentioned a man.'

Darragh was awed by the potency of that question. 'Was she interfered with?' he asked without hesitation.

'Not directly,' said the inspector, getting this matter out of the way. 'There was some stuff deposited on her, probably after-wards . . . a lot of stranglers are like that. They're better with the dead than the living.'

Darragh was chastened by the image of this frightful man. His awful masturbation made all the schoolboys in the confessional seem like cherubim.

'She mentioned a kindly man,' said Darragh. He was willing to help even an imperfect agent like Kearney. 'She knew it was a risk having him come to the house, but she said he wasn't demanding, and he helped her maintain her dignity.'

'How did he do that?'

Darragh knew how his answer would be interpreted. But there was no way of not saying it.

'He brought her things which she felt contributed to her dignity.'

'What sort of things?'

'Extra food . . .'

'Dignity,' said the monsignor with a feverish air of knowingness to Inspector Kearney. 'A woman making up her mind to adultery in return for a pair of stockings.'

Darragh thought he might punch him, which was a cause of automatic excommunication under canon law.

'That's an unfair view, Monsignor,' he said. He could feel his own face blazing to match the monsignor's. He and the monsignor were like two hot poles, with the cunning, cool terrain of the inspector connecting them. 'She had a genuine desire that she and her son wouldn't be degraded by want.'

'Such a sentiment,' said the monsignor, 'doesn't alter my first impression. Frank, if you don't see as much, then you need to take a few more courses in moral theology.'

Frank said, 'Monsignor, please stop pretending I'm stupid.'

'And you, Frankie, you stop pretending we're stupid. The inspector and I have in our different ways been round the block a few times. It isn't bush week, you know, not with us. You'll be treated as you treat us.'

Darragh found it hard to put in words, but it seemed to him that the monsignor was taking unnecessary and disloyal pains to do the policeman's work, while Inspector Kearney sat by with a priestly serenity on his broad and normally combative face.

'She told me she wasn't going to be one of those hypocritical

Catholics,' said Darragh, 'who risked sin and then crept back to the confessional. She said she wanted to be honest about it. She said her generous friend had not asked for anything, but she knew that he might, and told me that it was a moral risk she was willing to bear.'

'And she told you nothing about who this fellow was?' Kearney asked calmly.

'No.'

'An American soldier?'

'I don't know. She didn't make a point of that. She seemed to want God and me to be under no illusions.'

'A contract between unequal parties,' said angry Monsignor Carolan.

'I think you should have another drink, Vince,' the inspector told him. 'There are some things I haven't managed to tell you or ask Frank yet.'

The monsignor sat down, panting. Darragh sensed the shock his parish priest had suffered, and felt a fraternal sympathy for him.

'Did you ever visit her home?' asked Kearney.

'Yes,' said Frank. His memory of going there recurred to him as an indefinably sweet instant, a daydream exalted and enhanced by duty.

'Oh dear God,' said the monsignor.

'I hadn't told the monsignor,' said Kearney, 'but we found a letter of yours in her little lounge room.'

'I thought she was too fine a spirit to write off,' Darragh explained. 'I offered further spiritual counsel . . .'

The monsignor said, '*Spiritual counsel,*' as if he disbelieved both words.

'There was no stamp on the envelope,' the inspector observed. 'And no postmark.'

'I sent it home with her son.'

The monsignor's eyes were again engorged in a way that Darragh found himself tempted to detest. They were underlined by patches of furious red high on the cheeks. 'Infatuation's little messenger, eh Frank?' he asked.

'No,' said Darragh. 'No.' He would become angry with the monsignor, but later. Yet Darragh believed the fellow should know, if he was so damn experienced, that the worst thing one priest could do to another was to raise accusations of physical attraction in front of a layman.

The monsignor compounded the wrong by murmuring, 'Dean O'Haran again!'

Darragh understood the historic reference, knew that the policeman would too, and was grateful for the fury that rose in him. 'Monsignor, you have nothing to worry about on that score.'

'You've put yourself in it, Frank,' said the monsignor. 'How will it seem if the *Sunday Truth* or the *Telegraph* informs the world that a priest was corresponding with a murdered woman?'

'There is no reason for the *Truth* or anyone else to say so.'

'Well,' said Kearney mildly, 'there are Freemasons in the police force who would love to give a journalist such a set of details, Frank.'

'And the morning after it appears,' the monsignor continued, 'every Catholic in Australia gets mocked with it as he comes into work! Speak frankly to Mr Kearney here. He can help us prevent scandal.'

And that was why Kearney had conducted this interview in the monsignor's presence, so that he could have a barking dog to keep Darragh off balance. But then, if he used tricks like that to find . . . To find what? The ideas of a victim and a culprit were still equally beyond Darragh's normally pliant powers of belief.

'Tell me all about your last visit to see her,' Kearney suggested.

Darragh did that. He had Mrs Heggarty's letter, yes. He'd get it in a moment.

'Did you see any sign of her visitor?'

'Well, there was a visitor.'

'Who was it?'

He felt a strange brotherly guilt at mentioning Ross Trumble. 'A neighbour, Ross Trumble, called in.'

'Ah, we know Rossy,' the inspector asserted. 'What did he do there?'

Darragh found himself unwilling to say Trumble was drunk. 'He dropped in some meat from the abattoirs.'

'A gift?'

'I suppose so. He said it was part of the quota of a friend of his.'

'So Trumble might be her fellow, eh?'

'I don't think so.' He was affronted by the idea that a bundle of abattoir lamb chops could be the trigger for all Kate Heggarty's turmoil of soul. So he told how she tossed Ross Trumble out of the kitchen for repeating things he'd already said to Darragh. What things? asked Kearney. The normal Red things, Darragh told him.

'He was harmless,' said Darragh. 'I think.' Darragh told Kearney about Mrs Heggarty's humane remark, that Trumble was about to lose both a mother and a girlfriend, and his orphan soul wanted to find other kitchens where he was welcome.

Kearney sent him to his room to get the letter from Mrs Heggarty. On this errand, Darragh paused at his desk and touched his breviary. He opened it and found an ordination card of a classmate sitting there, Paul O'Brien. *Oremus pro invicem, Frank,* O'Brien had written. Let us pray for each other. And underneath was printed, 'Our Lady of Perpetual Succour, pray for me.' Indeed. And for Kate Heggarty's repute, blighted in death, even though the men downstairs cast her as victim while at the same time consigning her to hell's pit.

He got the plain letter, and took it downstairs. As he re-entered the study, the monsignor, beyond himself now and, Darragh noticed, possessing the emotional unreliability of someone who has gone over his normal quota of drink, said, 'Ha! The billet-doux arrives.' It was easy to forgive him since he looked, for the first time in Darragh's experience, sozzled.

Kearney read the brief letter Mrs Heggarty had written. Then he said, 'Do you mind if I show this to the monsignor?'

This put Darragh in an impossible situation—the monsignor was ready to take denial as an insult, but also to read too much into Mrs Heggarty's words. In the end, he nodded his consent, and the monsignor turned his enraged eyes to it, and his 'My good heavens!' and his 'Mother of God!' sounded like distant artillery. The monsignor looked up, almost pleading, 'Tell me what this means, Frank. "Except that I do not want to argue the matter with you again. I feel we argued the matter enough last time."'

'She didn't want me pointing out the danger she was in.'

'My God in heaven! Then why visit her?'

Darragh did not reply, and Kearney said, including both of them in the decision, 'I don't think there's anything here for my colleagues. I'll have to keep it though, Frank, in case. But you went, like the shepherd in search of the lost sheep, in good faith, even though she told you not to talk about the matter. But then, she would, wouldn't she?'

The monsignor tossed his head as Darragh saw with some amazement his letter from Kate Heggarty vanish into Kearney's breast pocket. Kearney said, 'You'll have to trust me with this, Frank and Vince. I'll let it into the file only if I have to. See, someone might think that "the matter" might refer to something else than spiritual advice.'

'That would be ridiculous,' said Darragh.

'Public opinion is ridiculous,' Kearney assured him. 'There's no justice and very little sense in it.'

Monsignor Carolan began mourning aloud, yet more or less to himself. 'There has not been a whiff of scandal here at St Margaret's. The parish was founded in 1872, and has been immaculate since . . .'

'Mrs Heggarty mentioned a neighbour. Thalia. Did she see visitors come to or go from Kate Heggarty's door?'

'She saw you, Frank,' said Kearney, with a false-shy smile. 'Her best friend, Thalia Stevens, who minds Anthony. She saw you. Saw Trumble. Saw a big black car, a Chrysler she thinks, once or twice on the corner of The Crescent and Rochester Street. Not yours, was it, Vince?'

The monsignor looked up with alarmed eyes and the hair on his skull distrait. 'Mine's a Buick,' said the monsignor, covering his mouth with his fist as the acid of what he had been drinking seemed to recur. 'Thank God, Frank doesn't have a car.'

'But does your mother have a car, Frank?'

'A Morris,' said Darragh. 'It belonged to my father. My mother doesn't drive it much.' He yearned for the father who had nursed the Morris so proudly along, swinging its bony steering wheel, or, in braces and a tie and vest, treating the leather upholstery with a soft cloth. So much is lost before you're thirty, and now it seemed Kate Heggarty was among the careful lost who cleaned their leather and linoleum and baked their fruit cake.

'Apparently it was all pretty secretive,' the inspector said. 'The coming and going of your kindly fellow, Father Frank. She was even secretive with Thalia Stevens, who really liked her. Mrs Stevens told me they were like sisters. Her old man is away too, but safe for the moment, in Western Australia. But far off enough for her to sympathise with Mrs Heggarty. She approved of her friend being pretty secretive, because people these days jump to conclusions. She knew this Heggarty girl had her pride. You'd picked her as a proud woman, Father Frank?'

The monsignor muttered, 'Strangling doesn't happen to proud women, but to fallen ones.'

'Well, that's not always true, Monsignor,' said Kearney moderately. 'Sometimes it happens to those who are too innocent.'

'I can't imagine that,' the monsignor remarked, locked into his own version of the death. His stubbornness about it made the story he had told about Mrs Heggarty, the absolution of her body, more and more credible to Darragh. He felt the shudder as truth entered his blood. No more spiritual advising for Kate, he thought for the first, freshly bewildered time.

'The truth is,' Kearney went on, yawning slyly as his argument turned a new corner, 'it's often a woman who is caught between two men. It's often jealousy or fear of losing her on the part of one of them, or of both. That can bring on a fatal result.'

'But there weren't two men,' Frank protested. 'Her husband is a prisoner.'

'But say there were people who didn't know you, Father Frank,' suggested Kearney. 'Think for a moment as they would. This fellow who wants the girl in one sense, and a priest who wants the woman in another sense, and sends her letters by way of her son, and visits her even though she says she has nothing more to say. I know you don't see it as a triangle, and I don't. But vulgar people, or people who didn't know your pure motives, might, you see. Sit down, Father Frank. Let's all sit.'

Darragh, taking the third seat, wanted to say, 'Call me Frank
or Father. Not Father Frank.' But he was pleased to suppress the
demand, since it might make him seem restively guilty in the face
of this outflanking line of argument. He felt restively guilty in any
case.

Kearney resettled himself and sighed. 'This is what I wanted
to tell you, Father Frank. I've done a lot of work with priests in
the past, and I know as well as anyone that they're human. If
you'll excuse me for saying, they're like the rest of us, all too
damn human. Now Kate Heggarty was a very beautiful young
woman, a genuine good sort. And not all young priests are very
worldly. They go into the seminary straight from the Brothers'
schools. They might have been to a Catholic Youth Organisation
dance. That's the extent of their knowledge of society between
men and women. You went to the seminary straight from
school, didn't you, Frank?'

Darragh admitted it. 'But you're going in the wrong direction,'
he said.

'I'm sure I am, but just tolerate me a little while. It would be
possible for a young fellow who was a priest, and who didn't
have a lot of worldly experience, to get infatuated and to have all
the human longings . . . And these could be in what you'd call a
very spiritual way. But still, human longings underneath.'

'Like St Francis and St Clare,' the monsignor annotated, for
once not disgusted, but still fearful.

'I am not saying for a moment that this happened,' Kearney
assured Darragh yet again. 'But imagine a young priest had built
a woman up in his mind as a model of what a woman should
be—good-looking, straight, virtuous. A fair dinkum Australian
woman of the best kind. And as I say, he doesn't have a romantic

attachment to her in any clear way, but he wants her maybe to go on being this model of Catholic womanhood. He wants her to be a fine daughter of the Blessed Mother, he wants her to be a Child of Mary. And then he discovers that it's not so. Like other woman under stress, their husbands POWs in Singapore or Germany, or just serving in the army, she falls. You see, good women can fall. If they didn't fall they wouldn't need confession. And so one way or another this young priest finds she's let herself down, and let down all the effort he's put into her soul. *And*, he finds out, she betrayed herself with some character who has bought his way into her affections, say with gifts of stockings or chocolate or gin, or something else as silly. A young priest might feel really outraged then. A young priest might feel a sort of fury . . . And he might find a lot of strength.'

Behind his instant rage, Darragh felt also an instant self-recognition. He managed though to glare at the two policemen, the one called the monsignor, and the other who was a servant of the Crown in New South Wales.

Kearney said, 'You're a slim, fit young fellow, Father Frank, a bit scrawny but long-armed and strong.'

As Kearney hypothesised, casting him as the potential strangler, the level of outrage Darragh felt was in fact not as extreme as he would have expected. Though his revulsion was profound, it was tempered by the suspicion that Kearney, as he had when he asked for a Lenten indulgence, was playing at a mental exercise at which he was skilled. He liked to have people flustered. He had succeeded with Monsignor Carolan, and turned him into an inquisitor to harry Darragh.

'You're not telling me that I'd hurt her?' asked Darragh, at a loss for convincing words, reduced to the plainest, most ordinary denial. 'Out of some sense of moral outrage?'

'Or out of a kind of justice,' Kearney said.

Darragh covered his face with his hands.

'It's ridiculous,' said Darragh. 'She has a little boy.'

The monsignor, weary now, his mouth aching open in a whisky yawn behind which he still managed to counsel Darragh. 'Frank, I adjure you, son. If there were anything at all to it, you're better off telling the inspector. Rather than becoming the suspect of some bigot who'd love to send you to gaol.'

Inspector Kearney nodded at that. 'Better to speak now, while you're among friends.' He reached for the near-empty whisky bottle. 'Have another drink, Father Frank. Ease it out. What is there you can tell?'

With both hands, Darragh dismissed the idea of a drink. His voice was taken over by some fury of contempt. 'Apart from the confessional, I met Mrs Heggarty five times, I believe. Once by accident on a train. Then in the playground, and in the parlour there. Then at her house with her child there, or at least running in and out, excited, with Mrs Stevens's children, and with Trumble calling in.' The memory took his breath a moment. 'Then at Mrs Flood's funeral. That's all. I won't waste time taking offence.'

The monsignor cast his eyes up. It was clear to Darragh that his parish priest did not accept a parity of insult and outrage had been achieved between them, and he was not yet finished with the just punishment of his curate. Kearney, however, remained as level and calm as ever. And began to question Darragh about how, apart from Mass, he had spent Sunday. Darragh explained that he had gone to his mother's for lunch. Aunt Madge drove him in the Morris down to Watsons Bay for a walk, and she had filled him in on the plots of pictures she had seen since Easter. Then tea, and Madge drove him to Central Station. Then back to the presbytery. 'I read a bit,' said Darragh, 'finished my office.'

'You weren't tempted to call in on Mrs Heggarty on your way from the station?'

Of course not, Darragh told him.

'And . . .' said Kearney, 'no night walks?'

Refusing to answer, Darragh cast his eyes to the far corner of the room. Kearney quietly dispensed with the lees of his whisky glass. He stood. 'Well, it looks like I can't help you any further then, Vince,' he told the monsignor. Darragh was aware in some amazement that both the monsignor and the policeman didn't fully believe him. Kearney fetched his hat, the clipped and multi-coloured feather in its brim.

'Father Frank,' he said, 'you look after yourself. I don't want you to suffer from guilt by association.'

For diplomacy's sake, Darragh stood and shook Kearney's hand, the hand he at least knew, which led by the ganglia of a big police arm to the brain which had made a cunning assessment of his preoccupation with Mrs Heggarty, though misreading his intentions.

After shaking the monsignor's hand, Kearney was gone.

Darragh said, 'Excuse me, Monsignor.'

'No,' ordered the monsignor, kneading his face. 'Sit down, Frank.'

Darragh took the seat recently occupied by the inspector. 'So, she is really dead?' he could not help asking.

'Oh, you're so bloody gormless,' said the monsignor. The corners of his broad head began to shine yet again with red dis-approval. 'My friend gives you a chance to confide in us, and all you can do is come up with a kind of prim outrage.'

'I'll attend the funeral,' said Frank.

'That's what I bloody well mean. That's a fence that's not even close, Frank. The body won't be released for burial for at least a week, ten days, Kearney told me. And imagine the newspapers there, round the grave. Thank God there's nothing too bad in her letter. As for yours, well, who could say?'

Until this moment, Darragh had not quite believed in the monsignor's warnings about a press scandal. He believed it had been a conjured-up stick to beat him with. But now he imagined the impact of such a thing in the *Sunday Truth*, his mother's surprise, Mr Regan's. Not exactly *Truth* readers, the Regans and the Darraghs, but they would have it gleefully pointed out to them by neighbours. It seemed both a small and a massive thing to care about when put beside the idea of Mrs Heggarty being finished with breath and all systems of hope.

'So *I* shall do the funeral,' continued the monsignor, pausing again to try to swallow his heartburn. 'You can take the child to Killcare, Frank, since he knows you. I'll get one of the parishioners to drive you up. A day in the bush. That's if you're here. I've spoken to the vicar-general and it's very likely the cathedral might want you to go to retreat, Frank. Seven days of contemplation. Or a month of it.' He shook his head in long sweeps, and his horror at having a priest ordered off on a compulsory retreat because his actions had been indiscreet obviously weighed on the monsignor.

'I'm sorry,' said Frank. Though he wondered if he could tolerate the silences of a retreat, he would argue that point if it became necessary.

'Oh Frank, you're encouraging me to become a tyrant, and supervise all your bloody stupid acts. I think I've said that once already, though.' And, having caught himself out in repetition, the monsignor sounded all at once as if he had become more lenient. With a further muttered apology, Darragh was let go to his room, but did not reach it before, on the first landing, the great loss of Mrs Heggarty and the cruelty she had somehow attracted to herself reduced him to crippling tears.

CHAPTER FIFTEEN

WHEN THE MONSIGNOR and Mrs Flannery had finished with them, it was natural that Darragh should hungrily read the newspaper reports of the death of Kate Heggarty, in the remaining mad expectation that at the end of one of the columns the journalists or Inspector Kearney would come clean and say, 'By the way, this is just a sample of what we can do to create realities where there were none and, far from being strangled, Mrs Heggarty, on her next day off work, will be found escorting her son, Anthony, up Homebush Road to St Margaret's primary school.' Neither *Telegraph* nor *Herald*, a Masonic rag according to the monsignor but necessary to buy on large occasions for its war maps and so that a fellow could be annoyed by its acidulous editorials, nor the vacuous afternoon *Sun* made this admission so desired by Frank Darragh, who was forced to put the print away from him so that his tears did not ruin the page.

But at least the newspapers pleased the monsignor by not mentioning Darragh, and by failing to cast any shadow over the monsignor's financial and sacramental polity of St Margaret's.

Apart from that, it was a pitiable story, and the newspapers were sympathetic to Mrs Heggarty, though they did not thoroughly excuse her. There was an editorial in the *Telegraph* which reminded soldiers' wives that as generous as they might be socially, they must be careful about the people they admitted to their houses in their husbands' absence. Neighbours had seen a man in a brown suit visit Mrs Heggarty one time in the early evening, and another man in a blue suit arrived from a large car parked around the corner about noon on a recent Saturday. He carried a suitcase like a commercial traveller.

Mrs Heggarty was well liked by neighbours, the papers said, though they said she did not go round attending tea parties. Her son could say nothing about the male visitor, except that he was strong—'He tossed me for fun,' said Anthony. 'He was named Johnny, and brought chocolate with him'. It seemed that sometimes when the visitor was there, Mrs Stevens minded Anthony.

Darragh's head, for spasms of perhaps twenty seconds at a time, and recurrently through the coming days, was possessed by the image of her face descending, the crown of her honest head exposed to God and to Darragh's gaze, to embrace with her lips the thin rim of a china cup. And somewhere, in Africa or Europe, Private Heggarty woke in his prison camp thinking himself still a man with a wife.

Darragh went to the school to see Anthony, but he was not there. The nuns said he was having some days off with Mrs Stevens.

The day after her death had been suitably one of neutral weather, and even early, when Darragh went to put on his vestments and say Mass, offering up the bread and the wine that Christ, who knew agony, might extend His mercy to Kate Heggarty, clouds had already cancelled sun, and sun the clouds.

The seasons were seized in place, he believed. After Mass and a poor breakfast, he felt in his shirtsleeves the need of a black cardigan, and when he put it on, the need to be bare-armed. He said his office in one session that morning, and the words evaded his attention, so that sometimes he would look back over the '*Veni Creator*' and ask, 'Did I recite that?'

The monsignor was not about at lunch time, and Darragh could not think of a single task for himself. If Kate Heggarty, disciple of *Rerum Novarum*, could not be helped, it was worth asking who might be.

The afternoon paper said that the observed wearer of the brown suit, an Italian door-to-door salesman of household products, was helping police with their enquiries. Darragh exclaimed at the newsprint. This could not be the man bearing gifts. Kate Heggarty would not admit a salesman and make him the crux of whether she remained a Catholic or not.

In the afternoon of that suspended day, Mrs Flannery found him in his room and told him there was a telephone call from the cathedral. It proved to be the vicar-general of the archdiocese, Monsignor Joe McCarthy. Standing in the hallway, phone to ear, Darragh felt chill break out on his underarms as if he would be unable ever again to accommodate himself to any climate.

'Frank, Joe McCarthy here. Sounds to us here as if you've had a hectic time. Shot at one week, and now this parishioner of yours. And the strangler.'

At the utterance of that word—*strangler*—Darragh felt, like an intimate revelation, the genuine existence of such a person. Until now the fellow had been a black vacancy, brown or blue-suited perhaps, carrying his bag of indefinite kindness, a force with the consistency of smoke. Not a defined man, with hands as rough and hurried as those of a rescuer. Nor did it seem to

Darragh, for once, that Inspector Kearney had the right level of urgency to match the concreteness of this clever, strong fellow, this murderer. With this idea of a definite, ten-fingered, two-handed man, Darragh was overtaken by a boiling rage, utterly unsuitable to bring to a telephone call from a vicar-general of an archdiocese. He scrambled in this tempest to hold to one small white area of reason, at the apex of his brain, with all the rest blood-red again, and suffocating.

'I feel very sorry for that woman,' were the tepid words he managed to emit from this cauldron.

'The world has gone utterly mad,' Monsignor McCarthy asserted. 'It is a time for God's special mercy. I hope we all get it, Frank.'

Darragh somehow managed to agree.

'His Grace the archbishop thinks that in these disturbing times you should go on retreat . . . you know, spend a bit of time in meditation and reflection. There is a Franciscan retreat house on the South Coast, or more exactly, Kangaroo Valley . . .'

Darragh knew, as any priest would, that to be told that the archbishop *thought* was not to hear an idle opinion but a command.

'It's very kind of His Grace,' said Darragh, trying to accept it all as a matter of the new, Australian-born archbishop's paternal concern. But he lacked the means of contemplation. He possessed only the means of rage. 'I keep myself very busy, Monsignor, and I doubt if Monsignor Carolan could easily get through all he has to do without my help. I mean, in the chief areas in which I am able to assist—ceremonies, confession, parish visitations . . .'

'Yes, you visited the poor woman, didn't you?'

'Yes.'

The vicar-general made a creaking noise over the phone, as if he were struggling to find arguments Darragh knew very well he already possessed, and had well calibrated from use on earlier problem priests.

'A–a–ah,' said McCarthy. 'It is precisely when a priest considers himself indispensable that he should take a retreat. I feel indispensable to His Grace, but if I were run over by a truck, he'd find a perfectly good new vicar-general in a moment.'

'For how long did His Grace want me to stay in retreat?'

'Well, that is flexible. For as long as we and Monsignor Carolan between us think it might benefit you, I suppose. Beginning next Monday. You could take the train to a bit beyond Wollongong, you see, and the Franciscan friars will pick you up and take you out to Kangaroo Valley. You'll miss your Monday off, I'm sorry, but the journey's very pleasant in its own right.'

'Next Monday,' Darragh repeated woodenly.

Not early enough to prevent him undertaking his full weekend workload, but soon enough after the event should the salacious Sunday press mention him. He was dolefully aware he would not escape making this retreat. Retreats were the Church's universal early response to all questionable incidents involving the clergy.

'We wouldn't want you to rush back, I don't think, Frank. Count on at least ten to twelve days.'

'I don't believe there's any need,' he still pleaded. It was no good being like an obedient monk. Not with all this fever in his soul, and the idea of the strangler born of woman and bearing a name. 'Look, it just seems to me . . . the country's about to be invaded, Monsignor, and whether by war or murder, children are becoming orphans. I don't think I can go away and meditate at such a time.'

'Frank,' the vicar-general told him with greater severity than had marked the discussion so far, 'your superiors think you have to. It's precisely at a time like this that you need to reflect. You've been through a great deal, a storm of the emotions. These events deprive a man of his compass. A retreat will get you back to your true north. Now, Frank, no more arguments. I'd be embarrassed to have to get the archbishop himself to talk to you.'

There was no arguing. '*May her soul, and all the souls of the faithful departed, rest in peace . . .*' he muttered at the phone when the vicar-general hung up. '*May her soul . . .*' He needed to act. In God's name he had been forbidden to act. Blessed be the Name of the Lord.

The monsignor was in, and so the dinner was uneasy at the presbytery table, Darragh sensing that as angry as the monsignor might be with him, he was, this sober, tea-drinking night, angry with himself as well, for his heated, whiskified feelings at the conference with Kearney yesterday. Perhaps, too, he harboured an edgy suspicion that there might have been a better way to do things, a more loyal way to Darragh, if only a man had not been so angry, and so shocked by anointing the strangled girl.

'Did you hear from the cathedral?' the monsignor asked with *basso* neutrality.

'They want me to go on a retreat,' said Frank. 'It seems you'll decide with them how long I should be there.'

'I think you need it, Frank,' said the monsignor.

'Why don't I go tomorrow then?'

'Tomorrow you have to take young Heggarty up to the orphanage at Killcare. I've got Mr Connors lined up to drive you and the little bloke.'

'Then why don't I go on retreat the next day?'

The monsignor's face was pained. 'Because you're needed over the weekend.'

'That's exactly right, Monsignor. I'm needed over next

weekend, and next Monday to Friday as well. Who'll do all your extra work for you?'

'Frank, is this the attitude?'

'Yes. It seems I'm getting worldly. Having been grilled by you and Kearney in tandem, I'm not nearly as innocent as I was.'

'Look, Frank, I made the best decision I could. I was too damned upset, Frank, even to pray over it. Perhaps you thought I threw you to him, but . . . As for false innocence, I can only hope you've turned that corner. You know what they say? In the world, but not of it. To be effective, a fellow has to know something of how the world works.'

'I won't learn much about the world in a Franciscan monastery in Kangaroo Valley.'

'I think you've acquired a bit of knowledge in the last few months, Frank, and now it's time to reflect on it.'

'With you the gaoler, Monsignor, to tell me when I can emerge?'

Darragh was delighted to see that his baiting had brought angry colour back to the monsignor's cheeks and scalp.

'His Grace will certainly discuss it with me.'

'And who will be your donkey when I'm not here the weekend after next?'

'Frank, I don't like that tone.'

'Do you think it's time some of your beloved finance committee went on retreat? They're in the world and totally of it.'

'Frank, watch what you're saying. This isn't you, I know. You've always been such a cooperative young bloke!'

'That was because I was a fool. Now I know a thing or two.'

'Well, one thing you ought to know is you don't talk to your parish priest like that. You ought to know that much if you're suddenly such a knowledgeable cleric.'

'Do you mind if I leave the table, Monsignor? I don't feel like any dinner.' In fact, mutton was setting in its own fat on his plate, and the peas too were being claimed by the unspecific, tepid gelatinous mixture which was Mrs Flannery's version of gravy.

'You can certainly go, Frank. You've just demonstrated why you need to go on retreat.'

Frank stood up and went to the foot of the stairs, where he savoured the small astringency of his vented anger.

'Don't forget you have to do the early Mass tomorrow,' called the monsignor.

The phone began to ring then. It was Captain O'Rourke, oblivious of murder, proposing, without any particular enthusiasm, a shared visit to Private Aspillon.

CHAPTER SIXTEEN

HE WAS PLEASED to decide he did not need to tell the monsignor of his intended visit to Gervaise. In any case, what harm could occur under the aegis of Captain O'Rourke? There were no jurisdictions to be violated. Bearing his grief, he would be a visitor, and he would behave like it. A seemly curate.

Darragh, the same purple stole in his pocket as he had taken into his first encounter with Private Aspillon, made the considerable journey by steam train to Liverpool. This was a town not so far beyond Sydney's outskirts, a place where by day the residual heat of summer seemed to arise from hard-baked earth in streets broadly surveyed as if for some British cantonment in India. By arrangement, Captain O'Rourke picked him up from the northern side of the station, opposite a straggle of garages, frock shops and little grocery stores of the kind his father had called Ned Kellys. The American chaplain was already waiting by a large khaki Buick appropriate, in Darragh's eyes, to General MacArthur. He was accompanied by a smartly dressed American soldier-driver who smoked while waiting for the visitor. Now he dispensed with his cigarette and came across the street to meet Darragh.

'Father Duggan?' said the driver.

'Darragh.'

'That's the one. Sorry sir. Any luggage?'

He reached for the small grip Darragh had brought with him and took it to the car. Captain O'Rourke, who looked like a slightly florid athlete, shook Darragh's hand as the driver opened the back door of the Buick for them to enter. O'Rourke wore no clerical collar but an army tie, and seemed very martial in a splendid peaked cap and tan suit, and his two bars, to signify his rank, at the collar of his shirt. He said it was nice to meet Darragh, but Darragh could tell that he was watchful for signs of eccentricity or excess in his visitor.

The car set off, the two priests in the back together. 'Okay,' said O'Rourke, 'as I told you on the phone, I set it up for you to visit this Aspillon guy, but it took some doing. His trial isn't up yet, and I know they'll come down heavy on him.'

'Heavy?' asked Darragh. A shiver ran through him. He had had enough of heavy comings-down.

'Depends whether they end up deciding he's AWOL or a deserter. And then of course there's the fact of cohabitation ... Some of these white girls! My guess is he'll get a five-year sentence.'

'*Five years?*'

'That's right. At least he wasn't in the face of the enemy when he went missing.'

'He sheltered me with his body,' said Darragh. 'I could tell the judges that.'

'Father, believe me. That's just a grace note. Counts for

nothing. Look, I went to see him and he's not a bad kid. Wild. Too much appetite. And an operator. Plausible. But when you go missing like he did, little positive traits of character don't add up to much at the court martial.'

They drew up to the camp gate in a country of stunted euca- lypts and acacia. The rituals of admission, the gestures of the military police, were all so emphatic. Americans were good at military liturgy, an art form much more casually attended to in the Australian army. No movement these men made seemed casual or negligent. In their standings-to-attention, in their impeccable webbing, they seemed to Darragh to have built a ritual bridgehead against the enemy.

It became apparent as Captain O'Rourke's car entered that the numbers of Americans within the gates had tested the accommo- dation provided by this complex of Great War huts in which the recruits of 1915, his father among them, had spent their last peaceful nights before the madness of France and Flanders. Barracks gave way to long rows of tents, aesthetically pleasing in their choreographed orderliness, the way the ropes of one echoed and ran parallel to the corresponding ropes of the next. The farther into the camp one went, the more tents proliferated. This was at some level a comfort to Darragh. Common wisdom had it that most American troops were either waiting in Melbourne or training in North Queensland. So if there were so many as these in the outer townships and suburbs of Sydney, Australia was not as wide open and bereft of support as was the popular belief.

Deeply into the camp, they came to a region of high wire gates and fences, surrounded by wooden watchtowers. Armed guards stood atop the towers, on watch against their own—at first sight, a peculiar task for a patriot. This detention compound was thickly tented out as well—so many misdemeanours and crimes had apparently been committed in a few months by the soldiers of Australia's great ally and best hope. Only one permanent structure lay in there—a guard hut to which, having dismounted from the Buick at the gate and entered an opened portal within it, Fathers O'Rourke and Darragh were led. They were offered a seat in a barred-off section of the structure, furnished with a table and chairs for interviews of this nature. The other part of the hut was a large holding cell, empty today. A natty military policeman waiting by the door pointed to Darragh's grip and asked him would he mind opening it, and whether he had brought anything for the prisoner. Darragh produced a pocket missal and a set of rosary beads.

The military policeman was half embarrassed in saying, 'He can have the book, Father. The rosary beads . . .'

'A prisoner could hang himself with those, see!' Father O'Rourke explained to Darragh. 'Don't worry, we have communal rosary and they use natural beads. Their fingers.'

'I brought some biscuits too,' said Darragh, reaching further into his little bag. 'Shortbread.'

The military policeman looked strickenly at Father O'Rourke, who said, 'Sorry, Father Darragh. It's always Lent in here. If you'd leave them with me, I'll make sure they get to some of the other guys.'

Of course, Darragh handed them over to O'Rourke, who seemed amused to receive them and asked a guard near the door to take them to his driver.

Before a proper conversation could develop between Darragh and O'Rourke, tall Gervaise Aspillon, accompanied by two MPs and chained at the wrists and the ankles, was brought in through the further door. The connecting links were loose so that at a nod from his mentors Gervaise was able to consider sitting, but not before, eyes aglow with modest hope, he greeted the priests, O'Rourke with an equally enthusiastic nod as Darragh. As Gervaise settled, O'Rourke leaned towards Darragh and murmured. 'Father, I might just leave you alone? Before I do, you wouldn't get a fellow priest into trouble, would you?'

Aspillon wore an expression of tranquil benevolence as he waited for this private discourse between the priests to end.

'I simply wanted to see the man.'

'No file in your pocket?' asked O'Rourke, winking.

'No file in my pocket, I promise, Father O'Rourke.'

'Okay. Just remember—for Gervaise, there's only one way out of here. Serving his time, here or wherever.' He looked away. 'I'll tell you something about wherever later.' He raised his voice for the prisoner. 'Gervaise, be good for Father Darragh.'

'Sure, Captain,' said Private Aspillon.

O'Rourke left and, in steadfast silence, Private Aspillon engaged Darragh's eye. Darragh felt for a moment like a public speaker who had suddenly lost his purpose for being on the rostrum. Aspillon said, 'How are you now, Father? After our big shake-up the other day.'

'On top of everything . . . well, a parishioner has died, Gervaise. I'm saddened. But how are you going?'

'One word, Father, I am happy to say. *Dull.* Dull I like. Lots of groceries in here. Time hanging heavy, but not burying a man. I think this is all gentler treatment than one of them solid-built prisons. Once they put those stone walls up, strange things are bound to happen. But wire and wooden posts, God's air can travel in and out. The same air other folk breathe. I'd be obliged if you'd pass that on to my friends in Lidcombe. You remember the house?'

'I don't think it's my business to communicate with them.

It's the area of another parish priest. Are you allowed to write?'

'Once a month, and this month is going to my mama.'

'I'll call the parish priest at Lidcombe, and see if he will contact your friends.'

'I would be *so* obliged,' said Gervaise smoothly, so that Darragh wondered: Is this a performance as others have warned me? A performance for an Australian curate who has seen Negro men only in the Saturday films of childhood?

'I brought you some biscuits, but you're not allowed them.'

'That's what you guys call cookies, isn't it?'

'That's right. Biscuits.' With any American you were always likely to end in a discussion about idiom.

'Twice-cooked,' said Gervaise. '*Bis–cuit*. That's what it means. Double cookies. I cherish the thought.'

The terror which had been in Private Aspillon during the siege and arrest seemed to have moderated in him. His body looked languid and un-tautened. But even as Darragh thought this, the muscles showed below his shirtsleeves and Gervaise began weeping softly. It looked such a manly, frank grief, empty of artifice, that the idea revived in Darragh that despite all warnings from Captain O'Rourke, some special effort must be made for this noble delinquent.

'Gervaise,' said Darragh, extending a lean, white hand to rest on Gervaise's wide shackled wrist, a lily laid on anthracite. 'I'll call the Lidcombe priest for you. What else can I do?'

Gervaise Aspillon, briskly drying his tears, declared, 'This is all my silliness.' He gestured towards the roof of the guard hut. Then he laid both cuffed hands on the table and talked at them. 'A man who hasn't travelled makes great journeys. Louisiana to California. Wow! And greater journeys still. Long Beach to Sydney, Australia. Across an ocean which just manages to come to an end. And see, a man's been through the mirror, over the equator, stewing on deck, broiled down below. And at the end, back in nice waters, the land comes up on the horizon and reaches out like the arms of God. And a man thinks, I am born anew in a different place and under a different law. It's new and it's grand to drink in white folks' bars and public houses. And the girl is well-favoured and she says, "Hello Yank", which is very funny and strange and turns a weak head. So this weak-minded nigger from Louisiana is thinking he must be good as whites here. I converse with this white woman. This girl. This cloud. This good woman with a hairdo from heaven. And no one comes up with rope or rifle to punish me. Or so it might seem to a simple man. But a fellow forgets, Father, there's lots of Aussies don't really like that, and there's mean Southern boys in the MPs. Punishment is punishment pole to pole. So the light's dawned for me. The light has dawned!' He wiped his eye with his massive chained hand. 'I broke laws written and not written, and I pay. Here, same as back home.'

'But you're going through a legal process, aren't you? Captain O'Rourke says you'll get a gaol sentence.' For Gervaise seemed to be conjuring up a more absolute punishment than that.

'That's true,' said Gervaise sunnily, 'I'll get a sentence. But it's funny, a lot of black men who go AWOL over white women end up hanging themselves in prison. An astonishing number, you'd say.' And he smiled, shook his head, and decided to wink at Darragh, whose stomach turned.

'No, Gervaise,' he said, full of fury against any hand raised to Private Aspillon. 'It won't happen. I'll come and visit you each week. Captain O'Rourke will keep watch over you . . .'

'Okay,' said Gervaise without conviction. There was a frantic silence for a while. 'But I'm out of reach here, in the stockade.

The MPs know how to tell army chaplains a consoling tale. "Prison's just too hard for them darkies," they say. "They're like that, you know, and it's damn sad but can't be helped." Don't tell my friends anything I've said, except you saw me looking pretty well.'

'It's iniquitous,' Darragh murmured, and Private Aspillon did not reply. Again, would God permit such flaws within the legions of right to go unpunished on the battlefield?

Gervaise said indulgently, 'It's kind, but you can't keep visiting me. The army won't permit it. And it'll upset the chaplains corps. And there are men in the towers or in the tents now, watching us, and they say, "How did that nigger get a priest in to visit him and confabulate at length?"'

'I'll write to General MacArthur if I need to,' Darragh promised.

'His provost-general would say, "That nigger's telling the priest this just to get him upset." And I do string people along, all right. I like to talk, and have a gift.'

'You do, Gervaise,' Darragh assented. 'You have a gift.'

Every other suggestion Darragh made for Gervaise Aspillon's rescue from unjust MPs was gently rebuffed. The black man gave the impression of being used to powerlessness, and reconciled to it after his AWOL adventure.

'Can I see you again?'

'Well,' said Gervaise, 'I'm permitted a monthly visit. But I might be somewhere else by then.'

'I'll keep track. I'll watch.'

'You know, Father, an old man I know says, "Don't start them dogs a-barkin' unless they's already at it." It's not bad advice.'

Two guards had re-entered the hut. Aspillon lowered his head while Darragh blessed him. The guards dragged Aspillon upright. Darragh was tempted to tell them, 'I'll be here to see Private

Aspillon again as soon as I can get permission.' But he did not
wish to start dogs barking, and so he watched as they jostled the
black man out of the hut.

By the Buick beyond the wooden postern of the gate, the
captain and his driver were fraternally smoking Lucky Strikes. As
Darragh was let through the gate, O'Rourke approached him in
a not unfriendly way.

'How did it go, Frank?'

'I'm concerned,' said Frank. He lowered his voice. 'He seems
convinced that sooner or later he'll be found dead.'

The captain looked away. There were a few seconds of
monsignor-like annoyance there. Darragh was bemused to find
that he consistently annoyed his fellow priests these days.
Something to reflect on in retreat. 'Look,' O'Rourke assured him,
'prisoners say these things, Frank. If they can get an outsider in,
they *always* say these things. They're starved for attention, and
they're self-dramatisers.'

'In my experience,' said Darragh, 'he's a reliable fellow.'

'Jesus, Mary and Joseph!' said Captain O'Rourke. 'The man
nearly got you killed, Frank.'

'The only question's whether there's any truth to what he
says.'

'The compound's full of exaggerators, Frank. Do me a favour
and let it go. Look, this is a specialist area of work—I'm sure
you'll agree with that. And I'm qualified to do it both by rank
and priesthood. Visitors only muddy the water, all due respect.'

'I feel a fraternal duty to him. And a pastoral one.'

'Look, get in the car, Frank,' muttered the chaplain, colouring,
'and I'll take you to the station.'

In the privacy of the back seat, Captain O'Rourke seemed to
have achieved an even temper. He looked out the window at the

proliferation of tents. At last he said, 'You're a scrupulous guy, Frank. We have 'em too. If they're not careful, they grow up to be oddballs. Old men with twitches.'

'Because I'm worried about Gervaise?'

But the captain was sure he knew of what he spoke. 'It isn't that you lack virtue. It's that you have too much of it for the world to work with. I hope you don't mind me talking out like this.'

'It isn't pleasant,' Darragh admitted. 'But I don't mind.'

'You're not responsible for that boy Aspillon. He's in the care of the chaplains corps. If we can't save him, he can't be saved. Now, come out here in a month if you like, but you won't find Aspillon. All the black troops will be gone. Don't say I told you. It's a military secret, but everyone round here seems to know it. And Aspillon stands for the reason why it's happening. Your government, and our army, both—they don't want black troops in your city, creating civil discord, attracting white women and the anger of white men. Within a week or two, every black soldier will be in farthest North Queensland. It looks like the government and the army are going to save you from yourself, Frank. And just in case you're wondering, we chaplains too believe in the Incarnation, the Communion of Saints, Transubstantiation and all the other Mysteries of Faith. We too have the charity of Christ urging us. Don't think you've got that on your own, Frank. Okay?'

This gentle but resonating rebuke depressed Darragh and made him suspect he might be ineffectual and silly. Even so, he was not rendered utterly repentant by it. 'Still,' he said, 'if you don't mind, I'll talk to you in a few weeks. To find out where I can write to Gervaise.' The Reverend Captain O'Rourke looked ahead towards Liverpool Station, sighed, and said okay.

CHAPTER SEVENTEEN

AT ODD HOURS it would penetrate and transfix Darragh's imagination: she was lying in the morgue. Did they treat well her body, which she had bathed for visitors and dressed in floral cloth? Who were these morgue-keepers, who were unordained for their job, who might as easily have worked in a cardboard-box factory? Her dignity had fallen into their hands, and society seemed calm about it, and waited without urgency for a coroner to have his court on her mute flesh.

A small amount of morning print was given to explaining that police had discharged the brown-suited man, the Italian salesman, since he was unable to assist them further.

Meantime, Kate's son had to be made an orphan pending his father's return. Darragh dreaded the arrival of Mr Connors, the member of the finance committee Darragh had recently slandered, the friend-of-the-parish appointed to conduct Anthony and Darragh to Killcare. Not that Darragh intended to use Mr Connors as a sounding-board, but he was the sort of man who wouldn't hear a word against 'the Mons', as all the finance committee called their parish priest. Yet when Connors came to the presbytery door to fetch him, Darragh found the man's demeanour calming. Despite the times, and two sons in the armed forces, one serving overseas, Connors was one of those people who possessed even in his eye such an unfeigned sense of the moment-by-moment mercies of life that he would suddenly sigh, not for loss of the moment but for its fullness. He was dressed like a very fortress of fatherhood, in a hound's-tooth suit and vest, and a slightly old-fashioned upright collar of the kind Mr Regan favoured, as had Darragh's own late father.

The leather of his car, a 1938 Dodge, squeaked with the enviable tidiness of a man whose life was an abundant tree—one son a doctor, or more accurately an army medical officer, another a lawyer, another a young pilot. Handsome grandchildren filled out the map of his life. Only the cosmic uncertainty of future Japanese intentions interposed any sort of cloud over the happy crown of righteousness which was the Connors family.

'Good morning, Father. A fine early autumn day for a drive up the coast! I hope the recent Lenten devotions don't leave you too weak to enjoy the scenery. You young fellows sometimes take all that too seriously!'

Settling into the front seat, Frank asked him how he had got enough petrol for the journey. Oh, said Mr Connors, he had an old school friend who was a garage owner in Burwood, a fellow member of the Knights of the Southern Cross. He didn't use the car much anyhow. 'It's not a time to be far from home for too long.'

In opinion, Mr Connors was a facsimile of Mr Regan, and to an extent of the monsignor. No question, said Mr Connors, that Mr Curtin, the Labor prime minister, had been placed in care of Australia by our Divine Lord. The Portuguese, first European discoverers of the continent, had called it Land of the Holy Spirit, and a country so named was surely not designed by God to fall to barbarians. Curtin certainly knew that and was fighting to save this holy land. He'd defied Churchill and had the Australian troops gradually coming home from the Middle East. (Not in time to save Lance Bombardier Heggarty, Darragh immediately and privately acknowledged.) And though Curtin had in his socialist youth abandoned the tenets of his faith, he was, by all that Mr Connors heard, very open, very attuned, for an ultimate return. A lonely spiritual sort of man, with the old Irish Catholic fallibility for the drink, which he seemed to have overcome recently. In the meantime, his lapse from Catholicism made him more attractive to the general population, including—even— members of the Masonic lodges. His brave plan to cooperate with the Americans—'because Mr Churchill isn't interested in our welfare, he thinks we're *bad stock*'—was something earlier prime ministers might not have been brave enough to do for fear of someone like Churchill. 'There are people who call themselves Australian,' said Mr Connors, 'who would rather save the Empire than save Australia! Honestly, Father!' Then Mr Connors wondered if he'd gone too far and offended Darragh's sense of charity. 'At least that's how it seems to me,' he said with less certainty.

Mr Connors turned then to the subject of his son who was learning to fly bombers in Canada. 'I hope he comes back here to fight our war, and doesn't stay over there in Churchill's,' he said. It developed that Churchill was one of Mr Connors's *bêtes noires*—it was an uneasy alliance in arms between the great British statesman and the Connors family of Homebush, New South Wales, Australia. Churchill, said Mr Connors, had been responsible, when First Lord of the Admiralty in 1915, for sending the Australians to Gallipoli. 'Look how that worked out!' Mr Connors suggested.

They were nearing the railway again, the region associated in Darragh's mind with Mrs Flood and Mrs Heggarty, his lost parishioners. Here in The Crescent, Mr Connors braked in front of a low, dank-looking house of plum-coloured brick some ten doors from Mrs Heggarty's place. Up its side laneway and through a gate came five children delighted to encounter Mr Connors's vehicle. Two jumped on the running board and looked in at him, one on the running board by Darragh's window, and one each on the rear and front bumper bars. It was as if they had planned this capture, so assured did they seem of their jolly, freckled possession.

'Hello, Curly,' said Mr Connors to one of the two children by his window.

A plump, sweet-faced woman of perhaps thirty years came out of the front door, carrying a suitcase and leading Anthony Heggarty by the hand. Thalia Stevens, whom Kate Heggarty had so respected. Mr Connors and Darragh ordered her children off the running board and emerged to greet her.

She looked with a concerned smile deep into the eyes first of one, then of the other man. 'He's a bit W–I–N–D–Y, poor little feller. He knows what happened, in so far as a kid does. I've tried to build him up.' She turned then to Anthony. 'What a beautiful car!' she told him. 'You know I didn't ride in a car until I was fifteen? You're a lucky little bloke. Say good morning to Father here.'

Anthony did it. Darragh said, 'You can sit in the front if you like, and have the window. Or have the back seat all to yourself.'

For a time Anthony was too reticent to say, but at last he decided he'd like to be in the front too. So he got aboard, as did

Mr Connors. As Darragh thanked Thalia Stevens and went to join them, she said, 'Just a word or two, Father.'

He paused, and saw her sad, earnest eyes, already webbed so early in life with incipient lines. 'Father, I'm going to miss the little fellow. I wanted to ask you, if I promised to raise him a Holy Roman, and I *would* promise, could you reconsider letting me have him?'

'I don't quite understand, Mrs Stevens,' said Darragh.

'Well, the nuns wouldn't have a bar of me, seeing I'm not of the Faith like. But I would go to Mass with him, or send my eldest, if you'd let me. Look, I know it would be all jake with Kate. She always trusted me with Anthony.'

'Are you telling me you would keep him?'

'And raise him a good little Tyke, Father. I mean, RC.'

'Do they know this up in Killcare?'

'I don't know. They came, two nuns, and inspected me over.' She smiled with the apologetic air of a person who has failed an exam. 'Made my brats sit up, I'll tell you!'

Darragh said, 'But I didn't know you were willing . . .'

'Well, I mean,' said Mrs Stevens, 'it isn't the Australia Hotel here or anything, and the kids are always messing up the kitchen . . .'

By now four of her children had ascended to the bonnet of the car and were making Anthony laugh beyond the windscreen.

'I don't think Monsignor Carolan knows this,' said Darragh. 'Is there a telephone?'

'There,' said Mrs Stevens, pointing urgently towards the Rochester Street corner, where at some stage one of Kate Heggarty's visitors had parked. 'Do you have any coppers, Father?'

Darragh hunted in his pockets and found only one George V penny. 'I can get you another,' said Mrs Stevens, rushing indoors.

Darragh told Mr Connors and Anthony to wait awhile—he had to call Monsignor Carolan. When Mrs Stevens was back with another penny, he jogged to the corner, delighted with the possibilities of the hour. He could do Kate Heggarty the intimate honour of saving her boy from Killcare and the automatic stigma of orphanhood.

In his excitement, his index finger seized in vain air before engaging and hauling round the number slot. He began to use his middle finger. Mrs Flannery answered and said the monsignor was in his study. Oh the promise of all this—car, boy, cave mother, wizard! Himself the Merlin who gave the boy-king the means of heroic life. So easy, so easy . . .

'Monsignor Carolan,' said Monsignor Carolan.

Darragh told him there might have been a mistake on the nuns' part, that Mrs Stevens had made it clear to him she would offer a home to the boy, and would raise him as a Catholic. It seemed there was no need for Killcare.

'Frank, Frank,' said the monsignor. 'She says that.'

'No, she's an honest woman, and I would make visitations and keep an eye on Anthony.'

'Stop it, Frank,' the monsignor roared. 'Stop it! You're hysterical!'

They shared a silence for a while. The monsignor broke it. 'The nuns who came to look at Mrs Stevens's are experts, Frank. Forgive me, I know you're an expert on everything, from women to black troops to God knows what. A bloody encyclopaedia, you are!' Darragh could hear the monsignor panting. 'You'll–bloody–kill–me–yet, Frank,' he yelled, a word at a time. 'The woman is poor, her husband's not there, she's already got five children, and she's not a Catholic. She wants him for the money the Commonwealth pays for foster care, Frank.'

'Monsignor, it doesn't seem to me . . .'

'Frank, I'm telling you. The people who know a thing or two have decided this. He's lucky to be taken in at Killcare. When his father comes back he can return home. But even if you were delivering the kid to the very pit of hell, on behalf of the arch-diocese I'm ordering you to do it. Do you understand, Frank? This is the end. I'm *ordering* you.'

Darragh covered his eyes with his non-phone-holding hands. The idea that he make a profound submission of soul and consign the child had its blind appeal. But, he thought, this isn't the end. He believed there must be ways to liberate the child.

'Are you going to Killcare, Frank?' the monsignor asked, a still, tired voice on the end of the line. 'Of would you prefer me to throw you to the archbishop?'

'I have no choice,' said Darragh. 'Do I?'

'The sooner we get you on retreat, son, the bloody better.'

Back at the house dispirited, he told Mrs Stevens that it was all arranged for Anthony at Killcare and couldn't be helped for now. Maybe later . . . He said this, 'Maybe later . . .' not to fob her off, but like a fellow-conspirator. At a level of his brain he was aware he was plotting with a plump, ordinary woman of non-Catholic background against a monsignor and nameless expert nuns. And he was willing to do it. That was a tendency he might expunge during his long and tedious retreat. Or perhaps not.

In any case, depression and anger possessed him as he got into the car, the middle of the front seat, allowing the window seat to Anthony. He patted the seat beside him for Anthony's sake, as if to say, 'Feel this luxury!' At the wheel, Mr Connors, jovially emitting such nicknames as 'Tiger,' 'Skeeter,' 'Popsy,' persuaded the frowning Mrs Stevens's brood to get down from various parts of his car and leave it free to move. They clapped when he managed to start the engine. As the Dodge began to draw away down The Crescent, in a street which seemed to refuse to carry in its blank bricks any of the weight of Mrs Heggarty's murder, the kids ran after it, shouting encouragement, and Anthony seemed cheered.

Driving down Parramatta Road towards town, Mr Connors told Anthony how well the nuns would look after him. 'Only you didn't have any brothers or sisters, did you? Well, now you'll have lots of brothers and sisters.'

'I only wanted a couple,' Anthony declared.

'Well, you'll have a couple of special mates, that's for certain. And the nuns will give you a big boy to yourself, to look after you. I've been up there. I've visited it with St Vincent de Paul.'

Anthony occasionally looked out, Darragh saw, at passing women toting or towing children along the shopfronts of the road. Current motherhood was a phenomenon all the way from Concord to Burwood to Petersham to Leichhardt. Darragh feared Anthony was thinking something along the lines of, 'If it's so plentiful and normal along here, how have I managed to lose it, this quantity. A mother.' The junior engineer in Anthony was awakened by their passage across Pyrmont Bridge, and the climax of the Harbour Bridge, its great steel arching like the flight of a sweet arrow towards the sun over North Sydney. Mr Connors knew how many bolts there were in it, and how only the other day a Yank in a Kittyhawk had flown beneath the bridge roadway. It was a great dare with the Yankee pilots!

Ultimately, through woodier and woodier northern suburbs, they were in the country. Beyond Hornsby, farmers kept their children on the edge of the road selling fresh eggs and oranges. 'They've escaped the rationing mania,' said Mr Connors with approval. Many dun hills gave way to the complex inland waters of the Hawkesbury River, and a long bridge, with a railway bridge *and* a train running parallel to it—another sign in Mr Connors's and even Anthony's eyes that the world was going to some trouble to accumulate its treasures before him. But then, more hillsides and their olive-green foliage, fascinating no doubt to a botanist but less so to an orphan and a priest.

At last a small post office store arrived, and visible beyond it the gothic sandstone of the orphanage. It was, thought Darragh, far too austere for an orphan from Homebush. Its architecture seemed designed more to affright than to mother.

'It's big,' he reassured Anthony, 'but that's only because it's a home for so many boys and girls.' Anthony began weeping, softly, so as not to appear ungrateful, as soon as they entered the polished-wood hallway. A statue of the Virgin by the door, delicate hands spread, seemed to offer young Heggarty the comfort of that which he could never again know on earth. A young nun showed them to the parlour with deep leather-covered armchairs in monastic black, and a desk. The boy's soft crying continued.

'Come on then,' said fatherly Mr Connors, helping Anthony to a chair. 'A lot of the kids in here have no mother and no father at all. Whereas your father will come back in a year or two and take you home.'

When this sensible idea did nothing to reach the small boy's grief, honest Mr Connors winced and exchanged a glance with Darragh.

At last a large, authoritative nun dressed all in black entered, papers in hand, and before she had reached the desk, said, 'Mother Augustine, gentlemen. Hello, Father. Come now, Anthony. That won't do!'

This command from a solemn presence did the trick, and

Anthony Heggarty, lost in a big black chair, achieved an awed composure. As for the nun herself, Mother Augustine, she was not awed at all by young priests or senior laymen, though she observed the forms of introduction and made note of their names as soon as she had sat down at the desk.

'You have the birth and baptismal certificates?' she asked Mr Connors, and Connors produced an envelope from his pocket.

'These are, of course, copies,' he said. 'The police . . . they didn't want Mrs Stevens or the nuns searching Mrs Heggarty's house for them.'

'Copies are excellent,' said Mother Augustine, reaching for them. She turned to the boy. 'You'll make your first communion here, Anthony,' she said. More than a promise, it sounded like a jovial command. 'Best to be brisk,' she murmured in Mr Connors's and Frank's direction. 'Causes fewer tears in the end.' She picked up a brass bell from her desk and rang it. Three children, two boys and a girl, aged ten or eleven years, entered the office.

'Paddy, Jim and Shirley will look after you, Anthony. Stand up. And your bag. Paddy, help him with his bag. If you wish to know anything, Anthony, ask these children. Oh dear heavens!'

For Anthony Heggarty, surrounded by his mentors under the pressure of the intentions of Mother Augustine and these unknown children, had urinated on the polished floor. His stricken eyes dared direct themselves at nobody other than Darragh. There was an extremity of desire in them, as if he believed that saving him was easy, and since Darragh was the Good Priest of the Playground, it was within his means. This terror, too, the strangler had made.

The drive back to Sydney could be engaged only at the cost of admitting to his soul an urgency to punish the violator and stran-

gler. What sort of man, presented with the bounty and honesty of
Mrs Heggarty, with that thirst for equity beneath green eyes,
would find the solution to her conundrum to be this: to constrict
her air, violently shut it off, to interdict the river of her blood as
well, to close her arteries? He wondered was it because of habits
of discipline, of tempering his taste for romanticism, of obeying
superiors even when their edicts did not pass the test of reason,
that he felt connected now by a tautened rope to the malefactor,
and felt that the quickest way to hauling him in might be, after
all, to go to the retreat house in Kangaroo Valley, since revelations could arise from passive submission as well as from active
rebellion. There must be some ultimate activity of course—
quietism was a temptation and a heresy. But revelation was
always unexpected—that was a long-established rule. 'Arise, and
go into the city,' God said to Paul, the persecutor of Christians,
when Paul was knocked from his horse by lightning or a flood of
light—the text of *The Acts of the Apostles* was a little obscure in
demotic Greek. But what was not obscure was that Paul had had
his enlightenment on a road, between Jerusalem and Damascus,
locked merely in the contemplation of his horse's hoof-beats.

   And Darragh began to grasp, as Mr Connors, making too
much conversation, drove him back to Sydney through forests
full of a brazen, questioning light, why he, like Paul, the former
Jewish flayer of Christians, had become a stranger to God. He
had not asked the correct questions, the questions a pilgrim
should ask. God, source of all I am and home to what I might be,
what would You have me know, and what have me do? And at
once he knew what he would do. That night, the eve of his depar-
ture for retreat, he must visit Mrs Heggarty's house, with no
object in mind than to bear home to the dead mother the message
of the son's anguish. This was something beyond the reasonable

net of what the monsignor would have him know, have him do. But he couldn't help that. It was something commanded by divinely implanted instinct. It was the same as to sneeze, to blink, to breathe: something above and something simultaneously below the poles of sin and virtue, will and submission.

CHAPTER EIGHTEEN

A ND SO HE SET out, unforbidden, after a solitary dinner, the monsignor absent, salving his soul at the table of one of the laymen. The Crescent, running die-straight east–west by the railway line, its embankments, its electric train stanchions, was, at half past seven at night, a contest between the homely smell of fried, rationed chops escaping the pore of the houses on the left, and the sintered, coaly metallic-electric aroma of rail lines to the right. But there was none of the warmth of raucous kitchens, of stew or vegetables or sago or bread pudding, about Mrs Heggarty's house, one of the twins separated by a fence of wood and wire, the shallow verandah full of the shadow of death. Three narrow strips of glass made up the front window where the bedroom always was in these houses, in this house as in Mrs Flood's. He hadn't paid particular note on his first visit, but now he knew that in there it had happened. Like a girl in a caution-ary tale about sin, she had given herself up to, of all the world's men, the exactly wrong fellow. Not the cynical fellow; not the normally main-chancing fellow. The lethal fellow. She had been struck by the thunderbolt of God's obscure will. It had avoided Mrs Flood, who had sinned lustily, and struck Kate Heggarty in her first lapse. And she had known as she fought the man that all her talk of dignity had been so much blather, that she could not have made a more extreme mistake. This thought gave him no joy at all, but deepened the poignancy of her loss.

Darragh opened the little wire gate to the side of the house and walked there in narrowed darkness, learning something, he believed, though he could not say what. The southern winter, barely begun, pricked at raw shave marks on his neck, and seemed to have pooled like a malign spirit around the sagging house where Kate Heggarty had brewed her last tea and smiled her last smile. How could Lance Bombardier Heggarty return here and remain sane?

Now into the backyard. The clothes lines ran slantwise across the night, one of them stretched tight with a timber prop. Down the yard, an iron shed slouched but with an exaggerated determination which almost promised it would still stand when Heggarty was at last released. Like a blessing from a well-meaning but immune heart, the sound of The Amateur Hour—to which the monsignor was probably at this moment listening at his parishioner's dinner table—surged across the dark from somebody else's kitchen, in momentary and doomed jolliness.

He nudged a laundry door and looked in at the cold washing coppers, and smelled the same smell he had got since childhood from his mother's laundry—Solvol, Reckitt's Blue, Sunlight Soap. Here *she* had attended to the pride of appearance, and achieved that cleanliness which is next to dignity, that quality which ensured that no child's mother said, 'Keep away from Anthony Heggarty—his clothes aren't properly laundered.' But there was only a ghost of warmth here, only a phantasm of Kate Heggarty retained in the fading scent of blue-bags and cornmeal starch. Not enough, and no declarations, no presence strong enough to explain itself and give instructions.

In deeper shadow of the narrow back verandah sat Lance Bombardier Heggarty's boyhood cricket bat—you could tell that by its age, and the sticking plaster around the handle, and the crack at the base. An inheritance for Anthony Heggarty. A bucket of clothes pegs kept it company. Relics of a marriage. Laundress and batsman, the notable incarnations of *mulier* and *homo Australis*. Over this little conjunction of objects in the near dark, Darragh wept. He raised a hand to the green-painted back door and pushed, but it was locked, and all further indications of the crime were locked within it. He walked down the yard towards the peach tree in its middle, hoping for some enlightenment beneath the cold wires of the clothes line. He still believed that she had infused all her familiar places with clues. This little back-yard geography offered something, but he could not sight it, it lay just around the angle of seen reality.

'Please God,' he said. 'Please God.'

In a retreat, in six or ten or twenty days of silence, the only word uttered being the recited office and the words of the liturgy of the Mass, something from this ordinary place might reveal itself.

She had left no trace for him in the air. He wiped his eyes with his right hand and stood still to assess whether this little rite gave him any clearer vision. When it failed to do so, he left by the side laneway, and out the wire gate to the browned-out street. Given that all window shades were drawn by order of the air-raid wardens, the most palpable reality was still the cooling odour of communal dinners, turning rancidly cold in the air. Darragh had given up that homeliness. The squalor of cheek-by-jowl domesticity. He was separated from his own human squalor by the thick walls of St Margaret's presbytery. Until the invaders came, he had no need to scrape congealed remnants in a sink. This is what it meant, he saw, to be a eunuch for the sake of Christ. And reflecting thus in The Crescent, he moved under the unlit streetlights, feeling his way by the pencils of light which evaded the best intentions of curtained rooms and which, later tonight, wardens under the management of Mr Conover would see it as their duty, moving about the streets, to eliminate.

On the pavement, a large hand descended on his shoulder, very nearly as a blow. He turned, and it was Ross Trumble. 'I saw you slinking along there, father of the people,' said Trumble. 'In a fucking cardigan tonight. Dressing humbly, eh?'

Trumble's fairish face and his breath as well were again heated by beer, hastily drunk somewhere else.

'Hello, Mr Trumble,' said Darragh. But he blushed too, caught in a strange endeavour some might think perverse, and others guilty.

'*Hello, Mr Trumble*,' Trumble repeated, and appealed to the dark railway embankment across the street. 'And everywhere this death bird goes creeping in his black cardigan, a woman dies. That poor little tart Heggarty. Do you think she's a poor little tart, or are you glad she got punished?'

Darragh burned with this insult, since Trumble didn't know that he, Darragh, was a flawed man, not a skilled robot of the Church, flawlessly uncompassionate.

'I think you ought to back off me, Trumble,' he said. 'I feel terrible enough about her and about Anthony.'

Trumble was a little surprised, but he rallied. 'The best girls are gone, and the people's chief hope is under fascist attack, but you have nothing better to do . . .'

His argument became leaden and died for a second, as he swallowed and moistened his dry mouth. Then he cast about him for something to say—one of his *argumenta ad hominem*. It was as if, while making up his mind what his next real decision would be, he must fill the space with the occasional music of his polemics.

'They told me,' said Trumble, 'that you had it in for me. You told the bastards about the chops. You really are a bastard. Visiting dead women in a cardigan. I know you blokes preach death-worship. Just look at your chief bloody image. Nailed-up pain. What a model to hold up to kids, eh? You got Rosie Flood. Did you manage to mess up that poor Heggarty sort, before her boyfriend strangled her?'

Darragh rallied under Trumble's normal hot breath and predictable interrogation.

'Her boyfriend,' asked Frank. 'Did you ever see him?'

Trumble seemed genuinely tickled. 'His Eminence as Sherlock Holmes! How do you know I'm not the monster? You told bloody Kearney I might be.'

'I didn't tell him that,' said Darragh. And then, as if by inspiration, 'Do you still believe everything the police tell you? Maybe you'll end up believing everything I tell you.'

Trumble shook his head. 'I know that bastard Kearney. He nearly had me in gaol in 1940. Now he comes round and tries to convince me I'm the fancy man. If I hadn't been out all night with a friend who's a journalist at the *Telegraph*, he would have had me for it, too. That bastard would like to hang me. Have me yelling, "Bless me Father" on the gallows. But he's only a straightforward cop, that Kearney.'

'*Straightforward?*'

'Yeah. You can see through him. You're the sort of bastard no one can see through.'

For a second Darragh had a giddy daydream of having Trumble write down and sign such a statement. It would amaze the monsignor, who found Darragh so transparent. 'You give me too much credit, Ross.'

'Don't bloody Ross me! You know, the day's not far off when we'll put you against the wall like we did to the priests in Madrid, and we'll put a hot bullet in your heart.' But Trumble paused and seemed to decide this would not be adequate. 'And still the ignorant will come creeping with their little handker-chiefs and mop up your blood and expect it to cure them of goitres.'

Darragh did not know where the impulse to confide in this hostile, half-tipsy Marxist came from. Darragh was God's storm-trooper only in Trumble's mind. In the monsignor's, in the vicar-general's, he was an ee-jit and a cautionary tale.

'I'm just another man, Ross. Just another confused battling yokel.'

'Oh yeah. You really loved it when I said that to you last time. Well, let me repeat, Sonny Jim. To me you *are* just another bloke. And there! You are!' And to emphasise the *there* he punched Darragh full force on the shoulder. But then he seemed to despair of blows. 'There's nothing I can do to you to make up for your bloody creeping influence on Rosie.'

'In the case of Mrs Flood,' Darragh told him, willing now to stoke the man's confusion of soul, his shoulder smarting, 'it wasn't me at work. It was something more than me.'

He was perversely delighted to see Trumble's certain fury return. When you strike again, he thought, I'll damn well strike you!

'Oh, save me from that I–am–but–an–instrument shit,' Trumble declared, showing in his maddened eyes how well

Darragh's line had worked. 'That makes me really fucking angry. I could beat the fucking certainty out of you.'

Darragh said, 'I think you might be more certain than me. We both try to live by great certainty, don't we?'

'Don't bloody say that,' shouted Trumble. 'That's utter bullshit! My certainties have a scientific, social and economic basis. Yours are fucking fairytales.'

'Maybe that's why I'm having a few problems with them,' Darragh admitted, ringing the changes now between divine messenger and ordinary fellow. Although, he noticed, even in the midst of all this yelling, it was easier to be frank with an enemy than with the guardians of the Faith.

Trumble asked, 'If you've got any doubts, why did you need to come hunting down Rosie and Kate?'

Darragh, the darkness of his rage a potent comfort, was enjoying himself. He had Trumble's head spinning, he could see. Darragh's mother had spoken in awe of his gentle father's Gaelic temper emerging in his youth, the power of his rage, his determination that the insulter should not walk away before blows were thrown and blood drawn. That madness was in him now, but he retained throughout his cunning in debate.

'Look, Ross,' he said, 'I believe in the flawed nature of humanity. I believe Stalin is as lustful for power as any man. I believe the Pope is subject to sin. You believe people are born perfect, and it's ownership that destroys them, that having it or not having it is all that makes them bad. You're more innocent than I am. You're touchingly innocent. You'd make a damn good student for the priesthood.'

'I can't bloody believe this,' said Trumble, casting his eyes to the mute-dark sky, and at a loss to take the discussion further, he threw a considerable punch at Darragh. It landed on the side of his neck, an improbable level of force and intent in it. Darragh, very satisfied, could not stop himself bending over, gagging, and thus inviting Trumble into his defences. It was easy for Trumble now to strike him again on the upper cheek, showing great accuracy for a man who had been drinking. It was as Darragh had read in the novels—the heavens lit up with whirling stars, and a bilious incredible day supplanted night. But he had his balance, at least, and grabbed the solidity of Trumble, driving him back in an imperfect but potent rugby tackle, the kind which the brothers of his boyhood would have considered a poor substitute to real sportsmanship. A short, half-smothered punch against his ear brought further foul comets into Darragh's vision. He began to pummel Trumble's kidney area, and stood up and reeled off one good blow against Trumble's left cheek. Even so concussed, he knew that this was not the Christian martyrs' way, to try to oppose one's own lions to the lions of the tyrant. The true way was to open one's breast to the claws, but Darragh could not manage it. He threw another truncated and worthy punch into the soft and—as he thought of it—beery flesh near Trumble's spine, where a rare area of flabbiness absorbed it and robbed it of some meaning. Then he pulled himself away and brought a short, satisfactory blow on Trumble's ear. But the man's forehead, fair, steely and dense, descended on Darragh's temple and proclaimed another brief, vicious, sickly day.

At that moment of pain, his anger departed. It occurred to him to ask what he was doing, brawling in a street, after hotel-closing, outside a dead woman's house. It means I must now take what he gives, Darragh concluded. Dull and vivid blows one after another. I am at last submissive, he declared to himself, with the faintest glow of pleasure and a larger fear of coming impacts.

But some ministers of mercy were all at once there, holding

him firmly by the shoulder, dragging Trumble off, and crying, 'Hang on! Whoa there! What the bloody hell!' Once he knew he was safe from further blows, he could tell at once these two men were plain-clothes policemen. They wore the suit, differentiated only by minutiae of pattern, which Inspector Kearney wore. They wore the same hat from Anthony Hordern's. Darragh saw the younger of the two men give Trumble a very effective crack across the back of the head, involving not just the fist but the forearm as well, and delivered with the laziness of long practice. 'What the fuck are you doing, Trumble? Beating up priests now? You ought to be fucking interned, you prick. Sorry, Father. Pardon my French.'

They were all saying that these days, all the profaners mild and heroic, even poor old Bert Flood. In this case, Darragh lacked the breath to forgive the policeman's French.

The older policeman told Trumble he was on a warning, he was watched, he was to go home. He ought to keep a bag packed too, because bastards like him could be interned any second. Just as well old Joe Stalin was on our side now, the younger suited cop remarked. Only thing that saved Trumble's rotten blood bacon. 'Unless you want to prefer charges, do you, Father?'

Darragh found the breath twice to say no. The older copper said he thought that was wise in these circumstances.

'What circumstances?' Trumble challenged.

'Well,' said the younger policeman, nodding towards Kate Heggarty's house.

'I didn't see him come out of there,' said Trumble, showing his solidarity with Darragh against the police.

'Don't argue with the bastard, Cliff. Haul off to buggery, Trumble.'

Trumble gathered his limbs, disordered by conflict, and began to slouch homeward up The Crescent. Still living with Bert Flood, it seemed. Brothers in lost love, of one kind or another.

Darragh, breathing, sore in the head but subject to no more false flashes of light, concluded the detectives wanted to get rid of Trumble because he did not hold any real interest for them. With him, their manner had been that of schoolteachers who subjected a bad student casually and daily to their contempt. But they found him, Darragh, more interesting, he surmised. 'Do you have a car here, Father?' asked the older policeman.

'I was just out for a walk,' said Darragh. It was so obvious— he knew from all the Saturday afternoon matinees that the murderer always returned. He could see in the older policeman's eye that this must be a valid principle, since there was a meaningfulness, and he turned to swap that meaningfulness with the younger policeman. Both of them were older than he was, and wise according to their way.

They said they had been keeping a watch on number 23, Mrs Heggarty's house. Indeed, their car was obvious now, under the embankment. Of course, given that the guilty did return, the police would keep their vigil, just as in the films. How could he have felt so unobserved? 'We saw you go in, Father.'

Both men then introduced themselves to him with a careful, wooden etiquette. The older policeman Soames, the younger Blainey. Darragh could tell instantly from a particular kind of incomprehension the secular always showed that they were not Catholics. There was no malice to it, rather a sort of wary astonishment. Priests were so used to seeing such manners in those who were not of the Faith, that some older clerics said you could tell, from the sanctifying grace in the eyes, who was and wasn't a Catholic. But to Darragh it was all a quirk of perception. Catholics knew how to fit a priest into the landscape. Others did not.

Soames asked him, 'Why did you go to number 23, Father?' Again a little incredulity in the *father*, arising in a man of perhaps fifty years who found himself calling a man of twenty-seven, bruised and in a cardigan, by that strange and potent honorific.

At once it was apparent, as pain faded, that there were no reasons that could be expressed to a plain-clothes policeman. A sort of wisdom told him to be frank.

'She was a parishioner of mine. I came to pray for her soul.'

'Oh yes,' said Soames. 'But you could have done that in the church.'

'At Mass. And in the church. That's right,' said Darragh.

'Do you usually come to the house of a dead person to pray?'

'Sometimes before their death. Sometimes after.'

'Yes,' said Soames, in a deadly neutral way. 'But you're not wearing vestments or any . . . you don't have your collar . . .'

'No. The truth is the monsignor would probably not want me to have come. But I wanted to pay tribute . . .'

'So you dressed as if you were just going out on a stroll?'

Darragh shrugged, conceding the point.

'But what did you think you'd find there?' asked Soames, his jaws blue even in this light beneath the brim of his hat, from the daily struggle between thorough shaving and the contrary force of his masculinity.

'I just don't know,' Darragh confessed. He engaged, by preference, Blainey's eyes. 'I felt so sorry for her. Her husband was taken prisoner. I doubt I can put it into so many words. I wish I could. Obviously.' He shrugged again, but they both waited for him to annotate what he had already said. 'When something like this happens, I feel anger against the man who did it. I feel disappointment that I was not able to . . . well, somehow prevent it. Find a better path.' That sounded pious, he thought;

in a way the average Australian policeman would not like.

'That's in your statement to Inspector Kearney,' Soames announced, almost as a request for something newer.

Darragh said, 'I can't tell you anything further, Mr Soames.'

'You didn't interfere with anything in there, did you?' asked Blainey.

'No.'

'Did you go inside the house?'

'It was locked.'

'Do you have a key?'

'No. *No.*' What a concept for them to favour—that he'd creep the vacated rooms! But they were right. If he'd had a key, he would have.

'You're sure you don't have a key, sir,' said Soames, suspending Darragh's clerical title until he was sure about this.

'I don't. I would have told Inspector Kearney.'

Soames said, 'It's not good though, for a priest to be prowling around an empty house like that. Cliff and I are experienced fellows, Father. And all our experience says it's not a good idea, you being here like this. There are enough . . . what would you call them? . . . enough little *items* running between you and Mrs Heggarty. I'm sure you know more ignorant fellows than Blainey and I might draw an unwarranted conclusion.'

Darragh was weary enough, ashamed enough, unsatisfied enough to tell them to draw whatever conclusion they chose. But he said nothing. More ignorant fellows were welcome to draw their unwarranted conclusions.

'We'd take you home,' Soames offered, 'but we won't be relieved for another hour.'

Of course, Darragh insisted he was happy to walk home. His delivery by police car would have confirmed the monsignor's

desperate sense that he had on his hands a rogue curate. And the
monsignor would soon enough hear of this encounter outside
number 23 from Kearney, his brother on the secular level, a
kinsman in enviable, shared worldliness. Darragh nodded to
number 23 and said, 'I was just hoping to pick up . . .' But he was
as inadequate as earlier at describing what. 'That it happened . . .
that's what I can't believe.'

Blainey said, 'Yes. Look, you'd better get cracking, Father.'

Darragh had nothing further to say and turned to go. Soames
called out to him. 'Sometimes these things are done by blokes
who have pretty straightforward ideas. Anger gives men and
women strength you wouldn't believe.'

Kearney had argued the same way. But Darragh had nothing
wise to utter in response, except another muttered goodnight.
And so he turned back, a shadow in a cardigan, priest, brawler,
disbeliever in Kate Heggarty's death, through streets where
almost from house after house he could hear the performance
of a yodeller on The Amateur Hour. Amateur hour. He had just
provided it.

CHAPTER NINETEEN

AFTER SAYING EARLY Mass for the repose of souls and capture of the guilty, he had a train to catch at a quarter past eight to make the connection at Central with the half-past-nine down the coast. The monsignor had his own Mass to say at eight o'clock, and Darragh met him briefly while divesting in the sacristy, as the monsignor tied his cincture.

'Monsignor, I have to tell you. I went to Mrs Heggarty's place last night. The police found me. I'm sorry about that.' As Darragh spoke, the monsignor's face sagged and his skull beneath his strands of hair took on the seamless hue of exhausted anger.

'I'm sorry for all the embarrassment to you. But it's a shock, isn't it, to find one of your penitents has been strangled . . .'

'She wasn't penitent, that's the point.' A suspicion entered the monsignor's eye. 'Are you going to Kangaroo Valley?'

'Yes. This morning.'

The monsignor exhaled. 'You had better come back a changed man, Frank.'

The monsignor had had the grace to whisper, but the altar

boys were beginning to sense his fury and to listen in. The monsignor put his lips close to Darragh's ear. 'I hate it that I can't predict what you'll do, Frank.'

'I hate it too, Monsignor.'

For this morning, after a little early reflection, he could see the fallacy of his behaviour. He had been wrong-headed enough, he confessed to himself, to think that to be a fool for Christ was better than to be wise after the manner of this earth. But he had tried to bring that trick off last night, and it had been a catastrophe. It seemed an outrageous vanity to believe that by breathing in the air of number 23's side lane and backyard, he could achieve more wisdom. And if he were set on being a fool, why try to explain himself away as a rational fellow to two policemen? You could not act on some ill-advised fervour and then expect sensible men and women to accept your explanation for it, so that you were left justifying yourself, in the darkness of The Crescent, like a high-school debater.

Before he left for Strathfield Station, he wrote a long note for Mrs Flannery. If an American chaplain called, would she kindly tell him that Father Darragh had been unexpectedly called away, and would telephone him as soon as he could. Imperilled Gervaise would have to wait Darragh's return.

Changing trains at Central, he went up long stairs to the country platforms, where it seemed a thousand soldiers were bidding goodbye to tribes of women and infants. Thousands of tales here too, of loyalty and folly, and if he could absorb them all, perhaps he could compete with the monsignor and Sergeant Kearney for being wise according to the manner of this earth.

The war itself and the fields of peril were, however, north and north-west, so there were hardly any soldiers and no dramatic tension on Darragh's southward train, with its old-fashioned third-class carriages and its unglamorous number 34 engine, the pony of iron horses. Darragh recited his office with the new energy of a self-declared parish clown. But as he read his way through the small hours of Prime, Terce, Sext, None, he was prey again to the idea that as much as he might have discomfited the monsignor and incurred the attention of an appropriately vigilant police, he had by his indefinite mission to number 23 kept faith with Mrs Heggarty. This was in its way both a welcome and a disturbing suspicion. It seemed to compel him to further acts of foolishness and disobedience.

Beyond the window, southern Sydney factories, having rusted in the Depression, looked newly redeemed by war. Girls in overalls wore business-like scarves on their heads, the kind Mrs Heggarty had worn the day Darragh had visited her for tea, as they walked from one dismal industrial hangar to another. By Vespers, a vivid blue Pacific could be seen to the left. The train was rolling south of Cronulla, ascending the sandstone plateau of low scrub with wonderful mountains a little off to the west. Vast places. How could the Japanese credibly claim every square inch of this? The British had, some one hundred and fifty years before, and yet when you saw the scale of things, the coastal valleys, the ranges, the breadth of the earth beyond, the idea that possession could be asserted seemed hard to believe. If the cities fell, he imagined, these mountains would harbour rebels, exactly as in the Philippines. There were in Poland, so the news came sporadically, resistance groups with priests. He was taken by the allure, the grand, moral simplicity of such a life. The Japanese though, unless he found his sure voice, would probably shoot him while he was still explaining himself, and make him an irrelevant contributor to any dissent from their world order.

Even in this reflection, he decided, lay all the contradictory impulses of his no doubt immature nature. There was a way, he was certain, to honour both Kate Heggarty and his priesthood. The retreat would help him reconcile them. And after the encounter of last evening, he was ready for some such revelation. He could not juggle these questions in a world where at any stage an enraged Communist might throw a punch at him, or police-man misinterpret his reasons for being abroad by darkness in The Crescent. He must reduce his grief and intentions and tendencies to a unity of the kind which shone from the pages of that great medieval Aristotelean, St Thomas Aquinas. No more acting on wild, Platonic shadows of feeling. Unity please, for everyone's sake, dear God! And if it were achieved, he had no doubt he would more readily appease and rescue the soul of Mrs Heggarty.

The railway line swung back to the coast. Saying Compline, reciting the '*Te lucis ante terminum*' by heart, Darragh saw the coal mines in the hillsides, the great cartwheels of apparatus which drew the coal trucks from below. The pits were reported to be the venue for a primal fight between the children of God and the children of darkness—Catholic Labor unionists, usually called the industrial groupers, and the Communists. Everyone knew the Communists considered the coal mines the cockpit for the establishment of the Communist state, and the Catholic men, who wanted merely social justice and not overthrow, were inevitably locked in political battle with them. Union ballot boxes were stolen or protected by armed factions, and pitched battles at dark of night involved bike chains and cricket stumps. This sunny autumn morning, however, the coal mines seemed to be exemplars of industry, the great cable-drawing wheels grind-ing above the Pacific.

The train dropped down to the town of Wollongong, where the steel mill sat right up against the blue sea. The coastal range was close here, and blue and dominant, and a little way south, as the train reached a bush siding, Darragh, his office completed, pulled his bag down off the wire rack and got out.

A Franciscan friar, brown-robed, white-cinctured, waited in his sandals by some milk cans on the siding. He seemed to be about the monsignor's age, and nodded to Darragh as if there were nothing remarkable about a curate from Strathfield; indeed, as if he had come to the station this forenoon more for the drive itself than the opportunity to meet such a normal phenomenon as a young priest needing a retreat.

'Father Matthew,' he said, 'Got everything, Father? Good.' He escorted Darragh to a Ford truck, in the back of which sat milk cans and a bale of fodder, and told him to lift his bag into the back as well and take the front passenger seat.

The friar drove and they ground their way up verdant valleys. 'The worst drought in Australian history has just broken,' said Father Matthew. 'If the Japs come, they'll inherit an emerald coast.'

Darragh felt he quite liked this hard-fisted monk. He had the bullish neck of a country boy, a good footballer. He would have made a credible and authoritative pub-owner.

'Your retreat master is Father Anselm,' said the monk, Matthew. 'He's a really gentle old bloke. Sometimes he might seem a little simple-minded, even our students poke mullock at him a bit. But my advice is, listen to him carefully. Because the truth can be simple, can't it?'

'I hope so,' said Darragh.

'All I know is the cathedral themselves rang us, so I understand there's some kind of shadow. But a fellow who doesn't get in some sort of trouble . . . well, God loves a rebel, I like to think. I hope you have a type of renewal here. You won't see much of me though, because I'm the bursar and I run the dairy farm.'

And his hands on the wheel could have been a dairy farmer's hands too.

'That woman in Sydney who was strangled,' said Darragh.

'Yes.'

'She was my parishioner. I'd written her some letters.'

'Boy!' said Father Matthew.

But Darragh for once was not tempted to explain further, to exhort Matthew to think the best. It seemed to him Matthew tended to.

'I just want to know when they release her body. It'll be in the papers. My parish priest will bury her. I'd like to know when all that happens. Not knowing would throw me off kilter.'

Father Matthew inhaled noisily, pleased to be safe on a monastery farm. 'I read the daily paper. There's no reason I can't let you know.'

'And remember her soul in your Masses.'

'I will,' agreed Matthew.

The retreat house was also a seminary for Franciscan students, and a monastery for a number of monks. Darragh, said Father Matthew, would lead the same life as the students—silence, reflection, but on top of that a daily conference with Father Anselm. He could do a little work on the farm, if he liked, cutting the chaff, for example. The students did that sort of thing. Sometimes periods of physical labour were of benefit to the soul, said Matthew.

The red-brick monastery appeared before them among gum trees. With a central garden and a cloister, it looked like a 1940s attempt at encompassing the medieval tradition. The wattles in the garden still displayed a profusion of sensual yellow which St Francis himself, by all accounts, would have delighted in. But the lanky, shedding eucalypts spread the baked clay of the court-yard with sloughed, tattered bark and thin-bladed leaves of a type St Francis had never laid eyes on and might have taken a little time to accustom himself to.

A muscular Franciscan brother carried Darragh's bag to his room, and told him that the students were about to recite the small hours in the chapel. Putting his soutane on, Darragh joined them, occupying one of the chairs at the back of the chapel where local laypersons who came to Mass sat during ceremonies. The students faced each other in classical monastic style, occupying stalls which ran very nearly the length of the chapel. But there were no more than fifteen of these young men, Darragh saw. They were exempt from military service even in this national crisis, but they all seemed fervent, none of them motivated by this benefit more apparent than real.

Afterwards, in the refectory, he was shown a place at the top table, where he sat in his black soutane at the end of a row of brown friars, beside Matthew and near a slim old man who con-centrated fixedly and delicately on his food. Anselm, he guessed. He was to meet him at five o'clock, the official start of his retreat.

Left to himself after the monks and students walked out of the refectory, he spent five minutes in silent reflection in the chapel. The students were free to talk now and, having stripped off in their rooms, could be heard running out in football jerseys and shorts to play soccer or kick a rugby ball. Darragh took advan-tage of an earlier remark of Matthew's that there were first-class walks to be had around the monastery. From the escarpment above one of the nearby gullies, he had said, you could see all the way to the Pacific.

Darragh took the way indicated by a scarring of pathway on the edge of the bush. There was an implicit promise in the tree-spaced plateau that here was the room to consider at length things he had not had the time to deal with. The business, again, of reducing things to one. The touchstone of unity could be picked up like a jewel at the base of the great Australian unity of nature. So one hoped; so one yearned. Here could be unified Gervaise, the black theologian and deserter; Sergeant Fratelli, the angel of thunder; Kate Heggarty and her son, and all else. The autumn light on the track was wonderfully strong, uncondi-tional. With the summer flies gone, it fell on Darragh like the purest mercy. He became a mute walker; no clever prayers escaped him. After two pleasantly sweaty miles, the earth fell away. He stood on a cliff of sandstone, with forested gulfs and green streams running off towards the blatant blue of the ocean. Surely, in such absolute tones and uncompromising distances, the great truth could be seized.

He expected it even on the way back from the sublime view. Nowadays, the sun had begun to decline by four, and when he went back to the monastery and knocked on the door of Father Anselm's study, he noticed on entering the tall shafts of the forest cast long, sharp, eastward-yearning shadows beyond the windows.

Anselm proved to be the tranquil, fixed chewer from the top table in the refectory. He showed Darragh to a chair by a little table covered with baize. The books in the shelves behind him looked old, heavily bound, lacking dust covers, as if Anselm had long since ceased pestering himself with ideas or with entertainment.

'To begin the retreat,' he said to Darragh, and kept silence for many seconds. 'To begin the retreat,' he then repeated, 'we must say some prayers together.' He took our his rosary beads and led Darragh in a decade of the Joyful Mysteries. The Joyful Mysteries suited Anselm, for the trace of a smile did not leave his face at any stage. 'Glory be to the Father,' he said when the decade was done, 'and to the Son, and to the Holy Ghost. As it was in the beginning, it is now and ever shall be, world without end, Amen.'

Darragh put his own rosary beads back in his pocket. 'Young man,' Anselm then said, 'I have some advice from the cathedral that you have had a hard time. Is that so?'

'Yes.'

Anselm said, 'Indeed, but not as hard as that poor child.' It was obvious he meant Kate Heggarty. 'But you have the duty of being one of the bystanders, and to a young man that can seem hard, an experience of conflicting voices, even for a priest. You've come here in some confusion?'

Darragh admitted it.

'Good,' said Anselm. 'God has given you an honest nature. He may have given you a vain one as well, but you would not be the only young chap that he so endowed. I was certainly similar. I did not want to be a bystander. I had the vanity, too, which said that salvation of the world was all my task. It is a terrible, scruple-ridden tendency. It is the work of fervour, but also of pride.'

'Yes,' Darragh assented. This old man, he thought, seemed a genuine seer.

'Do you and I think God exists to guarantee the two of us that we won't be failures? Think of this, my son. We were never guaranteed by Christ that we could save even ourselves. We were given hope, mind you, but no guarantee. And yet we demand success. Who are we, you and I, to demand success? We're nobodies. Aren't we?'

'That's true,' said Darragh.

'I say this, young fellow, not to make you more concerned, but to make you calmer. Christ did not wish you to suffer as you have chosen to suffer. He said, "Sufficient to the day is the evil thereof." That is, we may be sure to encounter the evil of the day without searching ambitiously for it. That may be why the cathedral wanted you to come here. They saw that you had become feverish.'

'And they're right,' Darragh admitted. He felt heady, as if the old monk could hold out the prospect of the oneness he wanted.

Anselm looked at Darragh with his pale, light-blue eyes, and asked, 'Did you desire that young woman? Your parishioner? It's not a shameful thing to admit. If we were not all capable of desire, our vows would mean nothing.'

'I think I did, Father,' Darragh said. 'But I was concerned for her salvation as well.'

'As any true admirer should be, Father Darragh.'

'I'm also concerned for her son.'

'Why? He's with the good sisters I believe.'

'A woman in Homebush was willing to take him in. But she was not Catholic.'

'And thus perhaps an unsuitable guardian,' the old priest suggested.

Darragh shook his head. He was not ready to yield that point yet. 'It might be that the boy would have been a better Catholic in a household where he was happy.'

'That's a very secular view.'

'I know. It's the sort of doubt I'm often prompted to.'

'Take all your doubts,' said Anselm, raising both his hands and making an encompassing motion, 'doubts of your superiors, doubts of articles of faith, and submit them at the feet of Our Blessed Mother. Her mercy is not the mercy of this world. Her compassion is not the mere compassion of neighbours. Commit the boy to her, also. And then . . .' He paused and dreamed away for ten seconds, in a way that reminded Darragh of the old exor-cist who had once urged him to be a merciful confessor. 'And *then*,' he resumed at length, 'live for the moment.'

'Ah!' said Anselm after Darragh had blinked. 'You are sur-prised to hear me say that? It's the sort of thing young men and women terrified of the war say. It's the cry of an unjust genera-tion. But in another sense it's the cry of those who are in peace. We do not own the past, with its grief and sin. The past imper-fect, as the grammarians say. We do not own the future. We own only a rag of time, this moment named the present. And to the present, I know, God gives the necessary grace—to enable us to glorify that second in His name. I learned in time that if I lived in any other way than the embrace of the divine second, I would certainly be damned. I was once in battles . . . in battles, a man can live only in the second, and sometimes not even in the second. I learned in battles . . . I learned in terrible battles that it is not necessary to expand the present with false imaginings and with peevishness, and the frenzy of our lives.'

He seemed to drowse off in remembrance of things known only to him and perhaps to the late Sergeant Darragh. Then he resumed. 'Time is like a meal—each mouthful is separate and glorious. Even the second of our death is to be lived and imbued with grace. That is why we accept . . . we accept what is on the plate. We accept the orders of our superiors when they defy reason. We do not give way to a fear that they might again sound unreasonable in the future. That is something to leave to the future. The limits of what we are permitted to do *now*—that's what we accept. If not, then the world and its manifold voices will certainly send a young man like you insane, and distract you from your priesthood. I know this because I have already trodden the path . . .'

The old man swallowed. This stratagem he held out—acceptance, and the certainty of grace of the moment—was splendid, and tempted Darragh the way desire might.

But you are damaged, Darragh was tempted to say. You are shell-shocked in some way, and your spiritual plan is the spiritual plan of the shell-shocked. It is achievable within the limits of your nature and your monastic career. My nature is not docile even when I play at it!

Thus, he secretly asked himself in fear and for the first time, 'Can I long remain a priest, and will I see the face of God?'

This question occupied the first three days of his retreat. He envied old Anselm, the peace the man had achieved. It was the triumph of one soul, a triumph suited to a monastery rather than to the rough-and-tumble of a parish. But he was not a Franciscan monk, living in reflection and devotional routine. He was a secular priest, visiting the Misses Clancy and Mrs Flood, mixing it in sick rooms with all types, walking the uncloistered street and subject to blows from Trumble. Occasionally, Darragh would feel a surge of optimism—yes, I could become that humble old man, the man who gives his seamless attention to every spoonful of time, to every obscure instant. And the reward would be, he was sure, some revelation. He would live to see the killer's face and revel in the capture.

But the wilful complexity of his nature would recur to him at odd moments: after a spartan breakfast, on his silent afternoon hike, or in the middle of the Vespers chant in the chapel. He could *not* become Father Anselm. He hadn't been chastened and simplified by the artillery barrages of the Great War. It was not simply that he was innocent in the wrong way, nor that he'd bristled with rashness. It was that he refused to delude himself that over a lifetime he could render the crass complications of his soul into that particular one thing, the joyful, smiling gratitude for the new second, already, in any case, fled.

Each morning, feeling halfway like an impostor, he said Mass at a small side chapel, assisted by two Franciscan students, one to ring the bell, one to raise the tail of his chasuble as he in turn raised the consecrated Host, the body and blood of Christ, his Friend, Saviour and God. And even at this moment he knew that his prayers were contrary to Anselm's great tenet of composure-in-Christ. They rushed to present to God the question of how the killer of Kate Heggarty could be found, and how soon. The question still placed a massive personal weight on him, and put paid to Anselm's great proposition that the Moment + Grace = Peace of Soul.

One morning, Father Matthew murmured to him after breakfast, 'Body's been released. Funeral's today, Frank.'

There was a persistent mist that day on the great plateau above the sea. Darragh lived in its midst in fragile numbness. She who had wanted dignity had become a byword for indignity! The recitation of his breviary became a long plaint for the redemption of her soul. The blue-and-white Virgin Mother who had always been like a member of his family, a prescence of childhood and yet remoter than Mars, could not be imagined as one who would reject Kate Heggarty's last, panicked regrets, or judge her for the confusion of her strangled mind.

So this day of the funeral continued as one hung between times and seasons, and the moments went, embraced or not, and graced or not.

The funeral was photographed by the newspapers, Darragh found out, since each day Father Matthew permitted him to take a glimpse at the monastery's *Daily Telegraph*. There was a confused picture of the monsignor, large in his lacy surplice, solemn

in his biretta, sprinkling the coffin on which a small scatter of
flowers lay. So she was in the earth now, despite all his impatience for this revelation whose nature he could barely specify.

Yet a Saturday came. And a Sunday.

After a midday meal of mutton and mint sauce on Sunday, as
the students and monks left the refectory, Father Matthew, dairy
farmer, again approached him at his place at table. He muttered
an invitation for Darragh to meet him in his study.

It proved to be a farmer's office—stock books, a pile of bills
waiting to be dealt with, journals, a calendar advertising dairy
feed, and by a bookshelf a tin can which claimed to contain a
drench suitable for use on cattle. Matthew went to the desk and
raised the *Sunday Telegraph*. The front page carried a horrifying
headline about an Australian ship sunk in the Sunda Strait with
great loss of men. Race results from Randwick, a banner promised, were further back in the paper, displaced by this futher
tragedy of the war. Father Matthew found the page within the
paper, and folded it back. 'Frank, I'm sorry to show you this, but
the cathedral called and said you should be told. We all know
that this is an anti-Catholic rag. The vicar-general at St Mary's
doesn't want you to take this too hard. Naturally, he wasn't too
happy. He said, you know . . . young fellows can be . . .'

'Imprudent,' Frank supplied, hearing his own thunderous
heart.

'CATHOLIC PRIEST HELPS POLICE IN STRANGLER
MURDER.' A lesser headline said, 'Exchanged Letters with
Murdered Woman.' He read the article a careful sentence at a
time, each word occupying seconds. Detective Inspector Kearney
of the CID had confirmed that the police had found a letter from
Father Francis Darragh at the residence of the murdered woman.
Other sources indicated that the priest had been intercepted

during a night-time visit to the premises. He had been involved in a scuffle outside the house and then approached by police on watch, and spoken with. Inspector Kearney had refused to say whether the priest was under a shadow.

At first reading the report felt weightily bad to Darragh, and he knew that a second reading would only reveal extra burdens of shame. But he sat and read the piece again, as a penance, to the end. The archbishop's office had told the newspaper that Father Darragh had been sent away for a time of reflection at a monastery. The vicar-general had made it very clear to the *Sunday Telegraph* that Father Darragh would speak to the police further should they require it. So they had got even by publishing a picture of the vicar-general.

Darragh was not aware, until it happened, that he was capable of groaning. 'It's a bugger of a thing,' said Father Matthew, the dairy farmer. 'At least no one gave them a photograph of *you*.'

'My mother,' said Darragh. 'It will kill my mother.' He could imagine Aunt Madge absorbing it, but Mr Regan, who had experienced the lechery of Yanks, and his mother, who had sent him through the seminary, relinquishing the chance of grand-children—they must be bewildered and suffering. 'Would it be possible to book a trunk call?'

'I'm sure we can do it through the local exchange,' said Father Matthew. He picked up the phone, cranked its handle, spoke to someone named Nora, discussed dairy cattle prices and Nora's children, said he wanted to book a call—he turned away from the receiver to get Mrs Darragh's telephone number from her dazed son—and ultimately hung up. 'The trunk call's booked for four o'clock,' said Matthew. 'Is there anything I can do?'

'I think . . . I need to reflect,' said Darragh. 'Maybe a walk . . .'

'And you're seeing Anselm at five?'

'That's right.'

'Did I mention Anselm was wounded and gassed? In France.'

Darragh thought with longing of such great, simplifying events.

He took the hiking trail again. There was in the Australian bush today, after yesterday's blankness of fog, an impassive air. The eucalypts gave the sense not only of being pre-Christian and thus indifferent, but pre-human and thus doubly indifferent. The trees, tall in knowledge, continued to keep to themselves all that Darragh had no doubt they possessed. The idea of an answer encoded among these great, shaggy-barked, smooth-fleshed shafts was sustaining, and he would not like to have been stripped of that expectation. He would not have minded being, for the next moment, hour, or forever, motherless Adam, and for this neutral vegetation to cover the entire planet not already covered by the chiding blue of the distant sea.

His mother and father had wished for him a career as a lawyer, a doctor, the sort of man whose life was unaffected by seasonal shifts, and of course, a father of a smiling family. They were good enough Catholics to accept it as God's will when he announced to them at sixteen his apparent calling to the priesthood. He had already fulfilled one ambition for them, having won in the Leaving Certificate exam an Exhibition—an all-paid scholarship to Sydney University, to the faculty of his choice. There had been no such exemption of fees for the seminary. Yet his mother, out of her savings and her war widow's pension (his deceased father having been considered, in view of his foreshortened life, a victim of the Great War) had seen him through the seminary, had bought his soutane, his surplice, his *Liber Usualis*—the book of plainchant—his textbooks of philosophy and theology, moral and doctrinal, his own *Summa Theologica*, his black suit, his black stock and celluloid white collars. What did she think today? The *Telegraph*'s story reeked of his infatuation, one way or another, with Kate Heggarty, and it was now clear to him, with the secular voice of journalism ripping away all self-deception, that indeed he had been, and indeed he still was infatuated.

At four o'clock he returned to Father Matthew's study to face what might be motherly reproach or, something worse, the lack of reproach. Father Matthew asked the woman at the telephone exchange if she would mind not listening to this conversation, because it was about matters to do with the archdiocese of Sydney. 'You always have to do that,' he murmured, one hand over the mouthpiece, in Darragh's direction. 'She listens to every-thing, but she's a good Catholic . . .' Something on the line had claimed Matthew's attention again, and he said into the receiver, 'Wait a second.' He handed the phone to Darragh.

It was Aunt Madge on the other end. 'Frank, you sound like you're in the other room,' she said, as if the entire point of this trunk call was to demonstrate the miracle of the telephone. She was breathless, as most people were, with the seriousness of trunk calls, with their expense, and the inroads they were said to make upon vital military communications. 'I hope you are well, dear Frank. Look, we read the paper. Believe me when I say it means nothing. It's always been an anti-Catholic rag, and like all rags it'll be tomorrow's steak wrapping, or cut up into strips to be used on backsides in country shouses. Don't let them make you feel shame, Frank. Do you hear? Now I'll get your mother. She's standing right here.'

Darragh's mother said, 'Darling. Are you well?'

'I'm well. I'm only worried about you.'

'I'm in first-class form,' asserted Mrs Darragh. 'It's always been an anti-Catholic rag, that *Telegraph*.' This was the antiphon Catholics were used to uttering when newspapers printed tales of scandal within the Church.

He said, 'It's a poor return for you, Mama, after all the years of expense in the seminary. I keep on thinking of the chalice you and Aunt Madge bought for my ordination.' Gilt and gold plate with enamelled medallions on sconces of the handle—the Lamb of God, the IHS (*Iesos Hristos Soter*, Jesus Christ Saviour). A miraculous vessel. A grail. And it must have cost his mother and Madge at least £50. Now it spent most of its year in a cupboard at St Margaret's sacristy. He sometimes remembered to bring it forth and use it at Mass at Easter or Christmas.

'It's the insinuation of it all,' said his mother. 'You can't help that the woman went to confession to you, can you? They just like to insinuate. You wonder if anything they say is the truth, even about the war.'

'Oh, I think a lot of that is reliable,' Darragh sadly assured her.

'They talk about a scuffle. Did anyone hit you, Frank?'

'I'm not hurt, Ma. It was just a local eccentric.'

'Now, don't you worry,' she said, a true warrior woman. 'No one is going to take any notice of this. Mr Regan was just in here and he said that everyone he's spoken to thinks it's ridiculous. They all know you, darling.'

Then they're doing well, Darragh thought. But it would be too cruel to say so to his mother. So they continued, for the remaining permitted minute of their trunk call, to play what Darragh thought of as a form of tennis of consolation—'I'm concerned for you,', 'But I'm only concerned for you.' The kindly myth that no damage had been done was piled up, house-of-cards-wise, in the ether between the Kangaroo Valley monastery and the Darragh bungalow in Rose Bay. Then the line was cut.

When Darragh went into Father Anselm's study that night, the old man looked at him with an acute and, for the first time, knowing kindliness in his eyes. 'I believe, young Darragh, you are in a hard position. A priest who falls, even for the moment, into the hands of the weekend press . . .'

What Darragh was most certain of, now that his follies had been published and there was no further need to keep him hidden, was that he would be released from his retreat after eleven days, on the coming Friday, to enable him to do the Saturday confessions and Benediction, and the early Sunday Masses. And so it happened. On Friday afternoon, the vicar-general called and said that the retreat was considered concluded, and that Darragh was to take the Saturday morning train back to Sydney. The cheering aspect of this recall was that it meant the cathedral did not expect him to appear in this coming Sunday's papers.

His last session with Father Anselm was five o'clock on Friday evening.

'It's possible,' the old monk told him in conclusion, 'for a man to be involved in scandal through very little fault of his own. His strongest impulse, his simplicity of heart, betrays him. But the world does not know how to use a simple heart.'

Father Anselm seemed for a time to think about unnamed instances, perhaps on battlefields, where the world had tried to violate with steel his own simple heart. 'It's the reason priests get hardened as they age. They were taken as fools in youth, and don't want it to happen again.' He thought about this phenomenon awhile, too. 'You bear for Christ this cross of notoriety. With any good fortune, it'll be a temporary affliction. I have in a long life, Father Frank, seen men bear themselves with dignity even when there are no grounds for dignity left. You must bear yourself with dignity now, administering the sacraments, giving good sermons, visiting the sick, living simply. And show your parishioners that you are conscious of no deliberate shame, or if you are, that you have taken account of it.'

That evening, after dinner, Father Matthew stopped him outside the refectory and took him to his office and poured him a whisky. 'I've got to say I wouldn't want to be in your position, mate,' said Matthew, and Darragh felt a vague and yet enjoyable vanity at being seen as a man on a frontline. 'I'm sure you've got the heart for it, but it's hard to face people, and you'll be facing a lot of them at Mass on Sunday. What'll you say to them?'

'I haven't thought of that,' said Frank, putting down his glass. It was a daunting idea. 'What do you reckon, Matthew? Do I address the subject? Or do I just give a regular Sunday sermon? Faith, hope and charity. The sacraments. The Blessed Virgin . . . Say this had happened to you—would you mention the *Telegraph*?'

'Some of your parishioners would want you to stand up for yourself. Some will have morbid interest. It's a hard one. But, bloody hell, I think I'd tell the truth and mention anti-Catholic newspaper talk—that sort of thing. I'd reckon you're entitled to say that.'

'Do I speak of the woman?' asked Darragh.

'That'd be brave. But look, even down this way, even in a country town, there's a new and dangerous air about. We used to visit the big world in the picture shows, but now the pictures have come to us. In the form of the Yanks. In the form of the Japs as well. I tell you, Frank, I'm glad I've got the dairy farm to concentrate my mind.'

CHAPTER TWENTY

HOME AFTER LUNCH on Saturday, Darragh found himself treated with a sort of edgy awe by Mrs Flannery, who gave him a canned salmon sandwich to compensate for his missed meal. Captain O'Rourke had called, and had reported that 'the person in question', who had been 'sentenced at court-martial', had been 'shipped north with a penal battalion'. These were words she read from notes she had taken, raising her eyes wonder-struck at 'court-martial', as if it were the measure of how utterly transformed Darragh now was.

Invigorated to know that Private Aspillon still breathed, Darragh washed his face and hands, put on his cassock, and went across to the church to hear confessions. As he approached his confessional, he was aware of the normal three or four pews of queued penitents. Some looked at him sideways; there was a shining fixity in the faces of the older women there. Yes, he had been in the papers. But they were sure the papers were wrong! Their loyalty abashed him. But there must have been some drawn into the ambit of his confessional by his notoriety, or even the possibility that being under question himself, he would not be too severe with them. Carrying his stole, he paused at the middle door of the confessional, kissed the cross embroidered on the purple, entered, closed the door on himself in this small, shadowy space, and took his position on the chair which enabled him to hear with equal ease confessions on the right and the left.

A shiver possessed him as his mind, his sacramental intent, settled itself to hear the whispered shame of his congregation. Whispers of desire and meannesses of love and of spirit entered the space where he sat. He told the masturbating boys that when they met their wives in ten years time, they would be ashamed of having yielded to their weaknesses now. Virtuous women who confessed to pride—the most suspicious confessions of all, since sometimes when women mentioned pride they also implied they had much reason for it—plagued his ears and eroded his spirit. He was aware of an impatience in his voice, and a slight astonishment in response from the other side of the wire grille, of the kind a child shows when a favourite and indulgent uncle becomes severe. He imposed the penalties appropriate to these small sins, but again he confused certain matrons of the parish by asking them to say entire decades of the rosary to expiate the pride they had so proudly confessed.

The radiance of afternoon faded in the small slit of beaded-glass window behind his head. He sat in an even more sombre half-dark, in which his folded hands shone dimly but luminously. Winter afternoon sun came down aslant the council chambers, leaving Darragh's confessional weakly lit. Yet, he knew, he spent twice, three times as long in the confessional as the monsignor. This small geographic injustice once more nagged away at him for half an hour, as he automatically bound and loosened his penitents, absolved the petty crimes of his parishioners, handed out penances and thought of tasks to be attended to among the living—the two chief issues being the tracking down of Gervaise, and a trunk call, if it could be arranged, to the orphanage in Killcare.

Nearly all the light was gone. Having concluded with a penitent in the box to the right, he slid the shutter on that side's grille closed, and opened the one to the left to find nobody there.

His mind took now to nudging round the rough tablets of his Sunday sermon, as yet unwritten. The story of the woman taken in adultery, whom Christ saved. There had been no merciful intervention in Kate Heggarty's case. Darragh knew he should not explicitly mention her name. It would only titillate people to do so—boys who had seen her in the pews on Sunday and thought she was a good sort. He also knew that to mention the murdered woman by her name would play into the monsignor's rampant idea of his, Darragh's, own folly, and it was best to satisfy that appetite only when conscience or instinct made it unavoidable.

He flinched as a penitent entered the left-hand confessional box, and he heard the whisper of cloth as whoever it was lowered himself to the kneeler there. He knew it was a man in a suit. In taking up the kneeling position, men's serge made a different noise from women's satin or cotton or wool. Though he did not even know he knew this, Darragh's mind accepted the newcomer as a male.

He made sure that the right-hand grille was definitely closed, lest a late-entering penitent in that box hear what this newcomer said.

'Bless me Father for I have sinned,' the penitent began, proving the universality of the rites of the Catholic Church by speaking in Fratelli's voice. Looking through the confusing window of the fine-mesh grille, Darragh saw a Fratelli-like bulk. This meant, he decided, with reasoning rendered leaden by the hour, that the penitent *was* Fratelli.

'It is a year and a half since my last confession.'

'So you missed your last Easter duty?' asked Darragh.

'That's a fact, Father. But a good angel is on me, and so I came now.'

'A good angel? What exactly does that mean?'

'It means that for the moment I'm not the Devil's property.' It sounded such a humble and gothically minded Fratelli, a Fratelli drawing on the robust Italian Catholicism of his parents, a Fratelli who for the moment renounced the shining nimbus of his helmet and the authority of his side-armed waist.

'Here,' said Darragh, coughing and regaining his breath, 'here you are within the reach of influence far greater than that of angels. That of Christ and His Blessed Mother.' Where did these sure assertions come from? Darragh wondered.

'I need to be under a better influence by far. You know that . . .'

'How do I know it? I'm not aware of that. Not yet.'

'Well, I always thought you saw through me.'

So, either I'm a fool or a seer! thought Darragh, his head spinning. What little ration of wisdom might be in him was underestimated by vicar-generals, and overstated by penitents.

'No,' said Darragh, wanting to clear away the idea that he had any special insight. 'Do you know what? I thought you looked like a courtier in a Renaissance painting. A handsome creature, virtuous and dangerous at the same time. That's all I thought. So don't make things up about me.'

'Okay,' Fratelli agreed, but he was not convinced. 'Now, no question I do my own sinning, but when I was a boy, I was misused by an older woman, and terrible things were let loose.

In an army in peacetime, you find plenty of guys with demons. The Corps of Military Police meets up with them in the stockade. Broken souls. At nineteen years, it's already too late to go back and untangle their lines. I feel a lot of anger when I see how like me they are. And how like I am to them.'

Darragh's instincts were against such an over-elaborated confession as Fratelli was making. He tried to get the man to the point. 'So you're confessing rage?'

'That's right. Rage.'

'Against prisoners? Or others?'

'Prisoners figure in it.'

'Do you inflict blows?'

'Yes. Them too.'

In silence, Darragh waited. He imagined bruised and contused jaws. 'I have sat at desks while men hanged themselves,' Fratelli continued at last. 'Sometimes it seemed to me a wise thing they did. I have given niggers in the stockade what they need to end things.'

Here, to Darragh's sudden outrage, was evidence for Gervaise's view of the world. 'How do you mean?' Darragh asked nonetheless.

'A man who wants can hang himself with a cut-up handtowel. If he's ambitious for it, he can do it with shoelaces or rosaries.'

So the foundations had shifted. Captain O'Rourke, as officer and priest, declared such tales apocryphal. Had O'Rourke never heard the confession of a prison guard?

'How often did this happen?' asked Darragh, fearing the answer, pleased that Gervaise was out of *these* hands, but alarmed he might be in ones of similar intentions.

Fratelli seemed, beneath the aegis of the angel he had invoked, to be counting. 'Five, maybe six times. You can't have too many prisoners die on your watch. But niggers—the army goes along easy with the idea coloureds hang themselves in prison. And the more who do it, the more the figures prove it.'

This was not the normal mumbling of a sheltered young man of scruples. Did all Americans make their confessions as fulsomely as this? Maybe they were told in childhood not to shilly-shally in front of the confessional grille. It had to be counted, too, that the parishioners he absolved were chiefly of Irish, Scottish or English descent, and had a more reticent, more stuttering nicety of guilt than Fratelli.

'This is a very serious matter. For you. For your superiors.' It was serious for Gervaise too.

'I did mention demons,' Fratelli pleaded.

'But it can't all be blamed on demons, can it? Your free will was involved.'

The penitent seemed to contemplate this and then concede the point. 'My free will runs to ruin. It chooses the bad from the bad.'

'But if you think that way all the time, then you expect to sin. You shouldn't expect to sin. You shouldn't think it can't be avoided.'

'But there are people round me who know too much about me. What people know of you is what you become.'

Is that true? Darragh was tempted to consider. It sounded true.

'Other MPs?' he asked.

'Other MPs,' Fratelli agreed. 'And other dangerous people in general.'

'You might have to stand up to them,' said Darragh. 'Defy their power over you. I'm not asking the impossible. But history is full of people who have stood up. They get mocked . . . It's a small price.'

Fratelli laughed, without any viciousness, but in a way that showed he thought mockery would be the least that would befall him should he desist from helping black men hang themselves.

'You're not talking about Private Aspillon?'

'Not that one. All the coloureds got shipped to North Queensland. He's not the question, that particular nigger of yours.'

'When Gervaise and I were together in that shed . . . did you want us both killed?'

Fratelli answered with some passion. 'I wanted you to learn a lesson. I wanted you to see the size of things. You'll see there were reasons I wanted to bring you to size. You were already in my sights.' Fratelli seemed to writhe within his suit. Body and fabric could be heard shifting. 'Be patient. You'll see.'

What would Father Anselm think of this, with his moment-by-moment theory? Darragh did not know what to make of it but horror.

He said, 'If you're really willing to amend, then I can absolve you of these sins. Even if you don't think you've got the strength, the desire to behave well is reinforced by what happens here, by the sacrament. The grace you need is not fully in your possession yet. You'll receive it with absolution, the grace to be a genuinely brave man. And you can stand up to them. If you can stand up to me . . . I can't complain that your confession hasn't been full and frank . . . then you can stand up to them.'

'But I'm not finished yet,' Fratelli assured him. 'I had you say a Mass for my aunt. Speak no ill of the dead, but she needed one. A married woman, and me thirteen or fourteen, getting at me in the empty pickers' huts at the back of the orchard. Making a man of me.'

Darragh wanted this torrent of confessed misuse to end. His

vanity as a confessor had kept him in place late enough for Fratelli to arrive and begin pouring these poisons in his ear.

'Are you saying you and your aunt . . .?'

'I didn't think I was used badly at the time. She was proud of me, I was proud of myself. She said, "I'd never find a boy like you among the skinny Protestants. Beside them, an Italian boy is a man." So you see, I had my full issue of pride before a fall. I didn't know anything. I was a straitlaced boy and I didn't know. And I was glad she was not a whore, and proud that she was older and saw me as a man, better than my uncle. "You're a better man than your uncle," she told me, and I was as proud as Satan. And for her I was a better man. In the sense she wanted.'

'You've surely confessed this in the past,' Darragh suggested hopefully.

Fratelli said, 'That's right. It's old stuff in a way.'

'And so it's forgiven. Unless there's something in it you go back to, or let influence you now.'

'There's an influence,' Fratelli admitted. 'She messed me for normal women. I was a man only for her. I was her man and never became anyone else's. I don't like whores. Whores are an abomination. I always thought so. I always wanted a decent woman. But I had no interest in kids my age. I wasn't interested in courting a Catholic girl, some lettuce-grower's daughter. When my aunt was praising me, I thought, watch out, you girls! Proud, you know. I thought I'd find a peach, a pearl. Easy work. But girls were nothing to me. It was married women, and women who looked married, like my aunt. I liked women with husbands and kids, women who'd been used and were kind of sad. Those who weren't left me ice-cold. But even now when I meet the sort of women I like, I've got the full intention to do the adultery. But

I can't make it work. Punishment, you see, for my old pride as a kid.'

Darragh shook his head. 'So, you have tried to have indecent relations with married women, but have been unable to?' he asked, wanting to move things along.

'That's true for the large part,' said Fratelli. *True for the large part* . . . Nothing was straightforward true for this man. He could keep me here for hours, Darragh thought in panic. He asked, 'Have you seen a doctor?'

Fratelli was a little amused in a brotherly way. 'Do you want a doctor to help me become the perfect fornicator?'

'I'd want you to marry, normally.'

'Normally,' conceded Fratelli. 'I wouldn't mind that myself.'

To reach a conclusion, Darragh found himself speaking of the Blessed Virgin, the image of womanhood. She wanted his happiness, Darragh assured Fratelli. Many men of perverse tendency had been helped to a normal life by faith in her powers of intercession with her son. Darragh, of course, did not know this from any experience, but he believed it absolutely, even in his present numb state.

Fratelli could not be dissuaded from further unnecessary explanations. 'I don't court women like a barbarian. I'm slow. I'm kind. I take care. I say gentle and tender things you would not expect of a rough soldier. I don't parade my uniform, never have. I dress like an ordinary Joe in an ordinary job. I am thoughtful of her children—though I want the woman, I know that this can be a hard thing for the child. For the way the child sees the mother, that's what I mean. I'm as scared as the woman that the child might see us doing something wrong. The woman is frightened of that too, but not as frightened as I am. I'm the one that's got good reason to be frightened. The woman meets me, and I'm as edgy as she is about what might happen. I'm as careful. Women aren't used to this. They're used to oafs blundering up, wanting them straight off.'

'All you tell me,' said Darragh, further and further out of his depth, 'confirms you have a good heart.'

'You don't know yet where I'm taking you. Anyhow, I don't visit often, I visit at discreet times. And as I said, dressed like a guy who works in a store somewhere. A guy in a cheap suit. Kind of threadbare and respectable. Grey or blue with little pinstripes. No two-tone shoes. Some dead guy's tie, bought in a second-hand shop. The dust of years in it. I'm so sincere, I'm pretty much invisible. I do this not so that people won't remember me, though that's often the case, I look like some Polack factory hand. I do it for her, too. I don't preen. I say, this is all I am, a poor mother-less child. So I kind of fall in love the normal way. I think it's the normal way. She's married, but her husband is away, working on a dam somewhere, or drilling for oil, or in the navy.'

With a tremor in his throat, Darragh said, 'Or serving in New Guinea or Africa . . .'

'I'm talking about my old life, in the States. Fort Ord, Camp Bullis, Fort Bragg. I've been ten years in the service.' Fear of what was imminent prevented Darragh from commending the earnestness, the care for avoiding scandal, in Fratelli's courtship methods. At the heart of lust there was meant to be no redeem-ing courtliness. 'I tell myself this is genuine love that I feel, and that, like they say, love conquers all. I'm behaving well. I even feel noble. I'm able to imagine what it'll be like when she and I say at last yes, and I get excited like a normal man, and want no other woman on earth. I even want her to leave her husband. I begin to talk to her about it before we've even done a thing.'

He considerately paused, in case Darragh wanted to annotate the issues raised to this stage. But Darragh had nothing to say, for Fratelli evaded all the skills of the confessor.

So the sergeant continued. 'Some night—or some daytime if the kid's at school—it comes. And this is perfect. This is a perfect union. No unwillingness in the woman—we're both past unwilling. She gives herself up. The one problem is, I can't give myself up. My aunt reaches out from the pickers' quarters, and I smell the smell of the place, and I'm done for. I'm part of a terrible greyness. I've died, I'm gone. This good woman lies there with a corpse, a rotting thing. Me. She knows it, and I can't begin to tolerate that she knows all this about me, that she sees me rotting like this. She's full of fear. She's sacrificed honour. For this? To lie with the dead?'

'You *must* see a doctor,' Darragh told him. A doctor might be the least of it.

'I *must* see a doctor,' Fratelli agreed. 'But at the time I'm not within reach of a doctor. Before I know, I've reached out and crushed her breath out of her. I save myself. I save her as fast and furious as I can. I manage, dear God, to crank off like a schoolboy. I put my suit back on, and I close the door and leave my saved love behind.'

Darragh, who had had rage for the imagined murderer, felt mere exhaustion now. 'You are in the greatest danger,' he said. Which was absurd.

'It happened three times in the States. Three angels I made and released from their own disgust. Only three. I don't go round talking to every woman I meet.'

'And one in Australia,' said Darragh with his dreadful certainty.

'An angel in Australia,' Fratelli assented.

'Don't you dare say angel!' Darragh, overtaken now by the appropriate fury, told him. 'I forbid you.'

'It's the way I think,' Fratelli murmured.

'No. You say angel to excuse yourself. You've done nothing but excuse yourself throughout.'

Darragh was aware his voice was growing somewhat heightened for the confessional. But the confessional lightning had struck him. The very woman whose salvation he so actively desired was connected to this wretch whose salvation he needed now to countenance. This case always advanced in Moral Theology classes, in the section *De Sacramentis*. The murderer comes to the confessional grille, to the curtain where God's omniscience begins, and the priest is left with the human knowledge of what has been savagely done. The confessor orders the killer to surrender himself—it is a condition of absolution that he should firmly intend to do so. The killer says he will, and the priest absolves him in the hope that the grace of the sacrament will fortify him for self-surrender to the state. But then the killer does not do so, reneges on the conditions of his absolution. When Dr Cleary, professor of moral theology, raised this issue, for some reason Darragh the student imagined an enclosed European village, sealed in by mountains, with the priest walking among gothic villagers, knowing they were endangered by the killer yet unable to tell them. As Darragh the student had imagined the scene, it had little to do with the suburbs of Sydney.

But it had happened to him and to those with whom he had broken the bread of heaven. It was not some alpine village of the kind he knew only from films set in Europe. It was a matter of *these* plain streets. A priest, whether in Homebush or in a mountain-girt Catholic village, could not break the seal of the confessional to save his life, to protect his good name, to refute a false accusation, to save the life of others, to aid the course of justice or to avert a public calamity. He was not bound by any oath in court when asked to reveal what was said in the confessional. A confessor who directly violated the seal of confession incurred an automatic excommunication, which only the Vatican could lift. The Fourth Lateran Council seven hundred years past had stated a sentiment Darragh was familiar with: 'Let the confessor take absolute care not to betray the sinner through word or sign, or in any other way whatsoever . . .' The Czech saint, St John Nepomucene, confessor to King Wenceslaus IV and to his queen, knew that the king was perverse in his sexual practice, and that the queen was utterly faithful to him. Wenceslaus tortured St John so that he might reveal the queen's sins, and when he would not he was thrown into the river Moldava and drowned, dying to preserve the seal.

The other law which Darragh knew from his student days and now could recount to himself instinctively was that he could not even raise the matter with Fratelli outside the confessional, unless by some miracle, some quirk of his madness or guilt, Fratelli himself raised it.

Darragh heard himself tell Fratelli flatly that he must turn himself over to the authorities, and heard Fratelli answering in a reasonable, doleful voice.

Darragh shook his head. 'What? What are you telling me?'

'I said, I am the authorities,' said Fratelli moderately, with the mildest sadness.

'You are not an authority. You are the authority for nothing.'

'Just now,' Fratelli said reasonably, 'you told me the grace of confession will help me not do any of this again. I wish never to do it again. But if I turn myself in, Father, I'll be hanged.'

'Don't you think that just?'

'Kind of just,' Fratelli conceded.

'You'll do this dreadful thing again.'

'Not if I pray.'

'This is hopeless,' said Darragh. 'Will you release me from the seal of the confessional, so that I can talk to you about this, face to face?'

'You can't tell anybody else?'

'No, I can talk only to you. In fact, if anyone else overheard us, they'd be bound to secrecy too. But nobody will overhear us.'

'Father, I have a purpose to amend myself.'

Darragh shook his head. 'When will we meet then?'

'Why not outside?' suggested Fratelli. 'Now.'

For some reason this made Darragh furious. 'Haven't you got any shame at all?'

'I have shame. And if you don't speak to me gentle, Father, whoever will?'

'I don't know if I can do that yet. Speak gently, I mean.'

Fratelli said, 'Maybe you'll be given the grace to do it. If I can be, you sure can too.'

'Stop this sophistry, for God's own sake.'

'I don't understand,' said Fratelli. 'All I understand is that I'm contrite.'

'God forgive you,' said Darragh, and then he absolved Fratelli of the crime of destroying Kate Heggarty. He imposed a penance of one whole rosary—the Joyful, Glorious and Sorrowful Mysteries—to be recited within the next twenty-four hours. It was such a fatuous penalty, Darragh thought, for the deaths by omission of Negroes, the deaths by commission of wives. He suspected that, after all, the sacrament of penance was not designed for such sins and Fratelli should have stayed, without approaching the confessional, in the habitation of the damned, some outer dark, awaiting capture.

By the time the stunned Darragh emerged thinking, *Surely he has gone*, it was full night. He looked automatically at his watch—it was only three-quarters of an hour before Saturday night Benediction, which meant a full church of people these anxious days. All attending to their contract with God: I will attend Benediction and Mass if you will let him live . . . If you make sure I die before him . . . If you give me a sign that he has gone to heaven . . . If you will turn the alien hosts away. God made no contracts, however. Except perhaps the long-term contract of redemption, longer running than the term set by the severest bank, the most avid insurance company.

He found Fratelli smoking calmly on the side steps of the church. The light in Mrs Flannery's presbytery kitchen thinly blinked between blackout curtains. Darragh snatched the cigarette from his hand and ground it out against the pavement. He was aware, from this sudden contact, of the meatiness of Fratelli's hand and thus, by implication, of the arm in which it ended. He took a step back in disgust.

'Father,' said Fratelli without sarcasm, 'I think you might hang me yourself.' And he held his hands up palm first. 'We can talk more about it. Tomorrow night. Are you free tomorrow night?'

Darragh tried to perceive some notional calendar of his coming activities. He saw only vacancy. He said, 'Yes, tomorrow night.'

Here, in the broader night, Fratelli was in command. 'Okay. I want you to dress like a normal Joe. My style. You got any civvies, Father? There's a pub in the Cross, Greenknowe Street. Open all hours to us and our friends. We'll find a quiet corner. A corner with walls behind us. Will you come, really?'

'I tell you to surrender yourself tonight. I don't want a drinking session with you.'

'It takes time and a bit of moral support before a guy can do that, Father. And I'm on duty tonight. So will you come tomorrow?'

'You're not in a position to order a priest around.'

'No, but you'll come. We'll settle everything that needs to be settled then.'

Darragh thought himself further into the meeting Fratelli proposed. There was something about those 'walls behind us,' Fratelli had mentioned that alarmed Darragh, who harboured a primal desire to live longer than Fratelli. No Moldava River for me, he pledged.

'I'll bring someone with me though,' he said. He could not imagine who it would be. 'Just someone to keep an eye on me. He can drink in another part of the bar. He won't know what we're saying.'

'Who will you bring?' asked Fratelli, sniffing the air, suddenly irritable. 'I don't want another guy. Another guy mightn't know that what I told you is sacred. I don't want eavesdroppers.'

'I can assure you, this fellow won't eavesdrop.'

'But he'll know you don't trust me.'

'I don't.'

'Says very little for the absolution you just gave. And all that grace you talk about.'

'I'm a human being, and I'm scared. I'll tell this . . .' Darragh was going to say *friend*, '. . . parishioner that I'm afraid you're such a sociable man I might get drunk, that he's there to get me home safe. I'll tell him we're talking, privately, about Private Aspillon.'

'It all comes back to niggers,' said Fratelli. 'You'll wear civvies . . .?'

'Yes. Out of positive shame for the company I'm keeping.'

Fratelli sighed at this. 'I'll meet you on the corner of Macleay and Greenknowe, eight o'clock. Is that set?'

'Of course it is,' Darragh assented. He was suddenly delighted that he would see Fratelli again. The more time he spent with the man, he believed, the closer he was to the necessary end, the punishment.

CHAPTER TWENTY-ONE

A S SOON AS HE entered the presbytery hallway, Darragh could hear the radio—a relayed BBC broadcast about the Afrika Korps and the British and Australian Eighth Army. He found, as he took a breath and went into the dining room, that the monsignor was eating chops with mint sauce and Worcestershire.

'Frank,' he said, looking up. He wore his usual cardigan and his black pants, was well-shaven and his thinning hair slicked. 'Sit down here,' he said, as if Darragh's sins had now been expiated. He called to Mrs Flannery, and Frank's meal was brought. It was touching, it was the affectionate gesture he so needed, and yet, seeing the glisten of fat on the meat, Darragh's gorge rose. He fought it, knowing that over-delicate sensibility must be conquered if he was to go drinking with Fratelli.

'Would you mind turning down the radio before you go, Mrs Flannery?' the monsignor asked, and the housekeeper did it and vanished.

'Frank,' said the monsignor, who had clearly examined his

conscience about his curate and come up with hopeful resolutions, 'I'm sorry you went through the mill last Sunday. Thank God you weren't here. You'll have enough ghouls turning up at tomorrow's Mass just to see you. But now you can understand the points I was making beforehand, points I made only for your sake. How were our friends the Franciscans, by the way?'

'They were very kind,' said Darragh. An instinct told him that he would do better with the monsignor if he gave fuller and more detailed answers, and he struggled to clear his head of Fratelli so that it could be done. 'My retreat master was a wise old priest. A former digger they told me. The fellow who runs the dairy down there, Father Matthew . . . Well, he broke the story to me very gently last Sunday.'

The monsignor seemed gratified. He nodded a few times. 'I rang him too. But you were not there at the time. I couldn't wangle two trunk calls in a day.'

'That's all right. You buried Mrs Heggarty.'

The monsignor made a pained face. 'I was harsh on her the day Kearney was here. I was somewhat shocked, Frank. When I buried her, I was aware of her neighbour weeping, and I had a suspicion, for what it was worth, that a woman who could be so mourned might attract the divine mercy.' The monsignor coughed. 'For what such a suspicion is worth,' he explained quickly.

Darragh was close to tears, of loss and hope both, so said nothing.

'You know,' said the monsignor, 'just let me say . . . be careful at Mass tomorrow. Don't do anything designed to satisfy the curious. Do you promise me? I know you're a good preacher. I hope that this Sunday you'll give a sermon no one will remember. A boring, boring sermon, Frank. God knows there's plenty of them. You could get one out of a book.'

'I'll do my best,' said Darragh. 'But I must—for my own honour—mention the thing, without going into details.'

The monsignor sighed. 'We're all hoping it'll be plain sailing for you from here on, Frank. It'll be a good thing when they catch the fellow, too. Excuse me now, I'm playing whist at the Gardners' tonight. I'll see you before the nine o'clock Mass.' He said a moment's grace after meals, knitting his brows, and stood.

'Monsignor,' said Darragh.

'Yes, Frank?'

'Thank you. A lot of men might have wanted to vet my sermon tomorrow.'

The monsignor laughed. 'Don't think I didn't consider it myself, Frank. But I think you've got to trust fellows. Even young Turks.'

Darragh ate his chops automatically and without the relish the ration coupon which had gone to buy them seemed to justify. It was considered that sermons should deal with the mysteries of faith in the abstract, and with biblical tales or events from the lives of saints. Many priests thought it best to avoid the individual, the anecdotal, the concrete. It was considered dangerous to talk about local illustrative cases, to use the suburban instance as a parable. The rule was sometimes broken to permit a priest to denounce a particular book, generally one he had not read, or a film—one he had not seen, or had seen and left at the end of the first reel. A politician might be denounced, although that had become more dangerous recently, since the war seemed to have driven people's opinions in various directions and produced in them an electoral wilfulness. But beyond that you stuck for your examples to the citizens of Christ's Aramaic-speaking locale. The prodigal son, the wedding feast at Cana, Christ walking on the water. And, of course, the woman taken in adultery.

When the monsignor was vanished to his whist, Darragh went

to the church for Benediction and to hear evening confessions. Though he encountered anxious souls, souls who thought they were damned for some lie they had told, some theft of a few pounds of steel or timber or food, some lunge driven by lust, he gratefully absolved them all. Their sins were human ones and radiant with absolvability. The last of them had been absolved, indeed, by half past eight. An idea about a protector, a body-guard, had come to him as well. He went back to the presbytery, changed out of his soutane into his suit, his stock and clerical collar, and set out down Homebush Road towards the railway line. He wondered if observant policemen were already on his track, but could see nothing much happening. Pedestrians were rarely thick on these streets, and the genuinely cold Saturday night air hung slackly over the wide pavements. If, before the encounters of the Coral Sea, there had been a lack of electric fear in the air, now there was a lack of joy at partial salvation. It all felt as it did before—ageless, and unimpressed by events.

In The Crescent he looked for the police car waiting under the railway embankment. He did not see one. Had they given up the watch? He entered the gate of what he thought of, even though she was now gone from it, as Mrs Flood's house. Ross Trumble answered the door, which was what he had hoped. He wore a woolly jumper and, hulking and good-looking, did resemble a revolutionary. It was impossible to believe that he was 4F. He seemed to Darragh acutely muscular. And he was sober tonight.

He was taken aback to see Darragh.

'You've come to see Bert?' he decided.

'No, Ross. You.'

'Me? Jesus, you're a game one. The scandalous priest, eh? Did the police spot you on your way past?'

'I don't think they're there tonight. I don't know.'

'Anyhow,' said Ross Trumble, his face cracking into a smile, a feature he had not yet displayed in any of his past meetings with Darragh, 'this'll confuse the buggers, won't it? Two suspects meeting. And what a two!' The idea tickled him. 'I mean,' he said, 'they had to separate us last time.'

He laid his eyes in comradely amusement on Darragh.

'Come in then. Bert's out at a World War I get-together.' People had now begun to call Darragh's father's Great War that. *World War I.* "I'll make you a cup of tea. Or pour you a beer.'

'I'd like a beer, in fact,' said Darragh. He thought of it as training for the next night, and as a consolation for the harsh day just past. They went through to the kitchen where Trumble switched off a radio. It had been broadcasting from the Trocadero in town, Andrews Sisters-style performers singing patriotic songs. *'It's a brown slouch hat with its side turned up, And it means the world to me . . .'* Ross Trumble seemed embarrassed to have such trite lyrics emanating from his radio, or Bert's. He switched the instrument off and went to the ice chest, from which he took out a half-drunk bottle of beer. He found a clean glass in a dresser, held it up to the light, considered it adequate and poured.

'Beer, the working man's religion,' he said. He shrugged. 'Just a thought. Not trying to rile you.' He laughed again. 'Given that up as a bad bloody job since the other night. Sit down.'

It seemed that the blows thrown and the attention of police had by some mysterious formula made them friends. Trumble's gibes were comradely now, for which Darragh was grateful. He half-smiled and began to drink the oaty dinner ale, tasting the gracious grain in it, and feeling a normal fellow.

'Did you get into much trouble with bishops and people like that?' asked Trumble.

'They sent me on a retreat.'

'A *retreat?*' He obviously and with some justice thought of the term in a military sense.

'You go away to a monastery, keep silent, pray and have sessions with a spiritual adviser.'

'And you were in the middle of that when the story came out in the papers?'

Darragh said yes.

'So it isn't all beer and skittles, this feeding people the opium of religion.'

'I don't mind admitting it's been pretty hard lately.'

Trumble himself had sat now. He lifted his own half-drunk glass of beer. 'I'm supposed to be happy when things go a bit bad for servants of the system. Priests and coppers. But it's different when you get to know somebody.'

Darragh thought that Trumble the revolutionary must, in fact, be a kind of sentimentalist, since he considered having a police-interrupted tussle with another man to be a valid form of getting to know him. There was a sort of innocence in this, and Darragh was surprised but strangely cheered by it.

'We're just ordinary blokes, you know,' said Darragh. 'Some of us very ordinary. And we don't see ourselves as you see us.'

'How *do* you see yourself?'

'As a servant of the people.'

'That *is* interesting,' said Trumble. 'When you bloody think about it.'

'Why?' asked Darragh.

'Well, you see, it makes you a poor bloody exploited sod as well.'

'I don't feel exploited,' said Darragh, though the temptation was there. 'I became a priest of my own free will. No one put a gun to my head.'

'No. I bet they just told you you'd go to hell if you didn't.'

'I had a profound desire for it,' said Darragh.

'Yeah. But they conditioned you, you see. They raised you to want it.'

'And did they raise you to want to be what you are?'

'My father bloody did, though I didn't see so much of him. He was without a job five years. Travelled round region to region by foot, and riding the rattler. They kept them on the road, town to town, but they didn't give them the means to travel. Railway police hunted them out from under the carriages. A great system, eh? Some fathers said, "Become a lawyer or a doctor, boy, because you'll never be hard up." But my father said when we met up again: "Change the world so that you can be a worker, and don't have to be a doctor or a lawyer to be safe." That was my education. It made some damn sense.'

'Everyone's childhood makes sense when you're in it,' Darragh said. 'That's when the world is simple.'

'And my world was simply bloody awful,' Trumble told him with a grin, but without the note of accusation which had marked their earlier discourses. 'If you blokes are the servants of the people, where were you? You were living in your presbyteries, weren't you, and we were lining up at the kitchen door.'

'I was at high school. My father was out of work too. He told me the Church didn't always act well. Some priests locked themselves in against the poor. But the Sisters of Charity were handing out tea and soup to anyone in the side streets. Just for the pure humanity of it.'

They were getting deeply into Kate Heggarty territory—social justice, *Rerum Novarum*, Marx, dignity. As much as these matters interested Darragh at normal times, they could not be permitted to dominate this kitchen conversation. Darragh took a long sip of the beer, and felt the first onset of deceptive, effervescent brotherliness in his blood. The thought struck him that men drank to achieve this platform of goodwill. The impulse itself was noble if benighted. His father had had a few episodes with whisky during days of unemployment, hiding it in the cistern of the toilet. It was his attempt to mould the world down to a graspable state. But spirits made Mr Darragh sad and aggressive, and broke down the coherence of his character. He became an unshaven stranger with a gap-toothed slash of a mouth who threw an inaccurate punch at Darragh's mother and told Darragh to fucking grow up, that his mother was making him a lily-fart. Darragh had especially noticed his own liking for liquor on the tennis Mondays. I'll have to be careful, he thought, or I'll become one of those red-nosed priests with the broken facial capillaries of the boozer—or, as they called it, the Tipperary tan. But none of that was as pressing an issue as Fratelli.

'Look, Ross,' Darragh said, leaning forward, getting down to business. 'I'm not a soldier because I'm a minister of religion, exempt. I believe you're 4F. I'm not saying this in any jingoistic way—I don't want you to go and get killed or anything like that. But it's just, you seemed so strong the other night, when we were having our . . . our little scrum . . . down the street.'

'I am 4F though, fair and square,' said Trumble. 'Had tuberculosis. And bad. Part of a lung gone. That's where I met Rosie. Up in the Boddington sanitarium in the Blue Mountains. It's easy to die in a place like that, but I thought: Build yourself up, son! I even chopped wood to the limit of what breath I had. And I wanted to live. Because wars always bring on a revolution, so I knew this one would too, if I could just stick around.' Darragh was tempted to say, 'Perhaps it'll be a revolution against Stalin,' but he didn't want to get into that argument.

'So I can hold my own,' Trumble concluded.

'I think you can too.' Once more a polemic urge surfaced in Darragh to ask, 'Can you really imagine the whole of Australia Communist?' But that would take the conversation in an unfruitful direction. He said instead, 'I came because I want you to do me a favour.'

'Here we go,' said Trumble with a broad smile, but again it had a jolliness to it.

Darragh told him about Private Aspillon. At least Trumble believed in the universal brotherhood of men, said Darragh. He and Darragh had that in common.

'But,' said Trumble, 'you've got to ask whether it's wise for a black man to strike up an acquaintance with a white woman. It's all bloody right in theory, but . . .'

'But society doesn't like it?'

'Bloody right,' agreed Trumble, suddenly like a gatekeeper of the known world.

Darragh expanded on his experience with Aspillon, leaving out the more pious aspects. Aspillon was now in a military prison, and Darragh claimed to be interested in his welfare. So he was to meet an American MP in a pub in the Cross, and he wasn't sure about the fellow, not after the events in the backyard in Lidcombe. He wanted to make sure he got home safely. Would Trumble consider coming? Except, said Darragh, he wasn't asking Trumble to take part in the dialogue. If he wouldn't mind sitting across the room, and just keeping an eye on things. They'd go into the Cross by train and bus. 'And I don't want to come home too late,' said Darragh. 'I always have the early Mass Monday.'

'Sounds like exploitation to me,' said Trumble with an enthusiastic grin. But the invitation had fascinated, and as far as

Darragh could tell, delighted him. 'Look, not only will we have a good night out on this Yank, and not only will I keep an eye on you, we'll get a cab home. It'll be easy to get a cab home if a Yank's with us.'

'Well, I'll pay for it,' said Darragh, in a rash burst of gratitude to Trumble. It would make a massive dent in his savings from the one pound ten shillings the archdiocese paid him a week.

'No,' said Trumble. 'I can handle it. It's good pay at the brickworks now. The capitalists want what we produce.'

He winked, and so it was agreed that the priest and the brickworker would meet at half past six on Sunday evening, at browned-out Homebush railway station, and it was Trumble who seemed more concerned about guilt by association than Darragh. 'One thing,' he said. 'Let's both catch it as individuals, and link up once it's on the way. I don't want to shock any of your parish people.'

'My parish people?' asked Darragh. 'Or yours?'

Even so, Trumble seemed so hugely tickled that Darragh himself felt partially appeased for the dreadful afternoon, partly reassured that the human species could be repaired and redeemed. In that spirit, he let Trumble pour him a second glass of beer.

CHAPTER TWENTY-TWO

A S THE MONSIGNOR had foretold, even Darragh's half-past-six Mass, a Mass recited in all-green vestments, and designed to accommodate the early risers—the penitential, the insomniacs—was considerably more crowded than usual. Some three hundred and fifty or more of the faithful, he would have guessed. The sermon he had prepared the previous night had been enriched and armoured by his alliance with Trumble.

The Gospel of the Mass, which Darragh read from St Margaret's pulpit of panelled native cedar, seemed crowded with omens and significance, perhaps to too great a degree. Christ, smelling bitter persecution in the air, warns his followers, 'They will put you out of the synagogues: yea, the hour cometh that whosoever killeth you will think that he does a service to God . . .'

He surveyed his congregation. Fortunately, not too many families at this time of morning. They were certainly attentive. Their frowns were the frowns of goodwill. He addressed them as priests were meant to. 'My dearly beloved brethren.' He began to speak of the incident of the adulteress, as related by St John. Jesus was on the Mount of Olives, approaching the Temple of Jerusalem whose stones would be in one generation tumbled by the Roman army. And the 'scribes and Pharisees', the members of priestly factions in the Temple, brought Him a woman who had been arrested for adultery and said, to test Him, that Moses's law decreed this woman must be stoned to death. 'But what sayest thou?' Christ bent and wrote in the dust of the ground, as if He did not hear them, but they kept pressing Him—they wanted His answer as potential evidence against Him. Then He rose and famously said, 'He that is without sin among you, let him cast the first stone . . .' Darragh could tell by the pale upturned faces below him that, of course—no fools—they caught his drift. They knew he spoke about the judgement which had been brought down on him by the press, and the fiercer one which had been brought down on Kate Heggarty.

'Stoned to death,' he said. 'We're used to that term. We first heard it as children, at a stage when we were involved in the stone fights boys enjoy, and it did not seem too terrible a death. Consider how ferocious it was to be in the centre of all the hurled stones though, to have the consciousness slowly bludgeoned out of you, and then at last, under the hail of rocks, to breathe for the last time, and to be still. Now the men who threw the stones felt gratified, and went back in that state to their homes, unaware they had been savages.'

The congregation looked very concerned. Some seemed ready to weep in compassion. Others were agog. In the back pews one of the few children was hushed.

'The stone-throwing impulse is very strong in humans,' he intoned fairly plainly, a banal but authoritative idea since it came from him. 'The papers are very good at it.' There was a faint knowing chuckle. 'The *Sunday Telegraph* are experts.' A relieved uproar of laughter enabled parishioners to glance at each other and grin. Darragh felt a little abashed, since it revealed they had all read the article about him, a thought which was for a moment oppressive. 'Christ realised that men with lumps of granite in their fists were not the best ministers to deal with the woman's sin. A woman who died in our parish in the past few weeks has been harshly judged in the manner of the Pharisees. It is all too human of us to judge her, because she paid the excessive price of being murdered for her sin. I believe that this woman needed our compassion and our considered help. We were not able to aid her in her daily life, to prevent her undertaking an association which has had this horrible result. Christ, who saved the woman so long ago, might have left the saving of this woman to us, particularly to her priest, and there's an extent to which we, and I, might have failed.

'I cannot think it right to judge her savagely after the fact. Let us remember that had she not suffered this dreadful result, if the breath had not been crushed from her, we would have known nothing about her supposed sin, and our judgement would be mild. It is the murderer who is the sinner. We should not burden her memory with the murderous guilt, any more than Christ saw fit to burden the woman taken in adultery with the guilt of a transgression which involved both a woman and a man.'

He felt a sudden tiredness and, like air from a tyre, the power went out of his oratory. He closed with the normal remarks about the services the faithful could provide the dead through their prayers. 'May their souls, and all the souls of the faithful departed, rest in peace, Amen.'

That same sermon, in essence, he gave again at the eight o'clock Mass, before a congregation containing more young families. Only children made noises during it.

As usual, he hoped to finish the eight o'clock Mass by seven minutes to nine at the latest, to ensure that he had unvested and had left the sacristy by a few minutes to nine, allowing Monsignor Carolan some moments of silent reflection before he went out to the altar to say the nine o'clock Mass. But the number of people receiving communion kept Darragh a minute or so over, and he was conscious as he left the altar and went into the sacristy that he might encounter an irritated monsignor.

The monsignor stood at the vestment bench in his white alb, with a cincture on, and a maniple at his wrist, while altar boys strained to lift an emerald, thread-of-gold decorated chasuble over his head, and arrange it on his shoulders. Darragh and his altar boys edged up to the long vestment drawers, and parallel to his parish priest he began disrobing, taking off his own chasuble as the monsignor in turn assumed his. He undid his white cincture and divested himself of his stole, kissing the cross embroidered on it.

'Is it true you told people they were to blame for that woman?' murmured the monsignor.

'That is not true,' said Darragh, in a supposedly easy voice, so that the altar boys would have no room for gossip about a falling out between the parish priest and the curate. But it was sickening that the monsignor had informants among the congregation.

'You remember last night I told you not to mention her.'

'I didn't mention her by name,' said Darragh. 'But there had to be some reference to her. If people were scandalised by last week's paper, it was up to me to stanch the scandal this week.'

The monsignor, a mountain of priesthood in his braided, threaded, looped and glittering robes, joined his hands and sunk his fine-cut nose between them in prayer. Having folded the chasuble, stole and maniple in its drawer—you could not trust the altar boys with that job—Darragh crossed the room and threw the white alb and maniple into a laundry basket, for Mrs Flannery always gave him fresh ones, heavily starched by lay nuns in Parramatta, to start the week.

Without looking at him, the monsignor put on his head the black four-cornered, three-peaked cap, the biretta, optional wear for priests which older men seemed to favour more than younger, and took up his chalice in its altar cloth, one hand beneath the chalice veil, the other laid flat across the embroidered burse, the customary posture of the priest approaching the altar. Anger was still in his face. He said sideways out of his mouth, 'Are you going out today, Father?'

'Not today,' said Darragh. He would visit his mother and Aunt Madge on some other Sabbath. 'This evening.'

'I'm going out to lunch. I'll leave you a note before I go.'

And he progressed through the door, and Darragh heard that peculiar unified sound of an entire Catholic congregation rising as one, a noise made up in part of sundry fabrics moving, of limbs of all ages straightening, of ankles hitting kneelers, of knees colliding with the pew in front. This was the nine o'clock Church militant ascending in its ranks to greet its monsignor.

Darragh ate another presbytery breakfast—a boiled egg, toast—and then, hunched down at the desk in his room, began to apply himself to reading the small hours for the Sunday within the Octave of the Ascension.

The psalms for the office of Prime were not particular to that Sunday; that is, they were the same psalms that priests, rattling through Prime, early or late at night, after a day in the sun, trying to make Matins and Lauds before midnight, said every Sunday. Deep in Psalm 17, a familiar verse stopped him in mid mutter. '*Lapis, quem reprobaverunt aedificantes, factus est caput anguli.* The stone which the builders have rejected has been made the keystone of the arch.'

It was not the first time a text penetrated him for good or ill. But by a hand which Darragh could only presume to be divine, the steepling weight of last Sunday's newspaper shame, which he now understood had been crushing him, crowding him nearer and nearer lunacy, was gone. He could not see how long the relief would last, but the sense of being a favoured child, or at least a being on a just course, returned like a gracious tide he seemed to experience even in his limbs. He dropped to his knees with an enthusiasm he had not felt for some months and offered thanks to Mary, the Mother of humankind, for her intercession, and to Christ, who had also tasted blood and ashes in the Garden of Gethsemane and written something mysterious in the dust of the Temple forecourt as the Pharisees bayed for His divine remission of a terrible sentence. Simultaneously, he felt confirmed in his intentions to meet with Fratelli. Efficacy returned to him like the rain, which even as he knelt began to fall outside. He had heard a distant radio report that in the parched interior, from which the weather came, there had been welcome torrents over the remaining areas held until recently by drought. He felt as graced by torrents as the inimitable earth itself.

He continued with Vespers and Compline: '*Ecce nunc tempus acceptabile, ecce nunc dies salutis* . . . Behold now is the proper time, now the day of deliverance . . .'

By the time he came downstairs, he was aware both the monsignor and Mrs Flannery would be gone from the house. Sunday midday was the one time of the week Mrs Flannery did not cook, but went to eat a baked dinner at her sister's house in Concord West. The dining room was empty and innocent of cooking odours. In the hall was an envelope addressed to him in Monsignor Carolan's handwriting. 'Dear Father Darragh,' it began rather formally. 'Don't go out tomorrow until we have discussed your future.' It was signed 'Vincent Carolan, PP.' Even that left him calm and armoured in new certainty. There was a second letter, and the monsignor added a note of regret to it that he had forgotten to give it to Darragh the day before, when he returned from retreat. It carried a design of a cross and eagles, and was from Captain O'Rourke. Aspillon, said O'Rourke briefly, was in a compound west of Townsville, more than a thousand miles north. 'I'm informed he's in good health. If you wish to write to him it is care of the Detention Compound, Camp Kenney, via Townsville. My unit will be on the move soon, so this is likely to be our last communication.'

Against what he knew from Fratelli, Captain O'Rourke's assurances counted for little. But for today, the amiable Gervaise would have to be committed to the care of God. Darragh had far too much else to attend to.

CHAPTER TWENTY-THREE

'JESUS,' SAID TRUMBLE, turning to him as Darragh stepped onto the train behind him. On the station, as earlier arranged, they had barely nodded to each other, but this train to Town Hall was nearly empty, and it was obvious they could travel together as a pair. 'You look like a dead giveaway, old sport. Let's find a seat.'

Trumble indicated facing seats by a window beyond which the occasional hooded lights of these suburbs could be seen. With benign amusement, he looked over his new friend's appearance. Darragh wore a pair of clerical black trousers, the seminary darkness of which he had tried to cancel out with his schooldays sports coat, a Fair Isle knit sweater, a white shirt left over from youth, and a broad woven tie of a fashion not much favoured in this time of war, dread and excitement. He had worn his black overcoat over it all while he waited to board the train at Homebush. Now, on the train, he and Trumble sat together companionably but not saying much, having talked so thoroughly the night before. At Town Hall Station, Darragh went to the men's lavatories, spending tuppence—such was the inflation of war—on a toilet cubicle in which he removed his coat and hat, packed them in the little grip he carried, and emerged, he dared hope, like a typical, undistinguished citizen of the world, out with a mate, looking for an after-hours drink.

'If you'd needed strides,' said Trumble, assessing him as he emerged from the lavatory, 'I could have given you a grey pair. You look like a bloody archbishop in mufti.' Darragh was disappointed the effect was not better, and Trumble, seeing this, relented. 'Don't worry. We'll pass you off as a . . . well, maybe a student of philosophy or some such. Let me carry the bloody grip for you. No, let me. Come on.'

Trumble, who in other circumstances was in favour of putting priests against the wall and shooting them, was taking his duty of care of Darragh with a thorough seriousness. As they moved up to street level on the corner opposite the wedding-cake architecture of the Town Hall, Darragh was aware of Trumble's hand extended behind his shoulder, as if to catch him should he suddenly fall back down the stairs.

Park Street did not seem to know quite what to make of its own blackout-cum-brownout. Department stores retained in their windows a few lights by which dress mannequins could be observed. Light spilled onto the pavement from occasional open cafes and pub doorways. Hoping to be a city hidden from bombers, it yet also hoped to be a city of discreet delights, of wares awaiting the next day's opening hour.

'Two Japanese reconnaissance planes over Sydney today, and the buggers can't give up their advertising,' said Trumble, sniffing at Grace Brothers' window. It was the first Darragh had heard of Japanese reconnaissance planes, but they were not Trumble's chief point. 'They're loyal to their credo, all right,' said

Trumble of the shopkeepers. 'They'd rather do business than live.'

They passed Hyde Park with its anti-aircraft battery, St Mary's Cathedral, where Darragh had been ordained a priest, looming dark behind. As they passed the Australian Museum, Trumble said jovially, 'Better watch out, Father. Between here and the Cross there are tarts on every corner. By the way, in the Soviet Union there's no prostitution. You ought to find that fact interesting.'

And indeed women in knee-length, low-cut dresses, early winter cardigans and flimsy coats, with acrid port and cigarettes on their breath, appeared from doorways to say, 'Hello boys!'; 'Out on the prowl, fellers?'; and, 'I always liked Australian blokes better than Yanks.' Though he had lived his boyhood four or five miles from this very point in William Street, Darragh had never before heard this sort of solicitation and found it a shocking yet exhilarating experience, as if he were getting closer to the unacknowledged core of the other reality, the one which did not present itself at the altar rails with shining face. A mysterious Sydney existed of which he had no knowledge, and he climbed with Trumble past car showrooms to the reputed parish of that other Australia, Kings Cross.

On its hill, and along the ridge of Darlinghurst Road, Kings Cross possessed a barely muted commercial energy of a particular kind. Though most doors were closed for the Sabbath, there was a sense of events occurring behind them, of drinks being poured, of jokes and touches exchanged in warm rooms closed to the sight of passers-by. Americans in crisp uniforms discussed their options by every corner.

Crass Darlinghurst Road led into more urbane Macleay Street, where naval and army officers with eagles on their peaked caps and surer social calendars than the enlisted men hurried towards their evening engagements, delighted—it seemed—that accidents of war had offered them such a pleasure port as Sydney.

'Our saviours,' Trumble told Darragh. 'They won't look so posh a week after the Japs arrive. The little yellow men will have 'em digging latrines.'

This sentiment of Trumble's was uttered just as he and Darragh passed a knot of American soldiers. It was spoken with undue volume, with Trumble staring ahead unblinking, with a kind of neutral certainty, into the eyes of the tallest of the men. It was one of those situations in which the victims of remarks are not sure that they have heard what they have heard, and would rather let ambiguity pass them by.

'They'll save us,' said Darragh, 'if anyone will.'

But it was apparent that Trumble was as full of a sense of a coming divine purge as was Mr Regan of Rose Bay. Trumble went on talking, as they moved down Macleay Street, about the fact that fashionable people entertained American officers in the flats around about, gin and whisky being provided from the horn of plenty which America seemed to be even in its retreat. 'And there they all stand,' asserted Trumble, on what authority Darragh was unsure, but with Mr Regan's intensity, 'glass in hand and weak as water. They don't seem to understand this is a world game.'

At the corner of Greenknowe Avenue, Trumble and Darragh waited where Fratelli had nominated. Darragh's heart seemed to try to find shelter in his throat. Mousy lights shone under the alcove of the post office. A young Australian pilot officer and his woman friend passed Trumble and Darragh, and seemed confused a little by their ill-assorted nature, by the question of what these two men had in common. But as they passed, Frank was relieved to see the couple return quickly to their mutual self-absorption. I shall never know that, he realised. Not that particular fierceness of attention for another. Were my mother and father like that? Did they have that triumphant air of having found together a sublime secret?

He felt cold. The sky was low and moist and a wind honed itself on the corner where they waited. Trumble showed a hardy indifference. He was underdressed for the night, Darragh thought, and lacked a sweater.

He sensed the question in Darragh's look. 'If I put on too many jumpers I get chills. Better to defy the bloody cold.' He seemed proud of the concept of defiance, and of how it had brought him to terms with his disease.

Long before the man himself went to the trouble of peering about in the near dark for Darragh, Darragh could see the square and somehow confident body of Fratelli approaching up Macleay Street from the direction of the naval base. He was dressed as he had described himself in the confessional: a normal citizen in a dark blue suit. Darragh decided to advance on him, and Fratelli's attention was jolted. Seeing Trumble waiting on the corner, he paused, lightly balanced, ready to flee.

'That's not a cop?' he asked.

'If only you knew, Sergeant,' uttered Darragh with an immediate ferocious laugh. 'He's a Red revolutionary. He wants to do away with you and me, all right. But not yet. Not tonight.'

'He's a big sonofabitch.'

'He's had TB. 4F. He'll sit across the room. He thinks we're talking about Aspillon. But he'll get me home safely. I thought you'd be in uniform.'

'Sometimes I work out of uniform. Sometimes I've got to. But I'm carrying my MP identity. I can get us into this club.' He reached into his pocket for it. 'Thanks for coming.'

Just short of some sort of primal grimace, Darragh said, 'There's only one reason I came.'

'Father, contempt won't do it for you,' Fratelli remarked with some sadness, his vast eyes encompassing the breadth and depth of all Darragh's compassion and ill will. 'Introduce me to your friend.'

So it was done, with appropriate mutual distrust between Trumble and Fratelli. 'Okay then,' said Fratelli, and he led them away from Macleay Street, down among browned-out flats, past a warden on the prowl for chinks of light, and into a small, darkened door which stood by steps leading down towards the waters of Elizabeth Bay.

Fratelli pushed the street door open, and stood back to let Trumble and Darragh enter a small, crowded alcove. In here, an American sailor—what they called shore patrol—stood smartly accoutred, and an old man in a white coat sat by a table on which a visitors' book waited.

'My guests,' said Fratelli to the old man in his authoritative, sunny manner, and signed himself in with his serial number and stood back to let Darragh and Trumble sign. Darragh, after considering the matter, signed himself as Father Francis Darragh, spelling 'Father' out in full so that there was no ambiguity. If he paid for it later in social odium or the disapproval of monsignors, so be it. It guaranteed he had left trace of himself. Fratelli led them through into a bar area, surprisingly cavernous. There were men and women in here, only perhaps half of them in uniform. An occasional Australian soldier or officer sat with his American hosts. Darragh turned to Trumble, who still carried Darragh's little grip, and said, for Fratelli's sake, 'I just have to have a word with the sergeant.'

Indeed, Fratelli seemed strangely sanguine about the coming

interview. 'Why don't you sit at the bar, mate?' he said, with a well-meaning attempt at an Australian accent. 'Tell the barman to put your beer on my tab. And any scotch too.'

Lugging the grip, Trumble went happily to the bar, which in the style of Sydney bars had no barstools, and leaned on the counter, observing Fratelli and Darragh make their way to a table against the far wall. As he settled, Fratelli began looking at the girls in sweaters and bright frocks who circulated around the room.

'These are good girls, not whores, Father,' Fratelli assured Darragh, pointing to the girls. 'They volunteer to work here. To sit and talk with us. We're under orders not to ask them for anything more.'

Darragh shook his head and gazed full at Fratelli, from whose murderous lips these irrelevant assurances came. They were interrupted by a frizzle-haired waitress from whom Fratelli ordered scotch and a beer chaser. Darragh said he'd have a pony, the smallest available measure of beer under New South Wales licensing laws.

'Come on, Frank,' said Fratelli, discreet about Darragh's priesthood, 'join me in the same. We can ease up after that. This is what working men drink in America.'

Darragh was persuaded, thinking that he could make his own pace in the drinking. But as well as that, as much as he needed to keep clear, he did desire something Lethean, something to blunt the import of the evening, something to encourage him in the silliness of this scene with blithe Fratelli, who must be rendered down to grave decisions.

Fratelli asserted his authority again by telling the waitress to send a hit of whisky Trumble's way as well—'That long drink of water at the bar.'

The waitress went.

'Sorry I was late,' said Fratelli at once, as Darragh himself opened his mouth. 'A big Saturday night in Sydney last night— still processing some of the fights. Air-raid warnings this morning. Did you know there were two Jap reconnaissance planes over us, right over here, this morning?'

'My friend told me.'

'Yeah. Round about the time you were getting up to say Mass.'

Darragh contested this glib truth. 'I didn't hear any sirens.'

'No. It was more an alert for us. Look, let's wait till she brings the drinks before we talk.'

'You mustn't settle yourself,' said Darragh. 'We're not here to drink.'

'Am I beneath talking and drinking with?'

'Of course not.'

'So you say,' Fratelli muttered with a small assuring nod, which carried its own ration of slyness. 'I *do* want to do the right thing, in case grace fails me.'

'In case you fail grace,' Darragh insisted.

'Easy to say, Father,' Fratelli complained. 'But I want to be good.' He held up both hands. 'I want to have a serious conversation that looks like normal talk.'

Darragh closed his eyes and put a hand to his forehead.

The drinks came quickly, and Fratelli paid for them with a ten-shilling note, telling the woman to keep the change. This, in a non-tipping nation, would give her a margin of shillings to take home. But she showed no special gratitude. She gave an appearance of boredom at the egregious generosity of Americans.

As the woman left, Fratelli was aware of Darragh's eyes on him.

'I'm not going to be spending much where I'm going, Father. Not if I take your advice. But, before I take the path, why do you think God made me like this?'

'He might want a special sacrifice in your case.'

Fratelli shook his head and looked at his whisky. 'Special sacrifice,' he murmured, picked up the whisky, and downed it. Darragh merely moistened the bow of his own lips with his.

'Look,' said Fratelli reasonably, 'if I was some hick in the infantry, you might tell me I can redeem myself in prison, or at the end of a rope. I might believe you, particularly as you seem to think that prisons are places where you expiate things. But that's not the way things are. Prison is a licensed hell. It doesn't elevate any soul. Not a guard. Not a prisoner. Yet you command me to walk out of here and martyr myself.' He was drinking beer reflectively.

Darragh took a small mouthful of the scotch, and as it juddered its way down the unsettled column of his body, he thought again how he could like some of this more regularly. If only there were not cautionary tales of the weaknesses for it which Australians got from Irish ancestors, from mad, alcoholic uncles, of whom Mr Darragh had told fantastic tales in Darragh's childhood.

'You know you have to do it, just the same,' said Darragh, feeling clear and certain. 'If *I'd* killed someone, I'd know I had to do it. The prison system wouldn't be a question. My guilt would be the question.'

'Yeah, but it's a theory with you. With me, it's my nature.' Fratelli drank a good draught of his beer, and sighing, told Darragh, 'You know I'm not like this with women. I'm not argumentative. I'm not a wise-ass. I'm soft. I agree. I raise points inch by inch, ounce by ounce. I'm a noble guy with women.'

'You already told me that,' Darragh murmured under his breath.

'Other guys are brutes. I know. You should hear the way they talk about women. In the camp. Their mouths are a running sewer. Their brains are savage. Normal men. Men who marry. You'd want me to be like them?'

Darragh finished his small glass of whisky, in an effort to relieve in himself the fear that he was achieving nothing.

'Good work,' said Fratelli. 'Join me in another of those.' And while Darragh's neck prickled with the heat of the liquor, Fratelli raised ten shillings to the waitress and made the sort of confident hand gestures Darragh had only seen in films, in nightclubs where men in tails and women in ball gowns waited with cigarettes and cocktails for Fred Astaire and Ginger Rogers to appear and dance. The word 'Copacabana' ran through Darragh's blood like a brilliant, alien viper.

More drinks arrived. Fratelli waved sagely to Trumble, and Trumble solemnly waved back. He had not turned his eyes or body from them at all, and still took his role of watchdog studiously.

Darragh considered the liquor before him: a shot glass of whisky, the tall drink of beer—double a pony, a schooner. His second schooner. In this mad place he had an appetite for it. But he must avoid it. For would he still be a wise counsellor when they were in him? In fact, was he a wise counsellor anyhow?

'Look,' said Darragh, 'this is not a social occasion. It's insane. This is not a party. Think for a second of Kate Heggarty. Those hands of yours . . .' Fratelli was persuaded to look at his massive hands for a while, and the experience made him reach for his second whisky and down it at a gulp.

'For most of the time,' Fratelli said, 'I was the best guy she ever met.'

'It's either to the police with me,' Darragh urged. 'Or we go to your own commanding officer.'

'They won't be happy, the brass. They like to pretend we're all nice boys.'

'You must come with me.'

Again Fratelli considered his hands. 'I guess I will.' But he reached out and drank a third of his schooner of beer. 'I guess I will,' he repeated, belching softly. 'Why don't you call me Gene?' he asked.

'Anthony said he called you John. A misunderstanding of vowels, perhaps. He heard your name as John, the orphan you made.'

'If I'd asked you here and you hadn't had my confession, you would have called me Gene. You would have said "Gene, mate". You would have said "cobber".'

'God help us, Gene,' said Darragh. 'Stop delaying.'

Fratelli murmured, 'I see that your big guy over there is keeping pace with me on the liquor.'

And again there were the hand signals to the barman, the calling of the wire-headed waitress, the furnishing of another ten-bob note. Looking with lowered eyes at Darragh's bewilderment, Fratelli asked, 'We don't have to go just now, do we?'

'Yes. I can't physically make you, but I would if I could. We should go *now*.'

'But I'll be a damn long time without the taste of John Barleycorn,' Fratelli muttered. 'Give me a moment.' He toasted Darragh. The weight of unreason and fear in the room caused Darragh to join him in a sip. Outside, an air-raid siren sounded, and the barman checked some curtained windows giving onto the laneway.

'I have to make a phone call,' said Fratelli, beginning to stand with a sigh. Darragh grabbed his left wrist as he rose.

'And then you'll come back and tell me that you are needed for duty, won't you?'

'I just want to check what's happening, Father. I won't leave. For God's sake, let's not have any fiasco with the big guy.'

And he walked away, decisively, and disappeared through the curtain to the entrance lobby. Left sitting, Darragh looked at the bar. Trumble was leaning there, glass in hand but still vigilant.

As Fratelli vanished from the room, a sailor entered, carrying phone messages to this or that officer, each of whom rose, apologised to their guests, and left—not without telling everyone to drink up and relax. In Fratelli's absence, Trumble came over and asked if everything was okay. Darragh reassured him.

'That's good whisky they're serving,' said Trumble, admiringly. 'Johnnie Walker Black.'

'He can afford it,' said Darragh.

Trumble nodded, winked and returned to his place at the bar.

'Sweet Mother of Christ, help me,' Darragh prayed, and sipped more whisky. Could he and Trumble make a citizen's arrest? Of course not. It would make Trumble privy to what only Darragh and Fratelli were permitted to know.

Fratelli came hustling back into the bar, his shoulders forward, a brave bull in appearance.

'Frank, sorry, we've got to go,' he said with new gravity. The presence of the sailor-courier added weight to his command. 'There's an emergency. We're better outside.'

He could see the doubt in Darragh's eyes. 'Bring your pal, too.' He gestured Trumble over from the bar. 'The Japanese are in the Harbour, gentlemen,' Fratelli told Darragh and Trumble. 'We are about to see the enemy face to face.'

The American knew, Darragh could see, how to confuse a

person—to appeal at the one time to a man's sense of peril and to his core curiosity. Trumble was already moving, and Darragh, a little distanced from himself by unaccustomed liquor, moved too. Out past the old man in the white coat, the tender of the visitors' book, who seemed unfussed about this moment of haste and history, and then beyond the door, into a sudden wall of dark.

CHAPTER TWENTY-FOUR

HERE IN THE night, Darragh could tell at once, Fratelli was the prince. 'Come on,' he said. 'Down the steps.' They descended among dim white mansions and harbourside flats towards a pool of light arising from the naval graving yard down on the shore, by which sat a huge battleship, moored.

'This is nothing to do with us,' said Darragh. 'Come with me now!'

'The *Chicago*,' Fratelli explained. And then, at his word, and as if he were conjuring events, the dockyard lights switched off, and so did all the lights aboard the battleship, and Darragh and Trumble were blind pilgrims again. As Darragh stumbled, feeling but not seeing the radiant heat of his fellow-drinkers, a set of dull but profound explosions from up the harbour became the chief sensory clue in their approach to the water. Suddenly an MP was shining a torch on them. A massive noise of firing broke out nearby, and in its pauses voices could be heard yelling in some heightened way, officers seeking information, the man on whatever trigger it was, something big, an artillery piece, at least an anti-aircraft gun, answering at the shout. The military policeman was shining the cautious ray of his torch over Fratelli's identification.

'These two gentlemen are from the New South Wales police,' Fratelli glibly told him. It was obvious to Darragh that Fratelli had the power to walk through any gate tonight. Fratelli seemed superior even to whatever was proceeding on the harbour, transcending both the friend and the enemy.

'Jap subs,' said the military policeman in an earnest, flat accent Darragh identified with the American South. 'Indefinite number. Right in the bay here. We got orders to look out for paratroopers. You seen any, Sergeant?'

'We've been drinking,' said Fratelli, a wink in his voice.

The MP's voice trembled. 'Wish I'd been.'

'You'll be fine, son,' Fratelli told him, a comforting captain in the darkness.

Trumble was grinning by torchlight, tickled to be cast as a cop, an oppressor of the workers, but keeping an eye on Darragh.

As they walked down a cement path, in spite of the overcast night Darragh could see palm fronds around him, promising themselves future botanical summers, admirably permanent in their expectations. In a corner between the parkland and the Elizabeth Bay jetty, an American anti-aircraft crew had their gun bent towards the water. There was heat from the gun platform, its breech, its long barrel. The entire crew of five men and an officer seemed to be talking at once, profaning under the weight of uncertainty. Their panic reached out to Darragh as he thought: These aren't warriors. Their uniforms are a masquerade. They asked each other if they'd seen something or other. Jesus Christ, they said, they weren't sure. They'd seen the hull, black as sin. 'I *saw*,' said one gunner, glimmering with certainty. 'We got it, Lieutenant.'

'No, you fucking didn't,' his young officer told him. And the debate went on. They could not leave it alone. It itched in them. As their dialogue eased a little, Fratelli introduced himself and said he'd been sent down in case of need for crowd control and other issues arising. He repeated, without naming names, his easy lie about Trumble and Darragh. The commander of the gun crew, the boy lieutenant, welcomed them. He seemed pleased to have them there. They could be his Dutch uncles, you could see him thinking. 'I'd say,' he announced respectfully, 'we should keep an eye for paratroopers. There's a crew at the end of the jetty with a Browning automatic. They're watching for that too.'

The harbour itself had become still now. No more booming. Yet shouts could be heard from the direction of the *Chicago* and the other ships moored by Garden Island, but every cry Darragh heard seemed more confused and informed by panic. Fratelli asked Darragh, confidentially, 'Can you see any paratroopers, Frank?' It was a jovial enquiry, as if Fratelli had some secret knowledge which made the possibility of paratroopers laughable. Frank peered up into the dark, low, inscrutable cloud. No threat that he could see was blossoming up there. Ten minutes passed quickly as Darragh and Trumble remained vigilant. But there were no sudden paratroopers nor any particular noise. The lieutenant told them that the bastards in the submarine he'd seen earlier and fired upon must have cleared out to the other side of the harbour, Neutral Bay maybe. No one knew how many subs there might be in the deep anchorages tonight. 'Hey, Lieutenant,' yelled the gun-trainer from his little seat, his hands still on the wheels which elevated and lowered the barrel. 'If we got that sonofabitch, we saved the *Chicago*.'

'Stop dreaming,' yelled the officer and shook his head, as if he were not a boy, nor claimed by boyish fantasies himself. And then a succession of profound thumps from further up-harbour—one, two, three, four, five! Each release of explosives echoed brutally in Darragh's spinal cord. He thought, 'Oh, God, the power . . .' At once, there was a frantic conversation about these noises among the members of the gun crew, and the young officer took the sights as the gun swivelled towards Rushcutters Bay. 'Fire!' he screamed, and the gun pumped out a thunderous rack of anti-aircraft shells into the water.

In hollow stillness afterwards, while Trumble's eyes darted around the clouds, Darragh heard a roar across the water. 'For Christ's sake, you Yanks. This is the cutter from HMAS *Geelong*.' The gunners looked at each other in amazement. Had they failed twice—in firing upon a friend, as well as in sinking nothing? 'You nearly sunk us, you stupid pricks!' roared the voice. Fratelli began laughing, and went so far as to dig Darragh in the ribs.

'Give us a fucking go!' cried a second voice from the Australian cutter.

'Godspeed,' called the lieutenant.

'Go to buggery!' called a sailor aboard the cutter as it increased speed to leave the bay.

This absurdity, doubt, horror were all overlaid in the air. 'There aren't any bloody paratroopers,' Trumble announced beside Darragh. He still loyally held Darragh's grip with his black overcoat in it.

'Neither there are,' said Fratelli with satisfaction.

'We should go,' Darragh told him, trying to find his eye in the dimness. But would he be obeyed in this darkness in which Fratelli reigned with such composure? Fratelli thought, and pulled a half-bottle of scotch from his suit pocket. Clearly he had bought it while making his phone call. He offered it to Darragh.

302

'No,' said Darragh. Now to Trumble, who was both willing to drink and could hardly be told not to—that the flask came from a murderous hand. This was a sort of triumph for Fratelli, who took the small bottle back and looked at Darragh by the remaining light shed by hooded lamps still undoused beneath the eaves of workshops and barracks and messes in the dockyard area.

'Father Darragh,' he said, in a voice so even Trumble could not have detected slyness in it, 'your friend drank. But you treat me as if you know something about me that keeps you from sharing a crock with me. Do you?' Darragh would not answer that serpentine question. 'Do you, Father?' Fratelli insisted.

'No,' said Darragh. He took the flask, and began to sip. Then he found that he drank hungrily, in the conventional desire of drinkers that the heat of the liquor would fuse a night in which there were too many elements to one reality. The mouthful tasted anciently familiar as if Darragh had been drinking it from childhood. To drink it standing in the dark was appealing, even in the dominant presence of Fratelli. What would Kate think of this men's ritual? But you are not forgotten, he promised. Not by a long way. Yet this is how it happens, thought Darragh, habituation to evil. Dangerous men do not wear horns. They carry a kindly whisky flask in their pocket. A shipyard siren wailed for no particular reason, and Fratelli accepted the whisky back from Darragh.

Did time still exist down here on the water? He had no certainty that it hadn't been blown out of the harbour by detonations. Ten past eleven. Searchlights sprang up from warships beyond the huge black bulk of the *Chicago*. They danced towards Bradleys Head and swept back again towards the Sydney foreshore, illuminating islands in midstream. Guns of ships at Garden Island began to fire into the mouth of Elizabeth

Bay, and Darragh could feel rather than see the gravity of the displaced water, and a presence out there. There was energetic turning of wheels and grinding of ratchets on the gun to which Fratelli, Darragh and Trumble were loosely attached. 'Hold fire,' said the lieutenant, at the sights himself. 'No, I see it!' cried the soldier in the little metal seat who had charge of training the gun, and—after a few orders from the officer—the gun, calibrated more in hope than certainty, howled and thumped again, and recoiled on its tyres, firing directly north. Three deafening racks of shells were shot off before there was silence.

Would my father, in his boyhood, have suffered this day after day, months at a time, in France? Darragh, dealing with the echo-speckled quietness after cannon, asked himself. Did I respect him sufficiently for it? But of course, no son did. The stories as related were hollow. The intimate shock even of one gun could not be rendered in words.

Into the pool of light thrown by warships moved a substantial silhouette. One of the gunners cried, 'That's *Perkins* putting to sea.' Across the molten light the ship edged, disappearing only by inches at a time into the darkness and shifting lights. For some reason, seeing the ship depart the scene of peril, Darragh began to breathe again and noticed the gun crew did too. 'One away,' said the lieutenant exultantly. In the past seconds, Darragh had all but forgotten Fratelli. He looked around, adverting to his presence, to Trumble's. The two men stood together, equally serious witnesses in the dark.

'I was sure that big bugger was going to blow up,' Trumble told him reverently.

The lieutenant and one of his men were peering across the water through binoculars, while a searchlight came from the great battleship, *Chicago*, and gun crews aboard it began firing across the harbour with scarlet tracer bullets. Thus a spine of periscope beyond Garden Island became clear to Darragh's vision and to others, for Trumble yelled in Darragh's ear, 'They're all round it.' He sounded an enthusiastic participant in the battle. 'All round it, but not on it!' The peculiarities of light and tracer and shadow which had enabled them all to see the tip of the submarine had passed and been replaced by raw, unregulated sound. So simultaneously did machine-gun fire and rifle shots and shells and depth-charge explosions occur, including here, with the gun crew and the men with the automatic rifle at the end of the ferry jetty all adding their foreground quotient to the body of sound, there was not room for a breath. Darragh was reminded of his loud day in Lidcombe with Gervaise, and found it hard amid the chaos to hold for much time at all to the bruised image of Kate Heggarty, still dear to him as the chief victim of this war and all its noise and lunacy.

He had just retrieved Kate's memory from the wreckage of noise when a new, dominant explosion occupied all his senses, searing his eyes, tearing at his eardrums, taking air from his mouth, bouncing his lungs off their accustomed walls and threatening their collapse. It lasted and lasted, and he had no rationality left as it passed—indeed, even as he knew it had ceased, it still ran crazily round the pan of his brain.

Darragh found himself senselessly running away from Trumble and Fratelli towards this recent explosion-in-chief. The earth took the vibrations from beyond the seawall, so that he ran like a peasant running in an earthquake, yet heading perversely towards the source, the volcano, the central unrest of the earth. There was a gate with an Australian sailor on it. He tried to block Darragh. But Fratelli was running too, to keep up with Darragh, and called, 'He's a priest, he's a priest,' and the sailor stepped back.

Darragh ran on at his frantic young man's pace through the darting searchlights of the high, moored *Chicago*, its sounds of bells and commands and its individual voices of bewilderment audible across the water. He saw a crowd of Australian sailors gathered, formlessly and without power, by a seawall. No, not utterly without power—some were leaning through a hole in the seawall and lifting drenched, bloodied men out of water which was nearly solid with the rack and ruin of something not yet defined. A submarine with the name *K9* on its conning tower stood offshore a little, but between it and the seawall lay, smashed and sunken, a bow of wood and a crowded wreckage of fragmented steel and timber. A black disembodied funnel emerged from the water and gave a dominant clue to what all this meant. A drenched sailor with a cut cheek and blood at his waist grasped Darragh.

'There were dozens on it,' he said, and Darragh knew he would tell anyone he met, all night, until he was taken away and his wounds dressed. 'They're down there!'

Whatever this ship had been, its ruin was final. Trumble was beside him, gasping and staring at the melee of wood and steel guy-rope. 'Jesus,' he said. Weeping, Darragh raised his hand over those who must still be drowning in this ruin.

'*Ego te absolvo*,' he intoned, more by instinct than by coolly arrived at intention. And as he did, he felt Fratelli's arm confidingly embracing him in brotherly shock for the unseen men seeking the mothering air in wreckage below them. Two further gashed sailors, rescuers or survivors, were hauled onto the seawall, retching and bleeding at the feet of other ratings and officers.

'Jesus,' said Trumble, 'poor buggers!' Naval police began walking along the edge of the seawall, ordering men back, warning of further undersea explosions. Precisely because Fratelli,

Trumble and Darragh were dressed as civilians, and might have authority of the kind to which Fratelli made such easy pretence, a naval policeman explained, 'The Japs were after the *Chicago*. They got this depot ship. Dozens of blokes. Dozens.'

Darragh wondered how the night could be expected to accommodate the scale of this, of the horror of those men whose lungs had flooded in the dark, bloody anchorage, as he and Fratelli stood there ineffectual by the cluttered surface water. More and more Australian sailors wearing the armbands which declared them to be police now proliferated, and Darragh found that even he and his companions were forced back from the calamity. Their right to be in the graving dock by the seawall was never challenged, but they found themselves further and further from it, walking backwards among sheds and barracks, but always pausing to look and exclaim. Fratelli handed around the remnants of the bottle, a badly needed mouthful each. Fratelli's arm played around Darragh's shoulder.

'This is the night, Frank,' he said. 'Even I know God is abroad.' He earnestly kissed Darragh's cheek, and Darragh did not recoil as much as he might have expected to. 'For Christ's sake, Father, you can't really expect me to do anything with the big guy here. Get rid of him, and you can take me to my medicine.' Under pressure of death barely achieved yet by the seawall, this seemed a peculiarly reasonable idea. It was, as Fratelli had said, a night when the relentlessness of destiny, the unarguable nature of punishment, seemed written on the air. 'Just get rid of the big guy,' Fratelli pleaded, throwing the empty whisky bottle on the pavement, indifferent to whether it shattered or not. 'He's not part of anything.' The anti-aircraft and other guns were firing again all round the harbour. There were the sea-bed sounds of depth charges. Darragh's brain jolted with fright for the Japanese submariners,

What must it be like to be encased in the silt, in the Christ-less dark of Sydney's profound moorage? What faith could soothe that bitter, thunderous dark?

Darragh turned to Trumble. 'Ross,' he said, 'I could be here till morning. I have to thank you, but everything's settled now and you ought to go. It's a long way to Homebush. Bert might need you.'

'I thought we were going back together?' said Trumble, his solemn eyes reminding Darragh of the possible dangers of Fratelli, which were greater than Trumble could know. Was Darragh sure? Darragh said that yes, everything was settled. He could see that Trumble, after all the liquor and row, was trying to remember how to make his way back to the world of taxis and electric trains.

'If that's the way you feel,' said Trumble, a little offended to be dismissed.

'Thank you,' said Darragh.

Trumble was all at once gone. Fratelli said, as thumps and thuds receded, 'I'd bet the sons of bitches in the subs are dead. And look.' He drew his hand up towards the overcast. 'No para-troopers.'

There was piping aboard the great battleship *Chicago* as it slipped its moorings and was all at once veering seaward, edging out towards the vast safety beyond the Sydney Heads. Darragh watched it, since its scale demanded watching, for an indefinite time.

'Bless 'em all,' said Fratelli in a dream. 'Let's go, Frank.'

He had talked like this to Kate Heggarty, with hypnotic author-ity, while she stayed stunned and fixed in place by her husband's capture. Darragh could well understand how she could have savoured his kindness, the powers of persuasion, the glittering

eyes that transcended the dull charities of the St Vincent de Paul
Society.

Darragh and Fratelli fell into step, moving as one being.

'Where are we going?' Darragh nonetheless asked.

'Up the steps again . . . A station at the corner of Darlinghurst
Road. I ought to know. MPs and Aussie cops.' They passed
through a gate guarded by two Australian sailors, who wanted to
hear anything Darragh and Fratelli could tell them. Fratelli did the
duty. A ship was sunk. The rumour was there were dozens on it.
A torpedo had missed *Chicago*, come right under the Dutch submarine, exploded under the seawall, and reduced the depot ship
to splinters. 'Christ,' said one of the young men. 'That must be
Kattabul. I know a bloke on that!'

'Yeah,' said Fratelli, moving on with Darragh. 'That's the war.'

They mounted the stone steps back to the world they had left
a few hours and some eras ago. Darragh hoped to retrieve the
known world at the head of the stairs, and Fratelli seemed light-
hearted, about to be rescued by grace at the plain desk of a police
station. He stopped, however, on one of the stone landings, by a
cement balustrade.

'Do you think you'll ever see the nigger, that Gervaise, again?'

'I hope so,' Frank confessed. 'He deserves to live and to go
home too, in the end.'

'Do you think he'll go home? Not if my kindred souls in the
corps have their way. Penal battalions of black men! Don't kid
yourself, Frank. You won't be seeing that boy again. Not ole
Gervaise! How sad! A big guy like that stepping into some mine-
field in New Guinea. Yeah. How sad!'

'Then we don't deserve to win,' said Darragh.

Fratelli waved that concept aside. 'Frank, you've ruined everything for me, you know,' he reproved Darragh. 'Frank,' He

wrapped his arms around Darragh with a ferocity Darragh could not have expected. 'You took her fucking soul, Frank.'

In that ferocious embrace, Darragh could barely move—he writhed but Fratelli had, as Inspector Kearney had warned, abnormal power. 'I'd led her to where we went, but you had her soul, Frank, fuck you!'

Fratelli's power seemed languid, but it put Darragh on his back, against harsh stone, or cement and gravel, nothing as erosive as Sydney's kindly sandstone, and Fratelli descended on him like a felled tree. Darragh was pinioned. I thought I was strong, Darragh told himself. But *this* was strength. Fratelli's massive hands were on his windpipe, and around the span of the throat. As in Kate Heggarty's case, there was knowledge and power here to crush the breath and interrupt the blood. If he, the Ordained of the Lord, a priest forever, could find himself in this choking situation, with the thunder of his blood detonating in the sky, providing the phantom paratroopers whose existence Fratelli had denied, how much more forgivable had this been in Kate Heggarty? Anyone could come to this end with such a powerful fellow! Darragh wanted only to tell the world that he had been validated in the sermon he had given that distant morning, twelve hours ago. The words of the Mass worked like solid lumps through his chest, up the column of his throat, taking on neon proportions in his brain. Wrestling with the power of this dark angel, he spread his hands, thumbs tucked in behind the two forefingers. For some reason, he thought liturgical correctness was required. '*Dignum et justum est. Vere dignum et justus est, aequum et salutare, nos tibi semper, et ubique gratias agere.* It is worthy and just. Truly worthy and just it is, truly proper and salutary, for us always and everywhere to give thee thanks . . . *Sanguis Domini Nostri Jesu Christi custodiat animam meam in vitam aeternam* . . . The blood of our Lord Jesus Christ, in His throat through which He deigned to share with us the prosaic air, guard my soul into eternal life.' Darragh struggled under the prodigious flashes of light he saw beyond the slope of Fratelli's omnipotent shoulder. When will the peace set in, he wanted to know, beneath Fratelli's crushing hands?

The jagged litanies continued to run out of him into a breathless sky, Jesus my Lord and my God, why has thou abandoned me? Jesus, Mary and Joseph, look down on thy servant in mercy. Sweet heart of Jesus . . . Tower of ivory . . . Morning star . . . Source of our joy, oh our joy. A dreadful thing to die with submariners, in the blossoming dark, with the merciless paratroopers descending and descending.

Now he could feel, even as his brain threatened to leave him, the hard bones of Fratelli's pelvis and the specific penis battering at his right thigh. He gagged for mercy but could feel his own penis engorged in a kind of vicious cooperation with Fratelli, who owned the night and all its mayhem, and had the power to evoke all squalor.

Among the multiplying parachutes of his last breath, a parachutist or minister of mercy appeared at Fratelli's shoulder. He wrestled without much effect at first, dragging at the shoulders of the succubus. Then, as the searchlights of vessels lit up the harbour again, Darragh saw Trumble the merciful creature lift a huge square of sandstone and drop it on Fratelli's head. Fratelli slid away, and Darragh was abandoned to a sudden ache for air. Trumble had lifted the successful lump of stone again and was about to let it fall from chest height on Sergeant Fratelli. Kearney preposterously arrived and prevented him. Kearney cried, 'Come on, come on, boys. Enough fun. Jesus, Trumble, let it go!' Two men in suits were lifting Darragh upright, and he saw before him

Kearney, framed by the lit harbour and honoured by a new set of deepwater explosions. Kearney reached out and shook his hand. 'What are you up to, Frank?' he asked. 'You'll never be a fucking bishop now, you know.'

CHAPTER TWENTY-FIVE

DARRAGH SPENT A drugged Monday in St Vincent's Hospital, attended by whispering nuns who had much to celebrate in God's benevolence. The *Chicago* had not been sunk, the young priest had been rescued, the killer detained! Though there were rumours that the mother submarines from which the swarm of midget subs had been released had shelled the innocent streets of Bondi or Bronte, the bodies of the Japanese submariners lay as deeply dead as that of Kate Heggarty, and the nameless citizens of the city walked abroad with tales to tell of the night of their survival.

Dear old Trumble, who had refused to leave his charge, was entitled to dream of his revolution at war's end—that was Darragh's view. He who loved the idea of the Madrid Republicans who massacred priests to save the populace from their influence was praised by the press for having saved the life of a priest. On the human plane, nothing was simple. And Darragh, who was co-hero of Fratelli's capture, did not feel a sense of triumph. Fratelli held him still by the throat. He was in purgatory with a barely saved and howling Kate. Fratelli seemed to have crushed the hope from his blood.

At one time he woke to find his mother and Aunt Madge sturdily present, and realised that contact with Fratelli had given him a disease, a membrane of dimness over his eyes. He began to shed tears when they spoke to him. Shame, which had been lifted from him yesterday morning, had returned at Fratelli's hands the night before.

He woke at three o'clock on Tuesday morning, recited the office from his breviary, which someone had taken the care to bring him from St Margaret's, and strained for the same level of gratitude as the Sisters of Charity. He was in feverish dread of the morning paper, and when the nuns did not bring him one, he went to the end of the corridor and found a *Herald*. After the passage of two nights, he was barely mentioned except as the victim of an assault. The oldest paper of the city, the most respectable, the paper of the ruling classes of Australia, had let him off lightly and with some generosity of soul.

For a time there was a hollow elation, but within half an hour it had evaporated, leaving an underlying landscape of ruin exposed. He felt a ridiculous tendency to tears when the monsignor visited him, spotting his grief in his eyes. 'Frank, please don't be upset. They have the killer safe contained.' The killer could not be contained though. He stained everything he touched; he spread darkness with his lunging penis. 'This is what comes of taking things too seriously, son,' said baffled Monsignor Carolan.

'I want to go back home,' Darragh told him. 'I want to work.'

The monsignor sighed. 'The hospital's ringed by journalists and their cockatoos, just waiting to get a picture of you leaving. Stay a while yet.'

Darragh continued inconsolable about Gervaise, dead sailors

and the wife of Lance Bombardier Heggarty, whose face was more
intimately clear to him than that of visitors. 'This is just a crack-
up you're having, Frank,' the monsignor advised him on a second
visit. 'You'll come out of this the wiser.' He reached out and took
Frank's wrist. 'Be a good fellow there.' Then he laughed, trying
to cheer Darragh up with ruefulness. 'Quite a trick even for you to
be out at the one time with a strangler and a Communist!'
Darragh was indeed consoled that the improbable comedy of it
had reached the monsignor. 'Where do you get 'em from, Frank?
You're a wonder in your way.'

Darragh did not want to look at newspapers again after that
first time. It was as if he learned through the pores of his skin
what others, even the nuns, knew from the newspapers of their
patients. Fratelli had been questioned by the Americans and the
CID. A fellow MP had by some accident, or led by a sense of
something awry in the master sergeant, searched Fratelli's locker
on Sunday evening before the emergency broke out, and found a
journal. The idea of a journal seemed all too credible to Darragh,
given Fratelli's confessional fervour, the fullness of his account,
the evasions, the qualifications he put on his own guilt. All that
took words. It took ink. There was not merely a journal, as the
CID, summoned by the corps, found in searching his locker.
There was as well a memento, a blouse. It was white, and of
embroidered linen, no obviously risqué item. Fratelli would have
prided himself on taking a worthy garment—no vulgar brassiere,
no satin lingerie.

By the afternoon following the submarine attack, a resident of
The Crescent, with the authority of the accumulated evidence
against the man, had identified Fratelli, and the earnest blue suit
in which he made his journeys to Mrs Heggarty's plain door.
Darragh could well imagine how Kearney would have skilfully

evoked information from the honest citizens of The Crescent, including Mrs Thalia Stevens.

Mrs Darragh came again, and Aunt Madge, and he found himself turned to stone or at least to silence by their tolerance of him, their cheery determination. That too brought tears to his eyes, which threatened to choke him if he let them free. They sat in light, looking in at him in his pit. His mother said that, darling, she was proud of him. He was earnest, she said, that was all. Earnestness could be cured, apparently, at St Vincent's. He had so shamed them, he wanted to confess, but the pills they began giving him on the second day bloated and dried his tongue. It lay in his mouth like a toadfish in a drying pool. Had the pills given him this tendency to be giddy and go liquid at the eyes? He asked a nun that, and she was evasive.

Vicar-general Monsignor McCarthy visited in his purple stock, and told Darragh that he was being prayed for. When he went outside, he could be heard holding half an hour's conversation with a specialist beyond the door. Darragh believed, though he could not swear to anything he heard or saw, that the specialist said, in a slightly raised voice, 'But he can't go on retreat. He needs a holiday.' The vicar-general re-entered the room, frowning about the purple of his stock. 'There's no rush for anyone to make up their minds on what should be done yet, Frank,' he said. 'Just rest for now.'

Darragh was appalled with himself for being challenged by a tendency to weep in the face of this official purple. 'I want to begin saying Mass again,' he declared. 'Hearing confessions. Anointing the sick.'

'In a day or so, Frank.' The vicar-general pointed to the breviary on the bedside table. 'And you don't need to worry about the office. You're dispensed from that for now. You're far too ill.'

'Dispensed,' said Frank. He hated the verb acutely.

Because the pills let the days slide away beneath his feet, it was Saturday before Inspector Kearney came with another senior detective. Kearney seemed tentative, and tender in a brotherly sort of way. 'Father Frank, we're not going to pursue the bugger for grievous bodily assault. It's the murder or nothing.'

'Of course it's the murder,' said Darragh, and again his eyes filled and threatened to unman him.

'The Yank authorities are right on our side. But the bastard's pleading insanity.'

Darragh felt laughter in him, as hectic as the monsignor's laughter had been earlier in the week. 'He zigs and he zags,' said Darragh, as if it were an endearing trait of Fratelli.

'He certainly does. Look, when things are better for you, I have to talk to you. Don't be alarmed. Our American friends don't want this to be a circus. They'll try him by closed court martial at Victoria Barracks. They're going to ask a New South Wales Supreme Court judge to sit with all the colonels. This won't be like a public court. No bigotry, no cross-examination. A court martial will give you a fair go. You should be out of the chair within an hour.'

'I can't break the seal,' Darragh explained. 'The archdiocese wouldn't know what to do with me then. They don't know what to do with me now. See, I feel I went down with all the sailaors.'

'No. No, Frank,' said the detective in an authoritative way. 'You're here, you see. You're *here*.'

Darragh frowned. Yes, he must be here, he decided, but he did not always feel as if he was.

Kearney smiled in a rough attempt at reassurance, and to signify Fratelli was a joke. 'See, he says you drove him to it, because he loved her and you put her in two minds. With your spiritual advice and all! He says *you* made him mad.'

Darragh laughed outright and without apology.

'That's zigging, all right,' he told Kearney. 'That's zagging.'

'Perhaps. But it's so easily disproved. I know one of the MP officers thinks Fratelli's actually courting death, but without so much as saying *I am guilty*. Because the madness thing . . . it won't stand up. The judges will give you an easy time, believe me. You deserve some consideration after what he did to you.'

'Oh he had me, all right,' Darragh assented. 'He had me, the old Fratelli.'

'He had a horn on him when we took him, Father.' Darragh did not want to hear that. He was burdened with shame not least because something in him had called out the beast in Fratelli. It seemed, therefore, like malice for Kearney to say it. 'He kept that awful erection of his for ten minutes after, it seemed. Built like a bloody draughthorse. Remember what he did on Kate Heggarty's body.'

Darragh instantly vomited over the bedsheets. Nuns came from every region of the hospital, and correctly looked reprovingly at Inspector Kearney, who to them was just an importunate layman.

Darragh lost many days now. He believed he remembered an elderly nun telling him, 'But you can't say Mass yet, Father. You'd upset the chalice. Then . . . Our Divine Lord's blood all over the place.'

That closed the matter. Yet suddenly, as if he had got immune to the sting of his pills, or as if the doctor had reduced them, he was able to go into a courtyard and sit in the sun. His grief came less frequently, more dully. Tears he shed chiefly in the secrecy of his room, since he knew by now that they seemed to throw everyone into disarray. One afternoon, he and Aunt Madge sat together at a table in this enclosed yard. He caught Aunt Madge watching

younger nuns, novices, of an age unlikely to be permitted to nurse
Darragh, spying on him for a second from this or that window.

'Women!' she told him, as if nuns in some ways participated
more heavily than others in whatever frailty she was remarking
on. She looked at him as if she knew that the abiding question in
his mind was, How do I get from this courtyard into the effectual
world? 'You think you're such a sinner, don't you, Frank?'

'I don't know whether I'm a sinner or a fool. It's the same
thing.' There was the thing of feeling unclean too, but he did not
burden Aunt Madge with that.

'Yes, you're such a wild man, aren't you? In your own head.
That's exactly what's wrong with you. I'll tell you, most of us have
buckets more shame than you. The archbishop has more shame;
I wouldn't mind betting that at all—I knew him when he was a
curate. The monsignor—that walking ledger. It's better to be like
you than like him! So I want you to cut out these tears, do you
hear me? Or if you want to let them flow, do so, but forget shame.
You have no shame to bear.'

He shook his head. Aunt Madge lowered her voice. 'So there's
this assumption around, isn't there, hinted at in the papers, that
you and the girl . . . that you had an infatuation for her. Well, say
it was the truth. So what? What does it matter? Priests have been
sillier by far than that. Believe me. Women *get* to men, and priests
are men. Therefore, women get to priests.'

He couldn't explain how much he was ashamed that his fascination for Mrs Heggarty was public property. And he couldn't
argue with Aunt Madge. She was so robust in debate, of so strong
a mind. She dropped her voice further and reached for his wrist,
holding it emphatically. 'I'll tell you this just to wake you up. Just
to make sure you know you've let no one down. Mr Regan and
I—do you believe this, your beloved, upright Mr Regan?—we had

a love affair. Twelve years ago. Yes. Lasted three months. Looked at purely from the point of view of being a lover, he was splendid. He put all his guilt and all his sense of damnation into it, big dear old Regan. Now this was all a terrible thing, Frank, on my part and his. His girls were young. His wife was loyal. But the terrible thing about the sixth commandment, Frank, is that when you're violating it, when you're wrapped up in the other person, the other person stands for the entire universe. You forget everything else. And the sinister thing is, you feel somehow that God's on your side. Or this or that god, anyhow. Venus, say! Well, *mea culpa*. I didn't go near the Regan family for eight years afterwards. I used to sneak into your place when you were young, so Mrs Regan wouldn't see me. Sneaked out. I'm sure your mother knew all about what had happened, but she never said. Anyhow, in the end I just went to Mrs Regan one day and pleaded for her pardon, and she'd already given it. Maybe—and this isn't an excuse—but maybe she knew that one fling would be more than enough to bind dear old Regan to her for life.'

If Aunt Madge's object had been to make him fascinated in an old-fashioned way, then he was fascinated and appalled in a general sense, but surprisingly not in any personal way at Aunt Madge, who had always seemed to carry with her the possibility of great passion.

'And believe me,' said Aunt Madge, not pausing to get his pardon, 'there would be bucketloads of parish priests and bishops who could make the same or similar confession. Sex is a grand and terrible thing, Frank. It makes everyone mad sooner or later. Now you read all these prayers every day that talk about what a sinful generation we are, how fallible, how we can't clean our own backsides without God's help. And it's all the truth, Frank, it's all the bloody truth. But the trouble is you believe it only applies to you. You don't look at all these other fellows and say, they're just as silly as I am. You only look at yourself, and condemn yourself. As if you are one of a kind.'

'The monsignor thinks I'm one of a kind,' Darragh asserted.

'And so is he. And so—*bloodywell*—is he. A pretty ordinary kind, too. Frank, your mother sheltered you too much when you were a kid. Your father had been round the traps, but she made sure you got none of his balance, none of his wisdom. You thought every monsignor had the authority of a god, of God himself. You were an angelic kid. But Australia's the wrong place for that. In any case, it's only because you've been in the news-papers by accident that the archdiocese is running round like headless chickens. And by the way, don't you think that's a bit infantile of them?'

'They don't want to have to deal with a scandal,' said Frank, to fight off Aunt Madge's superior wisdom. 'You can't say that they haven't been generous. All this . . .' He pointed about him. He meant the hospital, the medical treatment. Tears pricked his eyes at the idea of it.

'Why not? You're entitled to it, Frank. Don't let them make you feel guilty about that as well. You can't help being a bit knocked about, you know. As for newspapers and scandals, they're the stuff of a day. I'd say the chances of your being pointed to in your old age as someone notorious are pretty small.'

Darragh yielded to an unexpected laugh. He thought, as it came up his throat, this is a natural laugh. Perhaps this is not the laugh of a total fool and a scandal.

He said, 'They talk about people having a Dutch uncle. You're my Dutch aunt.'

'Someone's got to be,' said Aunt Madge. 'Are you shocked? Do you forgive me?'

'That's already been settled,' he said blithely, far from shocked, after Fratelli, at such normal sins as those of Regan and Madge. 'Ancient history.'

'Anyhow, I depend on your discretion, Frank, even if you're not feeling like yourself for the moment.'

'That's it,' said Frank. 'You've got it in one, Aunt Madge. Mad as a cut snake. At least, so I'm told.'

But he was, in his way, recovering. When the day came to attend Fratelli's court martial, Darragh was driven to the barracks by the archbishop's secretary and accompanied by a nurse. Darragh remembered the secretary from the seminary, a man a few years older than himself, extremely competent and clever. They chatted about former classmates all the way to Victoria Barracks, Darragh sitting in the front seat like a fully restored member of the archdiocese. Occasionally, something the other priest said would evoke in him a vast dread of the encounter about to take place. 'Thank God they've only let one news agency in to observe this court martial.' It was a sentiment he had heard before, but now it had immediate meaning. Monsignor Carolan, for whatever reason, had passed on to Darragh a bit of gossip—there had been a debate at the cathedral about whether Frank should give his evidence, as he had always intended to, in full clerical suit, or wearing a white shirt and tie, like a seminarian. The monsignor did not realise that since his conversation with Aunt Madge, Darragh had begun to see such fretful debate as inane.

On arrival at the barracks, the archbishop's secretary seemed somewhat abashed to be asked to sit outside the courtroom, whose door was guarded by the sort of splendidly turned-out and revolver-equipped American military police of whom Darragh felt he had already seen too many. The secretary muttered to an army officer at the courtroom door, obviously explaining that Darragh had not been himself and might need support within the chamber of the court martial. But his argument was politely rebuffed.

Darragh let himself sink into a daze, surrendered to the numb web of his blood, and so rose and was escorted through the door by a guard. The court-martial chamber was ballroom vast, with its windows taped for air raids and draped to exclude light. Eleven splendid officers of varying age sat at a high table decorated with a succession of American flags. Among the military judges was a bald, plump man in a dark suit, the observing judge from the New South Wales Supreme Court. In front of the president of the court, a stern, square-faced soldier, stood a microphone, and behind him the Stars and Stripes and various army banners crossed over each other to make an impressive pattern against the wall.

By contrast with this heavily populated upper table the court chamber itself seemed under-populated. At the table for the defence sat a captain of perhaps thirty years of age, and Fratelli waited beside him. Darragh found himself staring at Fratelli and was, for reasons he could not define, hungry for signs. Fratelli merely looked in his direction and nodded once, curtly. A man who had tried to throttle him seemed to owe him more, Darragh thought. But then, there was hatred, wasn't there? He remembered that. Inspector Kearney had told him. Darragh formed words in his head and tried to transmit them to Fratelli. *I no longer dread you.* Imprisonment and accusation had crushed all that force, that look and air of grandeur, out of Fratelli.

The prosecutor, an older officer, asked Darragh about his meetings with Master Sergeant Fratelli: the day when Fratelli had asked him to say Mass for his aunt, and then the capture of Private Aspillon. The man spoke about that incident in a way which implied it was well known and investigated, and so, in a way which seemed to promise Gervaise a continuing existence. Next, the prosecutor wanted to know what the Australian corporal had said about Fratelli's being the cause of the storm of fire in Lidcombe. In other matters, Darragh pleaded the seal of the confessional, and was able to say only that Fratelli had said to meet him, for the sake of spiritual guidance, outside the confessional. Then there was the issue of what Fratelli had said while trying to strangle him. No seal extended to that.

All that he was able quickly to recite, anxious to be let go again, back to the anonymity Aunt Madge had promised him was imminent.

Throughout, Fratelli seemed to be as abstracted from what was happening as Darragh was, and gazed fair ahead with a fixity alien to all his previous behaviour as the young officer appointed to defend him began to ask Darragh questions with an edge to them. Did Father Darragh think a sane man would have tried to open fire on the shed in Lidcombe where Aspillon and Darragh huddled together? Without violating what he heard in the confessional, had Darragh done his best to turn Mrs Heggarty away from Fratelli? Then, an irrational question as far as Darragh understood it: To what extent did his own feelings for Mrs Heggarty make him resent the idea that she would go with another man? This was a question the journalists at their table liked.

It was therefore very welcome to the numbed Darragh when the president of the court called for a suspension of that line of examination, put his hand over the microphone, and held an earnest discussion with the bald man in the suit. Fratelli seemed to have drifted to sleep, or perhaps it was an act. At last the president unclasped his hand from the microphone. 'I'm not going to let you pursue the direction you're heading in,' he told

Fratelli's defender. The defending officer could, said the president, call as many specialist witnesses as he chose on the matter of Fratelli's sanity. He could call the men with whom Fratelli lived. There was no profit in expecting a decent gentleman of the cloth to make judgements on how Fratelli might have felt about this or that.

With the polite thanks of the court, Darragh was told he could go. He rose with his eyes still on Fratelli, who did not look back. But it did not matter. They had sent *him* behind the wire. They had made *him* say the rosary on his fingers and live without shoelaces. Darragh could see that within the walls, as a prisoner, he was the mere mirror of the courtier and warrior, the ghost of the fellow who commanded angelic white helmets. Near the door, one of Darragh's knees gave way and he fell into an involuntary demi-genuflection. Feeling foolish, he struggled upright. He heard the president call to his accompanying military escort, 'Give the father a hand there, Private.'

And then he was outside, welcomed back by the secretary-priest and the nurse. As they descended the stairs and entered the large black car from the cathedral, the secretary murmured, as if it did not matter, 'Did anything painful come out, Frank?'

'Nothing painful,' said Darragh. 'He didn't look at me.'

After his hospital stay, they sent him to live at home, urging him not to forget to take his pills. The vicar-general had told him to go to the pictures, and for good long walks. 'Your mother's area of Sydney is full of them,' he said. When he had been home three days, the vicar-general visited him again, this time in his mother's living room. Mrs Darragh made tea, set out the finest cups, and then withdrew.

'Frank,' Monsignor McCarthy told him when they were alone, 'the archbishop has been very busy considering what is best for you. What you should do when you get your medical clearance. We think it might be best if you were laicised for a time, until you're completely fit to work again.'

A fury rose in Darragh. 'Laicised?' he said. He shielded his eyes from the idea. 'That's a punishment, isn't it? In melodramas, it's called being defrocked.'

'It's not meant to be a punishment, not in this case. It's to show great confidence in you. Many men who have crack-ups are given a few months off. To holiday. Even to do a bit of secular work. You see, we could get you work as a proofreader at the *Catholic Weekly*. And, of course, you could wear lay clothes for the time being.'

'So that everyone could tell I'm under some sort of probation,' Darragh said.

'That's not what it's meant to imply. It's meant to imply you're getting your health back. And there are many pleasant and untaxing jobs you could do ultimately, although you're not well enough now.'

'I don't have any suitable lay clothes.'

The vicar-general sighed. 'You were wearing them the night you went out with Fratelli.'

'It was like fancy dress. I looked ridiculous. Fratelli and Trumble both said so.'

'Frank, don't resist us on all this. The archbishop is doing his best by you. You'll be exempt from saying your office and administering the sacraments. You'll have nothing to burden you. We'll keep in constant contact, and when you're ready to return . . . As for celibacy, you're a seasoned hand at that, Frank, and that will stand, of course. You don't have to be told that.'

'I don't,' said Frank. 'I'll still have all the disadvantages of the priesthood.'

'You're sounding bitter, Frank. You'll see it's best. The arch-bishop wanted me to give you some . . . I suppose you could call it set-up money. To buy a suit, and all the rest. I expect you'll be back at your duties at St Margaret's or somewhere else by Advent. Or the New Year at the latest . . .'

The vicar-general took a sheet of paper from a satchel. 'This is a decree of laicisation. And a letter from the archbishop. You may use them in case there's any confusion over who you are, and to show you really are a cleric and a priest.'

'Especially to myself,' said Darragh, with a tight smile.

'Come on, Frank. Rally, son! Take this as it's intended.'

Eventually Darragh's mother was asked to join them, and the vicar-general told her with a brittle joviality that Frank was to have four or five months rest from work. That he ought to go on holidays—perhaps the Blue Mountains. 'I have a cousin who's on a farm at Gilgandra,' said Mrs Darragh. 'Maybe Frank would like to go out there and stay, help them with things.'

The vicar-general said that would be a superb idea, and soon it was time for the man to go. Mrs Darragh showed him off the premises, Darragh remaining behind so that he would not have to shake his hand.

Mrs Darragh returned to him with a fretful hope in her face. 'I think that's a good thing, don't you, Frank—a break? In mufti. You can go to race meetings in civvies. I wonder can I call Gilgandra? I wonder will the post office let me?'

For the sake of mercy to his mother, he announced with a demented emphasis, 'I think it's a very good idea. I'm going to put on a suit coat right now and take Aunt Madge to the pictures.'

Almost at once, Darragh had a polite call from Mrs Flannery. Another curate was coming to St Margaret's and Darragh would need to return to the presbytery to clear out his room, to take away his books and clothes. 'Is the monsignor there?' he asked, and Mrs Flannery, with a remarkable biddability, went to fetch him.

'When were you thinking of coming, Frank?' the monsignor asked him. The following afternoon, said Darragh. 'Oh,' said the monsignor, 'sadly I'll be out. But best of luck to you. Get well.'

'You *could* be there,' said Darragh. 'After all the confessions I've heard. After all the Benedictions and Masses. You could be there if you wanted.'

'I beg your pardon?'

'You *choose* not to be there.'

'I don't think you're considering your words, Frank, but I know you're not well.'

'You could be there to say, "Goodbye Frank. You've been a bloody awful curate. Best wishes." I don't bite, you know.'

'I've already given you my best wishes, Frank. And, I might say, a good quotient of patience.'

'Oh well,' said Frank, 'I've got all I deserve, in that case.'

'God bless you, Frank, and goodbye,' said the monsignor with finality.

Aunt Madge organised through a friend of hers, a man named Henry, the one who claimed to have been at Marist Brothers, Parramatta, with Errol Flynn, to drive Darragh all the way from Rose Bay to Strathfield, so that Darragh would not need to catch train and bus while hauling suitcases. Henry was a bachelor, an active man in his parish, and nervously chatty with this young man who was part priest, part layman, part scandal.

Darragh asked him was it possible to drop by The Crescent, and Mr Henry was accommodating, allowing the car to idle outside number 23.

'This is where it happened?' he asked tentatively, looking for signs of distress in Darragh.

'This is the place.'

'Doesn't seem possible, does it? I mean, it looks so ordinary.'

About a hundred yards away, a woman and some children turned the corner from Rochester Street. It was Mrs Thalia Stevens, around whom her five children cavorted like hectic minor planets to her sun. She held two-handed a large, unfashionable black handbag and a bulging string bag hung from her elbow. She was not like her late friend, Kate Heggarty, a gracious dresser—her green dress, her black coat and her lacquered black straw hat hung crookedly on her. Her ankles bulged like a promise of old age over her scuffed shoes. She paused at her gate to draw breath, while one of her sons somersaulted up the pathway to her door. Darragh told Henry to move further up the street. 'Just here,' said Darragh. 'I won't be a second.'

He knocked on Bert Flood's door. No answer came, but an instinct told Darragh the house was inhabited. At last the door opened.

'Oh,' said Bert, taking in Darragh's sports shirt, suspenders and blue trousers. 'You, eh? How are you, Frank?'

Darragh exchanged the pleasantries. Bert watched him closely, but in a new way, the way you might watch someone who had been marked by unlikely plague or preposterous chance. Darragh said, 'I came to thank Ross.'

'Oh,' said Bert. 'Want a cup of tea?'

The inexpressive generosity of Bert would until recently have brought on stupid tears. 'I'm sorry, Bert,' said Darragh. 'I've got to get on. I just wondered if Ross . . .'

'Well, look,' Bert said, his gaze wandering in a philosophic way, as if the answer were in a corner of the garden, a quadrant of the sky above the Western Line. 'It's lonely here. The old Rossy's gone off to Cobar. Working in the copper mine out there.'

'No,' said Darragh. 'Isn't that terrible for his lungs?'

'Oh, he got a job as tally clerk. I think the party wants him to ginger up the union out there. You know.'

'Do you have his address?'

'He's going to write when he's settled.'

'When you do, I'll write to him,' Darragh guaranteed.

'Okay. You know, he's pretty upset about everything. It was all a shock for him, too.'

Darragh grasped Bert's hand, and shook it.

After Henry delivered him to the presbytery, Darragh had the exciting feeling of being a trespasser in the familiar yet forever changed hallway, and on the stairwell. Everything looked, in fact, resonantly different. The parlour, the dining room he had shared with the monsignor, his room with its desk. He set to work packing his clothes and his small library, his devotional pictures off the wall. He cleaned out the drawers of his desk. Here, he was surprised to find, lay three pages of blank parish stationery which ages before, or more accurately, after Easter, the monsignor had signed in case there were problems at the bank about the rollover of a money bill, and the finance committee needed them. Darragh gathered these and took them downstairs. 'I wonder could I use the monsignor's typewriter just before I go?' he asked Mrs Flannery, and after a moment's consideration, she consented.

The letter he typed over the monsignor's signature was headed To whom it may concern, and declared that Mrs Thalia Stevens of 33 The Crescent, Homebush, was a practical Catholic in good odour with the parish. He took one of the parish envelopes, addressed it to Mrs Stevens, and pocketed it for posting on the way home. Then he carried the accumulated rags and pages of his priesthood out to the boot of Mr Henry's car.

After Fratelli was found guilty, Darragh could not sleep for dread. He returned to the doctor. His dosages were increased, so that his tongue swelled once more in his dry mouth and impeded his speech. It seemed horrifying now to Darragh that Fratelli would suffer the sorrowful mystery of asphyxiation, the gross bemusement of a cracked spine. Relieved of saying the office, Darragh spent hours in his boyhood bedroom saying rosaries for Fratelli, the Joyful, the Sorrowful, the Glorious Mysteries, all fifteen decades of ten 'Hail Marys', an 'Our Father', a 'Glory Be', no sooner ended than he began again and fell asleep at last, lolling forward on his swollen tongue, his head on the coverlet. His mother wanted to take him to Katoomba as the vicar-general had suggested, to a guesthouse above the great pit of eucalypts which was the Jamison Valley. But he fought her off and delayed her. On the eve of Fratelli's execution, a set of militia conscription papers came addressed to Francis Patrick Darragh.

'This is a total mistake,' said Mrs Darragh. 'I'll speak to the vicar-general.'

But Darragh was relieved to be distracted from Fratelli's execution, and went down to Old South Head Road, caught a tram to the city and enlisted in the army that very afternoon. A priest was automatically laicised, he knew, by joining any of the armed forces, except of course with episcopal permission, to become a chaplain. But if the archbishop could laicise him at a mere word, at least Darragh could laicise himself by signing his name to enlistment. So the equation of justice in Darragh's head ran.

'You won't have to worry about the conscription papers now,' the recruiting sergeant told him. Darragh was to report to the Sydney Showground the next morning. 'Bring a suitcase to put your normal clothes in,' the recruiter told him.

On the morning Fratelli died, Darragh filled his seminary suitcase with his banal clothes, and was at the Showground even
before the hour of execution.

CHAPTER TWENTY-SIX

IN AUGUST 1943, when it was known that Australia, still very much in mid-struggle, had nonetheless been definitely rescued by the valour of its citizens and the strength and gallantry of their great ally, Darragh was stationed as a corporal medical orderly at a hospital in Popondetta in New Guinea. It was a beautiful place on the northern side of Papua New Guinea's central spine of mountains. It possessed a foothills charm. The Australians had driven the Japanese from the southern shore of New Guinea back over these mountains and into the northern lowlands. Americans had landed on the Solomon Sea shore to take the Japanese from behind. The latter seemed no longer miraculously ordained by God as victors and punishers, but were still strongly dug in on the kunai grass plains which characterised the north coast of New Guinea. North of Popondetta, dreadful, intimate conflicts occurred along the roads driven among the giant grass of pre-war plantations. Men stumbled back from these encounters with bullets through their shins, or lumps of shrapnel in their bandaged heads, or raving with killing infections—dengue fever or cerebral malaria. New Guinean natives often guided them along, as they winced or raved, to the hospital of the 2/14th Field Ambulance. Gangrene and effulgent tropical ulcers, concussion, shell shock, and dizzying fever temperatures had taken their minds from them. In that condition they were often terrified, expecting attack at any second. The Japanese and they had inflicted dreadful, rampant fear on each other.

By the time they reached the hospital to which Darragh was almost inevitably attached—since he had been honest about his background, and since being a medical orderly seemed to be the best thing for a priest on sabbatical—many of the soldiers no longer knew where or who they were.

The climate was so much more pleasant here that sometimes Darragh, off-duty, would climb the hill above the tented hospital, where—for reasons known only to engineers—the deep latrines had been dug. Recuperating men, waiting to go back to the viciousness in the long grass, called it Shit Hill, and its minder was a sullen orderly who sat on oil drums reading American comics and, when he considered the disease peril from the pits had reached a certain point, throwing in gasoline and setting fire to it. Men swore that he had done it when they were occupying the seats, and burned the hair off their arses—but that was merely a story, for the fellow lacked the capacity to make a myth of himself.

Darragh sometimes went up there to look at the vaporous mountains behind, and the hazed vistas stretching away across the plain to the Solomon Sea. At some moments, far from the wards and the airstrip, Shit Hill was a tropic idyll, and could even, in the evening's advancing blue light, seem a backwater. But now and then he drove down with other orderlies to collect medical supplies from the airstrips at Buna and Gona, where terrible battles had been fought earlier in the year, and Darragh would inspect the faces of the black soldiers who unloaded the planes and looked after the aircrew messes there. His letters to Camp Kenney had never been answered, nor his letters to the Corps of Military Police. An Australian corporal did not merit such replies.

From Shit Hill one afternoon, Darragh saw yet another damaged soldier being walked up the trail by a New Guinean in a loincloth, for delivery to the 2/14th. The soldier, it became apparent as he got closer, was not so much walking as being directed and carried, as was the normal procedure anyhow. His faced seemed blackened with ash and sweat. Darragh descended the hill to go on duty.

The medical officer diagnosed the soldier, a second lieutenant, as suffering from well-developed cerebral malaria, and put him on a drip of saline and sulfa drugs. Darragh was to take his temperature at three-hourly intervals. The man's body was washed by Darragh and another orderly and as he was settled by flickering generator light on his hospital cot, his features became distinguishable to Darragh. He was at once recognisable as the brother—Howley, or some name of that nature—who in the days before the fall of Singapore had fled his superior and his confessor. Since he became disturbed when Darragh tried to place a thermometer in his armpit, Darragh took his temperature anally, and it was 105 degrees. There was already peril that if he should live, his brain might not return to him.

The man was not clear-headed enough, or even strong enough, to say much. His protests were many, but they came in murmurs. One day two ragged soldiers with slouch hats and lean bellies came to Popondetta to visit him, and seemed depressed by what they saw. As Darragh changed a saline and sulfa bag, one of them said, 'Look after him as well as you can, mate. He's the bloody best platoon leader we ever saw.'

'Complete bloody madman,' said the other soldier with approval of the patient. 'In the right way, I mean.'

One night a brief remission occurred, a phase of calm and clarity, or what resembled it. The lieutenant grabbed Darragh's hand when he came with the thermometer, and declared, 'Father . . .'

Darragh said, 'I'm just a medical orderly, son.'

But the lieutenant said, 'Father.'

'I can recite the Act of Contrition for you,' said Darragh.

'The rites,' said the young man. 'Please. The rites.'

Though all fluid was voided from the young officer's body, by way of hectic sweats, as soon as it entered his system, there were somehow compelling tears on his cheeks. Where did they come from? They were summoned by profound contrition, by urgency on a ferocious scale.

Darragh had been suspended, by archbishop's decree and by becoming a soldier, from giving absolution. He was far removed from the holy oils. Some chaplain or other down towards Gona would have them, but would take a greater time to get here than the brother who had disgraced his order but honoured his uniform had left. Yet the urgency and distress in the man were compelling.

The distant cautionary stories recurred in his imagination. The drunken renegade priest who consecrated the contents of a bakery shop. Who anointed the prostitute, in ironic charity, with butter.

And yet, Christ, bending and writing in the dust as they taunted Him with the woman taken in adultery. Christ who sanctified the dust with His Aramaic hand. Who made a sacrament out of banal things.

In any case, Darragh absolved the young officer, and for lack of chrism, and depending on the spaciousness of Christ, got some lard from the cookhouse and anointed all the lieutenant's organs of sin behind the pulled mosquito nets of a night-time military hospital.

Men perished suddenly of such diseases. You visited once, and there was some way to go. You visited them an hour later and some sort of quiet paroxysm had run through them and left them vacant. It proved to be the case now. As he cleansed the body, he thought of the lard and wondered, how can I get back to what I was from here? Later, he would need to go to Shit Hill, and look out in the clear dawn for signs and indications.